TONY GALLOWAY

SOLOMON'S RING

DEMON POWERS

BOOK ONE

Solomon's Ring

Demon Powers Book One

Tony Galloway

Chattooga Press

Cover images by Miblart

Print ISBN: 979-8-9868746-1-6

Contents

To my lovely wife Cara and wonderful children Adrian, Ariyanna, Bethany, and Natalee. You make life an adventure worth having.

Prologue

Belial could sense fear in the man he followed. The man was wiry, nimble, and nervous. Dressed all in black, a plain hoodie with jeans, and leather boots. Even his goatee was black. With the hood up, he cut a figure that might have been any of a hundred hipster wannabe university students, but he was something different. Something very different. The man glanced over his shoulder often, a ritual of paranoia, but he saw nothing. Belial had nicknamed him Twitch.

Belial crouched on the pavement behind a corner coffee shop where the university students would congregate in a few hours. For now, the place was dark, and that suited his purposes just fine. He peeked around the corner. Twitch was crossing the street into the university park, islands of street lit green beneath the reaching limbs of ancient oak and elm trees. He stepped into the sea of shadows between the islands and vanished from sight.

Belial took a breath to slow his heart and felt the tension ease. Someone screamed, a muffled sound that echoed in his skull like a voice in a cave. Another breath and a measured thought were all it took to restore silence. He chided himself for letting his concentration slip, then he climbed onto a nearby dumpster, leapt from there to a chain-link fence, cringed at the rattle it made, and then hoisted himself up by the storm gutter that ran along the back of the shop.

When Belial attained the roof, he crouched. He caught a flash of furtive eyes scanning the street from across the way. *They never look up*, he thought with a devilish grin. He crouched lower, relishing the sensations of his borrowed body, even the agonizing protest of his host's knees as he jumped onto the electrical line running from the building to a gazebo behind the target. Maybe he'd drop on top of Twitch and end this quickly.

Belial hung from his ankles and hands and began inch-worming across the street, focusing intently on the man, determined to be swift and silent. It was important he take this one down quietly.

He'd been following Twitch for weeks from university to university across the Southeast. What began as a routine assignment to capture a renegade demon had become a fascinating game of espionage. Despite housing one of the weaker classes of demons, he possessed amazing charisma and had accomplished things Belial had never seen done before. He couldn't say who was in control, the demon or his host. It was baffling.

Belial was more than halfway across the street when the car keys slipped from the pocket of his jeans. He snatched frantically with one hand, missed, and almost fell. Cursing silently, he caught them with his mind right before they hit the pavement, but the damage was done. The man saw them tumble and glint in the dim light and hover a few feet above the ground. For a heartbeat, Twitch looked perplexed; then he looked up. A half smile crossed his face, and he darted into the park and vanished. *Shit.* Belial let go; the pavement sent shock waves of agony through his host's knees. He cursed inwardly and dashed after his quarry.

They sprinted through the park at a breakneck pace. The man whirled and flung a handful of steel ball bearings at Belial as fast as bullets. Belial raised his hands to form a wedge, and the marbles veered off course, careening harmlessly into the trees.

"Stop, I just want to talk!" Belial shouted. There was some truth to it; he longed to sate his curiosity. In response, a park swing came spinning out of the darkness, its chains cutting the air like whips. Belial dropped to the ground, and the flailing chains touched the hairs on the back of his head as it passed over.

Twitch had gained a good lead now. Belial glanced around uncertainly for a way to stop him; he spotted a manhole cover near an outbuilding ahead. He called it with a whisper of willpower, and sent it slicing through the air toward the wiry man's knees. Twitch leapt down a side street just in time. The manhole cover crunched into the grill of a parked minivan, setting off the alarm.

Belial sprinted to where he'd last seen Twitch, a quiet residential area with long rows of brick houses and manicured lawns. This wasn't going well. He jogged down the street, sweeping the area with his senses. At the end of the street, he turned left and found himself in a construction zone. The pavement gave way to mud and gravel, and instead of houses and cars, there were dump trucks and excavators. He searched around the heavy equipment, some of it with tires taller than his host.

Belial listened hard, working to hear beyond the night sounds of katydids and tree frogs. To his right there was a scrape, faint enough to doubt it had been more than a rat scurrying from one hiding spot to the next. Belial stepped to the edge of a half-dug basement and dropped with feline surety into the darkness below.

Belial stifled a groan as the landing jarred his already abused knees. He sensed movement in the darkness. Three figures approaching swiftly, fanning out to flank him. He pretended not to have noticed them.

The first to reach him took a swing. Belial pivoted to the side and trapped the arm. With a fluid twist of his hips, he snapped it; before the assailant could cry out, Belial broke his neck on the return motion.

Then the other two were on him. He shoved the larger one and sent him sprawling over his fallen companion. The third slashed out with a wicked knife. Belial leapt back, but the blade drew a line of fire across his belly. *Too slow*, he scolded himself. He recovered in time to intercept a lethal overhead stab. His muscles quivered as he struggled for control. The tip of the blade hovered inches from his nose.

The second man recovered from his fall, hoisted a large rock over his head, and heaved it. The stone took Belial in the back with a meaty thwack. Belial stumbled forward under the impact, and the knife tip opened his cheek from just below the eye to his jaw. Smiling, the rock thrower drew a knife of his own and circled to Belial's left. The odds were never in his favor.

Belial pushed against the man in front of him with everything he had. The knife tip hovered just above his collarbone and angled down to slide behind it. The man was large and shifted to bring his weight to bear. Belial gave way and twisted, letting the attacker's own effort send him careening away into the mud wall.

The second man closed the distance and slashed wildly. Belial ducked under the blade and scooped up a handful of dirt, flinging it into his adversary's face. The man lashed out blindly as the fallen assailant regained his feet. Belial lunged in; an unexpected slash sliced his forearm to the bone. He felt the tendons let go like guitar strings, but he turned the knife with his good hand and shoved it up between the attacker's ribs. In one leonine motion, he spun around, pulling the blade free, and opened the last aggressor's throat. A shadow blotted out the dim starlight for an instant and the spilled blood shone blacker. He waited to see the demons in their true forms as the Pull drew them out of their dead hosts. Long seconds passed, but nothing happened. It was as if the men hadn't been possessed at all, though he had suspected otherwise.

He rolled them onto their backs with his foot. He couldn't see their features clearly in the pitch, but he touched their faces. Two were clean shaven and the third, though he had a beard, was much too tall and heavy to be his man. In a way, Belial was relieved. He had questions, and dead men didn't give answers.

He scaled the muddy wall with some difficulty, cursing his useless hand. When he reached the top, he slowed his breathing and listened. Eyes closed, he extended his senses, searching for some change in the night sounds, a flicker of arcane energy, anything that might warm the trail. After several long, unfruitful moments, Belial retraced his steps through the construction site.

He'd all but given up when the sudden yapping of a small dog down the street flushed his prey. Belial glimpsed him at the edge of the subdivision, weaving through the trees like a phantom. The chase was on again. Twitch was fast; Belial was faster. The distance between them shrank steadily. Beyond the subdivision, an apartment complex loomed dark, save a single lit window. Twitch vaulted the wooden privacy fence and landed softly on the asphalt beyond. As he topped the fence, Belial saw his target lounging against a streetlight. A handful of colored marbles orbited one another lazily above his open palm.

"What can I do for you tonight, Warden?" he asked in a smooth baritone. He was younger than Belial had realized. The pointed black goatee he wore might not have been real. It was absurdly immaculate. The young man's eyes danced with merriment and burned with ancient intelligence that belied his years. "You don't look well, Warden. Rough night?"

There was definitely a demon here, but Belial still wasn't sure it was in control. Bizarre. Time to get some answers.

"You know what I am, so you know how this ends. Just answer a few questions, and then we can get you back where you belong. There's no need for violence."

"Oh, I couldn't agree more, no call for unpleasantness."

Belial released a breath he hadn't realized he was holding. "Let's go somewhere a little more private to talk, then. I have ques—"

"You know, I made these myself," the man interrupted. "Each one has a unique set of microscopic passages through the interior. Listen." The marbles sped up, blurring into rings, and the rings circled one another like a floating gyroscope in the pale-yellow light.

Belial covered his ears as they began to emit terrible, familiar high-pitched shrieks. The wails and moans filled the parking lot. Filled Belial with dark, insatiable, hellish thoughts. Car alarms sounded from the street. "Stop that! You'll bring them all down on us."

"That's the Melody of Hell, or at least something close to it. That's what you'd send me back to? Back to 'where I belong'? What the fuck do you know about where I belong?"

Belial didn't get a chance to answer. One of the marbles careened out of orbit, struck him in the right shoulder, and spun him into the wooden fence. The arm hung limp, blood quickly seeping through his shirt. He could tell the bones were shattered. In his mind, his host screamed again. He was a man unaccustomed to pain, and Belial couldn't spare the concentration to shield him from it. He squinted and reached out with his power to snatch the remaining orbs. They slipped through his grasp as if they weren't solid. He tried again, but every time he thought he had them, he didn't. It was like scooping water with splayed fingers.

"I'm afraid that will not work, Warden," Twitch said with a rueful grin. "You should have brought friends. I did. They should be along any minute."

"Who are you?" Belial wheezed out between clenched teeth, trying to buy enough time to sort things out.

"My friends call me the Engineer."

"That's a stupid name, and your friends are dead."

"I'm disappointed! You're supposed to protect people," Twitch said grimly. "Those were just prospective recruits. My friends are still coming."

Belial's green eyes blazed arctic blue; he had to end this now before there were witnesses or reinforcements. He felt the blood on his shoulder crystallize. Twitch's marbles grew louder, shriller in the chill. Belial focused his attention on the orbs and one by one, they frosted and shattered into icy dust.

The Engineer struggled to raise his arms as heat leached from his body. His goatee hung heavy, now a comical icicle. His finger twitched, and the bloody marble behind Belial answered his call. Belial sensed the attack, but when he tried to stop the orb, it slipped through his mental grasp yet again and slammed into the back of his head and exited out of his left eye socket. Belial had the satisfaction of seeing the Engineer's ice-numbed finger twitch a half a second too late to stop it from plunging into his own stomach.

For a moment, the voice of his host was back, screaming in terror, but then Belial was drifting above the parking lot, watching the steam rise from the frosted asphalt. His former body spasmed and convulsed, smearing blood with its ruined face.

Twitch, the Engineer, whatever his name was, slumped against the light post, curled around his wound. Those friends he'd mentioned materialized from the shadows, a woman and two men. They ran to him, tried to pry his bloody fingers away from the hole in his stomach. Each of them had a golden gyroscope tattooed across the left sides of their necks. Even the Engineer had one; Belial tried to remember if it had been there before. If it had been, he had overlooked it somehow.

The woman looked up, sensing his presence; she tried to snare him with her mind, but the Pull had him and he sank willfully into it. Belial smiled and waved a claw-tipped hand in farewell. He never thought there was a time he might be happy to be in the Pull's grip. Tomekeepers said it was a created effect, but Belial thought of it more like spiritual gravity, or osmosis, a kind of drag effect tugging similar energies, a law of metaphysics.

Everything faded into patches of light and darkness as he transitioned from the physical realm. The entire world beneath him shrank into a pulsing patchwork of energy. The light was an ever-shifting pattern of new souls flaring into existence and the dying winking away to wherever they went.

Just before he slipped from the physical world entirely, he saw a great swath of darkness spreading in the west, hundreds of lives ending at once in some great tragedy, and as he pondered what it might have been, another light blazed into being, a hidden flame suddenly unshaded over a hundred miles north, and all the others, bright as they were, seemed dim by comparison.

This was a descendent of Solomon; of that he was sure. And so invitingly open and defenseless. He felt drained, but this was a rare opportunity. Using her, he could bring his full power to bear. He felt torn with indecision, and time was running out. Already at the edge of hearing, the keening screams of the Raff set his nerves on edge and made Twitch's parlor trick seem like a bad violin performance.

With a supreme effort, he willed himself toward that light, skating along the razor's edge between worlds. It was madness to think he could overcome one so bright if he managed to make it there at all. Twice he was almost yanked back as his strength failed, but excitement and curiosity filled him with giddy resolve.

As Belial drew near, her psychic radiance coalesced like a dying star, turning all else into shadow. *She's asleep. Good.* She slept deeply as he merged with her. The resistance was less than a child would have given. It was never so easy. Something was shifting on a cosmic level, playing havoc with all the rules tonight. The sensation of merging was like plunging into a vast ocean; fortunately, his brief splash didn't wake her as he slipped beneath the rolling waves of her subconscious. The Pull lessened and then was gone as he settled into place. Suddenly there were smells and the feel of sheets on his new host's bare legs. All he learned was her name, Brooklyn Amelia Evers, before exhaustion forced him to share her dreams.

1

Lost Day

Brooklyn leapt out of bed, looking around wildly for her cell phone. Sunlight streamed through translucent emerald curtains. What time was it? Being late for work again wasn't an option. She dropped to the carpeted floor and felt around under the bed, shoving shoes and books aside in the search. Somehow it always wound up under here. Her fingers bumped it further under the bed, out of reach.

"For Christ's sake . . . " Brooklyn looked around her room for something to fish it out with. Her eyes settled on the guitar that belonged to her boyfriend, David. She held it by the neck and slid it carefully under the bed. He would lose bladder control if he ever found out about this. Brooklyn couldn't see the phone; her eyes ached, and the sun lanced in the window, blinding her. She swung the guitar in a large arc, and the phone came sliding out across the carpet. The guitar got hung on something and one string popped with a twang. *Damn.* It was stuck and wouldn't budge either way. She left it. There would be time to lift the bed later when her head didn't throb. She'd need to pick up a package of strings, too. Brooklyn grabbed the phone and tapped the power button to see the time. Dead. Of course.

She bounded down the carpeted stairs two at a time. Her dad munched cereal on the couch in his underwear. No matter how many times she begged him to wear pajamas, a robe, anything! It was hopeless. Devin sat next to him in his SpongeBob pajamas with a stuffed dog clutched under his arm and a banana in his hand. Devin, almost four, favored Brooklyn's sister so much it made her heart ache.

Brooklyn kissed him on the head and said, "Morning, kiddo," then turned to her father. "Dad, what time is it?"

"Quarter of ten." He leaned to the side to see the cartoons around her. The gray hair at his temples trembling in time with his crunching cereal.

"I'm late for work."

"I'd say so. Supposed to be there yesterday." He dragged his eyes from the screen and fixed her with a reproachful stare. His eyes were blue like hers and held a hint of worry behind the anger.

She laughed. "What do you mean? I just overslept and—"

"Overslept? You were gone all day yesterday and half the night." She heard the cold fury and pain in his voice and cringed. "Are you on drugs? That's how it started with your sister."

"Jesus, Dad, not in front of him." Devin watched the exchange with wide-eyed interest. Brooklyn scooped him up and carried him into the kitchen and sat him on a stool. She plugged her phone into a charger, and the screen lit up. *Sunday? It's Sunday? Today is Saturday.* "Mom, what day is it?"

Her mom looked up from the dress she was ironing with tired, puffy eyes. "It's Sunday, Brooke."

"Well, I guess I don't have to work today after all," Brooklyn said as she glanced through her text messages. There were three from David.

U didn't go 2 work? R U sick??

Where R U??

Ur mom said U slept all day yesterday, I'll come over tonight after work, pizza and movie OK?

Brooklyn wrote back: *Sure, sounds great.*

Her mom focused intently on her ironing, not looking at Brooklyn at all. She pursed her lips several times. Finally, in a low voice, she asked, "What's going on with you?" She looked up then, teary eyed.

"I don't know. Just tired, I guess." She dropped a couple slices of bread in the toaster and began peeling an orange.

"Where were you yesterday? I told your boss you were in bed sick. What were you doing all day?"

"I was— I went hiking. I just needed a break." Her mind raced. Where had she been? She couldn't remember anything.

"Hiking, where?" Devin asked around a mouthful of banana.

"In the woods, kiddo. Where else is there?"

"What if you'd lost your job? School won't pay for itself; you can't—"

"Mom, I'm a grown woman. I don't need a lecture," she said as she rummaged through the fridge looking for the jelly. She turned with the jelly in one hand and the butter in the other. "Besides, don't you think—" Brooklyn stopped short. Her mom stared at her with a haunted expression, streaks of mascara running down both cheeks. "Oh, Mom, it's okay. It's not like that, I promise."

"What's wrong, Gammy?" Devin climbed off the stool and went to her, wrapping his arms around her thigh.

Her mom knelt and hugged him. "Nothing's wrong, baby. Gammy needs to talk to Aunt Brooke for a few minutes. That's all."

Brooklyn touched him on the shoulder. "Why don't you go back and watch cartoons with Gramps? I think he's lonely."

After he left, Brooklyn went to her mother and hugged her while she sobbed. "It's okay, I'm not going anywhere; I'm not her. Please don't worry, okay?" She laid her hands on her mom's shoulders and gently pushed her to arm's length. "Mom . . . okay?"

She gave a hesitant nod and wiped her eyes. "I'm sorry, it was three years ago today your sister went missing. I never heard you come back last night. I didn't think you would. Then I saw you back in your bed this morning, and I—"

"Let's just have some toast, okay? You want toast?" Brooklyn felt relieved when her mom nodded and wiped her eyes. "I'll get it." She did *not* want to have another conversation with her mom about Erin. Where had she been yesterday? She smeared the jelly and thought just for a moment it looked like congealed blood.

Brooklyn sat in the shower and let the heat beat down on her head and shoulders. A whole day missing. She'd gone somewhere, done something, but couldn't remember what. She hugged her knees to her breasts. Was this what it felt like to go crazy?

Brooklyn closed her eyes and breathed deeply. *Think. Think. Think.* Nothing. Had someone drugged her? Maybe it was a brain tumor? She couldn't let her mom know this was happening. She couldn't handle it; that was pretty clear. Had Erin felt this way? Had her big sister sat in this tub once trying to remember lost days before she lost herself? *Would she have told me?*

There had to be a way to figure this out. Check her phone, email, or maybe there was a clue in her car. She shampooed, rinsed, repeated, and tried to remember. She remembered going to bed Friday night, reading for a while, and turning off the lamp. Then, waking up in a blind panic this morning. Brooklyn closed her eyes tighter and ran the memories over and over. Bed on Friday, then up on Sunday . . . Friday, then Sunday. *Think. Think. Think.* It was there, nagging like a splinter in her mind. She strained to remember until the back of her eyes cramped. A memory surfaced slowly, but distorted, like watching television with bad reception.

It was dark. "Tell me what I want to know!" It was her voice, and it wasn't. She couldn't determine if she'd just said the words aloud or heard them in her head. Was she really losing it? She rested her chin on her knees.

Then she heard another voice. "More of us than you could imagine." The smell of copper, of blood, was nauseating. Like the way her hands smelled after sorting change at work, but worse. Then it was gone, leaving a dull ache behind her eyes.

After the shower, she started the computer and reviewed her bank transactions. For yesterday: one $200 withdrawal at an ATM west of town. That was pretty much all the money she'd had. Brooklyn raked fingers through her hair and tried to remember being at that ATM and couldn't. What happened to the money? She shuddered at the thought of asking her dad for money to pay her car insurance. Maybe she hadn't spent it, or maybe David could loan her some money. The thought of asking him didn't appeal either; he already did too much for her. A woman in her twenties needed a better job and her own place to live. Devin and poverty were the things that kept her here. Sometimes she hated Erin for leaving their family to pick up the pieces.

It was nearly noon when she stepped outside. The early autumn sun warmed her skin, but the wind bullied her into bringing a jacket anyway. She cast her eyes about with a sinking feeling in her stomach. Her car wasn't in the driveway. Her eyes roamed the pastures below the house. The creek cut a wandering line across the browning fields where the horses nibbled. Beyond the fields, mountains rose in a patchwork of reds, yellows, and oranges. Autumn was the best time of year, and North Carolina was the best place to be. The days seemed more precious as winter approached. She forgot the car and the lost time, closed her eyes, turned her face to the sun, and let the wind whip through her hair. She could count on at least another hour of peace. Everyone else had gone to church, and afterward they'd go somewhere for lunch. Something passed across the sun, a fleeting shadow that left the impression of great black wings. She opened her eyes and searched the sky, but it was vast, blue, and empty.

The car turned out to be behind the house directly under Brooklyn's bedroom window, the front tire resting in the soft black earth of her mother's rose garden. There were muddy footprints on the hood and roof. Little wonder no one heard her come home. She must have climbed in through the window. How was that possible? There were no handholds or footholds, and it was at least fifteen feet from the top of the car to the ledge. Muddy streaks marred the otherwise pristine shiplap siding.

The little silver Honda lurched out of the flower bed with a jolt. Brooklyn pulled it around front and searched the interior. There were burger wrappers, empty soda cans, and a couple of receipts printed on old-fashioned adding tape, showing the charges, the cash tendered, and the change, but nothing useful. No date, time, or store name. On a hunch, Brooklyn opened the fast-food bags and found a receipt with a Tennessee address inside each one. She folded them carefully and put them in her pocket. It was a start, and the best one she was going to get, apparently. David wouldn't be off from work for at least three hours. Good. She needed time to think, and nothing cleared her mind like a horse ride.

The Everses' farm backed up to heavily wooded national forests on two sides. Brooklyn rode northeast into the shadows of the foliage. It was cooler beneath the boughs, and the sun fell in a patchwork of narrow shafts and tree-limb shadows. The sounds of squirrels cutting hickory nuts and the thump of horse hooves blended with the trickling of water as the trail turned parallel to a mountain spring.

Brooklyn remembered playing up here with her sister; Erin would always say, "Up here, there is no down there." It was true. A hundred yards beyond the tree line, the rest of the world ceased to exist. There was only the mountain. The trail wound away from the water and took a steeper track. She squeezed with her upper thighs, careful of her knees lest she spur the horse unintentionally. She bent low beneath the limbs as they surged upward together.

They came to a clearing where the ridge topped out and leveled off. She swung down and led the horse to a massive shelf of rock that jutted from the side of the mountain at a severe angle, creating an alcove big enough for several people to sit protected from the rain. She swept the leaves from beneath it with her foot and found childhood artifacts. Barbie dolls with rotten wisps of hair, a crumbling shoe box of arrowheads and mica, a faded blue Igloo cooler where she and Erin had kept beer as teenagers, slipping out a window in the dead of night to meet boyfriends up here. A ring of soot-blackened stones circled a pit where they'd built campfires on chilly nights and watched the smoke spiral up thick and black to break against the stone ceiling.

She smiled at the memories, but only for a moment. Loss turns all things bitter, and soon she wished she could forget it all. She imagined the stone falling and sealing it all away forever. She screamed in frustration and choked back a sob. Earth and leaves showered down from around the rocks, and the great stone shuddered and settled in the earth like a tooth loose in its socket. Brooklyn tumbled backward into the leaves, and the horse bolted back the way they'd come.

The slant of the sun changed while she lay too tired to move. Black spots swamped her vision when at last she sat up. Was that an earthquake? She'd never been in an earthquake before. She eyed the great stone warily. Brooklyn tasted blood on her lips and swiped a sleeve across her mouth and nose; it came away red. Frost clung to her jeans in an icy sheet and had begun melting through. She dusted it away, struggled upright, and ran for home.

When she stumbled out of the trees, the horse was waiting, and so were her parents. Before they could ask, she told them she'd fallen and hit her nose during the earthquake. They exchanged worried looks with one another.

"What earthquake?" her mom asked in the same voice she used for skittish animals.

"You know. The earthquake. I felt it just for a second." She looked from her mom to her dad and back again. They didn't contradict her, but she could tell they didn't believe her either.

Her dad rested a heavy hand on her shoulder. "Honey, did you fall off the horse? Hit your head, maybe?"

"I don't know, maybe. I do have a terrible headache." It was a strange sensation, an uncomfortable thrumming in her ears like someone playing bass notes so low they were felt rather than heard.

Her dad looked at her like he couldn't decide whether to be angry or worried. Finally, he sighed. "You want me to put your horse back in the pasture?"

"No, I got her out. I'll put her up." She gave both of her parents a quick hug and a smile and hoped it would reassure them she wasn't a lunatic. Brooklyn led the horse back into the pasture and closed the gate. The mare gave a disdainful snort as Brooklyn turned away. *Everybody's a critic*, she thought.

Brooklyn barely had time to clean herself up and down some painkillers before David arrived. He was a little shy of six feet and in good shape. He had shaggy brown hair and eyes to match, more of a musician's look than that of an insurance salesman. But that was okay, because he was both. Though, it was clear which was his passion. She couldn't stop smiling as she walked out to meet him. He hugged her, and she relished it, enjoying his solidity and the sharp scent of aftershave. "Feeling better today?"

"Better than yesterday." *At least I remember today*, she didn't say. "How about you?"

"Fine, as working on your day off can be," he said, looking amused.

"Harold on your ass again?" she teased.

"Was on Friday. But I guess he's got someone else to be pissed at now, seeing as how I'm all caught up and you left him working the front desk all day yesterday."

Brooklyn winced. "That bad, huh?"

David shrugged. "It won't last long. It never does."

They both laughed. His brown eyes were always bright, and he was quick to smile. Everyone liked him, even her dad, and that was saying something, but Devin adored him most of all. They carried the pizzas inside, where everyone gathered around the coffee table and watched television while they ate.

David made small talk with her family, and Brooklyn loved him for it because she couldn't focus on the conversation. He asked her dad how things were coming on the farm and what he thought of the high school football team this year. She nodded and smiled and heard almost nothing. Maybe she had a concussion. That could explain the memory loss.

"—isn't that what you said, Brooke?"

Brooklyn looked up. Her mom was gesturing at her. "I . . . Um, which thing I said?"

Her mom gestured impatiently. "Didn't you say there was an earthquake?"

Brooklyn shrugged. "I felt something. I'm not sure what it was."

Her dad shook his head. "I think we would have felt it."

"It wasn't just me that felt it. It spooked Lilly bad enough she bolted and came all the way home."

"It could have been an earthquake. We were probably in the car. You wouldn't even notice a little tremor if you were driving on the roads around here, bumpy as they are," her mom said.

David turned the conversation to deer hunting, and that kept her dad and Devin engaged for the rest of dinner. Soon they could take the movie and go upstairs and she would finally have someone to talk to about everything.

Five slices of pizza later, her head felt almost normal. Maybe it was just a blood sugar thing? Could that cause memory loss? Probably not, but it would explain falling down and the hallucination with the earthquake and the rock. She snapped back to the dinner conversation. She nodded in agreement with a comment she hadn't heard, and the conversation rolled on without her.

After the plates were cleaned and the leftovers put away, Brooklyn suggested they go upstairs. David smiled politely at her parents and let her lead him away. Her room was dark; as soon as the door was closed, she pulled him close and told him everything. He stroked her hair while he listened.

"You don't remember anything about yesterday at all?" he asked.

"I don't know where I went, what I did. I don't know what to do. What if it happens again?"

Shadows played across his furrowed brows. "I think you should go see a doctor. What if it is something, you know, serious?"

She considered it, the nosebleed, the hallucination, lost memories, and the headache. "I'll make an appointment, but you can't say anything to my parents. They already think I'm on drugs. They're worried enough." She searched his eyes for doubts about her and found none. "Did you miss me?" she asked as she slid her hand across his chest playfully. He didn't answer right away, but the amusement was back in his eyes and a smile touched his lips as he looked her up and down.

"Yes," he admitted, "but everyone is still awake and—"

"Then try to keep your loud moaning to a minimum," she teased as they kissed and shuffled in lockstep to the bed. At least the day would not be all bad. She pushed him, and they tumbled into the unmade bed together with her on top. There was a loud crack and a sickening cacophony of guitar strings.

After he stormed out with the pieces of his grandfather's guitar in a box, she lay in bed and cried. In two days, one of which she couldn't even recall, she'd lost her money, her sanity, and now her boyfriend. It wasn't fair. How could things have spiraled out of control so quickly? Brooklyn wanted nothing more than to sleep and forget everything, but she was afraid to sleep, not knowing what day it would be when she woke up. What if she lost weeks this time? What if she never woke up? Maybe that would be better for everyone.

“I’m all alone.” Saying it out loud made it more real. Fresh tears welled. “I’m all alone, all alone,” she said again and again like a prayer. Eventually, the tears ran dry and she couldn’t stay awake. As she drifted off with her mantra ringing in her thoughts, she heard a brittle, frigid laugh tinkling like ice in a glass.

2

Playing Politics

Kurt Levin was the last one into the conference room, if you could call it that. It served many purposes, including acting as a formal dining area whenever the occasion warranted. It looked more like a courtroom today, with a dais and fifteen ornate mahogany tables in a semicircle. Of the thirty chairs, eight were occupied. More than normal but less than Kurt expected with the Heir's banquet drawing near.

To the far left sat Erina Craft and her daughter Bryssa, of the Wandering Witches, both raven haired and green eyed. Erina was solemn, with regal streaks of gray worn like a fashion statement rather than a visible sign of aging. It lent a certain levity to her otherwise somber bearing. Their family seldom came to meetings, and it surprised Kurt to see them here today. Of all the families who sat on the council, theirs was the most mysterious. If legends could be believed, and they probably couldn't, the Craft family had sole claim to the rare gift of elemental magic. He suspected they were likely just gifted illusionists. The Crafts spent much of their time as traveling stage performers, a nomadic life chosen by the family matriarch centuries ago somewhere in Europe and still proudly practiced by the main body of the family. Erina may have grown up in a circus tent, but Bryssa, he suspected, had never known discomfort or the hard work of stagecraft.

The next two tables sat empty, and then sat Tristan Barrett, tall and broad with impassive blue-gray eyes and a liver-spotted scalp, the head of a Scotch Irish family that traced origins back to the ancient Druids, and the only foreigner to respond to the meeting call. He spotted Kurt and nodded politely in greeting. Kurt returned the gesture.

At the next table, Father Dravin Logan scribbled in a notebook. He was in his late thirties but might have easily passed for much younger. His black hair curled tight against his scalp, and he bore the shadow of a beard. He led a religious group that called themselves the Prophets. Yet, to Kurt's knowledge, the Prophets had predicted nothing accurate in his lifetime. They were a small but tenacious sect that had drifted in and out of existence over the past few centuries. Recent reports showed their numbers had grown significantly in the past decade under Father Logan's leadership. Kurt wasn't particularly fond of Dravin; he was self-righteous, charismatic, and overzealous. His followers creepy in their absolute, unwavering devotion, too.

Several empty tables separated Father Logan and Nathan Goodrum, and for good reason. Nathan was an ambassador for the Demonriders. Kurt considered them little more than a glorified street gang, but they had their uses, he supposed. Other stakeholders had repeatedly challenged their standing as members of the council, but they always won out in the end.

Demonriders practiced intentional and persistent possession and earned their membership by bending demons to their wills, a secretive and risky art on the best of days and an invitation to disaster most any other time. Dominating demons gave them incredible reserves of energy to draw on, but you could never be sure their control would hold. Demonriders walked a razor's breadth from breaking the laws regarding demon summoning and possession, a fact that made them loathsome to most of the other Solomonians in the room. Some of Kurt's own followers were reformed Demonriders dismissed for losing control.

At the next-to-last table, Kurt saw two of his three counterparts for the districts of North America. Kurt himself handled law and order in the supernatural community for everything east of the Mississippi; Brianne Moore, a spindly woman in her early fifties, held everything west of the Mississippi; and Michael Benson, a skinny, dark-haired man with glasses who couldn't have been a day over twenty-five years old, kept order in Canada. Newly appointed, he still wore the traditional robes of his office Kurt had dispensed with such pretense the very day they had appointed him as a Protector. Comfort and utility trumped appearances.

The last of the eight was Eric Stewarth, a boy of about sixteen with fierce brown eyes, olive skin, and long black hair pulled back; he wore the Sigil of Solomon on his shirt, embroidered in golden thread.

"How's your father?" Kurt whispered.

"Some better, but still too tired for meetings," the boy murmured in his ear.

"You'll be speaking for him today, I suppose?"

"Yes," he said with a nod, "or more likely just listening and taking notes."

Kurt patted him on the shoulder and climbed the stairs to the podium. He fought to slow his racing heart. How frustrating to have faced things powerful enough to rip a man apart with a thought and yet, public speaking still left his legs trembling.

Eric's father was the Heir of Solomon, the closest thing they had to a sovereign. Normally this duty would have fallen to him, but unknown to most, he'd been battling a mysterious illness for the past three months. Such information was carefully guarded. The appearance of strength was imperative to keeping some groups under control. Kurt looked around the room at the gathering, his eyes settling on Nathan Goodrum. The Demonriders had the most to fear from the Heir because he possessed Solomon's ring and it gave absolute control over demons, even the ones they depended on for their unnatural power.

"Welcome, all," Kurt began with a smile, and let his eyes roam the room. "We've called this gathering because there have been many reports in the last few weeks of unusual disappearances." Murmurs of agreement broke out around the room. "Eleven of my own men have gone missing, and the Protectors of the North and West have suffered similar losses." He watched the faces of all present for a reaction. When no one sweated profusely, he continued. "There has been no communication from the Southern Protector. He's presumed dead." Kurt paused, knowing silence would fan the flames of discussion.

"Perhaps these men simply deserted," said Erina. "It wouldn't be the first time someone walked away from this life."

Sounds of agreement rumbled from several of those gathered. Kurt didn't disagree with the thought. Initiates remained affiliated with an established group, or they became fugitives.

"There's just too many in too short a time. Clearly someone orchestrated the disappearances, and it would have to be someone powerful," said Kurt, with a meaningful glance at each of them. *Like one of you, or someone who should be sitting in one of these empty chairs.*

Brianne steepled her fingers thoughtfully. "Thirty-four lost is a lot. Thirty-four people of power . . . Well, that's a small army."

Father Logan cleared his throat. "By my records, they were all novices and minor talents. Who would have a use for thirty-four with insignificant gifts?"

"There are ways to strengthen the weak," Nathan Goodrum reminded them all in a carefully controlled voice.

"And ways to make the strong weak again if they depend on unnatural paths to power," Eric added with a cocked brow.

Goodrum clenched his teeth but said nothing.

In all the meetings he'd ever been to, Eric sat meekly by his father and never uttered a word. Shocking that he'd spoken at all, let alone so boldly. Kurt hated facilitating the conclave. This was politicians' work. He didn't have the stomach for it.

The meeting teetered on the edge of discord. Clearly, open discussion wasn't going to get them very far.

"We have other items to discuss, so I will meet with Brianne and Michael afterward about our missing friends. Perhaps, if we compare notes regarding what they were working on when they disappeared, we may find a common thread." Kurt let the statement hang in the air for a moment. When no one objected, he pressed on. "Right then, so that issue we will table for later; what other business do we have for today?"

Bryssa Craft raised her hand meekly. "A request."

Kurt smiled. "Please go ahead."

"A grade-two demon took my fiancé, Evan." The room erupted in a clamor of incredulous commentary.

Kurt raised a hand for silence.

She continued tremulously. "Exorcism has never been a talent in our family. I came here to ask Heir Stewarth to banish the demon. I'm afraid Evan won't survive a lesser form of exorcism."

"And where is Evan now?" Kurt's mind floundered. Surely Erina would have verified the truth of this before allowing Bryssa to make such a fantastic claim in open council.

"In a storage unit just outside town, guarded by the rest of our family."

"Very well. I'll see what I can do after we conclude here." How could a grade-two demon be on Earth? It was unheard of. Summoning the Old Ones carried a penalty of death. And that assumed you survived the summoning. Every eye in the room turned to him, wide with disbelief.

Father Logan cleared his throat. "Perhaps I might be of help; I've dealt with—"

"Nothing of this magnitude," Kurt finished for him. "Thank you for the sentiment, but this is a job for the Protectors." *Something you will never be, Dravin.* He itched to say it aloud. He shuffled a stack of papers on the lectern. "It seems I have quite a busy day ahead, so let's keep this moving along. Mr. Goodrum, you had a petition, I believe."

"Well," he began in a carefully modulated, inflectionless voice, "we would like to formally disavow three of our members for desertion and be relieved of responsibility for anything they might do." He sniffed loudly. "Their names are—"

Kurt raised a hand to forestall him. "Hold up a minute. This is highly unusual. We allow a disavowal only when there is another council-approved group willing to accept responsibility. As you know, I have several of your former members in my service. So, you've made arrangements with someone?"

"Well, no, not exactly. They've gone rogue. There are rumors of a new, unsanctioned organization with practices like our own."

A chorus of murmurs rolled around the room until Kurt held up a hand for silence. "Give us the names."

"Hayleigh Vinson, Marco Goff, and Conner Day. Also, I have pictures to be dispersed."

"Very well." Kurt raised his voice, taking on a formal tenor. "I decree by the Wisdom of Solomon that the former Demonriders, Hayleigh Vinson, Marco Goff, and Conner Day, are fugitives. They are to be captured on sight and brought before the council for judgment. If they resist, it is just and proper to kill them. Brianne, please distribute pictures as soon as Mr. Goodrum provides them." He took a deep breath. "Now, the Demonriders will remain accountable. You took these three to train; they are your responsibility, whatever they may do. I can hardly make an unrecognized, rumored organization responsible." He paused until Goodrum ducked his head in acquiescence.

"All right, if there is no other business, I'll meet with the Protectors briefly and then we will attend to our other duties. Erina and Bryssa, if you'll wait outside, we won't be long."

"Grade two . . . Is that even possible?" Michael smoothed his robe nervously.

"It's exceedingly rare; someone powerful must have summoned it. I can't imagine one that old breaking free of the Pull without some significant help." Brianne reached inside her pocketbook and produced three Ziploc Baggies of peanut butter cookies. "We don't fully understand the Pull or how it works, but I think it would be about as likely as an elephant drifting off into outer space unassisted."

"These are fantastic." Kurt swallowed noisily. "So, you think this is something the three of us can handle safely?"

"Safely? I doubt it, but what choice do we have? Working together, we should be quite formidable." She offered a reassuring smile.

Kurt smiled through a mouthful of cookie. "This is going to be awesome! Who else can say they've confronted one of the Old Ones? It will be like standing in the eye of a supernatural hurricane or something." *And so much simpler than playing politics.* He itched to dispense with the pretense of political maneuvering and pit his will against an adversary.

"What happens if we fail?" Michael asked.

Kurt raised his eyebrows. "We die."

3

Changing Tides

They found Eric waiting with Mrs. Craft and her daughter. Kurt urged him to let them handle the demon alone, but as his father's proxy, Eric insisted on being present and agreed to make a quick exit if things got out of hand.

The drive took less than an hour. They wound through the mountains on a two-lane blacktop. No one spoke; Kurt could hear the SUV's tires whisper against the pavement as he navigated the curves. They arrived shortly before midnight at a nondescript self-storage facility with a gravel lot. The building, made of corrugated metal, sported long rows of roll-up doors. The lighting was poor. Kurt thought it seemed like a place you read about in the newspaper when a meth lab explodes.

They piled out of the vehicle and huddled like a small football team. Kurt looked around the circle, meeting everyone's eyes. "When we go in, I want the family out. Eric, stay near the door. If we get it out, the demon should fall to the Pull almost immediately. If things go sideways, get out and don't look back. Everybody clear?"

They all nodded.

Kurt grinned and said, "Okay, let's do this." He took a deep breath and heaved up on the metal door. It rolled up with a startling clatter, and they stepped in.

It was dim. Dust motes floated in the hazy light. A slim blond boy of about twenty sat cross-legged in the center of the concrete floor. Seven of the Craft family stood in the room, four occupying the corners and one on each of the three walls. They all had their right hands extended toward the center of the room. A circle of candles cast restless shadows across the ceiling. Kurt winced at the stifling heat. As his eyes adjusted, he discerned the sweaty faces of the seven. With each slow, deep breath the blond boy took, the other seven trembled with fatigue, their faces pinched and strained. Kurt stepped inside the ring of candles with the boy, Evan. Michael quickly ushered the others out and closed the door with a clang. He and Brianne each took a corner near the door. Eric stood against the door, forming a triangle spearheaded by Kurt.

Kurt stepped forward. What do you say to a demon at least as old as humanity? He nudged the boy with the toe of his boot. "So, what brings you to Tennessee?" No response came, just the same steady breathing. Kurt nudged him again. "Hey, you awake in there?" Every breath was an ocean tide, a wave of unstoppable energy expanding and contracting. Again and again, it rushed over him and flowed around him, cosmic and terrifying. "Eric, I really think you should go."

"I don't think so, Protector Levin," he replied. "You may need my help."

Kurt groaned inwardly. Eric was good. Kurt had trained him, so of course he was, but he wasn't *that* good.

"So, any idea how to wake this guy up? I'm—" He suddenly noticed the waves of energy had stilled. Not gone away so much as restrained in a way as shocking as if his own heart had stopped beating. The demon was awake. Its eyes were mismatched and hypnotically beautiful, one the steel gray of storm clouds with patterns of iridescent white lines that seemed lightning one instant and seafoam the next. The other eye shone a mixture of shimmering yellow and blue that reminded Kurt of nothing so much as the glint of sunlight on the Mediterranean Sea. "You have pretty eyes," Kurt heard himself say. *Stupid. What the hell kind of thing is that to say? Get a grip!*

"Thank you," the boy answered politely. His voice, though quiet, had a vastness, like the sound of far-off waves crashing against a cliff. "What are your names?"

"I'm Kurt, this is Brianne, and Michael," he replied, intentionally leaving Eric out.

The demon's eyes shifted from one face to the other, then he leaned to the side, looking past Kurt. "And you must be Eric?" He smiled like a shark. "I was a great friend to your family once; I returned something hopelessly lost . . . You wear it on your finger today."

Kurt turned to look at Eric; his fingers were bare, but his face had grown pale and expressionless.

"Why are you here, and what do you want?" Kurt asked, hoping to take the creature's attention off Eric.

"I've come for my children. Seven hundred and fourteen of them have come here and vanished. The Heir of Solomon must pay for his crimes and return my children. We had a covenant, Eric. Your family released your claim to the Element of Water when I returned Solomon's ring from the sea."

"We have taken none of your kin into service, ever, save the Wardens who serve under the First Treaty. If someone has summoned your scions, it wasn't us." Eric stepped forward past Kurt. "I swear it on the Seal of Solomon." He pressed three fingers against the golden embroidery over his heart.

Kurt tensed; he should have never brought the boy here. In seconds, the stakes had soared. He reached out with his mind, gently probing the demon, looking for a weakness or a way to unseat him. The demon was old, immense, and slippery as an eel. By now, the demon knew it was being probed but seemed indifferent, which was worrisome. Kurt gave a signal behind his back, and Brianne and Michael merged their power with his will.

"If what you say is true, show your good faith by returning the ring to my care. When you put aside your family's power, and it does not release my children, I'll know you've spoken true and return the ring. Do this; we may find we are allies with a common enemy. We've cooperated for millennia with the trust of mutual vulnerability and purpose. I want to believe you."

Eric took another step, and Kurt's heart skipped a beat; he leapt between Eric and the demon.

"How about you let the boy go and then we can discuss it?" Kurt said and ran a warm tongue over dry lips. "Or perhaps you'd like to tell us who summoned you here. The boy you're sitting in?" He glanced over his shoulder at Eric. "Go stand at the door like you promised." He opened his mouth to argue, and Kurt cut him off. "Go before you get us all killed." Eric's shoulders sagged, and he slowly backed away, but Kurt sensed his humiliation icing over into rage.

The demon looked genuinely perplexed. "A servant commands the Heir of the Wise King?"

"He's not the Heir; he's the Heir's heir." *Well, that was clear.* "What I mean is, your business is with his father, and he isn't available. Eric says his father had nothing to do with your um . . . children going missing." Kurt took a steadying breath and continued. "Now vacate that boy."

The demon's laughter was as merciless as a riptide. It seemed as good an opportunity as any, so Kurt pushed hard. The laughter died abruptly as they struggled in silence. Psychic battles were the most dangerous; broken bones would heal, but broken minds rarely did. Kurt drew steadily from his partners as he sought to safely break the demon's grip on Evan's fragile consciousness. The room thrummed with energy; the candles flared higher and higher. Kurt felt the demon's resistance recede, and he pressed his advantage, giving chase, letting his mind expand to fill the space. He felt the boy fighting, however feebly, for his freedom, and that gave Kurt heart; at least he wasn't broken. He closed his eyes and pushed with everything the three of them together could muster.

Brianne's voice came to him, faraway and frantic. "Tidal . . . you fool . . . tidal demon."

Ah, that was it. A demon of the ocean, Prosidris, returner of the ring, a demon of old myths and legends, but why was Brianne so worked up about that? Kurt felt like a god. The power he directed seemed limitless. What she was saying couldn't be that important, could it? This was no time to categorize demons by class, grade, or type. He didn't know why she kept going on about it, and he didn't have time to worry over it just now. Not with power thrumming through every fiber of his being like high-voltage electricity.

Kurt drew on his companions and gave a final, terrific thrust of psychic energy, and the demon receded further. He held strong, giving the Pull time to take hold, riding high on power, invincible, his being pressing outward, filling the room.

There was a tremendous roar as the tide came back in. A tsunami of energy slammed Kurt back into the steel door, severing the connection with his friends. Through a haze, he saw Eric standing over him, unaffected, a radiant glow emanating from his raised fist. Evan slumped across the floor, scattering candles. Kurt sensed Michael and Brianne behind him, unmoving, but alive. Eric gestured with his glowing hand, and the demon rose out of the unconscious boy. He looked terrifying. Twelve feet tall on a tangle of black tentacles, his torso the slick gray of shark skin. Four massive fins sprouted from his back like wings dotted with lidless eyes as large as grapefruits. His head was a roiling orb of storm-gray water, and faces, some of them bloodied, came and went in the shifting patterns. They were talking, but Kurt couldn't fathom the language. His ears buzzed with whistles and whooshes, long mournful wails and rumbles he felt more than heard. He ached all over but forced himself to stand. Kurt would never have brought Eric knowing his father had passed the ring. The ring itself was safe enough. No demon could take it by force, but Eric was just a boy and there were things he might not understand. Things Kurt didn't want him to discover. It was best if the father of the Demon Wardens and the son of the Heir didn't get too friendly.

"Cut him loose, Eric; everyone's hurt. We don't have time for this." Eric didn't seem to hear. "The boy may need a doctor." It was true. He hadn't moved since slumping over the candles, but Eric asked another question in that strange language. After the answer, he frowned, nodded, and made to remove the ring. Kurt's stomach lurched. If the ring came off, the Pull would take this demon, and if his children weren't released as well, he'd look under other stones. Kurt leapt to his feet and tackled Eric before the ring slipped free. They went down hard in a tangle of legs and arms. White light flickered. Kurt wasn't sure if it was the jolt of the impact or the ring going dark. He hoped for the latter. When he rolled off the boy, he smiled grimly; they were alone in the shadows.

4

Green Pastures

Belial sat in Brooklyn's car, watching the house across the street. The houses near the cul-de-sac were empty during the day, and the turnaround was on a knoll that gave a full view of the neighborhood, while low-hanging limbs and yard shrubbery gave partial cover to the car.

The days were certainly more comfortable than the nights spent crouching behind the shrubs or sitting in a tree to keep watch. Three full days and no one had come in or out. He wished he had been more patient during the bloody but brief interrogation. Perhaps the piss ant had lied. Belial couldn't see the golden gyroscope sigil through Brooklyn's eyes, but he remembered the faces well enough. Perhaps he had let revenge take higher priority than reconnaissance when he'd waylaid the Engineer's man. With patience and time, he might have led Belial right back to his boss. Belial was known for many things; patience wasn't one of them.

For the hundredth time, he considered breaking in. It worked so well in his mind. The door blasted from the hinges, his foes falling like wheat before a scythe, the cowards among them answering his questions, but recent experiences had bred a caution he'd never known before. There were too many unusual variables that troubled him. More than anything, he was unsettled by the Engineer, his arrogance, and his strange phantom marbles. Those orbs had slipped through his grasp again and again as if they weren't real, though the hole in his former host's skull had seemed real enough.

He sighed, shifting in the seat; his back ached. That was another thing. At least his last host had been easily controlled; not this one. If he could gain her submission, he could dispense with aches and pains and lots of other human distractions. Truly, she'd been a bitch about the whole thing. First, she'd set up a camcorder at night to monitor herself. When he'd tried to communicate, to reach some sort of agreement, she'd tried to rush off like a fool to a psychiatric hospital, convinced she had schizophrenia.

Even now, she believed herself mentally ill. Stubborn, strong willed, and idiotic; that was all he knew about her. Brooklyn had thwarted his attempts to access her memories from the beginning. She'd never been trained to use any of her gifts; that was obvious. Otherwise he could not have gotten in. It went further than that though. Not only untrained but sheltered by something or someone such that she'd never needed to be trained. That was another nagging, unanswered question. How did he escape the Pull and overcome Brooklyn in his weakened state? Both should have been near insurmountable obstacles. It defied logic and centuries of experience.

So, she was powerful, but not fully his. If he could just see her memories, he could take her resistance apart in no time at all. He knew it was crucial to gain full control before she wound up having herself committed or arrested. He brushed the hair from her face and reclined the seat. She was there, babbling, like always.

Why can't I move? What is wrong with me? I need a doctor. Her thoughts of frustration rattled around endlessly in the back of their shared mind.

He tried reaching out again. *Will you talk to me now?*

Just like before, she fell silent as if he might forget she was there.

I can help you understand what is happening if you'll let me.

Don't talk to the voices. Don't talk to the voices. Don't talk to the voices, she chanted.

You are being childish. First you pretend you are invisible, and now you stick your fingers in your ears and try to drown me out?

Don't talk to the voices. Don't talk to the voices. Don't talk to the voices.

Belial sighed audibly. So much for that. He focused on trying to recall her memories. He pictured her mother's face and sensed flashes of image and emotion, but just when the images took form, they slipped away. Belial tried her dad, her boyfriend, her sixth-grade science class. All her memories were annoyingly evanescent.

When Belial thought of Devin, he felt a swelling warmth and a hint of sadness mingled with uncertainty. Was this an opening? He pushed harder, fighting for the memories. They turned to ash and blew away. It stumped him. Every day, he focused on each of her family members. Her mom . . . nothing. Her dad . . . nothing. David, Devin, Erin . . . so little it might as well be nothing. Brooklyn had tapped into something on that mountain, but whatever had upset her eluded him.

"I could make you let me in, make you talk. You know that, right?" he said aloud. The threats sounded more intimidating when he thought them. A woman's voice just wasn't the same.

Then why haven't you?

Because I'd prefer a mutually beneficial arrangement, one that doesn't involve the destruction of your identity.

You're just a voice in my head. How can I believe anything you say, or anything I see? I'm crazy . . . I killed that man. I remember it . . .

Great, she could see his memories and he couldn't so much as glimpse hers. *That wasn't you, and that wasn't a man. Believe me; I'm here to help. Trust me? Okay?*

What are you?

I can show you if you are sure you'd like to see.

There was a hesitant pause before she said, *Okay.*

He made a place between them in her mind. A field because he thought she'd like that. The sunlit grass was greener, the sky bluer, the clouds more billowy than anything the real world offered. He conjured wild horses in the distance, a gentle breeze, the smell of freshly mown hay.

Ancient and gnarled shade trees sprouted, birds filled the limbs, and great rocks erupted like islands in the field. In the shadow of an immense and vague forest, a waterfall appeared and fed a sparkling pool. It was, he thought, just about perfect.

But what face to show her? He had four; he didn't think any of them would go over very well. The wolverine, the whale, the hawk, and the wolf. His four great wings covered front and back with lidless eyes set amid crystalline scales. Among the other spirits, he was considered exceedingly beautiful, but a doe couldn't be expected to appreciate the grace and splendor of a predator. So, he created a new form. Tall, pale, and wingless, he found it unappealing, but he looked something like David's more attractive younger brother. "You can come see," he whispered as he stepped slowly out from behind a tree and waited.

Brooklyn came, picking her way warily through the grass. It was disorienting to see her like this after more than a week of looking at that face in the mirror and thinking of it as his own. She was about five-eight, pretty in an athletic sort of way, and she moved with a strange and ungainly grace, dressed in jeans and a shirt as black as her hair. There was something amusing about the need humans had for clothing inside their own minds. The unnatural colors of the landscape gave her blue eyes an icy edge. *Truly, this one was made for me*, he thought. She stopped at what, he guessed, she perceived to be a safe distance.

"Who are you?"

He shrugged. "I'm Belial." The name was self-explanatory, but she didn't seem impressed. "I am a spirit; I mean you no harm or ill will." He spread his arms, palms up in welcome.

Her expression turned dark and sour. "Get out of my head! Give me my life back!" She rushed at him, swinging her fists. He vanished and reappeared behind her. Brooklyn whirled with another strike, and he blinked out of existence for half a heartbeat. She gave a howl of frustration as he vanished from blow after blow.

"BE STILL!" she howled. It wasn't a request; it was a command. There was willpower in those words, and the entire field seemed to shimmer as her edict echoed back from the hillside. The breeze was gone, and nothing stirred. Her next blow met his jaw with a wet, meaty thwack and drove him to his knees. Brooklyn hit him over and over, until the grass was bright with blood and his face swollen and misshapen. Until she was breathless and her right hand wouldn't open all the way. Brooklyn rolled off him onto her back, chest heaving. He sat up, rivulets of blood running off his chin from his broken nose and ruined lips. One eye swollen shut, he tilted his head until he had her squarely fixed with the other one.

"Let me see your hands," he whispered. She sat up and cringed at the damage she'd done. He smiled and, judging from her face, it was even more grotesque than he'd hoped. He took her hands deftly, before she could recoil, and ran his thumb across the torn and discolored skin. When he finished, her hands were healed.

"How did you—"

"Because I'm not evil," Belial said. "This"—he gestured to his broken face—"this was evil. You said be still, so I was still. I did not have to allow this, but I hope you feel better now. This, like most evil, was born of ignorance and fear, not malice. I forgive you." He touched his index finger to his forehead and dragged it slowly down the center of his face, and in its wake, the flesh knitted and his nose straightened. "Come," he said as he rose and walked to the pool beneath the waterfall to wash the blood off. He didn't dare look back to see if she'd believed his bluff and followed. The waterfall hung suspended in midair. There was no subtle way to do this, but better to do it than let her discover she could. Kneeling beside the pool, he closed his eyes and released the breeze and the waterfall. The sound of the little world coming back to life was deafening. Belial could sense her standing behind him as he scooped the water to his face and took a long drink to rinse his mouth.

"What is this place?"

"It's anything you want it to be, really. I've tried to make it a place you'd like, but you haven't been very forthcoming about yourself. If you would let me in, I could make this a haven for you. I could give you anything you can imagine. What do you want?"

"I want my body back, my life back, and I want you to get out of my head."

"My work is very important, and I need your body for a while. You ask the one thing I cannot give, and for that, I am truly sorry. When my work is done, perhaps we could reach an agreement, but for now would this suffice?" He gestured to a hill behind her.

Brooklyn turned slowly to find her parents' house, her car, and the landscape slowly becoming familiar as she remembered the way it was supposed to be. "None of the chairs need be empty," Belial whispered behind her. "Give me your memories, and I'll give you the people you love. Come," he said, taking her hand and leading her up the drive.

Minor details changed and shifted as she filled in the gaps. Rose bushes, cracks in the paint, a squeaky porch step. Inside, it was just like the first morning they remembered together. She felt a fragile smile and a desperate longing clawing inside her. Her dad was on the couch with Devin, watching cartoons, the smell of coffee and bacon. The hiss of her mom's steam iron in the kitchen. Devin's face was vague and undefined. She couldn't focus on it, and her father was just a ghost of himself, but for once wearing pajamas. Both of them were as inanimate as the couch they were sitting on. Poor copies of the people Brooklyn remembered. Her face grew hard and cold as stone. "Give me your memories, and I can give them to you the way they are supposed to be," Belial whispered urgently. "Let me in. Let me make them whole."

"They aren't real." Her voice sounded wooden, broken. "None of it is real."

"Nothing is real. Not this world and not the next. All that is real is what you feel. I can make it real, make *them* real for you, if you'll let me. Please let me help. You are suffering."

She blinked back tears, but when she spoke, her voice was firm. "No." Then she said it again, more forcefully, and everything dissolved in a swirl of color and light.

Belial gasped, sitting up in the car, looking around wildly. The sun was slanting through the trees as evening came on. Sweat beaded on his forehead, and he wiped it away with his sleeve. He laughed. The unexpected sound of his girlish laugh made him laugh all the harder. He laughed until tears streamed and his ribs ached. The seed now planted would grow.

5

David, PI

David spun back and forth in his office chair, ignoring the stack of insurance claims on the edge of the desk. The red light on the phone blinked lazily to indicate he had messages.

Outside the window, rain drizzled and turned the oily spots on the pavement into rainbow whorls. Beyond the parking lot, a ribbon of highway shrouded in fog birthed cars from the gloom. David sighed and ran fingers through his hair. It was only four thirty and already it seemed like nightfall. He walked down the corridor to Lee's office and pecked on the door with his fingertips.

"Yeah, come in."

They'd played football together in high school, but he looked much older than David. He'd gained weight and lost a lot of hair. He was usually in a good mood, and that's what David needed right now.

"Hey man, you got a minute?"

"Always, what's up?" He dropped his pen, leaned back, and smiled.

David closed the door and sat. "It's Brooklyn. She's missing again." Lee was the only person he'd trusted with knowledge of his office romance.

"How do you know? I mean, you said she left before but was back the next day."

"Her mom called. She's been gone since the day after we had that fight."

"The guitar?"

"Yeah, the guitar. Anyway, she hoped I'd heard from Brooklyn. I keep thinking maybe I pushed her over the edge or something. I mean, she was scared that night, confused."

"You said it yourself. She was already losing it. I know you don't want to hear it, but—"

"Don't." He pinched the bridge of his nose. "You're right. I don't want to hear you say she's crazy or on drugs. You don't know her like I do. She would never do drugs; that's what happened to her sister. At least that's what they say."

"Isn't it odd, two sisters vanishing? I'm just saying some mental illness, it's genetics."

"Come on, man."

"Okay, fine. But let's recap. She disappeared for a day, can't tell you where she was or what she did, spent all of her bill money on God knows what, parked her car in her mom's flower bed and walked on it, hallucinated an earthquake, destroyed your grandpa's very expensive guitar, asked to borrow money during your breakup fight, lost her job for not showing up, and now has taken off again." He shrugged. "If it's not drugs, and you don't think she is crazy, what does that leave?"

"I don't know." David sighed. This conversation wasn't really going the way he'd envisioned, but he pressed on. "Brooklyn's mom called me today. She doesn't feel like the cops are doing anything to find her."

"Brooklyn's an adult that left in her own car. They probably won't."

And she stole her mom's credit card. He wasn't going to share that and lend more fuel to the addiction theory. "I'm afraid she's in trouble and nobody is really looking for her."

"Why doesn't her family look for her?"

"I don't know, man"—David waved his hand dismissively—"her dad's a limp noodle, and her mom is kind of delicate."

Lee raised his eyebrows as if to say, *See. Crazy is genetic.*

"They've got the kid to take care of," David added quickly.

Lee leaned back in the chair with his hands behind his head. There were sweat stains on his shirt. "So what? They've asked you to find her?"

David shrugged. "Sort of, yeah." He leaned forward, staring intently. "What do you think I should do?"

"I don't know. How would you figure out where to look? What if she doesn't want to be found? You've got work, and I hate to bring it up, but we have a show in less than a week and you haven't been to the last two jam sessions."

"I know—"

"We've got to practice. Besides, it sounds like you guys are basically broken up."

David bit his bottom lip and pinched his chin into a cleft. "I know. It's just . . . You can't understand she was—"

"Delusional?"

"Haunted."

"If you run off on a wild goose chase, who will play the guitar Saturday? This gig could be a big thing for the band."

David shook his head. "You're right. We broke up. I'm the last person she'd want to see even if I could find her. Tomorrow night at Charlie's place?"

"Yeah, seven thirty."

David smiled. "I'll be there."

He tried to call again, and it went straight to voicemail. "Hi, this is Brooklyn. Leave a message." He hung up. Full, just like it had been every night for the past week.

He took a long sip of beer and picked up the folder again. Someone had taped it to his door. The credit card statement inside had several charges highlighted, all of them from the same few small towns in Tennessee. The most recent lay a good way northwest of Nashville. *Over four hundred miles. Christ.*

He put the papers aside and knelt by the coffee table, where lay the ruins of his grandfather's guitar. The music shop had been clear it wasn't salvageable, but he couldn't bear throwing it away. Instead, he'd made a coffee table shrine where, each night, he spent time on his knees bowed in monastic concentration as he puzzled and glued the pieces. On the edge of the table sat a cracked picture of him and Brooklyn, the one she'd hurled into the box of guitar splinters during the fight.

Lee made sense. She'd gone crazy. That stuff was genetic, and her mom was a little off. Her sister had pulled the same vanishing act a few years ago, so why was it so hard to swallow the logical explanation? Hell, she suggested it herself right before the fight.

On the other end of the table was a picture of his Grandpa Sterling smiling in his workshop, half-finished fiddles and guitars on the workbench behind him, thumbs hooked in the bib of his overalls. He looked really, really happy. He arranged the photos side by side so that Brooklyn was between him and his grandfather. The old man's eyes were full of light and life and a youthful vigor that belied his age. She wore a quirky smile, hair pulled into a high tail, and her eyes danced with mischief. Strange to think how oblivious they both were to what was coming. Within a month of that picture, his grandpa would be dead of a heart attack. Less than two weeks after the other picture had been taken, Brooklyn would be missing. David settled back on the couch and finished his beer. He looked at the remains of his guitar—and smiling side by side—the man who made it, and the woman who destroyed it.

The next day the rain had cleared and the morning, though damp and chilly, promised sunshine. David spent most of the day at his desk. By noon his muscles were stiff, and he had to rub his aching eyes, but the stack of claims was growing steadily smaller. He stretched and walked over to see if Lee wanted to grab some lunch.

Over corn chips, they talked about what songs to play at the show. Lee reminded him about practice that night at least five times before their orders came. David ordered a cheese dip and a bowl of pickled jalapenos. When they came, he dumped the peppers into the cheese and used the chips to scoop them out one by one, a quirky habit he'd picked up from Brooklyn. Behind Lee, a young couple shared bites of their entrees. He would find someone else to do that sort of sappy stuff with, a blonde maybe. But when he tried to imagine her, her hair was dark and framed the soft, round face and mischievous smile from the picture on his coffee table.

"—that's what Charlie thinks we should do."

David pulled his eyes away from the couple and feigned interest. "Yeah, that sounds good."

"Ah, the food is here." Lee pushed the chips, salsa, and cheese aside.

David smiled at the waiter. "Can I get a margarita, please?"

Lee lowered his voice. "You can't drink and go back to work. Are you trying to get fired?"

David just smiled.

By the end of the day, David was almost caught up and looking forward to making some music with the guys. He wanted supper, but more so he wanted a drink. The two he'd had at lunch had made the rest of the day tolerable, in no small part because of Lee's disapproval, but now he needed another to limber his fingers before practice.

Once home, he quickly swapped his briefcase for a double vodka and cranberry. He pulled his new guitar from its case. It looked beautiful and sounded like heaven, but it didn't *feel* right. He strummed chords absently as he stared at the coffee table. Both smiled at him, the maker and the breaker. What did she think about when she smiled like that? He laid the guitar back in its case and picked the picture up. They were together, leaning against the fence at her house. He had his arm around her. That had been a good day.

David had always known her, such a small town after all, but he never really *saw* her until she came to work at the insurance company. At first, they exchanged polite conversation between customers, then the smiles and looks they goaded each other on with, until finally she'd asked David to let her teach him to ride horses. He'd wanted to but said no because the company had strict policies about employee relationships. She had just smiled and gone back to her desk.

Later that day, when he had met Lee for lunch at the Chinese place, there she was. She smiled just like in the picture and patted the seat next to her. *Well*, he'd thought as he slid into the booth, *I'm sure as hell not going to sit beside Lee*. It was a group lunch, nothing more. By the end of the meal, they had a "horse lesson" scheduled for that Saturday.

That's when the picture was taken, their first sort of date. She'd taken him high into the mountains behind her house to a giant slanting rock that formed a shallow cave. They'd sat together under that rock and talked for hours. He'd fallen in love with her right there, and as the sun had set and the shadow of that rock crept over them, he kissed her. She had smiled at him after.

Just like this, he thought, as he rubbed his thumb across her lips in the picture. "Shit," he hissed, and he let it fall. Blood seeped from the pad of his thumb and looked more black than red in the low light. After he got a Band-Aid on it, he gingerly picked the frame up. The glass lay under it in several sizeable pieces. The edge of one smeared with blood and a wisp of white skin. He swept them up, removed the picture, and tossed the frame into the trash. Brooklyn smiled up at him with blood smeared across her lips. She'd gone from mischievous to sinister.

Charlie sighed and made a great show of handing Lee a twenty-dollar bill.

"I told you he'd come," laughed Lee.

David forced himself to smile. "Did you ever doubt me?"

"No, of course not!" Charlie rolled his eyes. Tall, painfully skinny, his bones seemed to stretch through his skin at odd angles. He wore a wispy goatee and had small close-set eyes that gave him a feral look. The hair on his head, which was as stringy as his beard, hung in a loose tangle down his back. Side by side, they made a study in antipodes. Lee easily made three of Charlie. In school, some of the crueler kids had called them Weasel and Whale. Looking at them both at once, it suddenly didn't seem so inaccurate an assessment. David felt ashamed for thinking it.

"Let's get started?" He pulled his guitar from its case and checked the tuning.

Charlie's parents were rich and subsequently—with no discernible effort on his part—Charlie had become wealthy as well. His basement recording studio rivaled the setups used by many major music labels. He seated himself behind the keyboard, and Lee took up his electric bass. They warmed up with a cover of "Freebird" and then followed with two originals they planned to use at the show.

After that, David called for a break. His thumb ached from holding the guitar pick, and blood was seeping through the Band-Aid. He walked to the car for another one; when he returned, they played a slow, soulful song that Charlie and Lee had written in his absence. They played it three times and by the last time, David had his part down. On the fourth pass, Lee sang about lost love and David remembered something his grandpa used to say: all music is about loving or dying. This one had flavors of both.

After about an hour, they took a break and ordered pizza. When Lee left to go to the bathroom, Charlie plopped down beside David on the sofa. "No news on your girl?"

"No, not really. We broke up before all of this so—"

"Yeah, of course, yeah, not your girl anymore. I bet it's still hard though, right? I mean, it's just so fucked up to think someone you know could just vanish like that."

"It's unsettling."

"Well, if there is anything I can do—" The doorbell chimed faintly from above. "That'll be the pizza!" he said with a smile as he jogged up the stairs two at a time.

Unsettling. Even if she were crazy or strung out, it was still unsettling. Disturbing. Wrong. Couldn't just happen. There were reasons, right? There were always reasons. He could hear Lee and Charlie arguing upstairs about who should pay the tip. Typical. Normal. It wasn't normal to just let people vanish from your life, was it? To just go on like nothing happened.

David made up his mind. He left his guitar in the case and beat the delivery woman out the front gate.

6

Bloody Dreams

Blood ran between Brooklyn's fingers in rivulets. The smell of blood and shit and piss made every breath an agony. Blood streaked her face and dripped from her hair.

I'm dead, she thought dizzily. Where was she, and how had she gotten there?

The house sported chic white carpet, beige walls, and a majestic stone fireplace. Soot-colored footprints led out of the dark hallway and gradually turned crimson in the sunlit living room. They circled the room and ended in the spreading red puddle at her feet.

I'm in shock; I'm bleeding out. Brooklyn searched her arms, touched her neck, and jerked her pants down to see her legs. There was nothing.

"I'm okay." Her voice echoed strangely in the cavernous house.

A hoarse, wet scream answered from the hallway and trailed off into agonized sobbing.

"Who's there?" Brooklyn took a step back, and her pants—still around her ankles—sent her sprawling. *Idiot.* She chided herself as she struggled to her feet and pulled her pants up. The sounds had stopped.

Brooklyn grabbed a fireplace poker and started down the hallway, searching her pockets for her phone with the other hand. It was gone. Fumbling along the wall, she found the light. The footprints ended at a door. *Here goes nothing—*

The door swung open on well-oiled hinges. It was freezing inside. Bloodcicles hung from the ceiling fan, and melting droplets fell from the incandescent bulbs. Along the wall, a tangle of naked, mutilated bodies lay like shattered ice sculptures. Brooklyn's stomach heaved. She closed her eyes until it subsided. The scent was a hundred times stronger here. This was butchery and blood, torture and death.

A massive puddle seeped from the bodies and turned the frost on the carpet to steam in a widening semicircle. It was like a '70s horror movie remade using modern gore-enhancing special effects. Brooklyn wanted to run away quickly, never to return, but someone in that pile whimpered. *This sucks*, she thought as she placed one foot in front of the other. She tried to breathe mostly through her mouth.

Here goes nothing.

Her shoe squished into the carpet and lifted with a sucking sigh. *Gross.* She grabbed the nearest guy by the wrist and pulled until he slid down into the puddle. *This isn't really happening*, Brooklyn assured herself as she pulled down the next body and the next. Near the bottom, she found him. With a gasp, she realized she knew his face. Brooklyn knew all of their faces. Because this was just a nightmare. Any moment she would wake up.

"Help me," he gasped, a froth of arterial blood bubbling between blue lips.

"Kill him," another voice whispered. Brooklyn whipped her head around so fast her hair slapped her in the face and stuck. *Double gross.* There was no one there. Just her and the dying man.

"I won't!"

"Why?" he sobbed. Tears carved trails in the blood on his cheeks.

"Wasn't talking to you. You are going to be okay." She got her arms under him and carried him like a child to the living room. If he'd been a larger man, it would have been impossible. Where was the damned phone in this place?

"What happened here?" Brooklyn asked as she lowered him to the floor.

In the better light, his rheumy eyes fastened on her face and he began to scream.

Trembling, she waited in the car until she heard sirens, then took a right turn out of the subdivision and headed back to the hotel. Brooklyn glanced in the rearview and grimaced. She looked as bad as she felt. There was so much blood it looked like badly applied Halloween makeup.

Getting to her hotel room unnoticed wouldn't be easy. Brooklyn tried waiting in the car until no one was around, but it was early evening and people came and went constantly from the nearby restaurants. She kept her head down so her matted hair shielded her face from view. The blood had dried and hardened into an uncomfortable, crumbly mess.

Brooklyn needed to go along the sidewalk, through the lobby, down the hall, up the stairs, and down another hall to her room. All without being mistaken for a psychotic serial killer, which, incidentally, might not be a case of mistaken identity at all. She had to be careful now. Her fingerprints were all over that house. The last thing Brooklyn wanted was a bunch of witnesses seeing her covered in blood. That's all it would take for the police to follow bloody footprints right to her hotel room door.

A sudden shiver rippled up her spine. When it reached the base of her skull, a vision flashed through her mind. She was standing below the outside fire escape on the back of the building. Brooklyn crouched and leapt impossibly high and pulled herself up on the second-floor balcony. At the end of the balcony was the emergency exit for her floor. She gasped. There was no way she could jump that high. Was there? Another image flashed: muddy footprints on blue shiplap siding.

Another ten minutes and it would be dark enough for the streetlights to click on. Brooklyn left her car in a crouching run across the parking lot, hugging the tree line and circling to the back of the building. Hidden in the trees, Brooklyn watched somebody's grandma sneaking a cigarette on the balcony. The old lady puffed languidly, looking out into the gloaming. Her eyes passed over Brooklyn without seeing her. Brooklyn had almost resolved herself to sleeping in the woods for the night when the lady finally went back inside.

Brooklyn flitted across the parking lot like a wraith. She looked up, judged the distance, and then jumped with all her might. She cleared almost three feet, lost her balance, and tumbled backward, banging her head on the bumper of someone's Camaro, which promptly began honking its horn and flashing its lights. *Great.* This was how it was going to end, captured by a car alarm.

The adrenaline hit Brooklyn hard. She crouched and felt a strange but familiar coldness making a bone-deep ache in her legs. She jumped, with screaming muscles, to the bottom of the second-floor railing, hung by her fingertips for a long moment, then with a grunt of effort clambered up and over onto the balcony. A door opened below. She pressed herself back against the building as the bewildered owner of the car shut off the alarm and looked around, grumbling profanities.

Just as she reached the glass door leading in, Brooklyn caught a glimpse of grandma-smokes-a-lot tottering back toward her, fumbling a cigarette out of a new pack with her palsied hands. Brooklyn sprinted back to the other side of the walkway and hugged the shadows. She found another door here, but it was locked. Meanwhile, Granny meandered toward her. She considered lying down and pretending she was a bloodied victim of some horrible crime or throwing the old woman off the balcony.

The second seemed more appealing, but either plan was bound to draw some unwanted attention.

Brooklyn's vision darkened again with a familiar shiver, and she saw herself standing at the locked door. She had a sense of reaching beyond the glass and pushing it open from the inside. Brooklyn remained crouched in the shadows and waddled to the door like a big bloody duck. She closed her eyes and reached outside herself like in the vision. Nothing happened. The footsteps were closer, and she felt like she was going to pee herself.

"Visualize," a voice whispered weakly.

Brooklyn closed her eyes and imagined it, just like in the vision. For a sickening moment, nothing happened, but then her fingers tingled and the sensation solidified into something real. She could feel the push bar on the inside of the door. *Come on . . .* She focused on pushing it, or pulling it, rather. Finally, it clanked open, and then the emergency alarm blared.

The shower was heaven, but it takes a long time to feel clean after that much blood dries in your hair and on your skin. She trimmed her nails short; there was stuff under there that wouldn't wash out. Brooklyn examined herself in the mirror, tucked a strand of hair behind an ear, and pushed her cheeks higher to make her face seem rounder. Why couldn't her face be a bit more like that? Clean clothes, brushed and dried hair, and some toothpaste and mouthwash left her feeling almost normal again.

Time to test out these abilities. She set the television remote on the table several feet away, pointed her finger, and ordered it to move. Nothing happened. Not to be discouraged, Brooklyn raised both hands in a lifting motion. That didn't work either. She slashed the air in front of her face and commanded the remote to obey. It didn't. Clearly this required coffee. Brooklyn slipped on her shoes and went down to the lobby.

The warm cup felt good in her hands. On a whim, she took a seat next to an older black man with a shaved head and the beginnings of a gray beard. He was nursing his own coffee and watching the news.

"Hi." She smiled from behind her steaming cup.

"Hello," he said pleasantly. "On vacation?"

No, just finishing up a demon-possessed killing spree, she didn't say. "Just business, mostly." She took another sip of coffee to chase the crazy away. She was starved for human interaction. "You?"

"Yeah, wife and I are taking a road trip. Florida to Maine."

"Oh, that's awesome. I'm heading home tomorrow morning." *Or maybe tonight, under cover of darkness.* Ugh . . . there was no way to go back and remove her fingerprints now. The place would be crawling with police.

"Have a safe drive home," he said with a smile.

"Yeah, you too." Brooklyn stood and on impulse bent to hug him. "It was nice talking to you."

As she pulled away, he asked, "Do I know you, honey?"

She shook her head. "I'm sorry. I haven't talked to anybody in a long time." She smiled. "I have to go."

Back in the room, Brooklyn put the coffee down and got to work. Nothing seemed to give results. She was tired, but afraid to sleep. The last thing the dying man had said kept ringing in her ears: *Don't go to sleep. Until you can control it, don't fall asleep.*

Brooklyn drained the coffee and sat it on the nightstand. *Here goes nothing.* She reached for the empty cup with her mind. Nothing happened. She tried hard, tensing every muscle with effort.

Just move, you bastard! she shouted in her mind. The cup ignored her.

She took a few deep breaths. Brooklyn visualized it happening, imagined the way it would fit in her hand, how it would float in the air. Then all at once, there it was: the sensation of a phantom hand. Slowly, the cup slid across the table. The icy thrill that rushed through her was more energizing than ten cups of coffee. *Deep breaths*, she reminded herself, and bit her lip. With an effort, the cup rose, hovering shakily in the air.

Brooklyn brought the remote control up next, tendrils of energy spiraling out of her body like taut fishing lines. She reached for one of her shoes while carefully keeping the remote and cup aloft. That was three things. It wasn't all that taxing apart from the concentration required. She willed them to spin around one another, and they did.

"I'm a Jedi!" Thinking of Luke on Dagobah, Brooklyn put her hands down on the bed and pushed herself into a sort of handstand, resting her heels against the wall for support. She added the Do Not Disturb sign to her galaxy of random implements. Coldness seeped through her stomach. Everything spun faster. Luke had done it one handed, so she lifted one hand from the bed, and her other arm promptly collapsed. Brooklyn toppled off the bed, taking the lamp from the nightstand with her. Her shoe hit the headboard where her face had been. The remote struck the dresser and shattered.

"We're trying to sleep!" a woman yelled, banging on the wall.

Brooklyn focused on getting some air back in her lungs. "Much to learn, I still have," she groaned.

Brooklyn had put this decision off as long as possible with coffee breaks and exploring her new abilities, so it was time to face her family or make some other plan. A part of her ached for home, but another part feared the reception that awaited. She'd lost her job by now for sure, disappeared without an explanation, and what if this whole murder thing followed her back to her parents' front door? When she thought of Devin, and how this must affect him, guilt made it hard to breathe.

Then there was the issue of control. Once he calmed down, the man Brooklyn had pulled from the pile of corpses had tried to convince her she could get the upper hand on this thing, even push it out in time, but he'd warned her against sleeping until it was under control. She hoped he had lived. *Christ, what was his name?*

If she went home, she might hurt her family. If she didn't go home, hurting them would be a sure thing, but at least they'd be alive. Brooklyn tugged at a strand of hair while she mulled it over. It was almost five in the morning when she packed her few belongings, slipped into some clean clothes, wiped the dried blood from her car, and left. Brooklyn was going home.

7

The God of Death

Azrael folded her wings and melted into the shadows in the corner of the small studio apartment. The place stank of sweaty clothing, old food, and vomit. The mattress on the living room floor near the television smelled faintly of mildew. It had no sheets. A pile of twisted blankets lay to the side on an open pizza box. Beer cans adorned the television. Save the mattress, the apartment was devoid of furniture.

The man who lived here came highly recommended; seeing how he lived left her with doubts. She flickered in and out of existence constantly while she waited. It was an uncontrollable reflex. An overturned bus in Cairo; she was there. A collapsed mine in Virginia; she was there. A mother smothered her infant in China, a tree crushed a man in Wisconsin, a teen leapt from the *Pont de Québec*, a woman in Russia poisoned her husband, a dozen heart attacks, half as many cancer cases, around eight car wrecks, and two house fires; Azrael was there and there and there and there all in the first minute of waiting. Sometimes she found herself at three or more places simultaneously. It was exhausting, and the population continued to explode. If there was one thing you could count on humans to do, it was reproduce.

The Black Death had kept her busy, or so she had thought. At least at the end of that, there were fewer people in the world. Now Azrael worked harder each year with no relief in sight. Already there were days she'd lost. The first time was an earthquake almost 500 years ago, but more recently there were terror attacks and tsunamis as well. Times when so many died so quickly, Azrael ceased to exist, literally pulled into so many pieces that she became a mindless global manifestation of natural law. It was the closest thing to dying she'd ever known; it was the only thing that had ever terrified her. Somehow, each time, Azrael had pulled herself back together. Each time grew harder.

Azrael had been waiting in the corner for two days when the tenant of the tiny apartment finally came stumbling in an hour shy of dawn. She stood motionless as he found the bathroom and relieved himself with a loud sigh. *I am the god of patience*, she thought with a sigh of her own. He came back to the sitting room wearing nothing but boxers. This had to be a joke.

There were two things you could say about him: he was hairy, and he was fat.

"I've been waiting for you." She stepped forward into a sliver of moonlight. "Are you Donald?"

He stumbled backward, tripped, and sat down hard on the mattress. "Who are you? How did you get in here?"

"I am Azrael; I have—"

"I'm not ready; please don't."

Well, he knew what she was at least. "I have work for you. Though I can see why you would fear me. Who could bear to part with all of *this*?" Azrael waved a pale arm to encompass the room. "You obviously lead a very fulfilling life."

"Yes, I—" He set his jaw as the jab hit home. "What do you want?" His chins and flabby pecs rippled as he struggled back to his feet.

"You were a Protector once, were you not?"

His eyes narrowed. "Half a lifetime ago."

"More than half; trust me, I can tell." She stepped closer, ignoring his sour odor. "I need a discreet exorcist; you come highly recommended, but from what I've seen so far, you're just a pathetic, old drunk waiting to die. Am I wrong?"

"No," he admitted.

"Yet you shrink away from death." Azrael ruffled her wings restlessly. "We have work to do. I'll wait while you wash the stink off. Don't be long."

Donald returned half an hour later, clean shaven, wearing faded jeans and a buttoned-up flannel shirt. With the gray hair and grime gone from his face, he was as black as her wings. Though the whites of his eyes were bloodshot and jaundiced, they were alive in a way they hadn't been before. Azrael held out her hand.

He did not take it. "Why do you care who's possessed? You're not a Warden or a Protector."

"My reasons are just that. Mine."

"I don't work for free. There must be some reason you don't just report this possession to the current Protector. Why is that?"

"Mine," Azrael repeated firmly. "I have no gold, but perhaps I should fix your failing liver so you can spend another twenty years drunk?"

He laughed. "Gold? When was the last time you bought something with gold?"

Azrael withdrew her hand. "What do you want, then?"

"I want my wife back." Donald's eyes narrowed dangerously. "You took her, and I want her back."

"Her soul has passed beyond my—"

"I don't care. You want my help; that's my price."

"Fine." She held out her hand again. She smiled as he recoiled from the icy touch. "Makes it hard to keep a boyfriend."

He took a deep breath and grabbed her hand again. She closed her own like a vise before he could let go, then she unfurled her wings, and they vanished.

Donald fell to his knees, pale and trembling, and retched in the nearby bushes.

"Every time I seem to flicker or grow transparent, that's where I go. You humans have a divine gift for finding creative fresh horrors to inflict on one another."

"That woman. Pitiful," he gasped as he pushed himself to his feet, spitting and wiping his mouth.

"She's his forty-seventh victim, by my count. Clever fellow, probably never get caught," she answered absently as she scanned the tree line.

"Why don't *you* kill him?"

"That's not how it works. Think about what you saw. Did I kill anyone?"

"No, but—"

"I am the God of Death, not the God of Murder. I release souls from the flesh, nothing more. If you want him dead, you kill him. Now, come on. We can talk about this later. She is just beyond these trees."

Together they climbed a small knoll and crouched, overlooking a subdivision. "That's her in the car. Name's Brooklyn. Demon is a grade three called Belial. Formerly an elemental Warden, seems to have gone rogue."

"Why would a Warden do that? What's your interest in any of this, anyway?"

"It's irrelevant."

"Well, I can't do this here, too public. I need a controlled environment where I can concentrate uninterrupted.

Azrael held out a scrap of paper. "She's been staying at this hotel."

"Well, how am I supposed to—"

"I don't care. Figure it out. What's important is this: the girl must not be harmed. If she dies, and obviously I'll know if she does, I will rip your family tree up by the roots. I'll kill your daughters, your grandchildren, your aunts and uncles, your cousins. I'll hire a team of genealogists to identify your most remote relatives. The things I'll do will have you spewing beer in the bushes for the rest of your life. I'll fill your stinking apartment with corpses and your bathtub with blood. And when you seek peace in death, I'll withhold it. Take this assignment seriously."

For the first time, Donald smiled. "And here I thought you just said you were not the God of Murder. Wow, you've got some skin in this game. I just can't figure what it is. That shit's biblical. So, what you are saying is, you'd rather the girl didn't die?"

"I'm not the God of Resurrection either, but if you succeed, I will return your wife. I must warn you it won't make you happy—"

"Had enough of your warnings for one day." He stood and slipped silently back into the trees.

Azrael reappeared in his path. "Fine, but there's one other thing." She paused and stretched her wings languidly. "I was never here. If you tell anyone about me, the deal is off. Got it?"

"I got it." He stomped around her and never looked back.

8

Death to Tyrants

Brooklyn felt tired. Not tired like after a sleepless night, or tired like after soccer practice, or even tired like after a marathon. Any of those would have been preferable to this flavor of exhaustion.

She'd been home three days. Three days of her mom's hugs interspersed with crying spells, endless barrages of questions, her dad's fake, half-formed smiles, and his silence that hurt worse than any words.

He had lost all faith in her, didn't believe her, and assumed the worst. That was okay because she'd expected it, but she'd expected him to yell and wave his arms. Instead, he treated her as if she were as fragile as glass. For some reason, that was worse. That alone left her emotionally exhausted, not to mention she hadn't slept in almost three days.

Each night she hugged her mom and said goodnight, then she sat on her bed and experimented, letting the power shock her awake with a sensation not unlike jumping into an icy lake. Empty soda cans lined the windowsill and filled the computer desk. That had worked until last night when she'd hit a wall.

The DVD had been floating through the air, spinning lazily like a flying saucer, and then it had fallen. Every effort to raise it had failed. When Brooklyn closed her eyes to try, it just didn't work. She could sense it, touch it, even grasp it a little, but it might have weighed two tons for the effort she spent failing to make it rise.

Her bones turned to jelly. Her head became a boulder and her neck the needle she balanced it on.

Brooklyn had made it through last night, but without the bracing thrill of the power, she was fading fast. When she wasn't focusing on staying awake, she was trying to figure out how to expel the thing inside. Search as she might, she couldn't find a trace. She imagined the field where they had met, but it was a dim recollection. It wasn't the true place. As far as Brooklyn could tell, she was alone in her head now. Maybe she always had been?

Her eyes wouldn't focus, and even breathing seemed laborious. By lunchtime her tongue had grown thick and clumsy, and in her father's eyes, the slurring confirmed addiction. The pale, hollow-eyed, bloodshot look didn't help either. After lunch, Brooklyn took a walk outside. The sun was unbearably bright, and if she sat down, her eyes rolled back almost immediately.

Everywhere she looked, there were flashes of blood. Once she even saw all the bodies in the pile lumbering toward her, groping for her with their fingerless hands; her screams jolted her awake. When her parents rushed out onto the porch, she told them she'd seen a scorpion. Brooklyn let her mother lead her inside. It was nearly time for supper, and she didn't see how she was going to make it through another night.

They piled the table high with food. Meatloaf, mashed potatoes, green beans, corn, salad, and buttered bread. There was hardly room left for their plates. *Does Mom think I ran away because the food was bad, or does she plan to fatten me up so I can't fit out my window?*

Brooklyn had been eating a lot since she stopped sleeping. It gave her energy, at least for a little while, so long as she didn't sit down. Staying focused enough to follow the conversation was a chore on par with learning a foreign language.

"Can we feed the horses after we eat?" Devin asked.

"Sure, we can do that." The muscles in her cheek twitched when she smiled. Her mom and dad exchanged a look.

"Maybe it would be better to wait," her mom said. "Brooke needs to get some sleep; she's exhausted." Her smile was strained and brittle.

The sun lanced through the kitchen window and made Brooklyn's tired eyes ache. She nodded and didn't say any of the smart-ass things that ran through her head. Likewise, she had bitten her tongue when both sets of her car keys mysteriously disappeared while she showered. It wasn't worth it. They thought her crazy, addicted, or both, and pretty much every time Brooklyn had tried to convince them otherwise had backfired. It wouldn't be long before they were coaxing her into the car like a cocker spaniel bound for the vet. She reached over and squeezed Devin's hand. "Maybe tomorrow."

She cleaned her plate and winced as she downed the last of her sweet tea. It was bitter, almost acrid. The conversation became a susurrus in her ears and she lost the thread for a while . . .

Then something moved behind her mom. The shadows rustled and shifted. The evening sun slanted in through the kitchen window, struck the dark figure, and simply vanished into blackness as if a piece of the world were missing. Brooklyn lurched to her feet.

Somewhere far away, her dad was yelling, "I've got her!" Then the kitchen turned sideways. The shadow came toward her. She tried to scoot away, but someone was holding her. It stretched great feathered wings high above its head and blotted out the sun.

Brooklyn found herself back in blood. It was a different bedroom than the one she remembered, but it had the same carpet and wallpaper. A man hung from one wrist. He writhed and clawed at his arm with his free hand. There were strange grooves in his wrist where a metal cable held him suspended from nothing. A kitchen knife floated casually beside the frost-covered stump where, once, a finger had been. No blood flowed past the strange icy scab.

"Be still," she heard herself saying in a voice that wasn't quite her own. She flicked a finger, and the knife traced a line from his jaw to his hip bone. "We wouldn't want an accident."

"Please, put me down and I'll talk. I swear it."

"Talk, and I'll put you down. I swear it." Her lips twisted in wry amusement. "How did so many of you cross together?"

"We didn't." He winced as the knife prodded him. "He brought us."

"Who?"

"We never knew his name. He made us call him the Engineer."

She smiled. "Now we are getting somewhere. How do I reach him?"

"He only talked to Sledgehammer."

"Where can I find Sledgehammer?"

"There," he groaned, pointing at a pile of bodies, "you already killed him."

"Well, that sucks. If what you say is true, that you were summoned, I mean, there is only one person who could do something like that. Tell me, do you know who holds the Ring of Solomon now? Is it this Engineer?"

"I don't know. Please put me down," he screamed as his shoulder dislocated, bringing his toes into firmer contact with the floor.

She ignored his plight. "How come some of you don't return to the Pull when your host dies?"

"Ascended. They've ascended."

"What does that mean?"

"I don't know. Nobody knows until the Engineer decides you're ready." He gasped.

"Well, you are fucking useless. Perhaps one of your friends in the other room can do better."

The knife flashed and Brooklyn screamed inside her own head while she watched the man die.

Everything faded, she was in a dark parking lot, and a man covered in frost gestured for her to step forward. Before she took the step, an unbelievable pain blossomed across the back of her head and Brooklyn untethered from her body. She saw black wings enfolding the world.

The scene shifted again, and she was staring into the mismatched eyes of a beautiful woman. Somehow, in this dream, Brooklyn had become a man. They kissed in the sand at the edge of an ocean. The rolling waves turned into rolling green pastures, and she was on her knees. Her twin punched her in the face again and again. She tried to move, to turn away, but she couldn't budge.

The field fell away; she was a kid again, eating ice cream on the front porch with Erin and her dad. Brooklyn held her bowl in her lap, one scoop of chocolate and one scoop strawberry. Erin was so young she still wore pigtails, her ice cream smeared all around her mouth. Her dad sat in his rocking chair drinking a beer. He'd parked the tractor in the driveway, and the porch fan turned in lazy circles that never seemed to move much air. Brooklyn held on to this. This dream felt right.

Brooklyn woke up with a hangover, and no doubt at all that her mom had drugged her. Her bed was damp with sweat, and hair stuck to her face. She reached for her phone, but it wasn't there.

"Ugh." Brooklyn rolled off the bed and looked underneath. It wasn't there either. After a shower, she made her way downstairs. The sunlit kitchen told her it was well past noon. That meant her dad would be out working on the farm somewhere, Devin would be napping, and her mom would be about the house. Brooklyn found her in the kitchen reading a magazine.

"Feeling better, honey?"

She was feeling better than she remembered in a long time, but she wasn't about to tell her mother that. "More like I was drugged, raped, and dumped in a ditch. What happened last night?"

"I guess you just pushed yourself too hard. You fell asleep at the table."

"Wow, well, I've got a killer headache," Brooklyn said, rummaging through the medicine cabinet until she found a bottle of Ambien with her father's name on it.

She slammed the bottle on the table beside her mom. "You roofied me!"

Her mom turned a page slowly and kept reading.

Brooklyn tried to stare holes through the top of her head. "Did you hear me?"

"Mhmm," she said, flipping another page, "I heard you."

"Well, are you going to say anything?"

Her mom shrugged.

"What you did was illegal! Maybe I'll call the cops." Brooklyn hated the shrillness creeping into her voice.

Her mom sighed and closed the magazine. "I did it because you needed to sleep. You looked like shit. You could barely hold your eyes open, and I hear you banging around in your room every night since you've been back. So go ahead. Call the cops. I've been giving you medicine since you were a baby. When you had a fever, I gave you Tylenol, Benadryl for a bee sting, the pink stuff for a stomachache, and if I think you need some sleep, I'll give you something for that too. It's your fault you are so damn stubborn that I have to slip it into your tea."

"I'm an adult," Brooklyn spluttered. "I don't need my *mother* to decide if I need medicine. And while we are on the topic, I want my car keys back."

"No."

"Where are they?"

Her mom made a marked effort not to look at her pocketbook hanging from one of the kitchen chairs.

Brooklyn grimaced and reached for it with her mind. It happened effortlessly. The purse flipped and dumped itself on the table. The keys were halfway to the floor when she caught them and they veered upward to her palm. Her mom's slack-jawed expression was as comical as a cartoon.

That was easy, Brooklyn thought. Apparently, the rest had done her some good after all. "I'm going to town for some ice cream. Be back in a while." She let the screen door slam on the way out.

It wasn't quite the same, eating ice cream alone in a booth instead of on the porch with family, but ice cream is good, regardless.

"Is this seat taken?" Belial asked, sitting before she could respond.

"How are you—"

"Oh, I'm not. I'm still in your head."

"Then get out." Brooklyn concentrated and she could sense him. She willed him away.

"I wouldn't do that," he said. "Let me explain."

"Explain what? That you're a psychotic killer?"

"Lower your voice. You're the crazy woman with ice cream on her chin yelling at thin air."

She looked around. There were indeed several other patrons watching her from the sides of their eyes. The color rose in her cheeks as she picked her cell phone up from the table and held it to her ear.

"They can't see me," he explained. "I'm still in your head." He tapped his temple for emphasis.

Her stomach lurched. What if none of it was real? What if she was still in the car, or the hotel, or a rubber room somewhere? Maybe she had never come home at all. The field had seemed real enough until they got to her personal details. Brooklyn pressed a palm against the cool tabletop. It felt real, but hadn't the grass felt real too?

Belial must have seen her thoughts spinning out of control. He reached his hand out and put it on hers.

"It's all real. You are home. I'm the only part of this that is in your head." He squeezed her hand, and her flesh prickled with chill bumps. "You must help me do something, something very important. Then I'll leave. No fight, no fuss; you'll get your life back."

"I want my life back now. I can make you leave; the man at that house said so."

Belial shrugged. "Sure, you are strong enough, but you don't know how." His voice turned grave. "Will you let me explain? I feel I owe you an explanation. I've kept much of what I've learned in the past weeks from you."

She wanted to throw her ice cream in his face. Instead, she nodded.

"Okay, without going into a lot of ancient history, what you should understand is this: there is a barrier between your world and mine. It's not a physical barrier like a wall, but more like a force of nature. It's a lot like gravity. Are you with me so far?"

"I think so, but what does it have to do with me?"

"Imagine if the gravity here on Earth weakened." He smiled grimly. "At first, you'd be able to jump higher, but as it worsened, your world would fall out of balance. Your atmosphere would drift off into space. Chaos and death."

"Okay, but how can you stop something like that?"

"By stopping the person who is causing it, and I know who that is now."

"Well, who is it?"

"His name is Alexander Stewarth. He's the Heir of Solomon. More commonly, he's simply called the Heir. You might consider him a king of sorts."

Brooklyn tucked a strand of hair behind her ear. "But how can some guy affect spiritual gravity or whatever?"

"The Pull. We call it the Pull. And he can't, not directly anyway, but he is the heir to an ancient, powerful artifact. A ring that gives him the ability to control any nonhuman spirit. If he can call a spirit by name, he can pull it to this side regardless of the Pull. Consider it a loophole. Normally, the Pull functions like a two-way vacuum cleaner. Spiritual matter is drawn to one side, and physical matter to the other.

"And now?"

He smiled. "Still working, but growing weaker. I wouldn't be here with you now if it wasn't."

"What do you mean?"

"Doesn't matter. The important thing is we have to stop him from bringing any more spirits across and make him release the ones he is holding in service now. If we don't, and if he continues to draw them across, we will soon reach a tipping point."

Brooklyn's head was spinning. *Could any of this be real?* "A tipping point?"

"Yes, a point where there is a greater mass of spirits on this side than on the other side. If that happens, I believe the Pull will start working in reverse, drawing the rest of the spirits to this world."

She was following the logic now. "So, kind of like two magnets. The heavier magnet will pull the other one to itself?"

"Yes, exactly like that."

"And would real, living people then be vacuumed into the spiritual world?"

He shrugged. "I don't know, and I don't think either of us wants to find out."

She took a deep breath. "And how would we stop him?"

"By killing him."

9

Fear No Evil

"No way! Find someone else!" Brooklyn shouted at Belial over melting ice cream. Several people got up and left the shop, eying her warily. He was suggesting cold-blooded murder. Bad enough he'd used her to kill already, but that wasn't her, not really. Now he wanted Brooklyn to be a willing accomplice? And why didn't he just ask this Stewarth man to stop summoning demons? Good questions with no one to ask. Belial had melted away like snow under the heat of her rage.

When Brooklyn finally got back home, her dad gave her a withering stare and there was something like fear in her mom's eyes. She didn't know exactly what her mother had told her father, but she was certain it wasn't that she had taken her car keys back telekinetically. Brooklyn nodded at them, an acknowledgment, and went up to her bedroom.

Alone, she stared at the bed, thinking of David. Terrible that their last memory together had been shouting insults at one another with his shattered guitar on the bedspread between them. Was he working today? Probably, and if so, small-town gossip would carry word of her crazy outburst at the ice-cream shop to him, confirming every bad thing he already suspected.

All that confusion, frustration, and anger poured into her fingertips. She gestured and sent the mattress drifting toward the ceiling, and a solar system of shoes and dirty socks leapt into existence around it. Brooklyn held her breath and sent them spinning faster.

So caught up in the rush of power, the way it infused her with clarity, that she didn't notice the temperature dropping or frost forming on the dresser mirror. Her lungs burned and ached. The released breath plumed into white mist. Everything drifted down softly, the mattress last of all.

Something tickled her lip. She scratched at it, and her fingers came away bloody.

Shit.

Brooklyn tilted her head back, stumbled to the bathroom for a tissue, and crammed tissue paper into her nostrils. The mental exertions left her with an afterglow of giddy tiredness. When she got back to the room, her identical twin lay naked on the sheets.

"Put some clothes on," Brooklyn said flatly as she turned away to wipe the mirror clean.

"Awww . . . you're no fun," Belial answered petulantly in her own voice.

She didn't answer.

"Come on, babe, it's been a long time." David's voice, plucked right from her most intimate memories. She whirled around. He smiled invitingly. Naked. And Brooklyn wanted nothing more than to go to him, but made herself pull back. It wasn't David. It was a monster. Her monster. And she knew what horror he was capable of.

"I've forced you to disappear twice now. I can do it again."

"Ah, I think not. You are too tired." His voice deepened as he changed back into the likeness Brooklyn knew from their first meeting—clothes and all, thankfully—and for the first time she realized how like David he looked.

"I'm not too tired. I burned your energy, not mine."

"Is that *my* blood dripping out of *your* brain, too?"

Unable to think of a witty retort, Brooklyn shrugged.

"Listen, I've tried to be nice, but what's happening is bigger than you, bigger than me. It's chaos and death on a global scale."

"I'm not a murderer. I won't help you kill someone. Besides, why not just ask this guy to stop?"

One second he was lounging on the bed, and the next he stood nose to nose with her. "You are a killer. You just don't know it yet. I've offered you a perfect dreamworld for your help, and you threw it in my face." His voice grew low and threatening. "Here's the alternative."

Belial grabbed Brooklyn's head between his hands, and the bright sunlit room swirled and became the living room. She walked down the stairs, and her family, busy watching television, didn't see her. Devin nestled between his grandparents on the couch.

A horrible dread blossomed as she stepped in front of the television. Her father opened his mouth to say something but never got the chance. She raised her hand and sent him careening into the stairway railing with a sickening crunch.

Stop it! she shrieked inside her own head.

I shielded your mind from the killing before, but if you make me do this, I promise you'll be awake for every second.

All the cutlery floated in from the kitchen, moving in formation like a squadron of jets. Her mom pushed Devin onto the floor and told him to run, just before the knives lanced across the room and pinned her to the sofa. Devin scrambled up the stairs.

Brooklyn stepped over her dad's limp body and climbed the stairs slowly, letting them creak, and calling Devin's name in a singsong voice not quite her own. He would be in his favorite hiding place: under his bed. *No, no, no, please!*

She pushed his bedroom door open, stepping over stuffed animals and toy trucks. With a thought, Brooklyn flipped the bed, and there he lay, big eyes, no tears, but trembling. She mentally brandished a small wooden baseball bat from the floor near his closet, raised it, and brought it down. Before it struck, everything swirled again and Brooklyn was back in her room, nose to nose with her tormentor, but on the floor, kneeling now. Her eyes blurred with tears, heart hammering.

"You can't hold me back forever," Belial said. "Either way, we begin tonight. You've got a decision to make." Then he vanished.

In the end, it hadn't been much of a decision at all.

Since Brooklyn came willingly, they worked together. No blackouts; she slept without worrying what day it would be when she woke. The days were uneventful: lots of time in the car, watching and waiting.

They had been gone about a week when the credit card stopped working. Brooklyn guessed the note she'd left wasn't very convincing. From her parents' perspective, she had done very little to inspire trust or confidence lately. Brooklyn was more alone than ever and spent a lot of time thinking about David.

The last couple of days and nights, they had hidden in the woods above an incredibly large mansion nestled in a cove between two prominent ridges. It backed up to the hills and faced a lawn that looked more like a golf course than a yard. To the east of the main building, a garage tunneled into the side of the mountain.

Occasionally, cars would enter or leave, and Belial would mark down information about the cars and their drivers.

When the massive doors opened, Brooklyn saw the garage extended out of sight into the hillside. With no visible machinery, the doors seemed to operate as if by magic.

Sometimes, when Belial was preoccupied with his reconnaissance, she wondered if her sister might be out there somewhere in a similar situation. Why did people disappear? Where did they go? Her parents probably wondered the same thing.

Occasionally, Brooklyn dared to consider pushing Belial out, taking control, but the images of his threat were never far from her thoughts. The cost of failing was too great, so she didn't try.

"That's him," Belial whispered. Brooklyn perked up, jarred from her daydream by his excitement. They watched through binoculars as a small turbo prop plane made an approach. It sat down on a long flat strip of cleverly camouflaged asphalt. The runway blended into the surrounding terrain almost seamlessly. The plane taxied around the back side of the garage hill and vanished.

Brooklyn swallowed. Facing the reality of what was about to happen was a lot harder now when it was time to act. No more abstractions. Somewhere inside that compound was a man with a family, and a beating heart, as human as her, and she, and the thing inside her, were going to kill him.

Brooklyn shivered. "So, what's the plan?"

Belial materialized in a crouch beside her. "A little shopping trip to gather the things we need. There is a banquet tonight being catered by a local company. You'll pose as an employee, serve Stewarth his meal, and cut his throat—"

"Wait a minute. I thought *you* were doing this. I can't kill a man!"

"You must. There is no room for failure. I cannot manifest while he's alive. He will sense me right away, and with Solomon's ring . . . Trust me, it has to be this way. As soon as it is done, I will take over and get you out safely. Trust me."

"Yeah right."

10

Killer Help

Brooklyn's arms were full as she opened the hotel room door. She had a mannequin, a wig, a stolen caterer's uniform, and a large carving knife still in the store packaging, along with a few other odds and ends. All of which went flying when something heavy slammed into her back and sent her sprawling.

"I don't want to hurt you," a harsh voice rasped in her ear. "Be still."

This is it. He pulled her arms behind her back and cuffed them. *I'm going to jail for murder.* In a way, it was a relief. She had felt incredible guilt since the bloody memories began to surface. Would she get the death penalty? He was on her back, and extremely *heavy*. Maybe he planned to simply suffocate her by crushing? Her spine could snap at any moment. She struggled to get a full breath. Finally, he rolled off and hauled her to her feet. For a moment, all she could do was gasp for air.

Brooklyn noted Belial, barely there below the surface of her thoughts, watching. A quick glance told her one thing: this guy wasn't a cop. He was an elderly black man in terrible shape. If possible, his exertions had left him more breathless than her.

"Who are you?" she asked.

"I'm here to help you." He wheezed.

"Great. How about you start by taking these cuffs off?"

"I don't think so, sweetheart." He wiped his hands on his shirt and pressed a still sweaty palm to her forehead.

He's afraid of me, Brooklyn realized as she tried to turn her face away. A steady pressure built in her skull and chest. She suddenly sensed everything. Her heartbeat, the elastic pulsing of arteries and veins, the noise of her own breathing, even the maddening electrical pulses zipping through her nerves. Her body became something alien. A disgusting writhing thing full of mucus and blood and meat. Those weren't her feelings; they were Belial's. For that moment, Brooklyn understood perfectly how it all worked. She sensed his tethers snapping like rubber bands.

"Help me, girl. Resist him," the man growled in a strained voice.

The Pull can't hold me. I'll be on my way back here as Devin before this guy catches his breath.

Brooklyn shuddered at the image. She could think of nothing more perverse. Reluctantly, Brooklyn reached for Belial, and the lines between them blurred again.

The room turned frigid in an instant, and all her senses came to life. Brooklyn kicked her would-be savior in the chest and sent them both sprawling. She glimpsed ethereal blue eyes in the mirror before it crashed down on top of him. Brooklyn rolled to her feet with a feline grace she wished she could call her own. The handcuff keys lay on the floor near her attacker. They came to her easily.

Her would-be savior lurched to his feet, shedding splintered wood and broken glass at the same moment the cuffs fell to the floor with a clatter. Brooklyn lifted the larger shards of the broken mirror, forming a razor-sharp semicircle around the old man. The pieces rocketed at him.

His hand shot up, the air shimmered, and the glass lodged in it and stuck.

"Thought you retired, Donald," Belial said, recognition flooding through him.

"And I thought you were a Warden," the man said. "Looks like we were both wrong." He flicked his wrist, and the rippling shield full of glass came careening across the room at them.

Belial rolled across the bed almost lazily, and the glass slammed into the wall. "You should have brought help." The mannequin floated up behind the old man. He flinched aside, and then the mattress flopped ponderously end over end across the room at him. Donald sat down, rolled backward out of the way, and was on his feet again near the dresser with a speed that belied his size.

Belial yanked the dresser drawers into the backs of his knees, knocking him forward toward the bed frame that was already rushing across the floor to slam into his shins. Donald made a spectacular somersault and landed hard on the center bed rail.

Brooklyn rolled him over carefully. "Will you stop now, and promise not to follow me?"

"Never stop until you let that girl go." Brooklyn felt a deep sorrow and regret, or was it Belial who felt it? She couldn't draw the line anymore. She pressed her hands across Donald's chest and watched the frost spread through him like liquid nitrogen until his eyes were blank and filmed over.

For half a second she sensed something at once familiar and foreboding, a shadow that haunted her memories. When she turned to look, the room was empty.

"Are you ready for this?" Belial asked.

"No." She didn't say more, her voice on the cusp of cracking. Brooklyn struggled to slow her heart and tried not to puke. He'd made her spend thirty minutes practicing on the mannequin, but it had been hard to focus with Donald the Exorcist thawing across the room.

"Nerves are probably a good sign." His lips quirked. "Means you're still human."

Brooklyn nodded.

"You'll do fine. I'll be with you and as soon as it is done, I'll get us both the hell out."

She didn't trust herself to speak, so she nodded again and adjusted her wig and uniform. As Brooklyn reached the front entrance to the mansion, Belial vaporized himself and grew still inside her.

A tall, slim man in a tuxedo opened the door for her and escorted her through a labyrinth of hallways to the kitchen. It was all stainless steel and half the size of her entire house. Cooks and servers bustled about. Brooklyn was dressed as a server. Despite her stomach doing acrobatics, she forced a smile, grabbed a platter, and followed a male server through the double doors into the dining room. She could do this. She'd been a waitress in high school.

Long tables covered in white linen filled the cavernous dining hall. Each table lined with dark, high-back wooden chairs. Only half a dozen tables were in use, each adorned with silverware and sparkling glasses, bottles of wine, baskets of bread, and bowls of fresh fruit. Brooklyn followed the waiter in front of her, watching him carefully and serving the next guest at the table from the same side and in the same manner. Would they see through the disguise? Her heart pounded, but for all the attention they paid, she could have dressed as a clown.

Being unnoticed is the point, Belial whispered in her mind.

She nodded imperceptibly and circled back toward the kitchen.

That's him. At the head of the middle table.

The Heir was a once handsome man, strong features, near to sixty, with the whitest hair she'd ever seen. It hung past his shoulders in a silky sheet, framing a well-worn face, but his chocolate eyes were sunken and tired. Despite the warm smile he gave the person speaking to him, fatigue and sickness showed in the slope of his shoulders and the way his custom suit didn't fit quite right.

Jesus, he doesn't look like he'd harm a fly. Are you sure you've got the right guy?

I'm sure. When they clear the plates, make sure you take his. Pick up the platter with your left and use the knife with your right as you turn to leave. One fluid motion like we practiced. You'll be halfway back to the kitchen before anyone realizes something's wrong.

She took her place with the other servers, waiting to clear this course and make way for the next.

"First night?" asked the woman beside her.

Brooklyn forced a nervous smile. "Is it that obvious?"

"You seem nervous. Try to relax. Most of these folks are nice. We work this place two or three times a year."

"I'll try." She fingered the knife hidden in the folds of her uniform.

"I'm Anna, by the way."

"Sarah." Brooklyn felt guilty for the lie and was searching for something more to say when the line of servers moved to clear the first course.

Brooklyn made a beeline for Stewarth as soon as she cleared the double doors. This was it. Everything depended on this. After tonight, she would have her life back. Devin would be safe. Brooklyn would be alone in her head again and free to start putting the shambles of her world back together. Maybe she'd patch things up with David. And, according to Belial, they would avert a world crisis. Only one little murder to go. One and done. She floated across the floor. Sweat trickled down her back, and her heart hammered.

Brooklyn hoisted Alexander Stewarth's salad plate. The knife slipped easily from its hiding place into her hand. He laughed at a joke, not even looking her way.

He turned and smiled at her. "Thank you, dear."

She couldn't do it. He wasn't even wearing a ring. A mistake. It was all a mistake. It had to be.

Do it! Belial hissed.

She stood there dumbly, the knife in her hand out of sight below the table's edge.

Tears blurred her vision. Stewarth and those closest to him stared at her curiously.

Devin, Belial breathed. The threat was enough to restore her resolve.

"What's wrong?" the Heir asked her. Concern playing across his sharp features. "Do you need to sit for a minute?"

She shook her head. "I'm sorry."

The knife whipped in a flashing arc, and then there was blood.

Brooklyn turned to flee and took several steps before what happened registered. Stewarth had gotten a hand between the blade and his throat.

Belial came to life like a bucket of ice water poured over her head. In one fluid motion, he flipped the knife, caught it by the bloodied blade, turned back toward Alexander Stewarth, dropped to one knee, and hurled it end over end right at his heart.

Through Belial's eyes, Brooklyn saw the ring. Glowing like a small sun on Stewarth's first finger.

The ring shimmered, and Belial's will buckled and snapped under the unrelenting force. The knife stopped and hung in the air, its tip brushing lightly against the Heir's breast pocket, and then it clattered to the floor.

As Stewarth gained his feet, the ring went supernova. Flooding the room with a light so absolute it banished even the memory of darkness. Brooklyn closed her eyes and covered them with her arms. She perceived the light all the same. It was inside her skull. She imagined twin beams shining from her eye sockets for years to come. So much light that it would take that long to disperse. The light wrapped itself around Belial—or was it her? Brooklyn couldn't tell anymore—and constricted like a snake. Pain blossomed so quickly and in so many places she couldn't scream or even breathe.

Brooklyn fell forward and collapsed into sweet, exquisite darkness.

11

Bar Room Banter

David sat in his car double-checking the address from Brooklyn's parents' credit card statement. There were charges almost every night at Macroy Diner and Bar. He couldn't imagine Brooklyn coming to a place like this. It was run down and seedy and had a dangerous vibe. Plywood covered the front window, the paint was peeling, and the glass in the front door had been blacked out. A row of motorcycles sat in a neat line out front.

David was more than a little nervous about going in. He rearranged the missing-person flyers in the manila folder. Ten in the evening, a lot later than most of Brooklyn's charges had been made, but hopefully one of the regulars had seen her. He took a deep breath. *Here goes nothing.*

Nothing could have prepared him for what he found on the other side of that door. He'd imagined a dim room filled with smoke, loud country music, guys crushing beer cans on their heads, and scantily clad women dancing on a plywood stage, but as soon as he crossed the threshold, a very sour-looking *maitre d'* in a black tuxedo and bow tie greeted him. The man's jet-black mustache made a stark contrast to his close-cropped salt-and-pepper haircut. The mustache had been twirled and oiled into ridiculous points and they bounced tremulously when he spoke. "We don't serve your kind here. Please leave by the way you came."

David stood in the foyer while the host looked over his spectacles as if he were addressing a particularly dimwitted child and repeated himself slowly.

It didn't compute. His kind? What did that mean? "I, uh, huh?"

"Clever. Well, you'll find that the door behind you will take you out as well as in."

"I'm looking for a girl, uh, woman, actually." He began fumbling with his folder. "If you could just have a look at this picture?"

"No."

David bristled. He'd never been treated like this. "Why the hell not?" he asked loud enough to be heard by everyone within.

"Because we don't serve the uninitiated," the *maitre d'* answered in a bitter voice. "Lucky, some assistance please."

David could do little more than stare with his mouth open as a stout man standing five foot nothing, with a four-leaf clover tattooed on his forehead, grabbed him by the belt, and with a strength that belied his size, carried him outside like a piece of luggage, and chucked him toward his car. He slid across the gravel on hands and knees. Flyers fluttered in his wake.

"Shit," he groaned.

"I'd say that's an apt description," said the man who presumably belonged to the boots David's chin rested on.

He looked up to see a hand being offered. He took it. "Thanks," he said, as he dusted himself off and started gathering up his papers.

"What in God's green earth happened to you?"

"They don't serve my kind here or something." He winced, looking at his raw palms. "I didn't take the hint quick enough, so they had a leprechaun throw me out."

The man laughed a deep belly laugh. "L-Lucky the Leprechaun! That's great, kid. He'll never live this down."

David looked at the man for the first time. He was tall and black with a buzz cut, a nose that looked like it had been broken a dozen times, and wild Einstein eyebrows. He wore formal wear, except for his scuffed-up work boots. Though his face looked weather worn, smile lines sprouted around his eyes as he chuckled. What hair he had was storm gray and his eyes the lightest caramel brown David had ever seen.

"What are you doing at a place like this, anyway?"

"I'm looking for a girl—"

"This ain't a place to pick up a date; maybe you should try—"

"It's my girlfriend. She's missing. She's been coming here the last few weeks and using her parents' credit card."

The man studied his face for a long moment, then bent over and picked up the last missing-person flyer off the ground and studied it. "Does she have blonde hair?"

"Dark brown."

He handed the poster back to David. "I haven't been here in a couple of months, but how about we have a beer and a bite to eat and you tell me more about this girl? Might be I can help?"

"That sounds great, but I don't think they are going to let me back in."

"Let's see." He grabbed David by the arm and dragged him back inside.

The *maitre d's* eyes bugged out of their sockets. "Mr. Levin, is this . . . this . . . person bothering you?"

"My *guest* and I would like a corner booth, please." Kurt smiled, but it never touched his eyes.

The host looked at David with disdain, and his absurd mustache twitched. "Of course."

A waiter quickly led them to the back corner of one of the fanciest restaurants David had ever seen. Oddly, the clientele looked exactly as he originally pictured: tattooed bikers in leather and jeans. He and this Mr. Levin were by far the best dressed in the whole place if you didn't count the *maitre d'.*

After they were seated and had ordered a first round, the man smiled again. "I'm Kurt, by the way, and I gathered from the poster that you must be David Sterling?"

David nodded.

"So, tell me, how did this, ah, Brooklyn, go missing?"

"Well, she lived with her parents, and one morning she just wasn't there. We work together, right? But she didn't show up for work or come home that night. The next day, pretty late in the morning, she comes down from her bedroom like she'd overslept. Thought she'd run late for work or something, but it was a Sunday."

"Wait, she didn't know the day of the week?"

"No, she—" David broke off as the waitress brought their drinks and took their orders. David ordered a burger and fries, the last thing you would expect to see on a menu at a restaurant this nice. After the server left, he continued. "She had no memory of the time she'd been gone. She was scared, worried, thought she'd lost her mind or something."

"Then she went missing again?"

"Hardly any time later. Like the very next day, I think."

"You don't know for sure?"

"Well, we sort of broke up after that first time. We had a fight; I left; you know how it goes . . . "

"Ah, well. Life is like that sometimes. We hurt the people we love just when we need each other the most." He looked pensively at his empty glass as if he might find some answers there. "Did she have any unusual beliefs or hobbies? An interest in the occult, for instance?"

"No drugs, nothing weird. She's a pretty normal person."

"Any theory at all about what happened to her? No suspicions? No trouble she might have been in?" Kurt motioned to the waitress for another drink.

"Nothing. She was fine and then next thing I know, she has amnesia. Then after that, she's gone again."

The waitress returned with Kurt's beer and David's food. David smiled and thanked her.

"You not eating?" David asked.

Kurt waved dismissively. "Can I see the picture again?"

"Sure." David fished a poster out for him.

He studied it for a long time. "She's pretty."

David nodded and grunted in agreement through a mouthful of food.

Kurt waved the waitress back over and handed her a twenty-dollar bill. "That's your tip. Give the bill to our host and bouncer and tell them Mr. Sterling accepts their apologies." She shrugged and took the tip.

"I have money if—"

"You had skin on your hands when you got here, too," Kurt said wryly. "Let's get going."

"Going where?"

"I think I know where you might find this girl you're looking for, but there's a lot to explain first. Shall we?"

"Is this some kind of joke?" David asked incredulously. "Demons, and crazy magical powers?"

"It's no joke," Kurt said. "I know it is a lot to take in, but your girlfriend is caught up in the middle of something a lot bigger than she is, and she is in some pretty serious trouble. She will go before our council for judgment tomorrow, and unless we convince them she was not a willing accomplice, they'll execute her."

They were back at Kurt's place, the biggest house, scratch that, mansion David had ever seen. The man had the whole inside of a mountain for a garage. Now, they lounged on leather chairs in front of the fireplace in his study. The rain that chased them from the bar to their cars made a distant roar.

"What can I do?" David asked. "Can I testify in her defense or something?"

"Essentially, there is nothing you can do. Your word would mean less than nothing. Everyone saw what she tried to do."

"But you just said she wasn't in control of it." David stood up, pacing in agitation. He wanted to believe none of this was real, but Kurt had put a quick end to that line of thinking with an irrefutable demonstration.

"It's more complicated than you can imagine. The man she attacked is basically the ruler of the supernatural community. If he doesn't deal with something like this so swiftly, violently, and publicly that it leaves a lasting impression, then he may as well cut his own throat." Kurt sighed. "I'll think of something. Meanwhile, let me show you to a guest room; I may need you tomorrow."

David found himself in a plush room with an attached bathroom, a mini fridge full of drinks and snacks, and cable television. There wasn't a phone in the room, and his cell couldn't get a signal. It wasn't until he had gone to the bathroom and come back that he noticed a flat metal panel on the door right where the knob should have been.

12

Best Laid Plans

Why he hadn't looked at that poster, shrugged, and walked away, Kurt did not know. Now he'd made promises with no idea how to keep them. Tomorrow morning, that girl was as good as dead. Ah, but there was something about the boy that Kurt couldn't quite put his finger on. Somehow, he reminded him of Tyler. He looked at a picture of his son above the fireplace. A family portrait of himself, his wife Mary, and Tyler at about age fourteen. That seemed like some other man's family, a better man's life. November would be twenty-two years. Truly, a lifetime ago. But now wasn't the time for that. Now there were problems to solve.

The law read simple. Being possessed was not an excuse for a crime. Possession was always a choice. If Stewarth set a precedent with Brooklyn, it wouldn't be long before every failed Demonrider expected the same leniency. Slippery slope. This really couldn't have happened at a worse time. With everyone in town for the banquet, there probably wouldn't be an empty seat in the council room tomorrow.

Kurt picked up the phone and called down to medical and quickly learned that Stewarth had been discharged after a quick bandaging and some pain medicine. Apart from the mysterious illness killing him, he was going to be just fine. He asked for word on Riley, too. As usual, no change. Selfish to think it, but Riley was the one person who could probably help him right now.

Unfortunately, his brother-in-law was still fighting a nasty septic infection from being shot in the stomach several weeks ago.

Next, Kurt called down to the basement to find out if Brooklyn had regained consciousness. She hadn't. He left instructions to be called when she woke up, even during the night.

Kurt might ask Stewarth to pardon the girl, but the man was a politician before all else. While just possessing the Ring of Solomon was enough to keep the Demonriders in check, the others would be emboldened by any show of weakness. Those without a demonic familiar had a lot less to fear from Solomon's Heir. Stewarth was a fair and sympathetic leader, but Kurt didn't imagine he'd feel particularly generous toward his would-be assassin.

Kurt might push for a council vote, but that was even less certain. He might call in favors for some votes, but it wouldn't begin to touch a majority, and he couldn't possibly do it in the next twelve hours. It would take a lot of talking to convince any of them to openly support an assassin.

Why did he care? It wasn't really his problem, right? Kurt already skated on thin ice with Stewarth because of tackling Eric and losing the tidal demon. The Heir hadn't seemed convinced when Kurt said there was a board flying at the back of Eric's head, probably because a demon enthralled by the ring couldn't do much without express permission. And, Kurt had thought wryly, because there weren't any loose boards lying around.

The phone jarred him awake, face down on the desk, in a puddle of drool. *Gross.*

"She's awake?" He looked at his clock. Seven in the morning and already light outside despite the persisting rain.

"How do you know she's awake?" Kurt rubbed his eyes.

"We can hear her talking," replied Caleb, Kurt's chief of house security.

"Talking to who? Herself?" His back ached, too damned old to sleep in a chair. He wiped a shirtsleeve across his cheek.

"We haven't been able to get close enough to learn more than that. Our men were *relieved* by the Heir's honor guard." Caleb tried to keep the bitterness out of his voice, but it seeped in around the edges.

Stewarth has his own people on guard? Shit.

"Okay, thanks." Kurt hung up the phone.

He looked around blearily, then poured half a shot of vodka to take the edge off. Orange juice would have made it better, but there wasn't time to send for it. Kurt didn't even remember falling asleep. He had two—maybe three—hours tops and no plan. As much as he hated to say it, this girl might just be fucked. He was headed for the bathroom to shave and get cleaned up when his gaze fell on the family photo above the fireplace.

Tyler.

Tyler seemed to stare at him with a look of disappointment. Kurt shook his head and rubbed his eyes. There, his son smiled again, the way Kurt remembered him.

"It's out of my hands," he said to the empty office. "Nothing I can do."

Did Tyler raise an eyebrow?

I'm going crazy. Then it hit him. Stewarth's own men working guard duty. Nobody even knew Brooklyn's name. If she disappeared now, there would be no repercussions for him. Stewarth could only blame his own people. Plus, they'd be looking for a blonde, and David said she was a brunette. A wig maybe? It would require a top-notch vanishing act. Something that would have Houdini scratching his head.

Tyler goaded him on with a reproachful stare.

"I can't. That's asking too much."

Tyler didn't answer.

"How much can one man owe?" Kurt screamed at his son. "How much?" He growled to keep from sobbing. A sudden draft caught the fire and sent a blaze of sparks up the chimney.

"Too much, apparently." A familiar female voice sent shivers up his spine. "But you're in luck, Protector; this one is on me."

Brooklyn woke up sore and sat with a groan, rubbing her eyes. *Eyes!* She'd been pretty sure they had melted right out of her face. The memory made her shiver. The mattress, the cell's only furnishing, had been thrown haphazardly into a corner. Damp, it smelled of mildew, sweat, and other things she'd rather not dwell on. A weak light filtered in from a high barred window and cast a grid of shadows on the stone wall. Her fingertips found the surface smooth and cold as glass, a solid slab of finished granite. Like a mausoleum.

Belial. Belial, come in Belial. No answer, but she sensed him inside, watching and listening.

There had to be a way out of this. She still wore the catering company uniform. Brooklyn made a careful circuit of the room. Flawless walls, no cracks, no seams, one solid steel door, and no bathroom. *Ugh.* She really had to pee. Down on her belly, peering under the door, the boot soles of two sentries were visible, one on each side of the door. Muffled sound came, a man talking on the phone, and then he spoke to the guards at the door.

"We need to sweep and secure the council room. Will the two of you be okay?"

"Yeah, sure," answered one of them.

There was a drumming of at least a dozen boots, and then the place grew silent as a crypt.

Belial, I need you. What's going on? You said you'd get us out.

Well, you said you'd kill the man with the ring. He answered so harshly it made her flinch. *I can't help you. I've been compelled to do nothing.*

I guess it's up to me . . .

I guess it is.

"Hey, I have to go to the bathroom," she shouted through the door.

"So go," one man answered.

"There's not a toilet in here."

"Not our problem," the other chimed in. "A couple more hours, it won't be your problem anymore either." They both laughed.

In less than a month, Brooklyn had lost her boyfriend, lost her family, lost her job, been used as a tool for bloody interrogations, and been coerced into attempting an assassination. Now she was imprisoned for something that wasn't her fault. The son of a bitch that got her into this mess couldn't get her out, and her jailers were douchebags. An icy rage built in the pit of her stomach. She'd had enough.

The room grew frigid. The moisture in the air coalesced around her. She began at the door and built a small ice ramp. Then Brooklyn hiked up her dress, squatted, and relieved herself. Piss ran down the ramp and under the door to puddle around her jailers' boots.

"Nasty bitch!" one of them shouted, and the key rattled in the lock.

Brooklyn reached deep into the darkest, coldest place within herself. A place in the human mind that most people won't acknowledge exists. The part where we know we are capable of anything, no matter how horrible. The place Belial lived inside her. Maybe he was compelled not to help her, but that didn't mean she couldn't use him to help herself.

Cold strength coursed through her like electricity. The door swung inward and lodged against her icy creation. She grabbed the first man's arm and yanked. The door wasn't open wide enough for him to fit through. Brooklyn pulled harder, the door shattered the ice, and he tumbled inside, most of one ear sheared off. She grabbed him by his jacket, pivoted, and flung him into the wall behind her. He groaned and fell into a heap.

Brooklyn slipped through the door cautiously. Without warning, something whipped through the air at her head. Though she tried to duck, it still caught her behind the left ear with enough force to drive her to her knees. For a moment, everything seemed to have warped out of focus, and a metallic taste flooded her mouth. Brooklyn struggled up as far as her hands and knees before taking a steel-toed boot to the stomach and ribs. She rolled over and scooted backward away from the man approaching her. Trying and failing to draw breath. The pain cleared her head some, but once she could breathe, it hurt to do so. In a frenzy, she flung things off a nearby desk with her mind. A stapler, two computer monitors, a phone, pens, but he deftly dodged them all. Brooklyn scrambled backward until her back found a wall.

In desperation, she conjured a wall of pure kinetic energy and sent it rushing across the room at him. Desks, chairs, and dozens of smaller things careened away from her. It tore at his clothing like a hurricane wind, but he kept coming, stepping through the wall of force. As the echoes of the commotion faded, her arms filled with lead until they were too heavy to raise. Her heart hammered like a frenetic bass drum in her ears. Her nose bled again, and she felt twitchy, like she'd latched onto an electric fence with her teeth.

"Better save a little strength," the guard grunted as he dragged her up by her hair, "for your execution. They say he's going to have you impale yourself on an icicle. Should be quite a show."

As the guard dragged her back to the cell, Brooklyn stumbled over something and looked down at a billy club. She giggled.

"Crazy bitch."

The energy that Brooklyn gathered in her hand was a lukewarm trickle, not an icy flood, but it called the club to her palm just the same. She pivoted and swung it underhand right into the family jewels. The guard collapsed. The air left him in something more a sigh than a scream.

Brooklyn dragged him through the urine slush and into the cell and slammed the door firmly. Black spots flitted like moths across her vision, and she couldn't seem to catch her breath. One of the two guards yelled into a walkie-talkie. There came a crackling reply. It seemed important, but Brooklyn couldn't remember why. Footsteps echoed in the stairwell.

She crawled over to a jumble of office furniture in the corner and wormed her way in, disappearing under the pile. Brooklyn tucked herself into a small space where the walls met and pulled her knees to her chin. She tried to breathe more slowly and quietly. It wasn't easy. The black spots were gone, and her heart slowed, but she felt cold. She bit down on a finger to keep her teeth from chattering.

A clatter of footsteps, then a dozen more guards flooded into the room. Brooklyn caught only glimpses but saw enough to know they wore the same uniforms and carried rifles. The man she'd thrown into the wall earlier was yelling through the door. "It was Levin; he was here; he helped her! Get us out of here."

Brooklyn barely dared to breathe. There was the clanking sound of a key turning in a big lock, and then the door swung open. She saw the second man doubled over the edge of the mattress, dry heaving over a puddle of vomit.

"What the hell happened to him?"

"She kicked him in the balls. Give me a gun. We've got to find that little bitch. Protector Levin; he was in on it somehow. He just appeared out of thin air."

"How did she open the door?" the newcomer asked in a neutral tone.

"She . . . She pissed on us!"

"So, *you* opened the door?"

The guard's silence was answer enough.

The man in charge grunted in disgust. "You, you, you, and you. Take them up to medical, get them cleaned up, and keep them there until I have time to debrief them."

Two of his comrades dragged the first man off, and he went out of hearing raving about someone named Levin. Two others hoisted the guard on the mattress between them. He was pale and trembling. He didn't look well at all.

"And that, men, is what happens when you underestimate a prisoner." The leader turned, surveying the room. "Especially one with nothing to lose." He stopped, staring right at the pile of furniture. "You and you, to the top of the stairs; you and you, at the first landing." Brooklyn heard footsteps receding. "You two, check the back stairwell, make sure the door up top is secured." She heard more footsteps pounding up another set of stairs.

"It's locked," a voice called back.

He squatted down and looked right at her. "Hey, honey." He smiled, not unkindly. "Come on out; nobody here is going to hurt you."

She didn't want to. She wanted to sleep. There was nowhere to run, and she knew if she didn't come willingly, they would drag her out. "Make them stop pointing those guns at me, then I'll come."

He tilted his head thoughtfully and raised his hand, and the men lowered their weapons.

Brooklyn crawled out, working her way carefully through the tangle. When she was out, four of them fell in around her, one with a stun gun held at the ready.

"Take her up to medical, but keep her as far from Dumb and Dumber as possible. Be gentle, but if she tries to run again, kill her."

13

Into the Fire

Kurt's stomach was roiling, but he kept his feet under him until he could sink into his office chair. They'd dropped right into the stone cell and found both guards locked inside, Brooklyn gone.

"How could she have gotten out?" Kurt asked.

"With help?" Azrael offered. She stretched her wings to their full span, a little over twelve feet. Kurt thought she was beautiful, not in a human way, more like a sculpture or a painting. Something that intimated perfection and in doing so lost its character.

"You are beautiful," he murmured.

She just smiled in response.

"Are you ready to pay what you owe and collect your prize?"

Kurt frowned. "I have most of it. Would you make the trade now and let me pay the rest as I can? I won't disappoint."

Azrael laughed. "All mortals disappoint me. If you give me most of what I've asked, I can give you most of what you desire." She laughed again, mockingly.

Kurt's face darkened. "Let's find the girl then, so I can get back to it." He picked up the phone and called downstairs. "I need you to make very discreet inquiries about the prisoner; there are . . . rumors that she has escaped. Find out what's happened. Remember, discreet."

Azrael folded her wings in tightly. "Let's assume they recapture her. Will the hearing continue as scheduled?"

"For sure."

"Then we should be there. I'll take her."

"In front of all those people? It's one thing to whisk her out of a jail cell and let the guards bear the blame, but to have her just vanish from a crowded council meeting under heavy guard? How will I explain that?"

"Why should anyone look to you for an explanation?"

"I'm responsible. Justice east of the Mississippi is my sole responsibility."

"And killing this girl is human justice?"

Kurt sighed.

"Would you hesitate to do the right thing if it were your son in her stead?" Azrael gestured toward the picture. "To turn your men against the Heir, cut his throat, take the ring for yourself, and finally pay me what is owed?"

"Murder is never the right thing." Kurt pulled a small golden trinket from his pocket. It was a three-sided Celtic knot. He traced the interlocked loops with his thumb. "Stewarth is my friend, but you're right, if it were my son, his life, I would do anything, but you already know that better than most."

"If he is truly your friend, ask him for a favor."

"I can't. He couldn't, even if he wanted to."

"It is simple. You save her or you don't." Azrael frowned and flickered furiously into translucency. "Tsunami." She grimaced.

The phone rang. Kurt snatched it up and listened. "How many with her?" he asked. Then he thanked the man and hung up. "They have her in the medical wing and will be bringing her to trial from there. Can you just pull her out?"

"It's too risky. I've never tried to take a demon on a ride along. That's why you were going to excise the demon in the cell before we zapped out." She continued distractedly. "Okay, how about I conceal myself in your council room? You play your silly political games, and if they try to execute her, I'll vanish her so fast their heads will spin? The Heir will remove the demon before the execution?"

"No, he will make the demon do the execution."

"That complicates things."

"A bit." Kurt poured himself a shot from a silver flask in his desk. "If we could, I don't know, get her locked back up or something . . . " He sat the glass back on his desk and picked up the Celtic knot. "An exorcism is going to take at least a little time, even with this thing." He tossed it in the air like a coin, watching the sunlight glinting off its intricate loops.

Azrael ripped across the room in an instant, her nose even with the talisman as it reached its apex and fell back to his palm. "Is that it? How does it work?"

"I'll show you when we complete our transaction." He slipped it back into his pocket.

She turned away as if she didn't care one way or the other, staring pensively out at the clearing sky. A shaft of sunlight fell on her and seemed to disappear as if she were a hole in the world, letting all the light seep out. "I wonder why the ocean spirits are so riled up?"

"Earthquakes cause tsunamis, not ocean spirits."

Azrael turned and laughed; it was the first genuine smile he'd ever seen on her face. "How can you be skeptical of anything? Haven't you seen enough?"

Kurt laughed too. "Seen too much. I'm full circle now, right back where I started."

When her smile faded, and her face grew solemn, it was like a lunar eclipse. "We must save this girl. She's going to be important. For both of us."

"Are you a prophet now? Important how?"

"Just trust me, I cannot say more, but what I said earlier about taking the ring by force . . . It's that serious. Kill everyone in the room before you allow the execution."

"Trust you? Murder a friend because you say it's the only way?"

She shrugged.

Kurt paced in front of the hearth. "What good is it to save a life if I become a monster in the process? You've tried to get me to do the same thing to pay your price, and I said no. How can I do for some girl what I couldn't do for my own son?"

"Do it for both of them."

"Why don't you? You're Death."

"It doesn't work that way. I have to use proxies, like you." She smiled. "I know you'll do the right thing." Azrael dimmed so that the sun passed through her like stained glass, and didn't speak for so long that Kurt wasn't sure if she was even still there. Then, like someone dialed up a rheostat, she pulsed back into solidity. "This is going to be a bad one." Azrael glanced at the clock on the wall. "It's time. Are you ready for this?"

"Not even a little." Kurt smiled grimly. "But we have work to do." He gathered a few papers and slipped a pouch of small metal marbles into his pocket with the Celtic talisman. When he looked up, she was already gone.

They brought biscuits, gravy, eggs, bacon, and orange juice. Brooklyn ate an embarrassing amount, but the more she ate, the better she felt. The nosebleed stopped, and the doctor put a stiff bandage over her bruised ribs. He listened to her heart and lungs. They even let her brush her hair—the wig had vanished in the scuffle—but she quickly learned not to brush anywhere near the throbbing knot behind her ear.

Brooklyn could hear Mr. Busted Balls groaning in agony down the hall, and it gave her a kind of perverse pleasure, especially the first time the brush grazed the injury. The doctor interrupted second helpings to shine a light in her eyes and ask her to follow his finger around her field of vision.

"Compliments of Mr. Levin," he said, placing a small stack of clothes at the foot of her bed. They were her own clothes from the suitcase in her car. Jeans, a T-shirt, a sweater, tennis shoes, underwear, socks. The guards politely averted their eyes while Brooklyn changed, but that was as much privacy as they would give. It was hard to move. Now that the adrenaline had worn off, everything ached. The pain in her ribs made it hard to get her shirt on, but she managed going slowly. Brooklyn wanted to pull her hair back, but she didn't have a rubber band or a clip. It felt good to be back in her own clothing, though. She sat cross-legged on the bed.

"So, can any of you guys tell me what's going on?" She paused, but when no one answered, Brooklyn continued. "Because usually when a person is accused of something, they get to know what it is, maybe get to make a phone call, talk to a lawyer?"

Silence.

"Any of that sound familiar?" She sighed. "Are we still in the United States? Because I feel like I've fallen down the rabbit hole and landed in North Korea."

Someone laughed behind her. Brooklyn turned to see who and instantly regretted it. She was sore in places she hadn't known she could be sore. It was the doctor.

"I thought you might want to brush your teeth." He held up a tray with a prepasted brush and a small bottle of mouthwash. He sat the tray carefully beside the small sink.

Brooklyn nodded her thanks.

"I assure you, you're still in the States, but you've stepped into a different world, just the same"—he paused—"and made a lot of trouble for yourself, it would seem."

She said nothing. There was nothing to say. An escape now was out of the question. Brooklyn brushed her teeth. When she finished, they told her it was time to go.

They fell in around her again, stun guns and all. They marched through a labyrinth of intersecting hallways and stairs. By the time they arrived at the council room, she couldn't have found her way back to the medical wing without a map.

The room had a soaring ceiling. Her captors nudged her toward a chair at the centermost of several fancy wooden tables arranged in a crescent beneath a dais. Several people were already seated at the other tables, most of them well dressed. She felt conspicuously under dressed in jeans and a sweater. Some of them stared curiously or frowned disapprovingly. Most averted their eyes. All of them fell silent. She must have served some of them dinner the previous night.

In the corner behind the dais, a shadow seemed to flicker. When Brooklyn blinked, it grew still, but if she stared for a few seconds, it seemed to writhe. She closed her eyes and rubbed her forehead. Clearly more than a minor concussion. So transfixed was Brooklyn by the shadow that she did not notice someone had taken a seat beside her.

"Hello."

She flinched when he spoke.

"I'm Kurt Levin. You must be Brooklyn." He held out his hand.

She shook it. "You my lawyer?"

He frowned. "Well, no. Technically speaking, I'm your prosecutor, though that isn't quite right either, because this isn't a court proceeding, not really."

"Well, what is it?"

"It's a judgment. It's hard to explain, but think of it as a whole series of court hearings rolled into one."

"Do you see that in the corner?" she asked. "That shadow."

He stared at where she was pointing for a long time before answering, "What about it? It's just a shadow. Are you sure you're okay?"

She nodded.

"May I see where you were hit?"

She tilted her head forward and lifted her hair out of the way.

He gave a low whistle. “That’s quite a lump. Though I hear you gave better than you got.”

She couldn’t stop the smile. “He got what he deserved.”

A frown darkened his face. “Probably he did, but what about you? Do you think you are going to get what you deserve?”

She shrugged and tried to keep the terror out of her eyes. “Guess we’ll see.”

14

JUDGMENT

Kurt shifted uncomfortably in his chair. What did Brooklyn mean? Did she know what was coming? Was she admitting to an active role in the assassination attempt? He couldn't make up his mind about this girl. Brooklyn held herself well, but fear haunted her eyes. Apparently, the girl sensed Azrael in the corner. As far as Kurt knew, no one else in this room besides himself saw the God of Death without her intending it.

"What's going to happen to me?"

Kurt met Brooklyn's eyes for a moment, then looked away. He didn't know how to answer and didn't want to answer. *Christ. She's somebody's kid.* "I don't know yet."

"One of the guards . . . One of them said"—Brooklyn turned away from him, looking hard into Azrael's corner—"said they were going to impale me with ice." The last part came out in a whisper. After a second, she turned back, searching his face for the truth. Brooklyn must have found something there to confirm her fears because she nodded, bowed her head, and said no more.

Kurt wasn't sure if she was crying or not. Hair hid her face. He was still trying to think of something comforting to say when Alexander Stewarth walked in and took a seat on the dais. One of his hands was wrapped in gauze and he had a butterfly bandage over a cut on his neck. Despite that, the Heir looked much better than he had the night before at dinner. He appeared well rested and wore a smile. That had to bode well for Brooklyn, didn't it? If

Stewarth wore the ring, it would be on the uncut hand, but how would Kurt steal something he could not see?

A quick glance around the room revealed plenty of familiar faces. Erina Craft and her daughter and several of their cousins stood along the wall behind them. He was pretty sure he had earned their allegiance, or at least a favor, the night of the exorcism. He'd shielded them from a lot of uncomfortable questions related to demon summoning.

Tristan Barrett had not returned to the States for last night's banquet. That was unfortunate; he was a levelheaded guy and Kurt could have counted on him for support.

Of course, *Father* Logan was here with a smattering of his zealots behind him; he'd find no support there. The next couple tables were filled with people he didn't know very well from one of the other regions.

He wished Brianne were here. She did a better job of keeping up with politics, but maybe it was better Brianne wasn't here. Like him, her allegiance was to Stewarth. He doubted she'd be up for a coup to overthrow their leader. Come to think of it, Kurt wasn't so sure he was up for it either.

Several older men, who came as a part of Stewarth's entourage, filled the next few tables. Then Kurt saw Eric, his long black hair tied with a ribbon, jaw set, eyes full of loathing that may have been meant for him, Brooklyn, or both.

The boy's mother, Del, sat beside him. Her dark eyes scanned the room like a lioness surveying a watering hole. Even after all these years, she possessed a delicate beauty. She had been the daughter of an Iranian revolutionary who had hoped to manipulate Stewarth and the rest of the supernatural community into aiding in his conflict. His quest for power had not ended well.

Nathan Goodrum sat with another Demonrider at the last table, and behind them in military formation were a dozen more, all wearing the blank, monastic expression of their order. They couldn't afford anger. Every emotion had to be moderated, or they risked losing control to their demons.

Shit. Maybe he really didn't have all that many friends here, after all. *I have Azrael,* Kurt reminded himself, but his stomach felt like it was trying to mimic the Celtic knot in his pocket.

"Welcome, friends." Stewarth smiled. "It saddens me that our celebration has taken such an ominous turn. These are dark times. Our centuries-long covenant with the Spirits of the Sea is broken, and now the Wardens, who have worked alongside us for so long to keep our worlds separate, send one of their own in a dress and wig to assassinate me."

Several people chuckled quietly.

Kurt glanced over his shoulder at his men lining the back wall near the exit. For each of his men, there were two of Stewarth's. Kurt couldn't kill a man in front of his family, especially not a man he considered a friend.

"Protector Levin?"

Kurt's eyes snapped up. "Yes sir?"

"Shall we proceed?"

"Ah yes, um, I've had an opportunity to make some inquiries, to conduct some interviews that is, or really I basically just talked with one person in particular so far, and I have good cause to believe—"

"Out with it already, Mr. Levin."

"I believe this was an involuntary possession, that this young woman did not attack you of her own free will."

There was no response for what seemed like a very long time. Kurt felt the blood rising in his face. He hated public speaking more than anything he could think of right now. Several of those present had raised eyebrows in expressions of incredulity.

Stewarth frowned. "Forceful possession is rare, unheard of . . . Surely someone possessing the talents displayed during the attempted escape this morning would easily shrug off such an intrusion."

"Perhaps this morning's display is a better example of the demon's abilities than of the young lady's."

Stewarth's brows knitted together. "Would you agree, Mr. Goodrum?" He smiled. "This is your area of expertise after all, is it not?"

Nathan looked like someone had slapped him. He wasn't accustomed to having his opinion solicited. He lurched to his feet. "It's common knowledge, sir," he answered in a slow, measured voice, "that even those without gifts are immune to a truly unwanted possession because of the Pull and the toll resisting it takes on a demon's strength. It should be impossible."

Kurt cleared his throat. "I've heard 'rare' and 'unheard of.'" Kurt swallowed. "Don't we have a responsibility to make certain?"

"Father Logan, do you concur with Mr. Goodrum's assessment?"

Dravin rose with imperial grace. "I do, sir. The last recorded incident of a completely involuntary possession was"—he grinned smugly—"biblical."

He's already made up his mind, Kurt realized. Alexander was simply gathering support, placing Kurt in the inconsequential minority. There was no way to compete with this political bullshit. People who might openly oppose an execution if Stewarth ordered it outright were falling all over themselves to help lay the groundwork for one now as they tried to curry favor.

"Mr. Levin is right," a high, clear voice rang out. Every eye turned to Erina Craft. "Less than a month ago, one of our own, my future son-in-law, was taken without consent." She let her gaze drift around the room, daring anyone to disagree. When no one did, she continued. "Mr. Levin was there"—Erina turned her eyes on Stewarth—"and so was your son, sir. They both saw something that most of the people in this room would call biblical as well."

Stewarth cleared his throat uncomfortably. "Thank you, Erina. I'll take that into consideration."

Erina shrugged and sat back down.

In the corner, Azrael flickered like an old eight-millimeter movie projector. Kurt noticed Brooklyn staring at the same spot.

"That's right. An involuntary possession is no less likely than a grade-two demon," Kurt added quickly.

Stewarth ran his fingers through his gleaming hair. "Protector Levin, tell me, what is the penalty for attempted murder?"

"Sir, there's no evidence of any involvement with the occult or—"

"What do our laws say happens to those who conspire with demons against the Heir of Solomon?"

The word tasted like bile on Kurt's tongue. Everyone in the room knew the answer. "Death."

"Death indeed," Stewarth agreed thoughtfully.

Kurt let the smooth colored orbs slip soundlessly into his palm. His last gift from Riley. When he attacked, Stewarth's men would react almost instantly. Hell, some of his own men would probably move against him. A chilling thought suddenly occurred. What if Eric had the ring again? How could he steal something he couldn't see? He glanced uneasily at Nathan and his men. The ring could turn every one of them against him in half a heartbeat. Demonriders traded some measure of their free will for power.

Brooklyn stood up beside Kurt. "I had no choice. I didn't want to do it. Belial made me."

"A demon can't *make* you do anything unless you give it control," Stewarth said. "We've heard that confirmed already this morning. It possessed you because you let yourself be possessed."

"No, I didn't!" Her voice grew thick with emotion. "He was going to make me kill my family, my nephew; he's four. Any choice I had wasn't really a choice at all."

Kurt put a hand on her shoulder.

"Dear, I've sat in judgment of many, many people over the years. I've already heard all the excuses and the sad stories. Perhaps you should have thought of your family *before* you dabbled in the occult, *before* you attempted to cut my throat."

"This is not fair! This is not how justice works. I want a real trial, in a real court, in front of a real judge. You can't do this!"

Alexander glared. "I sentence you to die."

"Now wait a minute," Kurt objected. "We can't just dismiss my findings. What happened with Bryssa's fiancé is—"

"Something we will discuss another day. I have ruled."

Yes. For too many years, Kurt thought bitterly. But he wasn't looking at Stewarth anymore. Kurt was looking at Azrael. "Death it is, sir." *For you, and probably for me too.* He gathered energy in his palm around the metal orbs that only he could control. Azrael wasn't moving. She wasn't following the plan. She flickered almost out of existence. *Take her!* Kurt screamed in his mind.

Stewarth's hand began to glow, and Brooklyn gasped in agony. She fell rigidly to the floor, eyes a ghastly, glowing blue. The temperature dropped so fast Kurt could see his breath condensing. Water flowed from all the cups in the room, bursting from plastic bottles. It coalesced into a wicked-looking icicle trident above where the girl lay prone on the floor.

"You were dead from the moment you tainted yourself and gave up the gift of your humanity. We always have a choice until we choose to give up on free will. You have chosen your own executioner."

Now goddammit! Kurt thought, and Azrael stopped flickering. She was more solid than he'd ever seen her. The God of Death crossed the room like a scythe and reached for Brooklyn, but something brought her up short. She flickered again, faster. The trident came down. With visible concentration, she solidified, grabbed the girl, and vanished. The ice shattered against the marble floor.

Unable to move, Brooklyn saw the wicked icy trident fall. She closed her eyes tight. That at least she could still do. This was it. She reached inside herself for that familiar, cold strength, but it wasn't hers to command anymore. Brooklyn could feel it coursing around her, shaping the icicle, forming the tips into daggers. She thought of her mom and dad, but mostly of her sister. *Are you out there somewhere, Erin?*

The pain never came. Just sudden icy fingers, an iron grip. Frigidity razored through her arm. It was like nothing Brooklyn had ever felt; it made her flesh prickle and her bones ache. She gasped and her mouth filled with salt water. *Is this what it feels like to die?* Brooklyn opened her eyes on the faces of death. Dozens of images flashed by in a coruscation of shocked expressions, grimaces, and gleaming, lifeless eyes. Some were drowned, some battered, a few burned, though she couldn't guess how when the entire world seemed to be made of water.

Suddenly, Brooklyn was on a beach, gasping for air. There were flopping fish all around on wet sand, and above her, a wave that seemed to touch the sky. The strange coldness came again, the ache in her bones familiar as it wrapped around her like steel bands. The world lurched and there were voices now, murmurs. Brooklyn rolled to her side—something crunching beneath her—and coughed up water. She wiped her eyes and found herself right back in the enormous room with her executioner.

She didn't question it. Nothing made sense anymore.

Stewarth stared at her wordlessly and raised his hands. The broken ice rose slowly from the floor around her, and the trident reformed.

T

here was an uproar. Stewarth's mouth hung open in astonishment for half a second before he pressed his lips into a hard line.

Azrael looked at Kurt and shook her head. A human emotion marred her inhuman beauty. Fear, maybe, or regret. Then she exploded in a flurry of black feathers and shadows that turned to wisps and vanished, burning an afterimage into his retina.

Kurt blinked once, and it was gone. He was on his own.

"Wait! There's something you should know before you do that, sir," Kurt said. The ice wavered over Brooklyn's prostrate form.

Stewarth raised a brow.

"I swore a vow when I took this job, a vow to protect humanity from the supernatural, and if you disregard what I've said here today and execute this girl, then I have failed and will have no choice but to resign."

"I'll gladly take up the mantle of Protector for this region, sir," Nathan Goodrum offered.

"As would I." Dravin Logan cut his eyes at Goodrum. "The region deserves a Protector with moral convictions, one that understands his role and place in the order of things."

Stewarth looked from one to the other, his face unreadable. He suddenly seemed frail, but his voice rang with authority. "Nathan. Dravin. I thank you for your eagerness to serve. But both of you, please, sit back down. Kurt, my old friend—

"What's her name?" Kurt demanded.

"Her name? I don't know her name."

"You sentenced her to die, and you don't even know her name."

Stewarth paused. "Do you really feel this strongly about this girl's life?" His tone was dangerously neutral.

"I do, sir. It would be a great injustice and a personal failure."

Brooklyn watched the exchange in silence, the icy blade poised above her heart.

Stewarth sat in silent thought for so long that when he finally spoke, it startled Kurt and he almost loosed one of the orbs.

"Then know this: she is your responsibility now. If she steps out of line, the next time we are here, there will be two executions rather than one."

"Yes, sir. What about the demon?"

"What part of 'your responsibility' wasn't clear?" he snapped.

"Of course, I'll take care of it. Thank you, sir."

"And Kurt, come see me after. We need to talk." With that, Stewarth rose and left through a back door with his family and four personal guards fast on his heels.

Brooklyn accepted Kurt's hand, and he pulled her up, a puddle of seawater spreading around her feet.

"That was a wild ride, I bet?" He smiled. The tension in Brooklyn's face gave way to relief, then trembling, and finally tears. "Come on,"—Kurt prodded her—"let's get this done."

15

Rekindled

Kurt led Brooklyn to a stone room not unlike the one she'd escaped this morning. This one held steel furniture and a collection of medieval restraints and implements.

"Uh . . . maybe we could skip this part?" she said, suddenly apprehensive. Some of these things looked a lot worse than the ice trident.

"Don't worry." Kurt clicked the lock on the door. "We won't need any of this stuff. This location is only a safety precaution."

"Will this hurt?" Brooklyn, already covered in bruises, wasn't sure why she cared to ask.

"Shouldn't, especially if you help me." Kurt fished something shiny out of his pocket. "You'll know what to do once it begins."

It will be like last time, Brooklyn told herself, *except this time I won't fight it.* She'd never been more ready to be rid of Belial. Even when this was over, Brooklyn wasn't sure how to pick up the pieces and mend all the bridges the demon had burned. One day, things would be the same. With some distance, all of this would be over and behind her. She could get back home to her family. Maybe even to David.

Kurt moved quick as a snake strike. His palm seemed to cover her entire skull. Something hard with sharp edges pressed into her forehead. Just like last time, blood pounded in her ears. Brooklyn became painfully aware of her body's machinery churning and pulsing until the demon's hold on her was a thousand throbbing microscopic tentacles. Brooklyn pushed Belial away and rejected him. He didn't plead this time or make threats, and as each tendril snapped, it felt like a splinter plucked from her mind.

When Belial was finally gone, everything seemed brighter. As if Brooklyn had been wearing sunglasses for the past month and they'd suddenly fallen away. Her whole being ached pleasantly with relief, like the twinge of having an IV removed. Every breath was sweet. Even the pungent, damp air down here smelled of freedom. Brooklyn realized her cheeks were wet and dabbed her eyes with a sleeve.

"Wow. I feel so much better." She felt warm inside, alive.

"You're okay?" Kurt asked. There was sweat on his forehead.

"Relieved, sore, but okay." She shivered. "And cold."

"Let's get you upstairs and into some dry clothes."

Kurt turned toward the door, but Brooklyn grabbed his arm. His bicep tensed up, but he didn't pull away.

"I wanted to say thank you for what you did up there. I know you didn't have to."

"Where did you go? When you vanished." He turned to face her, caramel eyes searching hers with veiled desperation.

"To the ocean. I'm not sure where. I almost drowned. There were fish everywhere, dying on the sand, and then this enormous wave, like a skyscraper. Right before it would have crashed down, I was back here." Brooklyn grimaced. "I saw corpses under the water. Flashes of them . . . " She trailed off, troubled by the memories.

"That was some powerful demon to almost escape like that," Kurt commented.

"I don't think it was Belial. Something cold grabbed me, but it was a different kind of cold. Plus, he said he was bound by your leader."

"Demons lie. Of course it was him. What else could it have been? Did you see . . . something else?" Kurt asked, searching her eyes as if he might find in them some ghostly image of what she'd seen.

Brooklyn bit her lip thoughtfully and pulled back a strand of dripping hair. "No, nothing."

"Come on," he said, turning back to the door, "let's get you taken care of. I have another appointment, as you'll recall." Kurt smiled wryly, opened the door, and strode out.

Brooklyn hurried to keep up, lest she get lost in the labyrinth he called home.

Brooklyn stepped off the elevator behind Kurt. *This man has an elevator in his house! What is this all about?* At the end of the hall and around the corner, they stopped at a simple door.

"You'll find everything you need inside. I'll be back as soon as I can. We have a lot to discuss."

She nodded and opened the door. It was dark when she stepped inside. The door closed behind her with an audible click.

"Who's there?" called a familiar voice from somewhere in the darkness, a voice Brooklyn would have recognized anywhere.

"David?" She fumbled along the wall for a switch and found it, the lights came on, and there he was.

"Brooklyn!" He hugged her right off her feet. "I was afraid they'd executed you."

"How are you here?" she asked.

"You're wet." They sat down on the bed. His shirt was soaked with salt water.

"Your bag is in the bathroom," he said. "Showed up here this morning. I've been going crazy wondering if you're okay."

"Wait, how long have you been here?"

"I've been locked up since last night."

Dread pooled in the pit of her stomach. "Locked up? Are you possessed?"

"Am I what?"

"Possessed."

"No, of course not. Look"—he gestured—"no doorknob. No windows. Just a fancy prison is all I meant."

Brooklyn nodded. "Mr. Levin said he'd be back soon."

David grabbed her shoulders, and she looked up at him. "What have you gotten yourself into?"

Brooklyn pulled away, stung. "I didn't get myself into anything. This isn't my fault."

"That's not what I meant." He looked up at the ceiling in exasperation. "I'm just trying to understand what's happening."

Brooklyn shrugged. "I don't really understand it myself."

"Are you okay? Kurt told me some of it . . . Sounded bad."

There wasn't an easy answer for that one. The silence stretched until David shrugged and said, "I'm sorry."

"Me too." Brooklyn shivered. "I need a shower and dry clothes. We can talk after." She kissed him lightly on the cheek before he could respond and left him to wait.

Brooklyn showered slowly, unsure she'd ever be clean again. And seeing David so unexpectedly hadn't quite been the reunion she was expecting. She'd already snapped at him. She was mad, she realized, but didn't know why. How had he found her? Brooklyn had told him everything that night, all she remembered at least, and ten minutes later they were breaking up.

Brooklyn brushed her teeth, flossed, brushed again, towel dried her hair, and brushed it, too. She availed herself of the toilet and was considering searching for a nail file, but realized she was stalling, afraid to face David again.

When Brooklyn finally emerged in a billow of steam, she felt almost human. David had ditched his wet shirt and sat on the bed watching television. Brooklyn wanted to lie down with him, a simple thing, like they used to, but couldn't for some reason. She watched him watching TV for a long time, trying to think of the right thing to say.

Brooklyn had been through so much, done things unbearable to consider, and all she kept thinking about right now was the broken guitar lying on the bed between them while they shouted at each other. What was different? What would he say if he learned she'd murdered a house full of people and stacked the bodies like firewood? Or iced the heart of an exorcist trying to save her? How much did he know already?

"Come sit down," David said, startling her out of thought. He slid over to make room.

"Okay." Brooklyn brushed her wet hair back, climbed into bed, and snuggled close. They shared a pillow and watched *I Love Lucy* reruns.

"Brooke," David began softly, "I'm really sorry about everything that happened."

"Me too," she murmured. "Your grandpa's guitar—"

"It's just a guitar."

Brooklyn didn't know what to say to that, so she just snuggled closer, pressing her back against his bare chest. He snaked an arm around her sore ribs and pulled her closer. It was a good ache. There was something honest about it.

"What did he tell you about me?"

Brooklyn heard him take a deep breath. "Not much, really. Just that you were possessed by . . . something. I didn't believe him at first, but then he levitated his couch with me on it. Made it a little harder to disbelieve. He asked a lot of questions about you, said you were in trouble, that he'd find a way to help you. Then he tricked me in here and I've been locked up since."

"He did. Help me, I mean. David, I've done bad things." She pushed the images out of her mind. "Things I don't want to think about."

"Whatever it is, I'm sure it wasn't your fault. When you are ready to talk, I'll be here." He kissed the back of her neck. "I'll always be here. I won't leave again."

Brooklyn turned to look over her shoulder. "I left, not you."

He traced a finger between her shoulder blades and down her back, trailing goosebumps on her skin. "Semantics."

"We're both here now."

"Yes." He moved against her.

"Kurt said he'd be back soon."

"I'm sure he'll knock," David said, sliding his hand over her hip.

Brooklyn half turned again and pressed her lips against his. *Sometimes*, she mused, *it is easier and better not to think*.

16

Three Wishes

When he awoke in his true form, Belial knew two things: he'd failed and the Pull had never taken him. This place was eerily silent. Hell was a noisy place, all the screams and wails blending into a kind of symphony. There was almost nowhere in the spirit world where the Melody of Hell was absent. He could think of only two places: the library and the Colossus.

Belial wondered what had become of Brooklyn. He reached for her with his mind, but it was like she no longer existed. Nothing existed. He was utterly alone in a perfectly round tunnel of immense proportions; the walls pulsed with a dim golden light. A path curved slightly to the left and vanished into a yellow gloom.

The Protectors had Brooklyn now. He wasn't sure what they'd do to her, but he feared it wouldn't be anything good. The Heir had forestalled the execution, a minor miracle, but now he'd set Brooklyn up as a target and tied a Protector's fate to hers. The thought grieved him. Brooklyn was a perfectly formed and powerful host, and Belial had only scratched the surface of what they were capable of together. There would be others like her in the future, and they couldn't possibly be any more recalcitrant than she had been. Still, losing her irked him. Willful little thing. He'd been harsh toward the end. Had to be. There was no bribing or seducing Brooklyn. Still, and despite all that, the thought of her in a cell somewhere or dead and bloody set a weight in his chest.

Though they looked and thought nothing alike, Brooklyn somehow reminded him of Tais. Belial turned his thoughts abruptly from her; that line of thinking would lead nowhere good.

Ahead, the tunnel came to a rounded point and curved away to the left at a harsh, new angle. Belial grew tired of walking, so he brought his hawk face to the front and spread his wings. The golden floor raced away beneath him; there was room enough to fly with comfort. Ahead, the tunnel slanted up. Belial beat his wings twice and rose with it, but just when he thought he'd found a way out, the tunnel sloped downward again. Further and further he raced, putting on speed until the path began to ascend again, but just like before, it apexed and turned down. When the tunnel rounded at a steep angle a second time, he wondered if this was the same place he'd already been.

Belial landed with a thud that echoed down the cavernous pipe in both directions. He turned his wolf and then his wolverine face to the floor and snuffed. He'd never been this way before. With a grunt of frustration, he took to the air again—this time in his true form—letting the many eyes on his four wings search the floor below and the ceiling above. He kept a rough count of the time he left the bend in the tunnel to the time it rose and subsequently fell again, then he measured the time to fly from the apex to the next bend in the tunnel. It wasn't much beyond there that he picked up his own scent again. He'd come full circle. Belial drifted down onto his stomach and stretched out languidly to think.

Three gently curving tunnels, each with a rise and a fall roughly in the middle, all connected by three corners or turning places that set the subsequent tunnels on a significantly changed angle. This labyrinth, if it could properly be called that, with no alternative passages, had to be triangular. He estimated each tunnel to be about three miles long. The sharp bends were the points. Belial tried to imagine the whole, but couldn't reconcile it in his mind.

He tucked his wings out of sight and rolled over onto his back. Belial rubbed a finger over the floor. It was gold. Actual gold. The world's most expensive prison. It didn't make sense. There had to be a way in and out; otherwise how did he get inside to start with?

With a sigh, he rose and took full wolf form. This was where he'd woken up, which was troubling. In a purely spiritual form, he didn't need sleep, but if he woke here, wouldn't this be the point of entry? He sniffed every square inch of the floor and walls. They were smooth, unbroken, and impenetrable.

Belial ran laps, flew laps, and if there had been water, he would have swum laps. There wasn't an entrance or an exit. He tried simply vanishing out and reappearing somewhere else, anywhere else, but that wasn't working either. He roared in frustration and coated the tunnel in ice out of sight in both directions.

Belial sat down. He tried to recall everything that had happened. Maybe he'd never been excised at all. Alexander Stewarth could have used the ring to trap him in some dusty corner of Brooklyn's mind, or drive him crazy with visions. Maybe he wasn't here at all. No prison could hold him. The Ring of Solomon and the Pull were the only things that could do that. Which had put him here? As a Warden, he'd sent his fair share of rogues back to the right side of the veil, but he'd just ripped them off like leeches and let the Pull do the rest.

This was maddening. When he got free of this prison, whoever put him here would pay. It was true; Belial didn't need to sleep unless he was in a mortal body, but he wasn't incapable of it. Maybe if he slept, he'd wake elsewhere. It wasn't much of a plan, but it was the only one he had.

Belial dreamed he was a man on a beach. The ocean stretched before him and disappeared where the world ended. Driftwood littered the beach, trees larger than anything the modern world had ever seen, toppled, their roots reaching skyward like the claws of a dragon. A river hundreds of feet wide emptied into the sea below. The waves dragged the river silt up onto the pristine sand and left intricate whorls of black and white.

"What are you seeking?" she asked in the Old Tongue. His stomach clenched. He knew that voice, a dagger in his heart.

"Tais!" Belial turned. She was just as he remembered. Hair so black the sun made it blue, one eye green and the other brown, a smile he couldn't help but return.

"Let's swim," Tais said, letting the linen of her simple robe slip off her bronzed shoulders. She stepped naked into the waves, and he followed, shedding clothing as he went.

Belial embraced her in the warm water. "We must flee. If we leave now, we can escape!"

She looked at him, confused. She didn't understand.

He tried again. "Something bad is going to happen."

"No," she said, reaching for him under the water, "something good."

He cupped a hand around her breast, and another slid down her sun-warmed back and beneath the water where her bottom swelled.

He always relished this part of the dream. The part before the sea erupted around them, but this time it didn't. The dream dissolved into a golden mist and when he opened his eyes, he was standing in a lavish office, nose to nose with Kurt Levin.

"Hello, Belial."

"Protector," Belial murmured guardedly, sweeping the cobwebs of the dream from his mind.

"You're probably wondering how you got here, why you aren't back in Hell? Maybe why you can stand here in your true form without the Pull dragging you back where you belong?"

"Is Brooklyn alive? Is she okay?" The words burst from his lips unbidden.

Kurt blinked. "She's fine, no thanks to you."

Belial's mind was working now, putting pieces together. "So, I had the wrong man all along; it was you. Taking demons, holding them somehow, and upsetting the balance between our worlds."

"Technically I work for Alexander. Who's to say you had the wrong man? Maybe it was both of us."

"I'm not stupid." He spread his wings and turned all his eyes on Kurt. "I see things quite clearly. My question is only why?"

"That's not your concern."

"Then perhaps I'll gut you and ask Alexander Stewarth." He flexed a claw suggestively.

Kurt smiled patiently. "You don't get it yet; you are a dog on a leash, bound to me." He held up a golden pendant. It was a three-sided Celtic knot interwoven with a circle. "You are a djinn and this is your lamp; I guess that makes me Aladdin?"

Belial tried to take it from him, but he couldn't move. His body felt numb.

"Now, you won't say a word about any of this to anyone. You cannot lie to me, so don't even try. I have a few tasks for you, and when they are complete—and I've put the girl safely beyond your reach—you have my word, I'll set you free."

"What tasks?"

"I need a Tome from your world. I don't know what it is called, but it describes the Incarnation of Death."

Belial laughed. "Even if I could get this book for you, you wouldn't be able to read it."

"Why not?"

"It's a part of the Eternal Collection, bound in dragon hide with scales so sharp they would cut your fingers to ribbons at a touch, scribed in dragon blood that is only visible at temperatures so high it would melt your face off to be within a hundred feet, and written in a language so old that only the eldest Tomekeepers have learned to read it. Brokenly."

"You're lying."

"I thought you said I couldn't?" He raised his eye horns mockingly. "What business have you mucking around with Death? And how did the girl travel to the sea and back?" Belial's mind spun. Imprisoning demons, stealing Tomes? What was this man up to?

"I don't explain myself to demons, and I can only assume you broke free somehow and disappeared with her."

"Oh yes," Belial replied sarcastically, "I broke free of the ring, thumbed my nose at the Pull, vanished to the sea, and then came back, only to fall victim to your little trinket."

"Will you bring me the book?"

"It's impossible."

"You're afraid?"

Belial bristled and put his wings away. *I'm afraid for you when I get free from this Celtic voodoo*, he thought to himself. "Even if I got the book, I'd never make it back."

"I freed you from the Pull. In some ways, you're freer and more powerful in my service than you've ever been."

Belial considered that for a moment while he watched Kurt pour himself a shot and down it. The Protector's caramel eyes were bloodshot and droopy; they drifted to the family portrait above the hearth.

"Suppose I bring back the book. You'll free me despite the fact you won't be able to read it, or even hold it?"

"Once you've delivered the book, and I've trained the girl enough to put her safely beyond your control, I'll set you free."

"That shouldn't take long. She's incredibly strong."

Kurt waved a hand dismissively. "Not strong enough, apparently, or none of us would be in this mess."

"That's your fault, not hers."

"How do you figure?" Kurt asked as he plopped down in his desk chair and poured another drink.

"You've pulled so many demons over here you've weakened the Pull. Getting here was easier than it should have been, though I can't explain why possessing her was so effortless."

"Hmm . . . " Kurt swilled his drink. "You can't lie, but you can be mistaken."

"I'm not."

"Let's hope you are because I have a quota to meet, and I'm going to meet it. How many does it take to break the Pull?"

"Is that your goal?"

Kurt frowned. "Of course not." His eyes flicked to the family portrait and then away.

Belial followed his gaze. "You can't bring them back. Even if I get the book."

"I'm well aware," Kurt answered coldly.

"Release the demons you hold, and I will renegotiate the agreement between the Wardens and the Protectors."

"No."

"You tread on rotten ice." Belial paused. "Weaken the barrier much more and the demons will finish the job for you. Once they start crossing on their own, the dam will break."

Kurt threw back his drink and slammed the glass down. "Well, I guess you better hurry back with that book, then."

17

Visiting Friends

With Belial off on his mission, Kurt turned to his next task; he'd put it off as long as he dared. The guards admitted him wordlessly into Stewarth's suite. He found the Heir at a desk, deeply engrossed in a book. He gestured for Kurt to sit but never looked up from the pages, so Kurt sat and waited. The study was lavish, with thick carpeting and plush leather furniture. Despite the day's warmth, a blaze crackled in the fireplace, making the room stifling.

Alexander closed the book with a thump and looked at Kurt as if just realizing he was there. "I know you don't mind waiting. You better not, anyway. You certainly kept me waiting long enough."

"I apologize, it took some time to—"

Stewarth held up his hand. "You think I rule because of my family name and because of this, don't you?" He dropped an ornate golden ring between them on the desk. It was inscribed with characters Kurt had never seen and set with a black stone that seemed to pulse like a living shadow. There were never so many shades of darkness in this world. It took a great effort to tear his gaze away, and before he could answer, Alexander continued. "Today I sentenced you. To die or kill the power-hungry parasites circling me like jackals, or to carry out justice and execute the girl assassin yourself. Maybe all three."

He was a clever bastard; Kurt couldn't deny that. "It was never my intention—"

"To make a fool of us both? That's really the problem, isn't it? You do things without intention, without understanding implications."

"Would you have me stand by while you execute an innocent girl?"

"Innocent girl? Demon whore assassin!" Stewarth pulled his collar down to show the bandage at his throat. "I didn't cut myself shaving, or have you forgotten that?"

"She was possessed against her will." Kurt leaned forward, hand on the edge of the desk. The ring was inches away; his fingers itched to touch it, but he forced himself to look at the sickly old man across the desk. "Can't you see the difference is about free will?"

"The man that killed your family. That was his excuse too, wasn't it? I don't recall you being particularly merciful that day."

The words were like a hammer to the head; he had no right to bring that up. Alexander thought he was so clever, yet he laid all his power on the desk between them, weakened as he was already.

The Heir cleared his throat. "Tell me how a girl vanishes and reappears drenched in sea water."

"Maybe the demon broke free or something. I don't know."

Stewarth laughed derisively and gestured at the ring. "Free of that? I think not." The lines on his face deepened as he shifted in his chair. "None of us will ever be free of it." He coughed. "My men say you appeared in the girl's cell and vanished again, right into thin air. Just like the girl."

It was Kurt's turn to laugh. "Are those the two that attacked the girl? The two you'll throw in jail as soon as they are well enough to leave a hospital bed?"

"Yes."

"Hardly credible."

Stewarth's gaze was unflinching. "No, I suppose not."

"You should put that away." Kurt gestured at the ring.

He smiled tiredly. "You know, I thought you were using the girl to paint me as a villain or to set the others on me if I made an exception. I even entertained the idea that you sent her in the first place, manufactured this whole situation, but this is really about right and wrong for you, isn't it?" He sighed deeply and went on. "That's why you are a great Protector, and why you should never touch this ring or try to rule. You've passed my test and reaffirmed my trust." He slapped the desk, and a circle of demons flickered into existence around them both. "This little incident made me realize I needed to beef up security a bit."

Kurt kept his voice level and neutral. "How? Without the ring?"

"My family is old; we have many secrets. We trace our line directly back to Solomon. We made the damned ring!" He slapped the desk again, and the demons flickered out of existence.

Try as he might, Kurt couldn't sense them. Which was scary as hell, pun and all.

Stewarth took a deep breath and picked up the ring. "You can go now."

"Thank you. I hope you feel well soon."

"It's Dravin Logan you should worry about. Goodrum despises you openly, but Logan is twice as clever and hates you for reasons you don't even know."

"He's no threat to me."

Stewarth laughed. "Just remember what I said. They'll use the girl against you. When she falls, you fall with her. Kill her now while you still have the chance, and let's be done with these games."

"I won't do that."

"Keep her close, then. I'm leaving tomorrow. I miss the ocean and the sun. Throw another log on the fire for me. Why is it always so damn cold in these mountains?"

With the most harrowing part of the day behind him and Stewarth's warnings still ringing in his ears, Kurt made his way to the medical wing. He was pleased that the injured guards had been moved to a local hospital. He wondered what Alexander would do with them when they were well again.

At the end of the curtained rooms and first-aid stations were a newly erected wall and door that gave Riley a private room apart from the usual patients who came and went. Kurt took a squirt from the hand sanitizer pump, slipped through the door, and closed it quietly behind him.

Riley had always been a slender man, but infection and fever had left him skeletal. His usually manicured beard had grown unruly. The last time he'd been awake, weeks ago, he had been delirious with fever. Kurt held his hand. It was cold and frail, devoid of the familiar strength.

Kurt watched the numbers on the heart monitor, the steady drip of IV fluids, then he lowered the blanket and peeled the bandage back to have a look. The flesh was pink and puckered. The hole was growing up but still sunken in the middle and wreathed in streaks of angry red. The infection had gotten into the blood and spread. The fevers had finally ended, but still Riley didn't wake. "My house is full of ghosts and broken things," he mused to no one in particular.

Kurt stayed there for a while, listening to the machines beep and hiss. When he squeezed Riley's hand, he squeezed back, but it seemed more a reflex than a conscious effort. Kurt had tried again and again to communicate with squeezes. It was an old game that never ended well.

The doctor said talking was good for Riley, so Kurt told him everything. He started with the deal he made all those years ago, the things he'd done to hold up his end, and ended with Azrael's death. Plenty enough of it Riley had surely pieced together over the years, but Kurt had spoken none of it aloud before. He peeked out the door to make sure there were no listeners. "He's out there somewhere, Riley. My boy. Alive. Somewhere. How will I ever find him now?"

If Riley knew, he wasn't saying.

After supper, Kurt returned to his study, took the photo from the wall, and looked at his once happy family. With the sun behind the mountains, the air had turned damp and chilly. It breezed in through an open window, raising goosebumps on his chest and arms. In the fireplace, the logs were stacked and ready. He walked to the window instead, letting the coldness seep in. The cicadas and night birds filled the darkness with noise. Sound was better than silence. Silence was intolerable.

Father Logan, Kurt mused. He was charismatic, self-righteous, but Nathan Goodrum was the only real threat. If anyone needed to be killed, it was him. Stewarth was a fool to think otherwise. *It is all political bullshit*, he thought. Let them straighten their spines and come, and he would deal with them.

"Azrael Uzrahai," he whispered softly into the night, but only the wind stirred in answer. The God of Death was gone, and with her all his hopes.

Kurt lit the fire and watched the flames grow. The flickering did strange things to the shadows. Gently, he placed the family portrait on the flames and watched it blacken and curl until it had gone up the chimney in an angry puff of black smoke.

It was past time. He'd been putting it off all day. Kurt poured a shot into his usual glass and stared at it for a long time. Somehow, life had gotten too complicated. What was he putting off? Seeing her cry? Not that. He'd delivered bad news plenty of times. Let wives and daughters and sons wail and sob while he waited like a lighthouse in a storm to answer the questions and offer empty reassurances.

Kurt couldn't remember what he'd said when he found out about his own family. He hadn't screamed or torn out his hair. He had given in, though . . . to his darker urges, and paid the debt in blood before he knew his son still survived. Kurt hurled the shot glass into the fireplace and the bottle behind it. The fire flared white hot and left him night blind.

Kurt found the door and knocked. Footsteps scrambled within, and a muffled shout from Brooklyn asked him to wait. He waited a moment until she called back that they were ready. Kurt took a breath and pushed the door open and closed it carefully behind him. They were standing awkwardly beside the bed, disheveled.

He hid a knowing smile with a pretend cough. "We need to talk." He smiled in what he hoped was a friendly way and pressed on. "I'm not sure how much you understood what they said today."

She sat on the edge of the bed, studying her toes. "I understood enough. More than enough."

"It's over, right?" David asked, looking from Kurt to Brooklyn and back again.

"I don't know an easy way to say it," Kurt said, "so I'll just say it. Brooklyn can't leave. She must stay here." He braced himself for the outrage, but she just sat there thinking it over while David looked on with disbelief.

Finally, she spoke. "For how long?"

"It's really difficult to say, but for a good while, at least."

"Why?" David asked. "Why can't she leave?"

"The Heir released her to me. She wasn't set free. I can't risk what might happen if she goes now. I'm responsible."

"Will I be able to visit my parents and my nephew?"

"I don't think that would be safe for you or them." He let that hang for a minute until he thought he saw understanding in her face.

"What about David?" She grabbed his hand like Kurt was going to snatch him away.

Kurt thought about that. If the boy left and could find his way back, the police would most likely become involved, which would complicate things. When at last he spoke, he spoke to David directly, weighing each word carefully. "David, I have no right to keep you here, and I won't try, but if you go home, you cannot come back. The risk is too great. At this point, you've both become potential bargaining chips."

"I can't stay here forever." Brooklyn searched his eyes. "You saved my life, but if I can't live it with my family, what's the point? I need to go home. Surely you can understand that?"

"I just need you to be patient." *When Riley wakes up, he will figure a way out of this mess.* "Just give me some time to find a way for you to do so without endangering your family, yourselves, or me. I took a great personal risk for you today, and I'm just asking for some time to manage the aftermath." When they didn't protest, he continued. "While we work on a solution to the target on your back, I think your time would be well spent learning a bit about your abilities so you can defend against Belial if he should come back." Of course, Belial would never trouble her again. Of that much, he was certain. There was a tense silence during which Brooklyn and David exchanged glances and communicated without words.

Finally, Brooklyn spoke. "We'll stay for a while. I think I need to learn what I can do, but this will not be permanent."

Nothing in life ever is. "Fair enough." He smiled. "Let's get you two a room. One with a doorknob this time."

18

THERE'S NO PLACE LIKE HOME

The sun lit a patchwork of muted greens and sickly yellows. The last vibrant autumn leaves were falling in droves. From his window, David had thought the day looked warm and inviting. It wasn't. The further they tramped through the drifts of leaves that obscured the ghost of a trail they were following, the more David wondered why it was necessary to hike into the wilderness to practice these magic tricks. Kurt had a house the size of a university. Surely there was a warm, cozy room where they could do this.

"Such a beautiful day!" Brooklyn exulted. "Today's the day. I'm going to lift the stone today."

She was referring to a large boulder the size of a riding lawn mower in the middle of the training area, but even so, David couldn't help but smile at her enthusiasm. "You'll do great." *And like always, I won't be able to move a speck of pollen.* He gave her hand a little squeeze as they both ducked under a low branch. For weeks David had watched Brooklyn's telekinesis progress from pebbles to stones, from stones to hefty rocks, and now she was after a boulder. David still couldn't move a pebble despite Kurt's assurances that anyone could learn with enough practice.

Kurt led the line, plowing ahead at a pace that left the rest of them panting and damp with sweat as they hurried to keep up. Finally, they plunged through the last cloister of foliage and arrived at the now familiar stone benches that circled the boulder like a miniature Stonehenge.

Their companions included Tessa, Raul, and Saul. Tessa was a woman of indeterminate age who was probably young but looked like every methamphetamine addict poster David had ever seen. When she smiled, it was nauseating. She was extremely twitchy and her most striking feature was her stringy brown hair. She had been pretty once, probably. Raul and Saul were identical twins, late twenties or early thirties. David wasn't sure which was which. Both were very fit and very blond.

To David, it seemed these training sessions were one part group therapy, one part meditation, and two parts frustration. Kurt sat on the center stone while the rest of them filled half the benches facing him. The cold of the granite quickly seeped through David's thin jeans. Brooklyn didn't seem to notice the cold as she listened to Kurt with rapt attention.

David wondered if Lee and Charlie had done the show without him. He felt guilty about leaving them in the lurch. Nobody knew where he had gone. It was possible they had reported him as missing. He lived alone, but by now his mom would have realized his absence, too. She was probably worried sick. He looked at Brooklyn. He was here for her and he couldn't just leave her here with these people, and who knew if he'd ever find her again if he left without her. He must have sighed because she whispered, "What's wrong?"

"Nothing." He forced a smile. Kurt explained, as he always did, the importance of going slowly, taking breaks if there were headaches or nosebleeds. Then they broke into pairs. The twins always worked together, and Brooklyn always worked with Tessa because nobody else wanted to. That left David with Kurt.

"Are you ready?" Kurt asked, levitating a pebble effortlessly between them.

David nodded.

"Okay." Kurt nudged the stone toward David. "Take it."

David imagined it happening, the stone floating. Imagined the heft, the way it would feel to wrap his mind around it, but it fell with a plop into the leaves as soon as Kurt let go. He looked around. Everywhere there were people levitating stones back and forth in a game of mental catch. It was frustrating.

"Again," Kurt said. "With enough practice, anyone can learn to do it. Just be patient."

If that is the case, why has telekinesis never been scientifically verified? He kept that thought to himself, however, and with a dutiful nod, he tried again. And again. And again. And again, so many times, he couldn't see straight. It was always the same frustrating failure.

"I just don't think it is going to work," he said finally.

"One more time," Kurt insisted.

David focused on the stone. He let the entire world fade away until he had tunnel vision. Kurt's eyes hovered like caramel moons behind the stone. David strained, at least as much as you can strain a nonexistent muscle. Suddenly he saw it, almost invisible even in the sunlight. It was like a strand of spiderweb, all but indiscernible except when the light struck it in just the right way. It ran from Kurt's palm to the bottom of the stone in what had to be the best balancing act in the world. Glancing around at the others, David saw similar threads flickering in and out of existence all around the little circle. Just then, a harsh beeping erupted from Kurt's pocket, and the stone fell. All the stones fell. Every eye turned toward them. David smiled at Brooklyn, but she didn't notice him, or if she did, she didn't smile back.

"He's awake?" Kurt asked excitedly. "Of course. That's great! I'll be right there." He lowered the phone and took a searching look around the circle. "Tessa. Lead everyone back to the house." Before anyone could respond, he darted down the trail at a sprint.

They left the stones where they'd fallen and began the descent, with Tessa in the lead. David and Brooklyn drifted together behind the twins. The chill air raised goosebumps on David's arms, but he didn't feel it. Adrenaline coursed through him. "We have to go now," he whispered to Brooklyn. "We might not get another chance like this."

"Go where?"

He glanced ahead to make sure the others weren't listening. "Home." He spoke the word reverently.

She held a limb to let him pass. "It isn't safe. What if . . . What if what Kurt said is true? We would endanger everyone."

"You can't live your life that way. Afraid of things that might never happen."

An image of stacked bodies flitted through her mind. "I'm learning things here; I don't think I'm ready to—"

"See Devin?" It wasn't fair, but he said it anyway. "He's already lost his mother, and now you're just going to vanish too?" Hurt flashed across her face. He'd struck a nerve. "I can't live here, Brooke, and I can't leave you here." He stopped her with a hand on her shoulder and turned himself gently to face her. "Town is northeast of here. We could leave the trail here, leave everything behind. If we avoid the roads and get to town, we can rent a car, or hitchhike, or call Lee or someone to pick us up." The others were passing in and out of sight through the branches ahead where the trail curved. "Please," he begged, "it's now or never."

"Okay, let's go." A mischievous smile spread uncertainly across her face. She kissed him hard and then they were running through the brush, jumping over logs, and ducking limbs. They followed a game trail around the ridge, keeping the sun over their left shoulders. It led them down a gentle but twisting slope into a deep hollow where a mountain spring trickled and mud, shiny and black, sucked and sighed with their footsteps.

"Maybe we could follow the water to a road?" Brooklyn suggested.

"I think it winds back toward the complex." They had both started calling it "the complex" a couple of weeks ago because it was too large for either of them to think of it as a house. "Let's avoid roads until we are closer to town." Over centuries, this trickle of water had cut a deep gash in the mountainside. They had just come down one side of it, and now they looked up at the daunting climb ahead.

"Do you think they will try to follow us?" Brooklyn asked as she slid a black rubber band off her wrist and deftly pulled her hair back into a ponytail.

"Definitely, but I think we will have a good head start, and I don't think he will try to send anyone through the woods. He will probably have people on the roads, maybe even in town, though."

"Too bad we can't just fly out of here." She looked wistfully upward.

David followed her line of sight, and something flashed high on the ridge. "What's that?" He pointed.

"I don't see anything."

"Right there." He turned her head gently.

"Just leaves and trees."

"Come on, let's climb up this way."

Together they struggled up out of the hollow, slipping noisily on the leaves and reaching for roots and saplings for support. The climb proved much harder than David had anticipated. The foliage was thick, but still from time to time as they climbed, he caught a glint of light off of something shiny. Brooklyn, though, never seemed to spot it. Their path took them into a thicket of bloomless rhododendron and gnarled laurel. Near the summit, it became so dense they were forced to stoop and, at times, to crawl.

"There's no way you saw anything through all this," Brooklyn said breathlessly.

David squinted, and it flickered just ahead. "Only a little further to the top."

They labored in silence. Heavy breathing and the rustling carpet of new leaves made talking a hardship, anyway. David saw it again, maddening, like a mirage. It always seemed to be just ahead. Frustration gave him a second wind. He plowed ahead through the slapping branches and deep drifts of leaves. All at once he emerged into a closet-sized clearing, and the flashes of light vanished. Directly ahead, a giant tangle of laurel impeded his way. It didn't blend well. It seemed to grow out of the slope at a ninety-degree angle instead of growing skyward like every other plant on the mountainside. He touched it. The leaves felt fake and waxy. He yanked on the whole thing. It wouldn't budge.

"What are you doing?" Brooklyn asked breathlessly.

"Help me pull this."

She grabbed a branch and together they heaved against it. Nothing happened. David ducked under the bushy branches and swept his arms across the leaves around the trunk. They rustled but didn't move. They were glued down.

"We need to go," Brooklyn said anxiously.

He didn't answer; instead he probed the earth all around this strange tree until he found something hard. His fingers worried with it until he identified it as a sliding latch. It disengaged soundlessly. David wriggled out and heaved on the bush again. A large square of earth, with the bush at its center, swung upward with unexpected ease and sent him tumbling back into the thicket.

"It's a cellar," Brooklyn called down to him. He watched her disappear behind the open door. When he scrambled back up the hill, David found her standing just inside the hatchway on a flight of concrete stairs that led down into the mountain where the sunlight didn't reach. Brooklyn looked back at him. "Do you have any kind of light?" she asked him.

He shook his head, joining her on the stairway. "Well, my watch has a light, but I don't think it is bright enough." He slipped it off, angled it down into the darkness, and pressed the button. The blue light did little to illuminate the way ahead, but they pressed on with it anyway. David pressed the button each time the light went off. He soon fell into the rhythm of it, steady as a heartbeat, and they inched forward, hand in hand, in three-second increments.

The walls were earthen, braced at intervals with hand-hewn timbers. It reminded David more of a coal mine than a cellar. The air grew unbearably chilly and damp. Brooklyn seemed unaffected, so David resolved to shiver in silence. Their footsteps and breathing seemed unnaturally loud in the confines of the tunnel.

"Hush," Brooklyn hissed. They both paused, listening. "Do you hear that?"

"Hear what?"

"Water. I think."

He heard it now, a faint trickling. They pressed on until the sound was unmistakable. It was water. Lots of water. The path spiraled downward in lazy loops until it opened into a cavern that blended their voices with the roaring water and sent it echoing crazily around the room. David could not judge the size of the room, but his general impression was very damn big. In many places, the walls glowed faintly with haphazard zigzags of pale white lines. "What are those?" David asked as he touched one with his finger. He felt only stone.

"What's what?"

"The glowing lines in the walls."

"Where? I don't see anything."

"Everywhere. They're like spiderwebs, but as big around as a finger."

"We should go back. It will be dark soon. And I'm sure they are already looking for us." Brooklyn held her voice steady, but it thrummed with anxious energy. David knew she was right. He turned reluctantly. Together, they climbed out in an intermittent bubble of bluish-green light. It made the world seem smaller, as if it were just big enough for the two of them.

When they emerged, the sun was low over the mountains and the temperature promised a pumpkin frost. David closed the hatch carefully, blinking against the shimmering that taunted the edges of his vision.

"Are you all right?" Brooklyn asked.

"Just getting used to the sun again." He smiled and took her hand. "Let's get going." They set off at a trot, following their shadows east.

19

Catching Up

Kurt's mind raced ahead of his feet, contemplating the merits of each possible path through the trees. *Riley. Awake!* He broke through the tree line and dashed across the lawn. Inside, he slowed his pace and collected his thoughts in the elevator, and by the time the silver doors opened on the medical wing, his purposeful composure was restored.

The doctor met him at the door, clipboard in hand. "He's awake, but weak."

"I'd like to see him, if he's up to visitors."

"When he woke, he asked for Mary." Kurt winced, and the doctor touched him on the arm. "He'll remember. He needs rest. Just . . . be brief, okay?" Kurt nodded.

Beyond the double doors, he was pleased to find familiar eyes, even if the face they were in had grown too thin to recognize. "You look hungry," Kurt said by way of greeting.

"Were my orbs recovered?" he asked in a rusty baritone that belied the fragility of his condition.

"Only one. It is safe and sound in my office," Kurt assured him as he pulled the chair close to the bed and sank into it. He couldn't stop smiling. "I thought we'd lost you."

"I thought we'd lost me too."

"Do you remember what happened to you?"

"Pieces. Only pieces. I was alone." He shifted on the bed. "My mouth tastes like ass. You hired someone to change my diaper but you couldn't get someone to brush my teeth? What kind of hospital are you running?" A hint of a smile played across his face, and he shook his head.

Kurt smiled back. "I promised your sister I'd keep you safe; I didn't sign up to be your dental hygienist."

A cloud passed over Riley's face. "Mary . . . When I woke, I thought—"

"I know."

Riley shook his head. "Well, stop grinning at me like a simpleton; tell me what I've missed."

"Well, without your wise counsel, I have offended one of the Old Ones and alienated the Heir and his whole family by protecting the assassin that tried to kill him, and in my spare time I enslaved a renegade Warden, adopted the assassin and her boyfriend, and watched Azrael die along with any chance I had of finding my boy." Kurt smiled ruefully. "It's damn good to have you back."

Riley coughed and winced. "How long did it take you to start this miniature apocalypse, unravel twenty years of political maneuvering, and ruin both our lives' work?"

Kurt shrugged. "You know, a few weeks."

"That's prodigious! Maybe if I take a nap, you'll have time to finish off humanity?"

"The doctor did say you need to rest," Kurt deadpanned.

"Well, what does he know? He's only a doctor. I think you better tell me everything."

"True." So, Kurt told him everything that had happened since the night Riley came stumbling in gutshot and half dead. When Kurt finished, Riley let out a low whistle.

He sat up straighter in the bed with a wince. "So, where do we start?"

"Well"—Kurt stroked the stubble on his chin—"if the Warden brings the book, do you think we can find a way to read it?"

"Maybe, but that is a huge if." His eyes stared at nothing, twitching back and forth at a speed that still left Kurt unsettled, even after all these years.

"Well, what did it say?" Kurt asked uncomfortably.

"There's no 'it' anymore, just me."

Kurt nodded and waited.

"If you get the Tome, I'll figure out how to read it." He took a sip of water through a straw. "We can worry about that when it is relevant. For now, we should focus on damage control. The simplest solution is to kill the girl before she's used against you."

"We can't just—"

"Let me finish!"

Kurt nodded and leaned back in the chair to listen.

"We have opposition on every side. You've made yourself a common enemy of the Prophets and the Demonriders. And despite what he may have said, Stewarth won't forget that you compromised him to protect a would-be assassin. He won't kill you outright, but he will continue to place you in dangerous predicaments, just like he has with this woman."

"Her name is Brooklyn, and Stewarth is dying."

"Yes, and his successor has even less cause to like you. Forcing him to break an ancient pact with the Old Ones will have earned him a severe rebuke from his father. Fortunately, restoring that alliance will be their obstacle to overcome, not yours."

"What do you suggest?"

"Killing the girl would appease Stewarth and leave your enemies without leverage. Then you could focus on completing your transaction, assuming there is a way to complete it." Riley sighed. "That would be the best way out of this mess, but you won't do that, will you?"

"No." Some dark part of him wanted to. To be done with all of this and focus on what he cared about, but he had come too far. And Azrael had been clear that Brooklyn was important, integral even, to something.

"Then imprison her, beyond anyone's reach . . . and divide your enemies. Turn them one against the other and look the other way."

"That is unethical. You're asking me to break my vows," Kurt grumbled.

"Don't go all moral on me. You've broken them before and you are breaking them right now, technically speaking. I'm merely asking you to survive the mess you've created."

"I'll do my best!"

Riley rolled his eyes. "That's what I'm afraid of."

They both laughed then, all the tension melting away.

"I'm glad you're okay." Kurt smiled.

"Me too, brother. Let's talk about the Pull. This rogue Warden may be right, especially if the Old Ones are crossing. You have to stop."

"I'm so close. Only need a few more. I didn't spend the last twenty years crawling through slime to stop now."

"Stubborn ass."

Kurt was contemplating a comeback when he heard a commotion just outside the double doors. He leapt to his feet and moved between the doors and Riley.

"Let me go. I have to see him!" a shrill voice screeched. It was Tessa.

"What are you doing here?" Kurt bellowed as the double doors clapped closed behind him.

"She's gone. She ran. They both ran." Tessa broke free and collided with Kurt.

He pushed her back to arm's length, his hands heavy on her bony shoulders. "How long ago? Which way did they run?"

"I don't know. At least two hours; I'm not sure. There was nothing I could do. Nobody would tell me where to find you."

Kurt could sense her trepidation. He nodded. "Thank you for finding me. Go back to your room now. No one speaks of this; tell the others. Business as usual."

Tessa nodded wordlessly until he released his grip. Then she fled.

Kurt's mind raced. If he organized a search, he'd draw attention to the fact she had gone. If his enemies' attention could be focused elsewhere, she might find her way home without being bothered. She would go home; he was sure of that. Back inside, Kurt caught Riley gingerly removing his IV lines.

"What do you think you are doing?"

"I am going to bring your acolytes here and lock down this infirmary. No one who might have overheard what just happened will leave my sight." He freed a line with a sigh and started on the remaining medical entanglements. "Meanwhile, you will find them and bring them back. Everything depends on it."

"You need your rest."

"Do I?" He opened his shirt, revealing only a hint of a pink dimple where there had been a puckered hole days before. "I'm not human, Kurt, haven't been for a long time."

"I know." Kurt didn't like to think of it in those terms. He often wondered what his wife would say if she could see how things had turned out for both of them, her husband and her baby brother. He couldn't think about that right now. Kurt yearned for a drink to calm his mind, but didn't dare risk one.

"They will head east toward town. Get there first and find them. Take your orbs." His fingers fumbled with the buttons of his shirt. Kurt was glad he'd had some clothes sent down the first time Riley had awakened. He reached out and embraced his brother-in-law, then dashed for the door.

Back in his office, Kurt opened a secret drawer in his desk and drew out a box. Inside on velvet were six multicolored orbs that looked like marbles. At a thought, they floated effortlessly into his pocket. They were, as far as he knew, a unique weapon. Riley made them himself, and it had taken weeks. Each tuned to respond only to one person, they could not be controlled by anyone else. When Kurt took control of them, his mental grasp was almost unbreakable. He grabbed a flashlight, his car keys, and a small knapsack of emergency supplies. Kurt took a moment to gaze at the blank spot on the wall above the fireplace, more from habit than anything. The tumbler on his desk sat empty; he left it that way.

He took the elevator down and walked leisurely, chatting with anyone he met in the hallway. The bag he tucked inconspicuously under one arm conveying—he hoped—the appearance of going out for supper or coffee as he made his way to the tunnel that connected the mansion to the garage. He trusted his people. He trusted them more when they didn't know anything.

20

Hell and Back

In all of Hell, the Tomekeepers' library and a tower known as the Colossus were the sole refuges of silence. Everywhere else, the rise and fall of voices, shrieks, snarls, and growls reverberated from every surface. Contrary to popular belief, Belial knew this spiritual netherworld was not inside the earth, and not the Hell described in the Abrahamic religions, but he could understand where those myths had originated. It was basically a great sphere, and instead of dwelling on it, they lived within, walking on the imperceptibly concave inner surface.

At the center of everything—seemingly held aloft by the Colossus—a great fiery nucleus radiated like a small sun. This was the source of, and muse for, the infamous Melody of Hell, and also the spiritual sustenance of all who lived here. Belial was grateful he had never been forced to make his home here. It was a cruel fate to depend on something so harsh for survival. He took one last look over his shoulder, where blackened stone and ash stretched into the distance, interspersed with crumbling stalagmites. At the edge of seeing, the spires of some vast structure cast a weak mirage through the shimmering heat.

Inside the labyrinth of caves, the screams and the heat faded away mercifully. Most entrances to the subterranean network beneath the library were jealously guarded, but this was an old way, little known, more sewer than passage. Still, the path ahead was likely dangerous. Not so long ago he could have walked right through the front doors of the library, but much had changed recently and Belial wasn't sure his status as a Warden carried the privileges it once had. He could always try to play that card if he were stopped, though.

The first obstacle appeared just as the last glimmers of soul light faded away behind him. Ahead, where the path angled down, an enormous section of the stone floor detached itself with a rasp. "Who's there?" Belial called softly.

He sensed movement from above and instinctively leapt to the side. Something heavy clacked into the stone floor where he'd been standing, and a milky liquid frothed around it. He glimpsed a long, segmented carapace. A scorpion, he realized as the tail withdrew with stunning speed. Before he could form a plan, jagged pincers lanced out of the shadows. Belial batted them away reflexively. The giant insect paused, befuddled. It advanced cautiously, emitting deafening cricket-like noises. He could flee; the way behind was open, but failure and a lifetime of being Kurt's prisoner didn't appeal to him.

The attacks came in a flurry now, each more narrowly avoided than the last. When its stinger gouged into the stone where he'd been standing a tenth of a second before, Belial reacted instinctively, flash freezing the white poison that pooled around it. The insect went wild, thrashing as it strained to free its tail. He knew the ice wouldn't hold for long, so he shifted into wolverine form and snapped his jaws on the taut tail. It was like biting steel. With a tremendous crack, the tail whipped free of the ice and sent Belial careening teeth first into the ceiling. As he fell and thc creature surged forward into the dim light, he got his first good look. It was black from claws to stinger and every bit of eighteen feet long. It was a jaekelop, Belial realized suddenly. He'd read about them but never seen one.

The floor rose to meet Belial, but he never got there. One pincer caught him about the waist with a bone-crunching snap. It was the first time in a long time he'd considered the possibility of a final death. Belial thought of his origins then, where prismatic glaciers mocked the sun and its false promises of warmth. Would some essential part of him return to the ice when he died? He didn't know. He hoped not. A part of him yearned for the Mediterranean of long ago. Another part yearned for nothing at all.

Belial shifted to his true form and, as the jaekelop tried to adjust its grip, he slipped free. He called for the cold, and the cold came. Droplets more precious than silver condensed from the dry air, and a sheen of frost covered the jaekelop's carapace. The effect was less than he had hoped. The giant scorpion lurched forward diligently, but marginally slower.

Belial shifted into a hawk, winging around the clumsy attacks, driving his beak into one black eye then the other, raking the rows of smaller eyes with taloned feet. The screech was unbearable. Belial flew behind the giant insect and landed silently in his true form to watch the jaekelop charge ahead blindly into the light it had likely avoided for centuries.

His hearing felt ragged after the insectile shrieks faded. The silence that followed unnerved him. He sat in the darkness thinking of Tais and her unmatched eyes, the mischief in them that belied her guarded cordiality when first they had met, and how in her innocent exuberance she goaded him into promises he could not keep. He treasured every memory of her except that last day beside the sea.

The jaekelop would wander blind until it starved, died from exposure, or if it was lucky, bumped into something bigger and hungrier. He was sure it would never find the hidden entrance to this tunnel again. He could have sat in silence forever, beyond the reach of responsibility, but given enough time Kurt Levin would yank the leash and he'd be back in the golden prison. Kurt had to die. He was a traitor of the worst kind, endangering everyone he was sworn to protect. Belial felt like a fool for attacking the Heir; he had been so sure that no one else could hold so many of his kind thrall. Levin would pay; Belial would make sure of it.

The tunnel narrowed and turned upward, forcing Belial to crawl and finally to slide on his stomach. The thought of encountering some predator in this confined space gave him a chill, but a few minutes later, the tunnel widened and the going got easier again. Within minutes, the ceiling sloped down and met the floor, an apparent dead end.

The smell of sulfur led him to the left wall, where he found a gash in the stone partially obstructed by a shelf of rock. The opening ran floor to ceiling but was so narrow he could only enter it sideways. It zigzagged, changing direction every few feet. When he felt a gust of heat, he knew he'd found the entrance. The hole was too small for him to pass except as an hawk, definitely too small for the Tome he hoped to bring back. *Complications. Always complications*, he thought as he bird walked through the crevice.

Beyond the crevice he found a storeroom, dimly lit, and a half-moon staircase cut into the concave wall. Belial proceeded swiftly, certain he was alone here. He emerged into an out-of-the-way alcove far in the back of the library. It took a few moments to dredge up a mental map. The Histories, a compilation of parallel accounts detailing the interplay of ancient events throughout the physical and metaphysical worlds, lay to his left. Ahead, he would find the Fountain of Dreaming and, beyond that, three additional wings dedicated to various arcane studies. He turned right toward the restricted wing. The marble flooring and vaulted ceiling ended abruptly, and he proceeded down rough hewn corridors, clearly the oldest and deepest of the tunnels.

The Tomekeepers, for all their knowledge and power, were largely oblivious to current happenings. Belial was counting on a certain amount of trickery to gain entrance to the study chambers that housed the Eternal Collection. He would, he had decided, use his father's name. None here would have ever seen his father before. Prosidris had made a pact very early on to avoid the common fate, but his name was known and feared.

As leader of the Wardens, in alliance with Solomon, Belial's father had remained in the seas, but the price was pacifism. He would no longer turn tides, raise waves, or capsize ships, not without breaking the agreement. While most of the Old Ones languished in an arid prison, bleached by soul light, the High Warden basked in his place of origin: the cool, briny waters of earth.

A set of double doors just ahead jarred Belial from his musings. The passage gradually widened and heightened until it accommodated the gargantuan doors at the other end. The tops of which rose to three times Belial's own height, sweeping from floor to ceiling in a graceful series of curves.

As Belial neared, he saw an elaborate carving joined the closed doors. At the top, a serpentine tail coiled threateningly. Below that, light pulsed through the silver inlay that ran like veined webbing through carved dragon wings. The neck turned elegantly near the floor and joined a protruding dragon head. Its mouth was open, fiercely displaying dagger-length fangs. Its eyes were of polished obsidian that drank the dim light.

"Why are you here?" a child's voice echoed around the chamber.

Belial whirled around, searching the tunnel in both directions while the inquiry faded into silence. "Who's there?"

"I am."

Turning back to the door, he found her at last, a dim figure rising to her feet in front of the dragon door, blocking the carved face from view. She was small, maybe ten years old. It was easy to see how he'd overlooked her in the shadows beneath the door. A silken green cloak swirled around her silently, shrouding her in its many loose folds. "Who are you?"

"I am."

"You are," he agreed amiably. As he drew closer, he could see the skin of her face was disfigured, scarlet, and scaly.

"I guard the way," she intoned solemnly.

"I am Prosidris, High Warden. Let me in," he said, invoking his father's common name.

"Liar," the little girl accused. She pulled back the cowl of her robe, revealing a hairless scalp where the skin affliction continued, giving her a reptilian look.

"I do not lie!" Belial blustered indignantly, drawing himself up to his full height. He glowered down at her, but she didn't flinch.

"Yes. You do," answered a third voice, and the door behind the girl split open. "You don't look anything like me," his father said, standing in the doorway with a sharkish grin.

Beyond the doors lay a cavern lit warmly with torches and candles. The floor was the same smooth stone from the tunnels, but covered haphazardly with rugs made from the pelts of many exotic and long-extinct animals. A row of stone pedestals lined the walls on either side and met to form a semicircle in the rear of the chamber. On each pedestal rested an enormous book. As they passed, Belial could see the symbols etched deep into the stone beneath each one. A language older than he was, one that had never been spoken by men. Even so, he recognized some scripts. *Book of Elements, Book of Knowing, Book of Worlds, Book of Beginnings, and Book of Endings.* There were many others on both sides that he could not identify.

"You are bound," his father mused.

Belial snapped his eyes up and found his father's gaze appraising and disappointed. "Temporarily."

Prosidris sighed, and it was like standing against gale-force winds of disapproval, though none of the candles flickered. "To whom?"

"A Protector, Kurt Levin." Belial regarded Prosidris with carefully concealed hatred. Then he changed the subject. "I'm surprised to find you here."

"They've turned on us, broken the old agreements; the boy is using the ring to enslave us." Prosidris paused, at a loss for words. "He used the ring on me!" he bellowed indignantly. "On me!" His voice shook with outrage. It rolled off him in dizzying waves that Belial endured with a grimace.

So, that's why he's here, cast down after all these thousands of years by a teenager, Belial thought smugly. "What are you looking for?" he asked, gesturing to the surrounding books.

"A way back."

"There is no way back without being summoned; you shouldn't have left the sea."

"There's always a way back. I'll climb the Colossus and jump if I must. If you and your siblings had done your jobs, I wouldn't have been awakened."

"You stole her from me," Belial said quietly. Centuries of repressed rage rose inside him with shocking immediacy. He knew he should stop, but he didn't. "To save your own skin, and for what? To end up here anyway?"

"And you? Why are you here?" his father asked jovially, as if no cross words had been uttered.

"Tome of Death. Levin wants it," Belial replied curtly.

"It's right there," Prosidris said, pointing to one in the back near the center.

"There's one missing," Belial commented as he approached. He focused on reigning in his emotions; there would be time for retribution when he broke free of Kurt Levin.

"The Book of Life," Prosidris said reverently in the old language, "stolen by the pretender eons ago."

"The vanishing god story?" Belial said slowly, remembering. It was a creation story, one of many such legends. In this one, a mysterious, unnamed god appearing as a humble scholar quietly joined the Tomekeepers. For centuries, he studied the texts, digging deeper than anyone before him. In time, he began to experiment, delving into the mysteries between the physical and spiritual worlds until one day he vanished along with the Tome of Life. Or something like that; there were many, often contradictory, variations.

"She was no god, just a pretender that got in over her head."

"She?"

"He, she, it doesn't matter. History lessons later. The Tomes and scrolls are well guarded. Your pompous master will have to do without. Although I wish you could play the vindictive djinn and drop it in his lap." He smiled and motioned to the dragon-scaled book, glittering black and sharp as broken glass.

Belial snatched it off the podium, immediately shocked by its weight and pulsing heat. It felt . . . alive.

"Put it back!" his father hissed with a hint of fear in his voice. Before Belial could process this, the double doors slammed open with a deafening thud.

"Tome. Back. Now." It was the little girl, but what had appeared to be diseased skin in the dim corridor glittered like rubies in the torchlight. She didn't have scale disease; she had scales. He advanced on her warily; she was only a child after all.

"Last warning," she intoned solemnly.

"Chill out, kid." He smiled, raised his hand without slowing, and called on the coldness inside. The surrounding floor iced, but the little dragon girl remained unaffected. That had never happened to Belial before. He didn't have time to think about it because she opened her mouth and fire blossomed around him, painting the room with impossible colors. He closed his eyes. This was it, the final death. He'd been so stupid to think the Tomekeepers would leave a mere disfigured child to guard their most prized collection. He gasped, then choked on something liquid.

Belial's eyes opened. He was inside a swirling pillar of water, which was quickly being vaporized. Through the water, flame, and steam, Belial could just discern the blob of his father in a similar elemental cocoon. *Run, fool!* His father's voice echoed inside his skull, deeper and more sonorous than it sounded in reality. *A life for a life; now we are even.*

Not even close, Belial thought, but he let the thought die without being sent. He ran without looking back. The protective shield hissed around him as he dove through the doors and raced for the tunnels beyond, the Book of Death clutched tightly to his chest. *We are a long way from even*, he thought as he scrambled ahead of the pursuing inferno.

21

THE FARMER

Brooklyn had spent many nights in the mountains behind her home, but there had always been a fire, a sleeping bag, and a flashlight. She pretended not to notice how uncomfortable the unfamiliar night sounds made David. They snuggled close for warmth. Brooklyn pulled her arms inside her shirt, leaving the sleeves hanging empty.

"We will find the town tomorrow. Get to a phone and call someone," David said.

"I'm worried I won't have a place to stay when we get back. I mean, what do I tell my parents? Obviously, I can't tell them the truth. I don't think they will let me move back in."

"Obviously. Being kidnapped by a magical cult probably isn't the excuse you want to give." He moved closer, his lips touching her ear. "Of course you know you could stay with me if you wanted."

She didn't know what to say. She'd spent the weekend with him before, but they had been early in their relationship and it seemed like such a commitment. But now? Now she didn't know. For all intents and purposes, they'd been living together for a month now.

"Only if you wanted to," he added, mistaking her silence for hesitation.

"I definitely want to." She turned to face him. "Like really want to."

David smiled. "I think your parents will be thrilled to know you are okay, even if you never tell them what happened."

Brooklyn wasn't so sure.

Brooklyn woke with the predawn light, left David snoring softly, and slipped into the bushes to take care of some personal business. Afterward, she watched him sleep as the hills came alive with morning sounds. The idea of moving in together made her nervous. It also thrilled her. He had given up so much to come find her, and more to stay with her. Would he resent her for it later? They were connected by these crazy weeks spent in a world that already seemed imagined. In ten years, would either of them talk about it? Would they believe it? Or pretend it never happened? Would the pebbles always rise when she willed it, or would a normal, boring life erode her abilities? Brooklyn had too many questions and not nearly enough answers.

"What are you thinking about?" David asked, startling her out of her musings.

"I was trying to decide if I should leave you or wait," Brooklyn answered seriously.

"What's the verdict?" he asked as he climbed to his feet and stretched.

"Guess I don't have to decide after all. Let's get moving."

They found their direction from the rising sun and set a brisk pace along the ridgeline, steep drops on either side. They talked quietly as they walked. David wondered if his absence had done in the band and, if not, would they take him back? Brooklyn wondered if either of them still had jobs; she suspected they did not. Really, she didn't care.

More and more, her mind wandered to the clearing and relished the memories of how it felt to take control of something, no matter how small, with her mind. Kurt had called her a prodigy; she had progressed more rapidly than anyone else in the group, accomplishing in a couple of weeks what others had labored months to achieve.

By midday, Brooklyn's stomach rumbled insistently. The day had turned unseasonably hot. A ribbon of two-lane road passed in and out of view in the distance on the left. Their path ran roughly parallel, and it was a reassuring reminder that this hike had an end.

"We have to make it out today," David insisted. "I'm not spending another night in these woods without food."

"We could go to the road and hitch into town." Brooklyn gazed vaguely into the distance.

"They're looking for us on the roads. I'm sure of it. He won't let us go; we know too much." He paused. "You know too much."

"Doesn't matter. We'll hit town before dark." She moved close; he smelled of earth, sweat, and pine needles. He was different, somehow. Unshaven, disheveled, irresistible. It was as if the last few weeks had stripped him of his boyish softness, left hard lines and a startling seriousness in its place. She traced a finger along the line of his jaw. His eyes found hers.

"Here?" he asked.

"Here."

They came upon a farm, hand in hand, acres of dead, brown cornstalks rustling softly in the twilight breeze leading up to a board-side farmhouse where they'd hoped to find a town. Beyond the house sat a barn and an enormous tractor beneath a shed. Lights winked on as the shadows lengthened.

"They might have a phone we could use."

"I think we should go around and find the town. Who would we call, anyway?" David pointed out.

"You're the one who doesn't want to spend another night in the cold, dark woods." As if to punctuate her remark, the wind picked up noticeably.

"They may know Kurt; we can't be the first people to run away from that prison."

Brooklyn cringed. She didn't really think of it as a prison, though to be fair he had locked up first David and then both of them. For her, it had been more like a school where she learned fascinating abilities, where she was the best at something.

Not for the first time Brooklyn missed her almost familiar bedroom, the twins, even Tessa, despite her unsettling appearance. She raised a twig mentally, just to make sure it still worked. She had practiced less today than yesterday; each time she did, she felt ravenous afterward. Brooklyn let the twig drop and turned her attention back to David, who was still talking to her.

"—like *Children of the Corn* or something."

"I know," Brooklyn said, though really she didn't, "but we need food. I'm going; are you coming or not?"

David sighed dramatically and shifted from one foot to the other, but when Brooklyn began walking, he hurried to catch up. Together they pushed through the rustling rows of corn until they stood on a small covered porch. Brooklyn banged on the door rapidly, her impatience fueled by an aching hunger.

They heard the squeak of a chair and slow, heavy footsteps. Brooklyn's stomach growled, and she knocked again. "Anyone home? We're lost; we need help. And," she added, "some food."

"I'm coming; hold your horses," bellowed a woman from within. The lady wrenched the door open and peered down at them like a couple of wayward children. Even David had to look up. She was the largest woman Brooklyn had ever seen.

"May we use your phone—" David began politely.

"And borrow some food?" Brooklyn cut in.

The woman turned her fierce gaze on Brooklyn. "Borrow some food?" she repeated slowly, as if it were the stupidest thing anyone had ever said. "Borrow some food?"

"That's what I said."

"Honey, when you borrow something, that means you plan to return it. Is that what you want to do? Borrow some food, keep it a while, and return it? Or do you want something to eat? I'll give you some food, but I'm not in the food-lending business. You see the difference?"

"Um, yeah—"

"Yes ma'am," the woman corrected.

"Yes ma'am," Brooklyn mumbled, exchanging a bewildered glance with David.

"I can't afford to heat the whole outdoors." She crossed her arms impatiently. "Either get in or get out."

In short order they were seated around a modest dining room table with plates of steaming vegetables, corn chief among them, and milk so cold the glasses wept. Their host, who identified herself as Mrs. Mays, flipped burgers with the widest spatula Brooklyn had ever seen. "What brings you kids out to Hansel and Gretel it?"

"We were camping—" David began tentatively.

Mrs. Mays slapped a still-sizzling patty onto his plate. "With no supplies?"

"We lost everything," Brooklyn finished for him with a reassuring wink. She nibbled at her mashed potatoes.

"We were hoping we could use your phone," David cut in, "to call someone to pick us up."

"Don't got a phone," she said sweetly. "In the morning, I'll drive you to town."

What kind of person doesn't have a phone? Brooklyn wondered. "How much further is it to town?"

"A long way," Mrs. Mays answered distractedly.

"How long?" Brooklyn pressed.

"Too far to walk tonight," she snapped, irritation showing on her face. After a moment, her expression softened. "Eat up. You both look like you could use a warm bath and a soft bed tonight."

Brooklyn wanted to press the issue, but David shook his head slightly, so she held her tongue. The food was rich and salty. Brooklyn ate three full plates and continued munching after both David and Mrs. Mays had retired their forks.

Mrs. Mays, it turned out, operated the largest farm in the region. Her husband, who had died in combat, left her to raise their son alone. That's when she had married Mr. Mays, who died several years later in a tractor accident, leaving Mrs. Mays with a vast farm and a steep learning curve. Brooklyn struggled to feign interest as the warm food settled heavily in her belly. As they migrated to the living room, Mrs. Mays pointed out her deceased husbands in pictures.

"That's my boy right there. I guess he was eight years old." She gestured at a bright-eyed boy with a mischievous smirk. "Weak minded, but strong willed. Stubborn as a mule and twice as stupid, but I love him."

"Mrs. Mays," Brooklyn said tentatively, "about that bath you mentioned?"

"Oh yes! Listen at me prattling on to you two youngsters and you filthy as hogs! Right this way." She led them upstairs to a guest room with an adjoined bathroom. "I think you'll find everything you need," she said to Brooklyn before firmly leading David across the hall to his own room. Brooklyn suppressed a smile.

The tub was an antique claw-foot design with no shower head. She ran it full and steaming, slipped into the water, and her muscles relaxed exquisitely. She closed her eyes and dreamed.

In the dream, her sister fled from her, climbing nimbly up a steep rocky face as Brooklyn struggled to keep pace. "Erin! Wait!" she called out breathlessly.

"Leave me alone!" she called back. The wind whipped her hair, so it obscured her face. Erin fumbled for a handhold, hauling herself over a ledge near the top and out of sight.

When Brooklyn reached the ledge, she struggled to pull herself up. Suddenly, Erin was standing above her. "Take my hand." She reached down.

The eyes were not her sister's. They were icy blue, Belial blue. "You're in over your head," he said, twisting Erin's face into a perverse smile. He went to his knees then and blew her a kiss. His breath stung sharp and pure like snow. Her fingers turned numb and icy. "Erin," she said, then she was falling.

22

The Price You Pay

Brooklyn gasped and clawed at the cast-iron tub to sit up. Cool water splashed over the side and ran along the tiled floor. She shivered violently as she stepped out and groped for a towel on the rack. "So much for a warm bath and a soft bed," she muttered as she toweled off.

The bedroom door burst open and Mrs. Mays loomed in the doorway. "Get dressed," she hissed, "you're leaving." David stood behind her dazed, pulling a shirt on over his head.

"They're here," he offered by way of explanation. Beyond him, she heard someone pounding on the front door and shouting.

"Who is?" Brooklyn asked as she struggled back into her clothes, trying to keep her teeth from clacking together. "Who's here?"

"The cult," Mrs. Mays interjected. "Why didn't you tell me you were running away from the cult?" She bustled them out into the hallway. "Never mind, I should have figured . . . You two just don't look the type." She led them down the back stairs in a flurry, robe whipping like a flag in a maelstrom. They emerged onto a flagstone patio. "Follow the moon, stick to the shadows, and you'll find town by sunup." She left them there, shivering and bewildered.

They set off across the field, weaving through the rustling stalks of dead corn. Brooklyn shivered, her hair an icy rope against her back. "Is it Kurt?"

"I don't know who it is," David told her. "Mrs. Mays just said they were downstairs, and they were looking for you."

They tried to be quiet, but it had rained during the night. The soft earth sucked at their shoes, and the stalks rustled at their passing.

"Down," David breathed in her ear as he drove them both down into the mud. A spotlight swept past them in a slow arc and then returned to the stalks still swaying lazily above them.

Brooklyn heard men shouting and the sound of running feet.

David tugged her back up. "Run. They've found us."

Together they stumbled headlong toward the woods. The corn fronds slapped Brooklyn and tore at her clothing. She heard a rumble of running feet and hasty shouts from their pursuers. They had a head start, but it wasn't a big one. The pursuers behind them arrowed through the field, barely disturbing the stalks.

"This way," David gasped as they broke free of the corn and scrambled up a bank toward the tree line. Halfway up, he paused.

"What are you doing? Run!" Brooklyn shouted as she passed him. Then she heard it, the baying of hounds ahead. She looked around desperately. The bank wrapped around the valley, steep and slick with rain. Below them, a cornfield full of pursuers, and above them, hounds. She returned to David's side. Together, they turned to face the pursuers.

"This is actually worse than *Children of the Corn*," David said, as about a dozen figures clad in black formed a semicircle beneath them, faces shrouded in shadows.

"Stop running. We are here to help you," a tall man said, stepping forward and pushing back his hood. It was Father Logan. Brooklyn recognized him from her trial. She could still hear his voice in her head, discrediting her claim of involuntary possession. He'd called it "biblical," with a smirk.

"You had a chance to help me, and you were happy to watch me be icicled to death. I think we'll take our chances on our own."

"You don't understand," he said soothingly. "Your story was unbelievable, but now I know you were telling the truth. Come with us. Let me help you." He held out his hand.

"If you want to help us, leave us alone." David put his arm around her shoulder protectively. His skin warm even in the damp night air.

"I understand—" Father Logan paused at the baying of the hounds, closer now. Another figure stepped up beside him.

"We don't have time for this bullshit," he boomed. Despite the volume, his voice was controlled, as if every word had been carefully weighed and practiced weeks before they were actually spoken. This was a voice from her trial as well. "Take the girl," he intoned without emotion. "Alive," he added as an afterthought.

"I don't want it to happen this way," Father Logan protested. "Let me talk to them."

"I'm done talking," Goodrum said over his shoulder as he walked away.

Several of the hooded figures broke away from the group and advanced silently. Brooklyn closed her fingers around the small practice stones in her pocket and drew them out. They felt warm enough to be alive. She shrugged David's arm away and, with less effort than she would have thought, sent both stones spiraling into their assailants. One of them went down with a shriek, but the other stopped the stone inches from his chest and wrenched it savagely from her mental grasp. The pain was sharp, like eating ice cream too fast. He smiled cruelly and hurled the stone. Brooklyn flinched and, beside her, David screamed and fell to the ground, writhing and clutching his leg.

Brooklyn knelt over him. "Are you okay?"

"Run," he groaned.

Instead, she turned, placing herself protectively between the hooded men and David. Her pockets were empty; she scanned the ground for something, anything, but there was nothing to find. They came on, but more cautiously now.

She remembered then, the room of blood, the bodies, how she had felt—no, that wasn't right—how Belial had felt as one by one they broke before him. Predatory, indomitable, a force of nature. She had never been like that before; it wasn't her nature. But could she be that way now? Without Belial? David lay writhing on the ground behind her. Because of her. She willed the water to her hands and felt her clothes and hair drying as rivulets snaked down her arms to form icy blades.

When the first man grabbed her wrist, Brooklyn turned, drawing the blade across his midsection. He stumbled back into his friends. They parted around him like water around a stone. She slashed and stabbed; another fell before they overwhelmed her. One man twisted the knives away with such force one of her wrists cracked. Then he hit her hard. Brooklyn tasted blood. The blows came in a flurry that left her curled on the ground. David shouted at them to leave her alone, sounding far away.

"I said bring her alive." The leader's voice lashed like a whip.

Brooklyn felt herself being hoisted over a shoulder. She saw David inside a ring of frost, clutching his leg and shivering. Beyond David, in the deeper shadows of the trees, something moved. Something big. As it came, her captor sensed it, too. He half turned before a massive dog leapt and sent them both tumbling toward the cornfield below. Her good wrist buckled painfully on impact, but she was free again. She struggled back up the bank toward David. Below her, the dog ravaged her attacker. His companions tried to save him, but two more hounds appeared and drove them back into a tight circle. They paced back and forth, hackles raised, teeth bared.

"David, David." She knelt over him, smacking his face lightly. Frost clung to his lashes. His body had contorted, curling protectively around his leg. There was a lot of blood.

"I'm fine." His voice was taut with pain.

A terrible yelp shattered the night. One hound landed beside Brooklyn like a sack of stones, its fur matted with blood and charred in places. It didn't move.

"We've got to go." Brooklyn struggled to lift David to his feet. He tried to rise, but as soon as the weight settled on his injured leg, he crumpled with a groan. "I can't lift you."

Several of the hooded figures clustered around Father Logan began climbing toward them. They walked past their companions, who were still battling with the remaining hounds. The dogs hardly paid them any attention. Brooklyn couldn't help but notice how they struggled and stumbled up the steep slope, totally lacking the speed and power of the others.

"We *are* here to help," the first offered breathlessly as they drew near. It was a woman's voice. "Come with us while the Demonriders are busy." She gestured toward the men battling the hounds. She held out her hand.

Hadn't they all come together? Brooklyn wasn't sure. The run through the field had been so frantic. "How do I know I can trust you?" Brooklyn asked uncertainly.

"Who else do you have to trust," the woman pointed out before adding with another gesture, "them?"

Brooklyn's shoulders slumped in defeat. "David's hurt. I can't get him up." Her voice sounded hysterical to her own ears.

"We can help," the lady offered again with a reassuring smile. "If you'll just let us."

"They don't want to drink your Kool-Aid," a familiar voice rang out coldly. The lady flinched as if slapped. Kurt ambled easily down the bank from the tree line. As he approached, the lady and her companions receded like water. His eyes roamed the scene below, moving over Brooklyn and David huddled in a circle of frost, to the hounds and Demonriders, and finally to Father Logan who had hastily drawn his hood up to shroud his face. "Snakes, all of you," he said loud enough for all to hear.

"Says the protector of murderers and assassins," sneered a familiar, emotionless voice. "Kill all three. No witnesses."

The Demonriders scrambled up the hill, more of them than Brooklyn realized. More still streamed out of the cornfield. Kurt met a volley of projectiles head on, deflecting a hail of stones, corncobs, and sticks away from Brooklyn and David. The air around Brooklyn crackled with static, as if she were standing near high-voltage lines. She saw a stream of colorful marbles rise from Kurt's pocket and careen wildly into the crowd in a way that reminded her of a pinball machine. Several struck home; she saw the unfortunate few fall and get trampled by their friends, but it wasn't enough. They reached Kurt and washed over him like an ocean tide.

She turned back to David. He was ashen, and she wondered with a jolt if he had lost too much blood. She turned him over and pulled his belt loose. Deftly, she looped it above the knee and tightened it with all her strength.

Below her, she caught glimpses of Kurt ghosting in and out of view in the horde of enemies below. To her left, where Father Logan and his hooded followers had been, the field stood empty. She didn't have time to wonder where they had gone; a lone man had broken away from the crowd and made his way easily up the slope. He approached with a predatory certainty that made Brooklyn's insides turn cold. She cast about for a weapon and came up with a shard of glass, part of the hail that Kurt had shielded them from. Her adversary came on without pausing, a dagger of black steel gleaming like a nightmare in the pale moonlight.

She moved to meet him, away from David. He raised the dagger and brought it down with inhuman speed. Brooklyn flung herself to the side, recovering after a stumble. He came again, slashing at her stomach, then her face. His eyes glittered under his drawn hood. The hood gave her an idea. She rushed forward; he met her with a thrust aimed at her throat. She wasn't there. Instead, Brooklyn tumbled, something she hadn't done since she'd been a little girl with her sister in gymnastics classes. Then she was behind him, the hood working against him. Before he could turn, she stabbed the glass into the back of his leg, ignoring the sharp pain in her palm. She twisted, pulled it out, and stabbed the other one. He howled as his legs crumpled beneath him, but somehow he whirled on his way down and sliced a cold line across Brooklyn's belly with the knife.

She fell back, clutching her stomach. He came after her, dragging his shredded legs behind him. She tried to scoot backward, but the effort left her dizzy and breathless. Blood welled warm between her fingers. He moved on top of her like a lover and placed the dagger tip against her chest, just above her heart. She closed one blood-slick hand around his wrist and the other around his throat. He bore down on the dagger, trying to get his weight on top of it to drive it into her. The slope of the hill made that hard, but still the tip pierced her skin, spreading what felt like molten lava through her chest. She shrieked in agony, pushing against his wrist frantically. His face, she noticed with unexpected clarity, had turned an interesting shade of purple. She clutched his throat tighter, digging nails into his flesh. Brooklyn recognized him at last: Nathan Goodrum. The dagger dug deeper, and new fire blossomed inside her chest like the explosion of a dying sun.

"Die, little bitch," he hissed with the first genuine emotion she'd ever heard in his voice. Behind him, she thought she saw tattered black wings spreading wide against the sky. *Are those his wings?* she wondered dully. She reached inside for the ice, but it wasn't there, only a terrible burning fire. Red seeped around the edges of her vision.

Just above her on the bank beside David, Brooklyn saw a beautiful woman, familiar, like someone dreamed of and forgotten a thousand times. Brooklyn tried not to breathe; every deep breath pressed her chest up against the knife. Her strength was gone. She only barely noticed Nathan drawing himself up, sitting on her, positioning himself over the knife, and wrapping both hands around the hilt purposefully.

Brooklyn didn't want to watch; she turned her head toward David. The woman was gone now, and David was flying like some dark angel. *He looks fierce*, she thought, as he slammed into Nathan, and the two of them went tumbling away from her into the battle below.

23

Bitter Work

Brooklyn pushed the hair off her sweaty forehead for what seemed like the hundredth time.

"Again," commanded an all-too-familiar voice. It was Riley. Since the battle at the farm, Kurt no longer allowed her to leave the complex, not even to train with the others. Instead, she had been given a private tutor. With a groan, she rose to her feet and tried to focus, reaching out with her mind to form a wedge of energy between them. In a blur, a dozen tennis balls rose into the air and launched at her. They pelted her shield hard, bounced off, or veered along its edges, arcing away from her. She felt every impact, like a finger jabbing into her forehead. Without warning, several of the deflected balls veered around the outer edges of her shield and struck her in the back with a hail of blows that drove her to the ground. She stayed there for a long moment, experiencing the pain, greeting the aches like old friends before pushing herself back to her feet. "I think that's enough for—"

"Again," Brooklyn interrupted, struggling to stay steady on her feet. A part of her wanted nothing more than to collapse into a soft bed, but another part, filled with bitter determination, remembered how easily she'd been defeated that night at the farm. And David—well, she couldn't let her thoughts go there right now.

"Your nose is bleeding," he pointed out, "and pushing yourself like this won't bring him—"

She hit him with a ball, a cheap shot right in the chest, hard enough to make him stumble. “Again, again, again.” She emphasized each word by launching a barrage of tennis balls at him.

His look of incredulity melted into the lopsided smile she’d become familiar with over the past few weeks. “Again,” he agreed, wrenching the remaining ammunition from her with unnerving ease.

After the training session, Riley walked her back to her bedroom. “Bedroom” was a nice word for it. In truth, it was a beautiful, lavish jail cell with a steel plate where the doorknob should have been.

“If you need anything, just call.” He gestured to the phone on the nightstand. She nodded. There wasn’t anything to say, not really.

After the lock clicked, Brooklyn shed her sweaty clothes and examined her chest in the bathroom mirror. The wound had healed crudely, leaving a scar that blossomed into swirls of angry black and red. It was pretty, in a dark sort of way, like a hellish barbed-wire tattoo. Riley attributed it to some rare poison, but she couldn’t remember the name. She traced the scar across her belly as well. It had healed better, but would never fully fade. Once, such scars would have horrified her, but now she barely cared at all.

Death Kisses. That’s what Kurt called them when he visited her in the infirmary. Brooklyn rubbed her finger over the chest scar. She remembered asking about David, pleading with Kurt to find him and bring him back. He had looked pained; it had been Riley who explained what happened at the cornfield after she passed out.

He’d touched her gently on the arm and told her there were too many of them, even for a Protector. *That’s what they all call*

Kurt, Brooklyn thought bitterly, *a Protector, but in the end he only protects himself.* The way she saw it, protecting her was just an extension of protecting himself.

"You should have saved him." Her words were harsher than she'd meant them to be, and though Brooklyn aimed them at Kurt, they cut her too. She should have saved him, should have found a way. Kurt had opened his mouth to respond and then closed it again, vanishing beyond the curtains that surrounded her bed space. She didn't call after him.

"He did all anyone could," Riley had admonished, "and he lost all but one of his dogs."

"We must get David back." She'd uttered the words with a fragile hopefulness, knowing somehow what the answer would be.

His gentle tone, the hand on her arm, none of it softened the truth. David died. Died to save her. Kurt last saw him in the thickest part of the fight, trampled in the tumult, still and lifeless. "There's nothing anyone could have done—"

"I don't want to talk about it right now," she'd snipped, staring up at the ceiling and counting the tiles.

"Okay, I just need to check your wounds and then I'll give you some space."

When she didn't answer, he'd lowered the blankets and opened the thin fabric of her gown. His fingers tested the firmness of the flesh around the wounds.

"You are going to be okay," he'd said, closing the gown and pulling the sheet up to her chin.

Going to be okay, going to be okay, going to be okay. She had said the words like a mantra until, long after he left, they became meaningless syllables. With a great effort, she pulled herself free of the memories. There was nothing to be gained by dwelling.

After a quick shower, she coiled her wet hair inside a towel. Sitting cross legged on the bed, she practiced levitating objects. She needed desperately to rest, and her head continued pounding, but she persisted. She'd managed seven small objects, including a television remote, orbiting her towel turban when a series of abrupt knocks sounded at her door. Everything clattered to the floor.

"Just a minute," she called out as she hastily pulled on a T-shirt and rumpled jeans. She tossed the towel into the hamper, reached for the nonexistent doorknob without thinking, and then intoned as sweetly as she could, "Come in."

The door swung open and in came Kurt Levin. Brooklyn was surprised; he hadn't spoken to her since the infirmary. His eyes were bloodshot, with bags under them as if he hadn't slept in weeks.

"Look," he said without preamble, "if I'm going to need to keep you locked up all the time, I might as well shoot you and save us both a lot of misery."

"Wow. You should write Hallmark cards."

He shrugged. "Being sarcastic doesn't change the truth. I've gone to a lot of effort, risked my life twice even, to save you, but I can't keep you from doing stupid things. If you two hadn't run off—" He saw her cringe and stopped.

"You didn't even try to save him. You just ran away and left him to die." Pain made her voice shrill. "You—"

"Did exactly what David wanted me to do," he finished. His eyes met hers firmly. "He sacrificed himself for you. We are alive, both of us, because of him. All I have done has been to keep you alive."

"You're right. Running away was stupid. If we hadn't tried . . . "

Kurt cleared his throat. "I find it is better not to dwell on these sorts of things; it will make you crazy. Instead, let's talk about where we stand—if you are up to it?"

She nodded. Everything he said made sense. Something about him reminded her of her father. In appearance they couldn't be further apart, but she thought they shared a certain gruff kindness and maybe a lingering sadness too.

"I didn't leave him there. Once you were safe, I went back with reinforcements. It was as if the whole thing never happened, only a few trampled cornstalks, nothing else to mark our passing."

"What about the lady that owns the farm? Did they hurt her?"

"Mrs. Mays? She's fine. Not a woman you'd want to pick a fight with." Kurt crossed the room and sat tiredly at the foot of the bed. "Before sunrise, we were scouring the Demonriders' lodge. They left only two guards, both new recruits. They were expecting all the others back before dawn, and didn't know where they had gone. The place was cleaned out. Pretty obvious they never planned to come back."

"What if they were lying?"

"I interrogated them personally, and I am very good at interrogation." He smiled grimly.

Brooklyn shivered. Something about the intensity of his statement left her feeling like she'd gone a few steps too far out on a frozen lake and the ice was beginning to groan. "What about the others, the religious group?"

He shrugged. "They own land adjacent to the farm and hold meetings there sometimes. They're pacifists. Claimed they were trying to avoid violence, apprehend you peacefully before the Demonriders could do you harm."

"And you believe that?" she asked in disbelief.

"Not at all, but I can't prove otherwise. They withdrew immediately and never took part in the fighting. When I arrived, they were offering you help, such that it was."

"But they were together, all together!" she spluttered.

Kurt ran his fingers over the stubble on his head. "I know. Don't take this the wrong way, but you wouldn't be a credible witness, because Stewarth would be the judge."

It wasn't fair. First, they accused her of a crime that she hadn't committed, well, not willingly committed at least, then held her prisoner, and finally attacked her for no reason. Almost murdered even, and then there was David. No justice for David. Brooklyn felt the tears burn hot and didn't bother to blink them back. "If I can't have justice for David," she said icily, "then let's talk about revenge."

24

Loyalty Lies

"You came!" Del rushed forward to embrace, greeting him with a kiss on each cheek.

Kurt shrugged and returned an awkward hug. Beyond her he could see Alexander Stewarth in a hospital bed. His son Eric knelt beside the bed, clasping one of his father's hands between his own. He glowered up at Kurt through his lashes.

"He's not dead yet, Mother." Eric's voice cracked like a whip. She stiffened visibly, like a puppet whose strings had been yanked.

Kurt followed Del into the room. Stewarth's eyes were closed; tubes, wires, and hoses crisscrossed his body and disappeared into various machines, including a ventilator that caused his chest to rise and fall off kilter, as if one lung were inflating more than the other.

"What happened?" The question escaped in a rush of breath Kurt had not realized he was holding.

Eric shrugged without answering, eyes lingering on his father with something like regret. Kurt could sympathize with regret. He thought of his son. *Tyler*, he corrected himself. Start thinking of them as "wife" or "son" and pretty soon they weren't real anymore. That had been a hard time in his life. When Kurt arrived at the hospital, Mary had already passed, but not Tyler. He clung to life with a ferocity that surprised even the doctors. How many weeks had Kurt sat beside a bed just like this one oscillating between hope and despair? He shook his head, and with a start, realized Eric had been talking to him.

"So, you refuse?" Eric asked.

"Do what? I'm sorry," Kurt replied sheepishly. "I was remembering when I first met your father." It wasn't a lie, not exactly.

For the first time, Eric's face softened. "I said, Mother and I need to take care of some family business, and we want you to stay with him and keep him safe. He was very explicit that you were the only person we should trust. I cannot take the ring until he passes, or we risk any portion of its power that resides in him being lost."

How interesting, Kurt thought. Some of the ring's power could seep into the user. That explained how Alexander had compelled his demonic bodyguards the last time they spoke, despite the ring lying between them on the desk. For a moment, he heard Stewarth's voice again. *My family is old. We trace our line directly back to Solomon. We have many secrets.* What an old blowhard! Kurt smiled at Eric. "Of course, it's my honor to keep him safe until you return."

"Call us if anything—you know, if he—"

If he dies you mean, Kurt thought, but he said, "I'll call you if there is any change, I promise."

Eric gathered their things, Del cast a wistful smile in his direction, and then they were gone. Kurt watched them go and then turned his eyes back to his dying friend. Absently, he traced a finger along the interlocking loops of his Celtic pendant. He felt it pulse coolly in response. Belial had been resting since he returned with Azrael's Tome. Apparently, it had been a brutal trip. Kurt had been sitting at his desk enjoying a drink when Belial materialized with a hiss and a pop, his wings singed and blackened, and dropped the Tome onto Kurt's desk. The dragon-scale binding had gouged deep furrows in the mahogany and begun to smoke and sizzle. Little flames sprang up around it and filled the room with an acrid stench. Awkwardly, he and Riley had maneuvered it onto a steel gurney without actually touching it.

It was hidden now, behind a secret door in Riley's basement lab. Kurt considered calling him to see if he had made any progress with reading the thing, but he knew Riley would call if there was anything to report. The problem was twofold. First, creating and maintaining enough heat to make the text in the book appear was difficult and dangerous. The second problem was finding a way to view the pages and survive at those temperatures.

Riley would figure it out, eventually; Kurt had faith. But every day of uncertainty—of knowing his son was out there somewhere, reincarnated, alive, a needle in a haystack—was maddening. The right demon could read it, one of the Tomekeepers. They were beyond his ability to summon or compel, though. He supposed there was no rush. Even if he could resurrect Azrael, he didn't have the agreed upon number of demons yet. Though perhaps the ones he had and the favor of bringing her back would tip the scales in his favor. *Yeah, right.*

Stewarth had lost weight. The hospital blanket outlined his narrow legs and sunken stomach. *How has he deteriorated so much in only two months?* Kurt, suddenly curious, rose from his chair and moved soundlessly to Alexander's side. Kneeling as Eric had, he took Stewarth's hand between his own. He felt it then, the invisible ring pulsing like a living thing between his fingers. Kurt's heart hammered as he traced his fingers over it, remembering the stone, so black it was like a hole in the world. The ring that could compel Hell.

Tais's green eye twinkled like the sea, and her brown one darkened with unspoken promises. Behind her, beyond the river, the sun sank slowly into the ocean. Her hair drank the dusky light and obscured her face in shadow.

"My father says the world is changing, and he wants me to be a part of that, but I know he only wants to be favored by this . . . *king*." She spat the word as if it left a bad taste, but then her voice softened. "I shouldn't speak of my father this way. A good daughter would obey."

"So don't be a good daughter," Belial suggested impishly. "Be a very bad one." He smiled and touched her cheek.

Tais sighed. "This king does not want me. He wants my eyes because I see things differently.

"Stop brooding about this king. What a fool he must be if all he wants are your eyes. Beautiful though they are," he amended playfully.

"I see you," she said in the Old Tongue. The syllables rolled from her lips like exotic music. "The real you. Savage and cold."

He shivered, his host's heart pounding. Belial always felt exposed when she looked through the flesh like this, but not unpleasantly so. "I will never let this king take you, Tais. He has already turned against all the gods and spirits of this world, against the natural order. He calls us demons, this faraway king in a faraway land. If he ever comes here, I will kill him."

"My father says the Magus are losing their powers to this king. Yesterday in our village, one turned a stick into a snake and couldn't turn it back again. It bit him and he died."

Belial stifled laughter. "He must have angered his Familiar."

"But my father said—"

"Your father"—he leaned forward and pressed his lips to hers for a long moment—"talks too much. A trait, I regret to say, you may have inherited. Besides, what do you think your father would say about me? Have you told him?"

The way she cast her eyes over her shoulder toward the delta was answer enough. "Let's take a walk." She rose without looking to see if he followed.

He hurried to catch up. They took off their sandals and walked ankle deep in the evening tide, hand in hand. The moon shone bright, and ahead where the ancient roots of overturned trees jutted up like bony fingers, they paused and embraced. This was their spot. When she came at dawn to gather the seaweed and clams that washed up during the night, he would be here. When she came later in the day to wash clothing in the ocean, he would help her drape the long swathes of linen along these upturned roots, and while they steamed in the sun the two of them would steal behind them, shielded from the view of passersby in their alcove.

"I have to go soon, before he comes looking." Without waiting for a response, she kissed him.

He closed his eyes. Human lips were undeniably fascinating. They kissed hungrily, hands exploring. Belial's fingers fumbled with the cord that bound her linen shift in place, but gently, almost apologetically, Tais pushed him away.

"We don't have time," she said breathlessly. "Tomorrow?"

"Tomorrow," he agreed.

He stood there a long time, watching her dash along the beach. Her white garment shone like a star beneath the full moon. By the time she reached the delta to turn upriver, he caught only glimpses of her flitting through the trees like a wraith. Then she was gone.

"She's beautiful as humans go, isn't she?" a familiar voice called from the water's edge.

Belial ambled down to where his father stood. "Exceptionally so," he replied evenly.

Prosidris's face split into a feral grin. "Is that why you've taken to your assignment with such zeal?"

"I've watched over her, as you asked me to, but you should know her father is brokering some bargain with this king across the sea, the one who speaks against us and names us demons."

Prosidris's face darkened at the mention of the king. "You just do your part and I promise you this king will never conclude his bargaining with her father."

At last Belial understood. His father planned to kill the king. "Will you travel to Israel to kill him yourself?"

"I plan to deal with him personally," Prosidris replied with a toothy smile, and then he shifted into something with tentacles and vanished beneath the waves.

25

Good Intentions

"Here we are," Riley said proudly. Brooklyn blinked against the bright fluorescent lighting. They were in a room that married the ultramodern shine of stainless steel and laboratory equipment to medieval alchemy and arcane practices.

In one corner, a microscope perched atop an overturned cauldron. In another, a sleek metal workbench held an ancient-looking mortar and pestle and a rack containing bottles of powder and liquids of various muted colors. Centered against the back wall loomed the largest fireplace Brooklyn had ever seen. It rose to such a height that she thought she could step into it without stooping. Inside the fireplace, an enormous, ancient-looking book rested on a scorched and blackened granite podium. Beside the podium, there was what appeared to be a welder or torch attached to a bank of green tanks.

"What is this place?" She turned in a slow circle, taking it all in.

"My lab. Come here." He gestured to what looked like a dental exam chair. "Sit." He turned away from her, placing a hypodermic and several other implements on a rolling cart.

Brooklyn shivered inwardly as she sat. She hated needles. "Will it hurt much?"

"Yes, it is painful, but I believe you'll be pleased with the results." He turned with a smile, a single metallic blue orb floating lazily above his palm. She reached for it with her mind, but it slipped through her grasp like oil.

"I can't," Brooklyn admitted after several failed attempts.

"It works based on the first law of physio-spiritual integrity."

Brooklyn stared at him.

"Okay, think about it this way. Remember when you tried to escape, and you attacked the guard? What happened?"

She did remember. Furniture had been blown across the room with incredible force, but the man had stepped right through her wall of energy as if it were a stiff breeze and nothing more. "It didn't hurt him."

"Exactly. He only felt the air molecules you pushed against him. You can't affect another person directly. Even though my psychokinetic abilities are much greater than yours, I cannot reach inside you and stop your heart, for instance. Your spiritual energy repels other spiritual energies to maintain its integrity."

"Okay, that makes sense, but what does it have to do with the marbles?"

The blue sphere rose into the air again. "It's permeated with my essence, like an extension of my body."

"How do you—"

"Ah, ah," he said with a grin. "Trade secret."

"And how long until they are ready?"

"About three days on average. My first batch took weeks." He rolled the cart of gleaming implements over to her.

"And you need my blood to make this work?" she asked nervously.

"I can make it work with blood," he answered, "but if you want the full effect, spinal fluid is preferable and much quicker."

Brooklyn gulped. The thought of a needle in her back made her cringe and shift in the chair, but then she remembered the cornfield and how the Demonriders had taken her weapons like it was nothing, and turned them on David. Something cold stirred in her chest. Resolution maybe. She wasn't sure, but when at last she spoke, it was with certainty. In a voice she hardly recognized as her own. "Spinal fluid it is, then."

Kurt noticed, with an odd detachment, that his hands were shaking as he pulled the ring from Stewarth's finger and slipped it on his own. "I'm just borrowing this for a little while, old friend."

Alexander didn't answer, but his silence seemed like an accusation.

"I'll have it back before you even notice it is gone; I promise." Kurt turned away and walked right into Azrael. He yelped in surprise and leapt back. His heart tried to break free of his chest. "You're—But I saw you—How?" he spluttered. Had Riley unlocked the secrets in the Tome of Death already?

"Yes, I'm still alive." She sighed almost sorrowfully. When she stretched her wings, Kurt noticed they were damaged. Great patches of feathers were broken or missing, and there were even a few small pinholes that let light shine through. Stars in a new moon sky.

"What happened?" He gestured to her tattered wings.

She stepped forward, and the light fell on her alabaster face. He stifled a gasp. "The last few weeks have been very difficult for me." Great fissures crisscrossed her flesh, making a jigsaw puzzle of her face. "And for you too? It seems you've abandoned your beliefs and loyalties. You should have taken that ring long ago, and we could have been done with our transaction."

Instinctively, Kurt covered the ring with his other hand. "What are you doing here?"

"He's dying." Her voice was soft, almost human. "How are your two charges?"

"One is dead, and the other is crippled with grief and guilt."

Azrael's eyes widened.

"It's not every day that I get to surprise Death with an obituary, but don't worry, the girl you've so mysteriously deemed 'important for both of us' is still alive." Kurt watched her, but Azrael's face had returned to its usual inhuman placidity. "You know, you never told me *why* she is important."

"And perhaps I never will." Azrael yawned. "Our time is short. How soon can we make the trade?"

"I've never used an artifact like this to work a summoning." *I'm not even sure how it works*, he thought to himself. "If you could take me home, it would save eight hours of driving. I must return the ring before his family knows it is gone, and before he dies." Kurt looked at Azrael. "How long does he have?"

"Long enough." She reached for him.

He darted deftly out of her reach. "One more thing." Kurt reached for the Celtic knot and awakened Belial from its depths.

He appeared as a handsome bronze-skinned man wearing little more than a loincloth, blushed, and shifted into his more familiar form, wrapping his wings about himself indignantly. "You woke me," he said by way of explanation.

"I need you to stand guard, make sure no harm comes to the Heir."

"No harm, got it."

"Don't get any ideas about finishing what you started," Kurt cautioned.

"That was misguided." His unfathomable eyes pierced Kurt. "Clearly, I tried to kill the wrong man."

Kurt nodded, stepped toward Azrael, and hoped there wouldn't be too much of the macabre to attend between here and home.

Brooklyn peered over Riley's shoulder through her shaded safety goggles. She was blind until the torch in his hand flared like a dying star. Even from behind him, the heat was such that she began to back away almost immediately. He applied the heat in sweeping motions across the pages of the giant book in the fireplace. She expected it to burst into flames, but it never did. Several minutes later, when Riley gave up and Brooklyn removed the goggles, she could see the stone pedestal smoking with fresh scorch marks, but the book lay defiant and untouched.

"It's no use." He shrugged. "We are reaching temperatures in excess of 3200 degrees Celsius and not a glimmer."

"What did you say this book is made of?"

"Dragon hide, dragon scales, and dragon blood. Under the heat of soul light, the blood ink glows like sterling silver, but that is a different sort of heat. It can't be measured by the same scales as earthly heat." He moved to an enormous machine that looked like an industrial oven and adjusted a dial. "These spheres may be done sooner than we thought. I lost mine, so I'm glad for the excuse to make more."

"Who else has these?" Brooklyn asked curiously.

"Nobody. They are something of a trade secret. Since Kurt insisted you be well armed, you will be number three. Welcome to the club." Riley smiled.

"So, how do you know so much about all this stuff?" Brooklyn waved vaguely to encompass the entirety of the bizarre laboratory.

He hesitated.

"I know, I know, trade secrets," she said with a frustrated sigh. "The two of you have so many. It seems like I can't get through a conversation with either of you without stumbling across something top secret."

"I'll tell you if you really want to know," Riley said seriously. "The fact is that I'm not human, not anymore."

Brooklyn eyed him. "What do you mean? You a vampire?"

He laughed. Really laughed. For so long she grew annoyed, but at last he answered, "No, nothing as glamorous as that."

"Well, what then?" she demanded.

Riley laughed again and Brooklyn considered punching him. "I don't know that there is a word for what I am. I was born as human as you, but through a series of unlikely events, I met a benign demon, a scholar of sorts, and we . . . connected."

"Well, that would explain it if this story were about your parents, but I don't understand how falling in love with a demon makes you part demon."

"When spirits marry, it is not like when humans marry. A spiritual union is a joining, a melding of two energies into one. I'm unique because, by nature, demons loathe humans. The idea of spirits permanently intertwined with flesh enrages and disgusts them. They consider us abominations as much or more than we consider them the same. They believe in a firm separation of the physical and spiritual bodies."

"You're a Demonrider?" Horror and revulsion rose like vomit in her throat. Brooklyn swallowed hard, pushing those feelings away. *He's just like the things that killed David*, a little voice whispered.

"Not at all." Riley reached to touch her shoulder, but she flinched away. His hand hung there for a moment as if he weren't sure what to do with it. He shrugged and put it in his pocket. "Possession and demonriding are both acts of domination. I am the result of a consensual and mutually beneficial arrangement. The person I was and the spirit she was, now I'm the sum of the two. I'm ascended."

"Is it possible to get a spiritual divorce?" Brooklyn asked in a neutral voice.

"No," Riley replied, "and even if there were, I wouldn't. I like who I am."

Brooklyn grimaced. She did not want to offend Riley. He was, after all, her only remaining friend, but she could not understand why anyone would love a demon, how anyone could. She remembered Nathan Goodrum's cold, inhuman eyes. She also remembered Belial. The thought sent a shudder down her spine.

He had made her do things that would haunt her forever. Every night she revisited the house of frozen horrors in her dreams, and every morning she pushed the fresh memories from her mind. It was as if sleep were slowly brushing away the cobwebs in which he had shrouded their shared experiences. "I didn't mean to upset you," she murmured. "It's just that I can't understand how anyone could. I mean, they are so cold and . . . " She trailed off.

His face softened. "Not all demons are like Belial, and not all demons were always called demons. Many were once minor gods, elemental spirits, the essences of places and cultures long gone, but none of them are those things anymore." Seeing her confusion, he continued. "Do you like me? Do I seem like a nice person?"

"Well, yeah." She blushed, suddenly flustered. "I wasn't saying that you were evil or anything."

"Ah, but you were about to, and I get it. You've had nothing but bad experiences with spirits, as most people have, but give me a chance to show you that—just like people—not all of them are the same."

Brooklyn nodded. "Okay, I'll try to keep an open mind, but I have some pretty striking images burned into my brain already. I can't change that."

It was his turn to nod. "Fair enough."

Brooklyn felt suddenly self-conscious, so she changed the subject. "So, in this book, the ink glows at high temperatures?"

"That's the basic idea, yes, but I think it has something to do with the temperature differential between the blood and the dragon-skin page. You see, dragon blood is endothermic in nature—"

"Whoa, slow down, Professor." Brooklyn smiled. "I was just going to ask at what temperature dragon blood freezes."

"Freezes?" Riley blinked at her in astonishment.

"Yeah, maybe if the ink crystallizes, it will change color. I don't know, it's just an idea." She shrugged.

"You're a genius!" He clapped a hand on her shoulder.

This time, Brooklyn didn't flinch away from his touch. Instead, Riley's excitement seemed to infect her. Her own face stretched into a matching grin. "You think my idea will work?"

"No way. Freezing dragon blood is the most absurd idea I've ever heard, but it gives me an idea." Riley hugged her, mumbling something about genius.

"Sure, yeah, that's all I was trying to do. Give you an idea." The sarcasm seemed lost on him.

"As I was saying, the blood has endothermic properties. It will absorb heat faster and hold heat longer than the surrounding page. I believe that if we heat the page, as we've just done, and then . . . " He trailed off, rummaging around in a large metal cabinet before pulling another stainless-steel tank and apparatus from the cabinet with a triumphant grunt. "And then we flash freeze it with liquid nitrogen, forming an opaque layer of frost across the entire page."

"Of course, yes, that's what I was going to suggest next," she deadpanned.

He looked up in obvious confusion, but then his eyes lit up with comprehension. "Well, let's see if your idea works, then."

She watched as he turned to the book and applied the liquid nitrogen. A thick low-lying fog erupted and spread around Riley, giving him a creepy mad-scientist vibe that somehow suited him.

"Is it working?"

He didn't answer, but gestured for her to join him. She moved forward through the spreading mist. He blew the fog away from the book gently. As they watched the strange symbols materialize in the frost, it reminded Brooklyn of nothing so much as the messages her sister used to write on the bathroom mirror that remained invisible until you stepped out of a steamy shower to find the words revealed in her lovely looping hand.

"You're a genius," he said, grabbing her hand and squeezing it.

"I know," she said, turning to look at him. His smile—she realized—made her want to reciprocate.

26

The Summoning

Kurt hit the couch with a thump. Azrael was already gone, leaving him alone in the dark office. He wondered where Nathan Goodrum and his men were hiding. He needed demons and could think of nothing more satisfying than stripping each and every one of them of their supernatural companions. But as it was, he needed a lot of demons, and he needed them fast. That meant he had no time to search out his enemies, and it meant he had no choice but to take a more dangerous path: a summoning.

Kurt tried not to think about what Mary would have said of his plans. The irony was not lost on him. Sometimes it was better if family didn't know everything you did for them. Over the years, he'd often struggled with the moral implications of his job. Things it demanded. The first time he'd killed someone during an exorcism, he had rationalized that the person brought it on themselves by consorting with demons. The first time it had been a child, he told himself the same thing but had needed to get very drunk to believe it. The worst had been a nineteen-year-old summoner.

If Demonriders were comparable to drug addicts, then summoners were dealers. It was justified, he had told himself as he stepped over her lifeless corpse to bag up the summoning implements scattered around her summoning circle. Kurt had taken them to the incinerator but couldn't throw them in. Those damned things had been all that remained of someone's daughter. Kurt imagined a family somewhere that would never know what happened, another girl missing without a trace. So, he'd taken her belongings and hidden them. A capital offense in his world.

What a mistake that had been. The girl, it turned out, came from a family of summoners, and through some dark art they had tracked the girl's things to his home. If only *he* had been home. But he hadn't been. Only Mary and Tyler had been home. He couldn't think about that right now. Soon he would have his son back. That's what deserved his attention.

Kurt wasn't sure exactly when things had changed, when the guilt had transformed from sharp pangs into inconsequential prickles, but right now it threatened to overwhelm him, and he couldn't have that; he was so close. So close to the good ending that would validate all the questionable paths he'd followed. Kurt told himself, as he often did, if he could bend Hell to this task, he could buy Heaven. He shook his head. A drink, he knew, would clear the cobwebs. Kurt moved through the dark like a wraith, not daring to turn on the lights in his office and risk being noticed. His hands shook, clinking the bottle against the glass. He downed the bourbon in a gulp, grimacing against the burn.

Kurt ran fingers lightly over the stonework on the left side of the fireplace. He found the one he was looking for and began wiggling it free. With a grating sound, the stone slid out. Kurt reached into the dark recess, feeling for the familiar handle. He found it and pulled slowly until a small box—perfectly fitted to the opening—slid out. Inside were the things his family had died for. He always kept them carefully hidden, but the time for caution had passed. Kurt shoved the box into a backpack and hastily thrust the stone back into place. He spared the blank space above the fireplace a furtive glance. He hoped to be hanging a new family portrait soon.

Brooklyn felt inexplicably at home in Riley's strange laboratory. While he worked tirelessly with the liquid nitrogen, transcribing the Tome, she discovered an adjacent room with all the amenities of a small apartment. Brooklyn rummaged through the fridge and made a snack of grapes and cheese while dutifully ignoring something educational on the Discovery Channel.

The clock on the nightstand read 2:03 a.m. It was impossible to keep track of time underground. She cut off the lamp and fell back amid the pillows, willing herself to sleep. Brooklyn could hear the almost familiar bustling from the laboratory. *Riley is fascinating*, she mused. Smart. Good smile. Not bad looking either.

With a stab of guilt, Brooklyn realized she was smiling. David had died less than two months ago and here she was thinking about someone else. She let her mind wander to other places: the rock shelf and overhang above her home and the days spent there with Erin, ice cream trips with Devin, dates with David, riding the tractor with her dad as a little girl, and helping her mom in the rose garden. Brooklyn hoped—as she slipped into dreams—that her family was okay and that they truly were made safer by her absence. After what happened to David, Brooklyn had not even considered trying to contact them.

Sleep came, and as always, the dreams came too. The room's white plaster walls were stained with a series of brown splatters that seemed to radiate outward from a nucleus like the petals of some grotesque flower. With a wet sound and a flash of silver, a burst of vibrant arterial red misted the collage. As life left her victim, Brooklyn saw the demon drawn out violently by an unseen force, whisked away as easily as a leaf fallen into a river.

She tossed the limp body into a pile and dragged the next person from the adjoining bathroom. She wiped the knife clean on the lady's white blouse, ruining it. Then began the now familiar speech. "I am a Warden; will you answer my questions?"

The woman's eyes were bloodshot, full of terror. "I don't know what you are talking about. Please let me go." She wailed in terror and shock. Brooklyn cut her. A long, shallow cut that brought the demon raging and spitting to the surface.

"Will you answer my questions now?" Brooklyn asked pointedly. The demon did not respond. Brooklyn pressed on doggedly. "I know you work for someone, small guy, pointy beard, calls himself the Engineer. Any of this ringing a bell?"

"I work for the Heir, Alexander Stewarth," she intoned in a robotic voice, just like the others. Belial had dismissed the first as a lie, but fifteen identical interrogations later and he felt uncertainty gnawing at his insides.

"Tell me about the Engineer."

Again in the same emotionless voice: "I don't know anyone by that name."

There was a sound like a sling blade passing through briers, and the woman doubled over clutching her stomach. "How about now?" Brooklyn's voice resonated in a way she never knew it could. The woman was screaming now, blood rushing out between her fingers. It was a piteous animal sound full of horror and disbelief.

"Brooklyn, wake up!"

She opened her eyes.

Riley was shaking her, his arm behind her shoulders propping her into a semi-sitting position. "What's wrong?" he asked. Concern drew his lips down into a frown.

"Just a nightmare."

His face relaxed. "I thought something was happening to you. You were screaming bloody murder."

"Bloody murder? Was I?" Her mouth quirked.

"What was it about? The nightmare I mean."

"Nothing," she answered airily. "I've slept enough."

He took her chin between his thumb and forefinger and turned her face to his. "You're not alone," he said simply.

"That's what I'm afraid of."

Brisk autumn had become bone-chilling winter without Kurt's notice. He noticed now as he climbed high into the mountains behind his home. The hike left him damp with sweat and when he stopped to prepare for the summoning, it turned clammy. Kurt filled his pockets with Celtic knots from his bag, small golden trinkets modeled after the one he currently wore on a chain around his neck.

Kurt cleared an area of all leaves and debris and dug a small pit. He filled it with deadwood and lit a small, cheery fire. By the flickering flame, he unpacked the remaining items as the last rays of sunshine lingered in the treetops and then gave way to twilight. More specifically: a silver bowl, a strangely colored shard of crystal about as long as a drumstick, and a thin leather book with a clasp. Kurt handled the book as carefully as a piece of broken glass.

He spread all the implements on an enormous tree stump, opened the book, and examined the handwritten pages. There were several writing styles, and Kurt suspected they had passed the book down through generations, each owner noting new observations or discoveries. Each page contained a carefully drawn sigil, a pictograph that captured the essence of each individual demon in a way that words or names never could. Some were as complex as a labyrinth, and others were as simple as a circle with lines through the middle.

While wearing the ring, the sigils resonated with Kurt in a way they never had before, as if they contained a certain internal logic and familiarity, like music. "All right," he said aloud, "let's get this over with." Normally, the procedure would involve carefully tracing a sigil on vellum in the summoner's own blood, chanting, performing an elaborate ritual, and eventually burning the blood sigil to pull the trigger on the whole deal. But tonight, he had Solomon's ring.

Kurt focused on the first name in the book, letting the image sink into his mind until he could envision it perfectly with his eyes closed. It was a simple one, all points and sharp angles, like a throwing star with teeth. The ring pulsed erratically, not unlike the sensation of having a fish on a line. Kurt exerted his will and felt the ring respond like a living thing.

He had summoned demons before, less formidable than this one, and the mental effort had been tremendous. Now, with a firm tug, this one coalesced in front of him. As soon as he saw it, the sigil made perfect sense. It bristled, scaled and spiky like a man-sized porcupine with the claws and teeth of a lion. Before it could communicate, Kurt stepped forward and pressed one of the Celtic traps against its forehead, and it vanished as silently as it had appeared.

The night progressed rapidly. One after another, he summoned and trapped them. There were many more pages on the left side of the book than on the right when he came across an unusual symbol that defied angles or straight lines. This one spoke of curves, swells, and hollows. It made supple promises. Something stirred inside of Kurt. The design evoked rolling mountains and the rise and fall of waves, the swollen roundness of a full moon, but more than anything else, it oozed femininity. Beside the design, which seemed more elaborate for its elegant simplicity, was written a single Latin word: *Infesta*.

Exhilaration and exhaustion were at war with one another as Kurt began to pull this mysterious spirit into the physical world. It was like tearing something from the grasp of a raging river. A shape appeared and resolved itself slowly into a beautiful woman with eyes like granite.

Kurt stumbled backward with his mouth opened in disbelief. She looked as she had the first time he had ever seen her, untouched by care or time. “M-Mary,” he stammered, “is it really you?”

“It’s really me,” she said with a warm smile.

27

Blurring Lines

"Why do you flicker like that?" Belial asked curiously as they stared at one another across the hospital bed.

Azrael did not answer.

"And your face, it's like a broken china doll that's glued back together. How did that happen?"

She watched him impassively through lowered lashes.

Belial grinned inwardly and spread his wings, turning all his many eyes in her direction. "I thought so," he began smugly. "I've seen you many times before, death in the shadows." Each time she flickered, for the barest instant, an Azrael-shaped hole appeared in the world. Through it he caught glimpses: first a man with a gun in a wooded glade, then a hospital room very similar to the one they stood in, a crowded street and a crumpled body under a car, a bloody knife gleaming dully in candlelight. Belial folded his wings tightly, a tremulous falling sensation washing through him, as if he'd stepped off the edge of a cliff and found himself suddenly wingless.

Azrael smiled knowingly. "It's a lot to take in, isn't it?"

Her voice washed the images away like a bucket of ice water. "It's like that all the time?"

"Never stops," she admitted wistfully. "I was a goddess of fertility and life once. I refused to submit to the new order, so my mother bound me to death as punishment."

"Why not toss you in Hell with everyone else?"

"I'm not fallen. I can't be bound there."

"Everyone's fallen. You take sustenance from humans, you sit under the soul sun, or you wither away. Just the three options."

"Not everyone."

"If your fate is decided, inescapable, then why struggle against it? Why pull yourself back together and resume the burden?"

"It's beyond your understanding."

"Come on."

"I will find a way out and back to my rightful place. I just need to buy more time."

"It seems like a very human response, struggling against the inevitable." When she didn't answer, he went on. "Fertility and life, you said? For what people?"

"An island people from very long ago. It has grown and gone beneath the waves now. The scions of my people are scattered."

Her fate was an exceptionally cruel one, but when Azrael spoke of these islanders, a strange tenderness twisted her pristine features like old grief. She grew still, as if listening to something far away. "It's his time," Azrael said, turning her brooding gaze on Alexander Stewarth.

Belial moved like a panther. In an instant, he placed himself between her and the Heir. "Not until Kurt returns with the ring."

"You are a simpleton if you think he ever intends to lay down such power. The sun is rising and still the fool has not returned, has not contacted either of us."

"Maybe he recognized the danger of summoning so many and decided not to risk weakening the Pull any further."

She laughed. It was terrible and beautiful at once. "He does not care about the separation of spirit and flesh. He wants one thing, and he will do anything to have it. Perhaps he means to break down the barrier, to tear down both worlds and build anew. Let him do it. Humans are destined to be destroyed one way or another."

"Like your island children?" Belial said without thinking.

Azrael's hand flashed faster than the anger in her eyes. The blow cracked across Belial's face like a whip and sent him spinning end over end into the far wall. He had never seen anything move so fast.

"You, fallen scum"—Azrael's voice shook with rage—"do not speak of them."

"I can't let you take this one. Not yet." Belial took up the position between Azrael and Alexander Stewarth again.

Her eyes smoldered like twin coals. "Let me?" she asked with outrage. "You? Let me? You'd do well to remember, humans aren't the only things that can die."

Ignoring the threat, he continued. "Let me contact him. You could bring him back in time to return the ring."

Azrael looked down at a hand on her shoulder. It was his hand, Belial realized with a start. He withdrew it quickly. She shrugged, a gesture that touched her wings and her shoulders. "I'll give you five minutes."

He hid his relief. He did not want to fight Azrael. It was true he could be killed, but whether or not she could accomplish the task remained to be seen. Getting the ring out of Kurt's grasp was a necessity if he ever wanted to be free again. The mere act of stealing the ring proved he was unbalanced, not to mention the reckless decision to summon more demons across an already failing barrier.

Belial reached out mentally, found the thread that bound him to Kurt's trinket, and followed it. Something felt different. At the other end of the connection, instead of the now familiar and warm presence, there was something alien, cold, and insectile. "Something is wrong," he said softly to Azrael. "Something is very wrong."

Brooklyn's stomach fluttered with anticipation. Riley lifted a stainless-steel tray from the innards of an ancient-looking machine with cogs and bursts of escaping steam that reminded her of the hiss and clatter of old trains. She craned her head to see over his shoulder. As the mist cleared, Brooklyn could see three orbs, each a bit larger than a marble. One gleamed a mixture of pink and silver like the inside of a seashell, another contained shifting hues of blue ranging from the color of the sunlit sea to the lightest flecks of a robin's egg, and the last made a perfect contrast to the others, a green so dark and deep it verged on blackness. Brooklyn's eyes widened. "How did you choose the colors?"

"I didn't. No two spheres are ever the same. The colors seem to develop randomly, though Kurt believes there is something spiritual about it."

"And you don't?" she asked without taking her eyes off the beautiful orbs.

He smiled. "I don't buy into all that mystical crap. Everything has a reasonable and logical explanation. Sometimes the connections are beyond our understanding. My best guess is that the coloration is a byproduct of undetectable contaminants in the spinal fluid, a speck of dust even."

"Can I?" She reached toward the gleaming trio.

"Not"—he closed his fingers firmly around her wrist—"with your hands. They are still very hot."

Brooklyn nodded and Riley released her. Tentatively she stretched out her mind, exploring with a sense that buzzed at the back of her skull like a cross between hearing and touching. Brooklyn found them as easily as she might locate her own toes. As she prepared her focus to lift them, they seemed to rise of their own accord. Almost before the thought had formed, they began to orbit one another, anticipating her desire. A smile of elation spread across her face.

"Now I'll try to wrestle them away from you," Riley said, taking a few steps back. Brooklyn braced for a struggle. The spheres continued a lazy orbit and then she felt the resistance. It was slight, like cobwebs, present, but insubstantial. The fingers of a ghost. Riley frowned. "I never realized how annoying that is from this side."

With a thought, Brooklyn brought the green one to a standstill and set the other two into a whirring chase around it.

"What are they called? Does this type of weapon have a name?"

"Balls," he replied.

"Balls?"

"Yes," he deadpanned, "every time Kurt rushes out on some mission or other, I have to remind him to take his balls."

Brooklyn was trying to formulate a snappy retort when a red strobe flashed, accompanied by a faint buzzing sound. "What's that?" she asked, letting her new weapons settle gently back into the steel tray.

"A phone call. See if those have cooled enough to carry." He darted into the bedroom and closed the door. Brooklyn touched the glassy surface of each one. They were hot to the touch, but not unbearably so. Gingerly, she placed them into the pocket of her jeans.

When Riley returned, he had her jacket in his hands. He tossed it to her and removed his own from a hook near the door. "What's going on?" Brooklyn asked.

"You and I have to handle something in town." He bustled around the lab, shutting down equipment and blowing out candles. In a flash, he was out the door calling, "Come on," over his shoulder. "And bring your balls."

Brooklyn rolled her eyes and hurried to catch up.

"Mary!" Kurt's heart leapt. He rushed forward and wrapped his arms around her. She felt as real as she looked. The familiar smell of her shampoo summoned a flood of memories. His eyes stung with tears, and he didn't try to stop them. For the first time in a very long time, Kurt was happy. "I don't understand. It's you, it's really you! But how?"

"There will be time to explain later, but right now the sun is rising and we still have work to do. How many more do you need to pay the debt?"

Kurt checked his notes. "About eighteen more."

"There isn't time to do it individually; summon them all at once."

"I can't control that many; that would be—"

"Suicide?" she asked. "I think not. You've only scratched the surface. With that ring on your finger, you can move worlds." Mary knelt in the leaves, flipping quickly through the pages of the summoning book. Arriving at a blank page, she pricked her finger with an earring and drew a strange twining symbol on the page. "Here, use this." She thrust the book into his hands.

"What does this say? Many and one?"

"Legion." Her voice caressed the word in a way that stirred something inside Kurt. "It says Legion." He nodded, drawing one of the Celtic traps from his pocket. "That will not hold Legion." She rested her hand on his. "These are mere replicas. Where is the original?"

"It's in use already." He scrounged it from another pocket. "I have a Warden bound; I can't—"

"Sever the connection," she insisted. "Our time is almost up. Do it for our son, for Tyler."

"For Tyler," Kurt agreed. Belial had retrieved the Tome, after all. The agreement had been fulfilled. Neither had any obligation to the other now. Kurt's mind whirled with unanswered questions, but the horizon lightened with every passing second. There simply wasn't enough time. He severed the connection, casting Belial adrift. Then he turned his mind to the strange symbol in the book. He let the twisting, writhing lines come alive in his mind and brought the power of Solomon's ring to bear.

It was harder than the others, but determination and the power of the ring brought it through. Legion was monstrous and scaled with as many heads as a Hydra. Maintaining control of so many at once was nearly impossible. Kurt's legs trembled with exhaustion, and black spots swam across his vision. Belatedly, he realized that he should have brought food. He needed energy. Raising the Celtic talisman was like lifting a bucket of lead.

Legion was slipping through his fingers like sand. Splitting itself into more and more pieces. Those that wriggled free swarmed about the clearing like angry bees. When Kurt tried to corral them back to the larger whole, more escaped. He couldn't focus on both tasks at once. *Mary! Where is Mary?* The thought sent a jolt of adrenaline and fear through him. Kurt lost his hold on Legion entirely as he whirled around and around calling Mary's name.

28

Water over the Levee

The morning sun hit Brooklyn like a slap. Her eyes watered and forced her to turn away. “Thought it was late evening,” she mumbled grumpily, realizing just how much time had passed since she last slept. The corners of Riley’s mouth quirked up in response. He seemed to experience none of the disorientation or fatiguc that she suffered as he wheeled them free of the underground garage with practiced deftness. *When does he sleep?* Brooklyn wondered. *Does he sleep at all?*

“Our contact with the police called for Kurt, but since Kurt is indisposed”—he turned a roguish smile in her direction—“they will have to settle for us.” His smile was infectious, transparent like a child’s. The kind of honest smile that seemed never to have been used as a tool for manipulation or deception.

“I imagine we will be an improvement over what they were expecting.”

“There is a lot of awesomeness in this car,” he agreed cheerfully. Brooklyn slid her fingers into her jeans pocket. The three orbs were there, a warm reassurance. To her fingers, they felt the same, but to her mind, each was unique and identifiable. “This could be a little unsettling. If you want to stay in the car, that might be best.”

“No, I want to help. I need to learn my way around this world if I’m going to be a part of it.”

Riley nodded. “You still miss your family, don’t you?”

Brooklyn felt a pang of guilt. She hadn't been thinking about her family at all, actually. She thought about them every day, but somehow it seemed distant. They may as well have been separated by centuries or vast distances or oceans. They couldn't understand all of this. She wasn't certain she understood it herself. Instead of answering, she asked a question of her own. "Do you have a family?" She had only ever heard him talk about Kurt.

"Not really." He shrugged. "Parents died when I was young. Mary—that's my older sister—and Kurt took me in. After she died, he raised me. Now it's just the two of us."

"And your sister? What happened to her?"

Riley looked out the window away from her, feigning interest in a field of cattle. He looked for so long that she thought he hadn't heard or simply wouldn't answer. When he finally spoke, his voice had grown strangely flat and detached. "She was murdered."

Belial felt Kurt cut their connection a moment before the familiar fingers of the Pull clawed at him. It was—had always been—nearly impossible to fight the Pull, so for most it was a waste to try. As he began to cross dimensions, Azrael's inky aura fell away, and she shone like a star. She shouted something, but he had passed beyond the realm of hearing now. Still, her words rose and fluttered like golden birds from her lips. Her lips kept moving, forming the same words over and over. She wanted to tell him something, but soon the room faded from view. He drifted, and the world shrank away from him as wholly as Brooklyn had.

Part of him realized he would likely never see her again. Her grandchildren might be old before he clawed his way topside. If only he could have told her why he ruined her quaint little life. Explain how she had flared up like a beacon, the brightest he'd ever seen, in a moment of desperation just like this one. He approached the apex. Just before the last of the material world slipped from his vision, the Earth burst into brightness. Every soul, every spirit, every demon a pinprick of light in the vast darkness. If he tried, he might have distinguished Brooklyn from the others, but he did not. She deserved what peace she could find now. And surely she had been trained enough to hide herself by now.

Hell resolved itself into the familiar arid landscape of ruined structures and razor rocks around the same pitiless nucleus. Something was different. The Melody of Hell, the endless cacophony of screams and wails and wild roaring, had changed. In place of the screams, he heard shouts, cheering, and wild, frantic laughter. It seemed as if all the legions of Hell had gathered. They amassed around a shimmer in the air that rose and wavered like a plume of gasoline fumes. As he fell closer, he could see through the distortion as if it were a window. He saw a sun rising over blue mountains, then a great expanse of stormy sea, a city, an endless kaleidoscope of earthly vistas. Similar columns dotted the plains. Dozens of them, tattered holes in the veil.

Those closest to the breach in the barrier between the worlds jockeyed for position, diving into it again and again, but not passing through, only landing in disgruntled heaps on the other side of the mirage, where they were kicked and clawed with disdain. *How weak has the Pull become?* Belial wondered. With an effort of will, he began to rise back the way he'd come. It was not easy, but it could be done; the Pull verged on collapse, but even as he rose, he sensed it recovering, knitting itself back together like a living thing. Across the plains beneath him there were other openings with demons, old gods, spirits, and creatures gathered like hyenas around fresh meat. A sudden series of wails drew his eyes. In the distance, one portal had winked out in a flash of light. As he watched, another closed. Each time one of them vanished, the effort of rising grew harder.

Belial gathered his will and pushed ahead with all his might. His wings spread and beat furiously, but as the windows slowly flickered into nothingness, he lost altitude. He hovered above one of the last of the portals where demons sliced one another to shreds just to reach the edge of it or to hold their place nearby. Belial drifted toward this chaos, toward the snapping jaws and venom and pain.

He flapped harder as he drew near those others with wings who were engaged in a fierce battle just above the throng of ground-bound demons, some of whom looked up with naked envy. It was little use. The fall between worlds was notoriously taxing, and his energy failed him. Belial folded his wings tightly and surrendered to the Pull, plummeting like a meteor toward the ravenous hoard below.

Brooklyn stood with Riley and Officer Santimo in the ruins of the local hardware store. Officer Santimo, who towered over both of them, explained that they had ten minutes before he had to call it in. Brooklyn and Riley entered the building while Santimo stayed outside to assure any early morning passersby that all was well in hand.

Inside they found a smoldering circle in the floor, fifteen meters in diameter according to Riley, and on the ceiling was its twin. As if a cylinder of fire had shot out of the earth and been instantly extinguished. Water cascaded down from neatly severed pipes. The store was filled with a haze of bluish smoke that smelled strongly of ammonia. *What happened here?* Brooklyn wondered, but didn't ask.

While Riley scrutinized the perimeter of the scorched floor, Brooklyn picked her way gingerly away from the epicenter, carefully navigating the overturned displays and splintered flooring toward the smoky and dimly lit back half of the store. The air grew steadily cooler. Near the back, she found an overturned worktable and a mound of tools. Brooklyn rummaged around, sending a pile of razor-tipped arrows cascading from the mound.

In the far back, beyond a steel support beam with a fire extinguisher mounted on it, a set of wrought iron spiral stairs wound upward. Brooklyn trailed her hand over the well-worn railing as she climbed. Each step sent an unsettling tremor through the ancient stairway. The summit revealed a sea of clothing racks packed with denim pants, flannel shirts, hunting coats, and overalls. It was the sort of place her dad would shop. She patted the orbs in her pocket to be sure they were still there.

A chill wind gusted through the open roof. Brooklyn pulled a blue-and-black jacket off a rack and slipped it on, ripping the tags off as she went. She felt a twinge of guilt for stealing. She imagined she could hear her mom's disapproval from a few hundred miles away. Brooklyn had stolen a candy bar from the grocery store at age four and gotten caught trying to open it in the car. She still remembered the shame of being dragged back inside to apologize to the cashier. The thought brought a wistful smile; it had seemed like a very big deal to a four-year-old.

Brooklyn approached the center of the room carefully. The singed and smoking hole from downstairs was mirrored in the floor here and in the roof above. The flooring around the perimeter was splintered and crumbling. She stood motionless; there were voices from below, muffled but intelligible.

"Many of us . . . Help us . . . Not one of them," said a strained voice in a series of gasps.

"How many came through?" Riley's voice rose through the floor clearly.

"Many rifts . . . Hundreds, maybe . . . Help us."

"I will not help you," Riley replied coolly. "I am of this world now and will not jeopardize it."

"Coward and traitor!" the voice roared.

Riley ignored the outburst. "Who worked the summoning?"

Brooklyn inched around the circle until she could see them below her. Riley crouched on the opposite side from her and looked down at a creature with a face wreathed in squirming tentacles. The lower half of its body had been neatly severed by whatever had blasted the hole in the floor. It laughed wetly. "Don't answer for traitors." It sagged backward with the effort of speaking, and its unfathomable black eyes met hers. Brooklyn thought she saw something like shock cross its face just before it spoke. "Well, well, the Warden's bitch."

Riley spoke without looking up, his eyes on the demon. "I take it you've met?"

It ignored Riley. "Remember me, you little whore? I'll be back for you when I'm whole again. Gut you . . . " It flexed its slimy fingers, and wicked black claws unfolded like switchblades.

Brooklyn remembered then the house of blood, and the people, all the possessed people, and a glimpse of each demon being whisked away as its host died. Something icy stirred in the pit of her stomach at the memory. Her voice came out low and dangerous. "We want an answer." The orbs clicked like tumblers in a lock as they moved restlessly in her pocket. *No*, she thought, *they aren't the right tool for this*. A large hunting knife rose from the shattered remains of a glass display and slipped itself snugly into her palm. They both looked at her in wordless shock as she stepped off the edge, turned expertly in midair, and landed lightly in front of the squirming creature. "We will have an answer."

"Nobody summoned me. Passages opened and some of us came through on our own."

The knife whipped across its face again and again in a flurry, opening deep gashes in its gelatinous flesh. "Give. Us. A. Name," she growled, punctuating each word with a savage cut.

"I will tell you what I know because I pity you, because you are a broken thing, infected with the Warden's thoughts. You speak his words and raise your hand like a puppet on a string. When he comes back to you, you will open for him. Whore. You are lost."

"Yeah, yeah, can you get on with it?" Brooklyn insisted with the knife raised threateningly.

The creature gave her a contemptuous look, deigning to speak only when the last of the cuts had sealed shut with a disgusting sucking sound. "A Legion was summoned from Hell. A short time later, the rifts opened."

"Do you know who did this or not?" Riley interrupted.

"Only the Ring of Solomon could compel so many."

Brooklyn could see Riley's mind whirring like clockwork. "Oh hell," he said softly. "We have to go now!" He stepped forward and pressed his palm against the gelatinous head of the creature. It screeched like his touch burned, and then it was ethereal, whole again, and drifting. When it was gone, Riley turned to her again. His voice shook when he spoke. "We have to find Kurt."

"You think he knows who is behind this?"

Riley nodded. "I'm afraid he might."

29

Falling Short

The impact Belial expected never came. Instead of scorched earth and claws, something plucked him from the air. When he opened his eyes, he saw the demons below cowering, scurrying for cover, scattering like mice before a hawk.

Twist and turn as he might. He could not see what had him, only the scorched landscape rushing below. His wings and their many eyes were pinned firmly against his back. They passed over a river of molten lava and turned, following it upstream. The heat and fumes were overwhelming. They spiraled through a narrow canyon without slowing. One of Belial's dangling legs smacked against an outcrop of rock and drew an agonized yelp. His captor's only response was to squeeze him tighter in the iron talons that encircled him.

He drifted in and out of wakefulness, not that his kind needed sleep, but struggling against the fall had left him depleted and the trip seemed to go on forever, an endless series of rises and dips. Time had lost all meaning when the most unexpected thing woke him: a breath of chill air. They were weaving amid the snow-capped peaks of strange barren mountains toward what appeared to be a long-dead volcano. They ascended steeply and followed the contours of the volcano until, at last, impossibly high, they broke the top, climbed higher, and flipped backward in a maneuver that made Belial squirm in panic. The world tilted sickeningly on its axis for a long moment, Belial thought fleetingly of Tais that day beside the sea, snatched away by an unstoppable force, and then they plunged headfirst into the darkness below.

The talons, which had banded his body into immobility for the last several hours, were gone. Half a thought formed regarding his own wings but was cut short by a bone-rattling impact. He tumbled blindly down a steep incline, bounced twice, and came to rest on his back. He looked up and saw the silhouette of his captor drifting down in languid circles. Belial's thoughts leapt from question to question. Where was he? Certainly not Hell. What had snatched him from the jaws of death? Why?

His captor landed silently beyond sight and reach. "Who are you?" he called out in the oldest language he knew. Sometimes old words still held power, but no answer came.

Belial spread his wings and launched himself upward. He climbed furiously toward the opening above. Just audible over the windy rush of his efforts, he heard the rasp of scales. An orange glow climbed the walls all around him. He dipped hard to one side and sheltered on a small platform as a ball of fire rolled past and disappeared out the opening above. The projectile's passing left him badly singed. Belial looked over the tiny ledge he clung to and saw nothing below but darkness. The air, now acrid and sulfurous, burned his insides. He leapt into the air, shifting into hawk form as he went. Perhaps a smaller target would go unnoticed.

He flapped with fury. The rim and the stars beyond loomed large. The walls danced with orange light again. Belial spiraled evasively, but the flames raced past him with room to spare and slammed into the walls above. *Must be hard to hit something as small as a hawk*, he thought with jubilation, but the thought was short lived. Debris rained down from the impact above, pelting him like hail. A softball-sized chunk of ice struck his wing, breaking it like a twig. It folded involuntarily and sent him spinning downward. His concentration ebbed, and he shifted back to his true form. Belial spread four unharmed wings, but they only served to lessen the impact.

"Who are you?" He repeated the inquiry with a groan. Small delicately taloned feet appeared just before his face.

Then his captor spoke in a familiar voice, one he had expected to never hear again. "I am."

Kurt awoke with the sunlight warm on his face and familiar fingers in his hair. It was a dream he knew, and so he delayed opening his eyes for as long as possible, relishing the moment. The morning sounds were summer sounds: birds chirping, the thrum of carpenter bees, and cicadas singing. Kurt felt warm and relaxed, but he knew it was well into winter and that cicadas rarely sang in the morning. With that acknowledgment, ice raced through his limbs and fingers and toes. The sounds of summer fell away, but the fingers in his hair remained.

"Are you okay?" The voice, laced with concern, was Mary's.

Kurt opened his eyes. She was above him, sitting with his head cradled in her lap. Her breath turned to mist in the early morning air. Her hands slid down to his cheeks, and he placed his over hers. The ring pulsed hotly against his finger like a second heartbeat. Kurt ignored it. Mary was real. This part was no dream. He felt a smile spread across his face, and his eyes blurred with tears. All these years and she was back, somehow. "How is this possible?" He reached up to touch her cheek, and she pulled away.

"It's been a long time," Mary offered with a shrug. "I took care of this for you." She dropped the intricate golden talisman onto his chest. "They are in there, all of them."

He slipped it into his shirt pocket and sat up. The clearing seemed to darken and spin for a moment, but then it passed. The air still thrummed faintly with hellish power. "Too much has happened here. We need to head home. I need food and you—"

"I like it here," Mary interrupted softly. Her eyes were lit with wonder, as if she'd never seen trees before. "We should stay here," she went on absently.

"You hate camping."

"Yes, but it's been so long; I'm not sure I'm ready to go back just yet."

They stood, and he moved up behind her, touching her shoulders softly. "Mary, where have you been? What do you remember?"

"Trapped inside that ring for so long. You released me, accidentally."

Kurt was dumbfounded. It didn't make sense. Nothing seemed to add up anymore.

"You have the ring now," Mary went on earnestly. "You can't give it back to him. You can't. He is a bad person, kept us apart, wrecked our family."

"Why would Alexander do that?" Kurt's thoughts were molasses. His head throbbed and sweat trickled icily down his spine.

"He was afraid of losing you. A Protector with a family, it's uncommon. He knew I wanted you to step down and he could not afford to lose you." She ran her fingers lightly over the bark of a pine tree. "Tyler fought so bravely to protect me. He had to," she said as she turned back to face Kurt, "because you weren't there when we needed you."

Her voice was petulant and sad, but her eyes seemed to dance with mirth. Kurt winced. "Mary, I'm sorry, if I had it to do over—"

"But you do, don't you?" She turned her back on him again. "You have the ring, you have me, and soon we will have our son again."

Kurt sat back down heavily. "Of course, I'll quit as soon as we have Tyler back. We can all go away together. Maybe somewhere warm?"

She moved to sit beside him. Her hand lay across his; the ring still pulsed insistently. "I don't want you to quit," she said softly. "I want *us* to rule."

The machines began to blare shrilly as Azrael withdrew her hand. The freed soul of Alexander Stewarth fluttered brightly in an invisible breeze and was swept away. Kurt had never returned. Things were not going as planned; she hated it when things didn't go as planned.

The room rapidly became overcrowded with medical staff trying to undo her work. She watched them charge the paddles and force his heart to beat. The other machine inflated and deflated his lungs like meaty balloons. It was all so perverse. These creatures were so mired in the physical world they could not fathom that life did not come from it.

"He's dead," she said. Nobody heard her, of course. *Apes with tools trying to fix a broken machine*, she thought angrily as they continued their ministries. The rage came then, shocking her with its force. Sparks showered from the monitors, and the fluorescent bulbs gave up their lives with soft pops and exhalations. The room was silent. Azrael stood nose to nose with the doctor, the paddles still clutched in his hands. "He's dead," she breathed softly. For a moment, the doctor seemed to hear her, maybe even to see her. "All of you are." She spread her wings and vanished.

Every time the death rate spiked even a little, it felt like being pulled apart again. She had a lot of things to do and very little time left to do them. Once there had been hundreds of paths that led to her goal; now there remained but two distinct series of events that led to victory and an infinite number that led to the final death. No middle ground.

Not for the first time, she wondered if Kurt Levin was a mistake. He had done nothing but fail. Failed to meet his quota again and again, failed to keep the girl safe, failed even to return the ring before the Heir died. Azrael wished she had the luxury of disposing of Kurt and starting again with someone new, but time was stacked against her now.

Kurt's office sat empty, but she could tell he'd left in haste. Azrael did not know where to look, and couldn't afford to wait for him. Perhaps he had banished Belial in order to sever all connections with her. But, no, she still held the secret of his child's whereabouts. Hastily, Azrael scribbled a note for Kurt to contact her. She did not sign it, but instead plucked a single black feather from her plumage and laid it gently across the words. Kurt would know what to do.

Azrael had to find a prophet for the next part of the plan. She thought back to the before-times, to the generations of priestesses who worshiped and served her when she had been a goddess of life rather than a slave of death. Some of that lineage still existed, but the connection had long ago withered. Hers had been a gentle people, it wouldn't be right to ask the next task of their children. They deserved better than that. Azrael had two candidates in mind, but which to choose? The killer or the broken boy?

She visited the killer. His was a familiar face. She watched him torment girl number fifty-one. His smile was a fragile thing, trembling lips stretched like worms across perfect teeth. He traced the blade across her flesh with practiced grace. A violinist drawing a bow across the strings. He fancied himself an artist, she knew. The girl barely reacted. She was near death, but he would not kill her yet. In that way, he was like the doctor from the hospital. Cultured barbarians. Her prophet needed respect for both life and death.

"We have weeks left together," the killer whispered into the girl's ear. His words seemed a greater torment than his blade. "Don't go to sleep just yet. The night is young." He slapped her face playfully.

Azrael frowned, remembering what she had said to Donald when he had asked why she let this killer live. *I am the God of Death, not the God of Murder.* Maybe gods were defined more by what they didn't do than what they did. Maybe murderers needed gods, too. She reached out with a single slender finger and brushed the man between his eyes. He gasped and stumbled back several steps; the bloody knife clattered to the floor.

"What are—"

"I wanted you to see me." She matched his retreating steps.

"Why?"

"Don't you like them to see you?" She gestured in the direction of the girl bound to the table behind them.

Slow understanding dawned on his face, and then he laughed mirthfully. The girl whimpered in response. "I'm not afraid of you," he spat venomously.

Azrael knelt to retrieve the fallen knife. "Fortunately"—she erased the distance between them—"fear is not a prerequisite for me." The knife slid neatly between his ribs and into the paneling behind him. Arterial blood gushed from the wound and dribbled from his wormy lips. He never stopped smiling.

The girl's belly and breasts were a road map of red. Azrael gently brushed the brown hair back from her sweaty forehead. "We all make sacrifices," she said to nobody in particular. The girl moaned weakly. Life still pulsed inside her, frantic and hopeful. Azrael leaned forward and kissed away the light.

She left the bodies for some mortal to find and piece together an explanation. Azrael paused in front of a hanging mirror to inspect herself. Her face was young and perfect again. The fissures had closed, but some part of her wanted them back. They represented strength and restraint. She touched her skin so her fingers could confirm the smoothness her eyes saw. Azrael had expected something different, a wart, a crimson streak in her hair, bat wings, maybe even horns, something ugly to signify her failure. Instead, she was cold and porcelain perfect. There was no going back now. Some things could not be undone. For the first time she felt the subtle tug of the Pull urging her from this world to the next. "We all make sacrifices," she said again to the lifeless girl.

30

Tracing Scars

"You want to tell me what that was back there?" Riley asked as he slid the car through a curve with inhuman precision.

"Why don't you slow down?" Brooklyn clutched the grab handle as they sailed through another curve with the tires shrieking in protest.

Riley looked at her and then nodded, slowing enough for the knot in her stomach to loosen. "That wasn't you back there. The acrobatics. The violence. Where did that come from?" He shrugged. "Didn't feel like you."

"You don't know me. You don't know anything about me."

"You're right. I don't," he said softly.

More rage and anger bubbled up like acid in her throat. She closed her eyes and focused on breathing deeply. "I'm sorry," she said when the anger receded. "That demon, I recognized it. Belial tortured it when we were, you know."

Riley nodded slightly.

They rode in silence until Kurt's mansion loomed like a solitary tooth grown from the earth.

"I don't know how I did those things at the hardware store." Brooklyn looked out the window, away from him. "It just happened like instinct."

Riley put his hand on her forearm. "We'll figure it out. But first, let's get some food."

She smiled. Food sounded good.

The dining room was empty when they arrived. Most of the others had eaten hours ago. Riley brought them each a plate from the kitchen piled high with bacon, eggs, pancakes, and fresh fruit. Brooklyn's stomach rumbled; she was hungrier than she'd realized.

"That's a lot of food," she commented as the Styrofoam plate sagged under the weight.

"We burn more calories than normal people. Haven't you been reading the book I gave you?"

Brooklyn thought guiltily of the dictionary-sized tome under her bed about the history of this new world she'd fallen into. "Not much," she admitted between bites. "I've been busy."

"Well, on the best of days, we use more energy than normal people, and many times more when we exert ourselves mentally. Be careful."

Brooklyn nodded in agreement. "So, what's the plan? Do you have any idea where to look for Kurt?"

"Not really, but I think we can assume some proximity to the breach this morning and the house. If we can pinpoint other breaches on a map, we can assume the summoning occurred roughly in the center. The thing is, Kurt was out of town on Protector business, so it doesn't make sense—"

"That demon said only the Ring of Solomon could have summoned so many. Do you think Kurt was trying to stop Stewarth? Or maybe his son?"

Riley put his fork down and looked at her. "Alexander Stewarth is dying. He called Kurt to his bedside to guard the ring until his passing. Stewarth believed someone was poisoning him. He went crazy, grew suspicious of everyone around him. There are rumors he had his personal guards put to death shortly before sending for Kurt and falling into a coma."

"You think Kurt stole it?" Brooklyn asked in a hushed voice.

"It's a capital *C* capital offense," Riley said, "but you are alive because of Kurt's actions as am I; he deserves our loyalty and the benefit of the doubt."

"I remember that he saved me," Brooklyn said, taken aback. "I wasn't suggesting we turn him in or anything." She drained her cup of juice. "Why would he want to summon demons? He hates demons."

Riley shrugged. "If we find him, you can ask him. Let's head back to the lab and see if we can triangulate a search area."

Brooklyn scoured local news stations for strange happenings while Riley placed calls to contacts in several surrounding counties. While he worked the phone, her mind wandered back to the hardware store and the demon's taunts. Was it right? Was she dancing on puppet strings? Where had the calm coldness come from? How had she moved with such precision? Despite her assurances to Riley that nothing was wrong, questions unspooled endlessly in her mind.

Absently, Brooklyn drew the orbs from her pocket and willed them into intricate orbits around her outstretched hand but didn't watch them. She didn't need to look at them to sense their position any more than she needed to look down to see the position of her foot. *If only I'd had these at the cornfield, David would be alive.* Brooklyn felt weary. Riley was at his workbench, engaged in deep conversation. She went to the bedroom and flopped down on the mattress with her legs hanging off the side.

Brooklyn awoke with a shiver. Vaguely uneasy from dreams she couldn't remember. The room was dark; someone, Riley, had removed her shoes. She called his name softly, but he didn't answer. Brooklyn padded silently into the lab. It, too, was empty. Riley had not left a note. That meant that he thought he would be back before she woke. Her eyes came to rest on the massive Tome in the fireplace. It seemed to push her away, exuding malice almost palpably. Brooklyn set her chin stubbornly and resisted the instinct to flee. Step by step, she forced herself to approach it. The hair on the back of her neck prickled. She held her breath and pressed her palm against the open page. It was hot to the touch, like fevered flesh. It was *alive*. Brooklyn jerked her hand back and fled the lab.

She wandered up several flights of stairs and down a maze of hallways, nodding to the few people she passed. Nobody seemed to pay her any mind, as if a woman with tangled hair and no shoes were a common sight these days.

The next hallway switched from ultramodern and sterile to antiquated and rustic. Wooden tables with embroidered doilies, elaborate unlit candelabras, and vases of freshly cut flowers were spaced at intervals. Ornate silver fixtures curled like teardrops from the walls and cast a warm glow in sharp contrast with the cold fluorescent lighting from the previous hallways. This new passage ended at a wooden door with a polished brass handle.

Brooklyn pushed it open to reveal a massive office containing a sofa and fireplace. A large mahogany desk gleamed like a museum showpiece, but there were great gashes in the top of it. There were several glasses and a bottle of bourbon, neatly arranged on a towel. She moved around the desk and sat. The chair was of a supple leather that cradled her exquisitely.

Somehow, Brooklyn intuited this was Kurt's office even before her eyes drifted to the framed family photograph on the desk. She picked it up. Kurt had his arm around his wife and his son on his lap. He looked like a different person, not because he had been so much younger, but because he smiled in a way she had never seen him smile before. In fact, Brooklyn was not entirely certain she had ever seen him smile, not really. Beside the picture was a black feather across a hastily scribbled note. It read: Contact me immediately. The note had not been signed.

"So, this is where he spends his time," she said to herself. Something about Kurt fascinated her. Brooklyn experienced fleeting guilt for invading his privacy, but curiosity was always her weakness. She searched the desk drawers one by one, careful to leave everything as she found it. Even though Brooklyn figured Kurt was unlikely to catch her, her pulse quickened as she plundered.

Nothing remarkable caught her eye; though, something simple did. Stationery. A drawer with stamps, envelopes, expensive writing paper, and pens. Since coming here, she'd been given no real freedom. She didn't leave the estate by herself and had no access to phones or the internet, and writing a letter had never occurred to her until this very moment. Brooklyn drew a sheet from the drawer and uncapped a hefty metal pen and wrote:

Mom,

I'm not sure how to explain things to you or even where to begin. So much has happened since I left that I am not even sure I'm the me you remember. I want you to know that David found me. Please don't send anyone else. I am safe. Please forgive me for leaving and for not knowing how to explain.

She paused, the pen poised thoughtfully. What if she explained? Would that be so bad? Something like: "Dear Mom, I was recently possessed by an arctic demon and used as a part of his failed assassination plot against the ruler of a supernatural secret society. I avoided execution, but now I must remain here and train to use my new telekinetic powers." Brooklyn sighed. That sounded crazy to her, and she had lived it. She quickly scribbled the ending:

Don't worry about me. I'm so sorry for the pain I've caused. Please give Dad and Devin hugs for me.

Love Brooklyn

She folded it quickly before the tears could start, put on two stamps to be sure, and scrawled the familiar address. Brooklyn wondered belatedly how she might go about getting it into the mail. For now, she slid it carefully into her back pocket and crossed the room to the window that looked out on the back portion of the estate.

The mountains rose cold and dark behind the manor and tapered into ridges that ran like outspread arms to either side of the enormous house, poised to embrace. Below the window where Brooklyn stood, a lone hound looked up at her. He was a lone hound because of her, she reminded herself. The others had died in the fight at the cornfield, died protecting her, just like David.

Brooklyn traced a finger absently along the scar on her chest, a habit she had developed when lost in thought or worry. Kurt was out there. Brooklyn didn't know how she knew, but she was suddenly certain. Kurt would go to the mountain. He had trained her there, and the hidden tunnels she and David stumbled across couldn't be a mere coincidence. These mountains kept secrets. Kurt's secrets.

The hound stood as still as a palace guard with his eyes turned upward to her window. He could find Kurt. Brooklyn knew it. She turned from the window and her eyes settled on a pair of black leather shoes beside the hearth.

31

Finding Kurt

Water beaded invitingly between Mary's breasts. The steam from the hot tub floated in spiraling columns and condensed on the cool glass of the hotel mirror. Everything was right with the world. The heat soothed Kurt's aching muscles, and the pain seemed to float away with the steam, leaving him tired and delightfully drowsy, but he could not sleep. His finger throbbed like a toothache. No amount of relaxation could ease the pulsing discomfort. Mary must have noticed because her languid smile turned to one of concern.

"You aren't going to take it off, are you?"

Kurt smiled reassuringly, blocking the pain of the ring out. He imagined a wall rising in his mind between himself and the jolts that came slow and steady as a heartbeat. "Of course not." Kurt knew the prospect of the ring falling back into the Heir's hands frightened her. Mary had examined it on his finger after they arrived at the hotel with an expression of fascination and revulsion. He still hadn't worked out how a person could be captured within such an artifact, but that was a problem for later, a puzzle for Riley. For now, he only wanted to reconnect, to relish this miracle he never dreamed could be possible.

Mary seemed satisfied with his reassurances. Though her brow creased with concern. "Does it hurt much?"

"Some," he admitted. "Nothing I can't handle."

"I'm sorry," she said. "Turn around."

He turned, and she kneaded the knotted muscles in his back and shoulders. The ring pulse quickened and sent aching jolts through his wrist and elbow. In time with each pulse, and just for an instant, her fingers felt like thousands of insect legs skittering across his flesh. He shivered. "Don't be sorry," he breathed. "I'd endure anything in Heaven or Hell to be with you."

"I know," she said softly, and nibbled his ear. "I know."

Belial had known the voice even before the dragon girl stepped into the dim light. Prosidris wasn't here to save him now. "What do you want?" He edged his voice with indifference and hoped it didn't tremble too much.

"We want out," she said, turning her eyes upward where a sliver of moon shone through the opening above.

"You and me both," Belial grumbled, "so let's get out. Why drag me here if you don't want to be here?"

She considered him for a long time, looking so much like a child he could almost forget what she really was, then asked, "Would it upset you to learn that your father is dead?"

"Not at all," Belial replied smugly, and had the satisfaction of seeing her poise falter.

She drew herself upright and swirled her green cloak indignantly. "I am the youngest, the smallest, and the weakest. I am the only one that can cross from here to where we were. I was taken through the barrier very long ago when I was smaller still. My mother sacrificed herself to ensure my hatching. She arranged for me to be taken in and sheltered at the library. There I grew too large to return here. I was content to guard the Tomes for the rest of my life." She paused, her scaly face contorted by some inscrutable emotion. "Then you stole from me."

Heat radiated off her in agonizing waves, but Belial endured it. He held her gaze for a long minute. "I stole from the library, not from you."

"They kicked me out. I am homeless because of you . . . " She trailed off.

"I'm sorry," he said, and he meant it. When she didn't respond, he went on. "What do you want from me? I doubt you brought me all this way to kill me?"

"The eggs do not hatch here in the cold; the walls between the worlds are weakened, but the time is short." She gestured and flames rose along the walls, casting an eerie flickering around the cave. Dancing light gleamed on the eggs, dozens upon dozens, and behind them the walls seemed to writhe against the vanishing splash of heat.

Brooklyn slipped like a ghost from the manor and into the chilly evening air. Riley, to her knowledge, had not returned. Kurt's hound gave an eager whimper as she approached. "Good dog," she cooed as she lifted the latch. He padded out of the lot and she coaxed him closer, pressing the opening of Kurt's shoes under the dog's wet nose. "Find him," she whispered. "Find Kurt." He whined and tilted his head.

The massive dog circled the backyard, dragging Brooklyn along as she clung to his collar. In short order, he lurched forward toward the edge of the woods with such zeal that Brooklyn thought her arm might be ripped from her body. He bayed eagerly. Brooklyn felt the vibrations in her bones as the sound rose up and rolled across the fields and up the mountain, echoing and dying amid the trees.

The limbs in the tree line tore at her clothes and hair as she sprinted up the familiar trail. Within minutes, the air grew cold; she regretted her choice to wear such light clothing. Fading evening light shone through the bare tree limbs, making them forlorn, reaching. Brooklyn remembered the many camping trips she had taken in the mountains behind her own home and wondered if she would ever walk those familiar trails again. She thought of her family, as she often did in solitude, and wondered what her mother was doing even now, and her father, and little Devin. She thought of him most often and wondered how her absence affected the twice abandoned boy.

The ridge ahead sloped up sharply and seemed to bend back on itself, wrapping around a large boulder. The dog paused and whined uncertainly. Brooklyn thought maybe she should let him go, but feared once he found the scent again, she wouldn't be able to keep up. Though the sun still smoldered against the horizon, the first signs of night were beginning around her in the shadow of the mountain.

At last the dog gave a victorious bay and began to drag her again along the rim of the ridge and down the hollow on the other side.

Kurt was on his back when she found him, eyes open, lips moving soundlessly. He lay sprawled in a clearing, surrounded by strange artifacts, the ground swept bare of leaves in a large circle around him. Smoldering embers and a coil of smoke marked a recent fire. An old and tattered book lay in the dirt surrounded by vials of strange colored powders and various other instruments that she did not recognize. As she drew closer, Brooklyn released the dog, and he made a great show, sniffing and licking Kurt's hands and face. Kurt did not respond. Were it not for the moving of his lips, Brooklyn might have thought him dead. She lifted his hand to take his pulse and noticed one of Kurt's fingers had turned blue and purplish with an angry bruise. As she ran her fingers over the discoloration, Brooklyn felt the angry heat of infection. Unexpectedly, her fingers closed around an invisible ring.

"What is this?" Brooklyn said to herself. As if hearing her words, the hound came over and began to sniff and lick the swollen finger and Brooklyn's fingers as well. She pushed him away and grasped the ring firmly to pull it off. The flesh was too swollen for the ring to pass over his knuckle. She tried twice before giving up for fear of doing more damage. Kurt's other hand was closed into a tight fist, and a slender golden chain trailed from his palm. Brooklyn coaxed his fingers open to reveal a familiar Celtic pendant that Kurt had once pressed to her forehead to remove Belial from her mind. Gently, she closed his hand back around it.

Kurt's breath came in short, shallow exhalations. At the end of each breath there was a faint insectile buzzing, as if something were softly rattling inside his throat. Carefully, Brooklyn opened his jaws and peered inside his mouth. It was hard to see in the dim light, but there was something black and shiny protruding from his throat.

Suddenly, his eyes met hers, and his teeth snapped shut. Brooklyn yanked her hand back, narrowly avoiding being bitten. Kurt sat up, wild eyed, and shoved her away. "What are you doing here?" he asked. His voice retained the strange rattling quality.

"I was searching for you," she said. And then she added softly, "Riley is worried about you."

Kurt's eyes darted back and forth rapidly, as if he were reading words on an invisible page. "Where is Riley Martin?"

"Not sure where he is right now. When I woke, he was gone. He's working, I think. Earlier, portals were opened by someone; a number of demons came through."

"Yes, yes," Kurt rasped, waving a hand dismissively. "It is of no consequence. There are bigger things going on. Things you and Riley know nothing about."

Brooklyn could not shake the feeling that something was not quite right here. She could not put her finger on it, but it was something in the way Kurt spoke, the delay in his answers as if he were reading from cue cards. The way he had pushed her as if in that moment he had not known who she was. "Are you okay?" Brooklyn reached out to touch his swollen hand, but Kurt recoiled.

"I'm fine." He enunciated each word slowly, as if he didn't trust his tongue to form them properly. The hound was circling and sniffing Kurt. Not in the familiar way he had when they first entered the clearing, but in a standoffish kind of way, as if he were trying to identify something unfamiliar. Kurt took a step toward Brooklyn, reaching for her shoulder, and without warning the dog leapt between them, knocking Kurt backward. The hound took up a position in front of her with his hackles raised. A low, steady growl rolling from his throat. Kurt did not look alarmed, only surprised and a little perplexed.

Brooklyn squatted behind the dog, holding tightly to his collar more for security than as a restraint. Things were happening here beyond her understanding. She had only just begun to scratch the surface of the supernatural world, but something, some instinct deep in her guts, told her that what had happened here, and was still happening now, was very bad. "What have you done?"

"Complicated, you wouldn't understand." He rose, dusting himself off carefully. "And it's private. Nothing is wrong; no cause for concern."

"If there is nothing wrong, open your mouth. Let me look into your throat."

Kurt's eyes narrowed menacingly. "There's nothing in my throat."

With her eyes locked on Kurt, Brooklyn began to back away. First one step, then another, moving slowly down the hill away from him, dragging the dog with her. "We are leaving." She cast a quick glance over her shoulder to the edge of the clearing. "I'm going to get Riley; something is not right here."

"You need to stay with me." Kurt said it gently, but there was a steely threat behind the words. Brooklyn had been training with Riley since that night at the cornfield. After she ran away, Kurt refused to work with her directly. It seemed he could hardly stand the sight of her. So why would he care now if she stayed or if she went? Her training with Riley had been thrilling and extreme. Where Kurt coaxed her to levitate rocks, Riley had thrown rocks at her and challenged her not to be hit. Where Kurt had cautioned slow, steady progress, Riley had demanded results. So, an instant before a large limb would have slammed into the back of her head, Brooklyn rolled fluidly to the side and back to her feet.

Icy rage rolled up her spine as it had in the hardware store, but she also remembered the words of the demon. With an effort, she pushed it down, separated it from herself, and raised her arms to defend against Kurt's next attack.

As soon as Brooklyn released him, the hound dove for Kurt. Kurt sidestepped and snapped a contemptuous kick that sent the dog spinning away into a tree. Brooklyn heard a sickening thud, a crunch, and a yelp of agony. That's when she knew for certain Kurt was not in control anymore. Brooklyn had seen the way he doted on his hounds, and she had seen the way he grieved for the ones who had died at the cornfield, saving her. "Let me help you. Let Riley help. You are possessed, but I know you're in there. I know you can hear me, and I know you want my help. So, take control and let us help you."

He laughed. A sickening sound like the wings of a thousand angry bees. "He is not possessed," the thing inside Kurt clacked at her. And without further explanation, the clearing erupted around Brooklyn. A torrent of sticks, pine cones, and other debris hurled at her.

Brooklyn brought her will to bear, as Riley had taught her to do with tennis balls, then later with rocks and baseballs. Instinctively, it rose around her like a concave triangle, shunting aside most of the debris. Her mind went to the spheres nestled deep in her pocket, warm against her thigh. She could feel them there waiting and ready to be called up as easily as one of her own limbs, but they were weapons for killing and she did not want to kill Kurt.

"What are you?" Brooklyn spat at the thing.

"Wouldn't you like to know?" it buzzed mockingly, and without warning, a large limb struck Brooklyn behind the knees and sent her tumbling backward into the thicket below.

The limbs that raked the back of her neck drew blood. She was acutely aware of that one small fact as she struggled to right herself and gather her scattered defenses. From where Brooklyn lay, she could see beneath the scraggly limbs where the hound slumped against a tree, still breathing. Brooklyn's instinct to run—to disappear into the trees and find help—threatened to overwhelm her.

Brooklyn knew it was not practical—knew it to be risky, maybe even suicidal—but she would not leave without the dog. Too many had died for her protection already. Brooklyn rolled to her knees. Nothing seemed to be broken, but she was sure that if she had the luxury of living until tomorrow, she would be sore in the morning.

Brooklyn ran her fingers hastily over the nape of her neck. They came away bloody. She climbed upward, back toward the clearing, and the limbs in her path bent out of her way, moved by an unseen wedge of energy. As she entered the clearing, insects that should have already gone to ground for winter emerged. Flies, gnats, bees, mosquitoes, ants, and hundreds of others she couldn't name converged on the clearing. There were many things scattered around that she might use as nonlethal weapons against Kurt. But already the insects were bludgeoning themselves against her defenses, and she knew from experience that she did not have the skill to maintain her shields and launch an attack. Reluctantly she called the orbs from her pocket and set them to spinning in the familiar patterns and orbits that Riley had taught her. They moved with such blinding speed that they blurred into circles like the rings of exotic planets.

Kurt looked alarmed. Brooklyn was not quite sure when it started, but the whizzing sound of the orbs cutting through the air changed to something higher and almost musical. The insects that had been intent on devouring her flesh only moments before drifted away from the sound like smoke being blown away by the wind.

The hound, roused from unconsciousness by this strange music, rose heavily to its paws and then sank back down with a mournful howl. Brooklyn inched forward step by step until the fiercely orbiting spheres occupied all the free space between her and Kurt.

"I will kill him before I see him live like this," Brooklyn said, and she meant it. Kurt's eyes moved rapidly as the thing inside accessed everything he knew about her. "Release him now, and I will let you go," Brooklyn said. "If you make me kill him, I will find a way to kill you, too."

"He doesn't think you have the spine."

"The Kurt I know would not want to live his life being controlled by something else; the Kurt I know would rather die. Maybe you should check that part of his mind."

"Actually, he's quite content with the arrangement. Very happy."

Brooklyn remembered the field Belial had tried to create inside her mind, the idealized approximation of those she loved. She suspected Kurt was experiencing something like that right now. "Go," she said, a feeling of dead, calm certainty frosting her words. The thing looked at her for a long moment with some emotion worse than hatred playing across Kurt's features, and then his mouth fell open. Brooklyn's stomach turned as the most misshapen insect she had ever seen emerged wetly from Kurt's mouth. Innumerable multijointed legs, each tipped with a glistening stinger, sprouted from the shiny black carapace. Its faceted eyes were milky white. Gold and purple bands alternated up and down the length of its body, lending it an exotic and lethal look. Then, before her eyes, it became David.

32

Strange Partners

Brooklyn lurched backward, away from the David-thing. She knew it wasn't David, but his likeness tore at something inside her and when he spoke in that familiar voice, she thought she might come undone.

"Brooklyn." He said her name tenderly. There was none of that insectile buzzing she had heard in Kurt's voice. He reached out to cup her cheek; her name rolled from his tongue again, like a plea.

"Stay back," she commanded. The look of hurt on his face struck her like a spear in the stomach. The orbs lay in the leaves, forgotten. Behind David, Kurt was motionless, still breathing shallowly.

"You can be with me, with him. Everything can be perfect again. He doesn't have to be dead, not to you, anyway."

"Trade my life for an illusion, for a dream? Why would I do that?"

"It's not your life I want, just your body. You never have to think again, or worry, or feel cold, or sad. What I'm offering you is heaven. All experience is illusory. Why not choose happiness?"

She knew the offer was nothing but a dream. Unreal. But some part of her wondered how real it could feel. What life lay ahead of her now, anyway? Real was better than illusion, wasn't it? For how long? "It's not real." Her voice rose several octaves. "It's not real." Fear and desperate desire settled like lead in her chest.

"I can offer you so much more." David's voice had grown low and suggestive. "If you can imagine it, I can give it to you." As if to make his point, he suddenly shifted. One second David stood before her, and the next second it was Devin reaching up to be lifted into her arms. A moment later, her father touched her hair with calloused fingers. He looked much younger, the way she remembered him from childhood, before her sister left and he gave up. Then her mother appeared, with fewer wrinkles, standing a little straighter, smiling a little wider. The face of her sister urged her to step forward into open arms, but Brooklyn just stared, rooted in place by disbelief and a symphony of conflicting emotions. In the next second, it was David again stepping forward, and this time she didn't step back. She let him touch her on the face lightly, just the way he used to. She closed her eyes, savoring the familiar gesture.

When she opened them, the clearing had become sunlit and warm like spring. She no longer saw Kurt on the ground behind David or the hound struggling to rise. They were completely and utterly alone. He bent to kiss her, to brush his lips against hers. "Not. Real," she breathed against his cheek with regret before she shoved him away.

"You choose your reality," he hissed. "This"—he transformed into another version of David with milky worm-filled eyes, a bloody mouth, and sallow, rotting skin—"or this." He became David as she had always known him: strong, happy, and full of life.

"No," she said weakly, sinking to her knees in the leaves. She looked up at David as he was when he haunted her dreams. She looked past him where the people who were supposed to help her should have been. Instead, she found the spheres amid the leaves, as easily and naturally as finding her own toes. "I choose Hell if that's what's real." She sent the spheres spiraling through David, and then, mercifully, it wasn't David anymore. It was that large and disgusting insect that had climbed out of Kurt's mouth. It shrieked and cursed her as its insides spilled from a shattered carapace, and then it was gone in a flash of light. The afterimage burned in her eyes until she blinked, and the ghost fled.

Brooklyn lay down, breathing deeply, trying not to dissolve into hysterical laughter. Though shaky and lethargic, she knew she had to get Kurt home. The hound too. Brooklyn fumbled the orbs back into her pocket and struggled to her feet.

At once, and without warning, the largest raven she had ever seen swooped down near Kurt's injured hand. There was a wet popping sound followed by a gurgling scream, and then the raven flapped over her head, a bloody ring clutched in its claws. Brooklyn hurried over to Kurt. The flesh of his finger was badly mangled and bleeding, but the pain seemed to have brought him back to consciousness. On his chest was the same black feather she had seen on the desk in his office.

"Are you okay?" She slipped her shoulder under his arm to help him to his feet. He turned to her. They were nose to nose; he looked at her for a long time as if seeing her for the first time.

"I'm fine," he grunted gruffly. Together, they checked on the dog. He had a broken leg, and perhaps some broken ribs, but he wagged his tail and licked them both affectionately.

Kurt examined his mangled finger and then frantically searched his pockets, muttering to himself.

"It's gone." Brooklyn touched him gently on the arm. "It's gone." She scooped up the feather that had fallen from his chest and handed it to him. "A giant raven took the ring and flew away."

Kurt crumpled the feather in his fist and threw it into the trees with a shriek of outrage.

Belial eyed the dragonling. "What's in it for me? Besides not being incinerated and left to die here."

She considered the question thoughtfully. "I could give you the Tomes. They are written on dragon skin in dragon blood, bound in dragon scales. They are my birthright."

"What do I need with ancient histories I cannot read?"

"What do you want?" she countered softly.

"Can you bring back the dead?" he snapped.

"I cannot." She crossed her arms and looked more like a child than any other time he'd seen her.

"Then you have nothing I want," he said scornfully. He had known the answer before he asked, but some small part of him still hoped to see Tais again one day.

"There must be something, some trade we can make," she pleaded. "I have sacrificed myself to bring you here. I am too big now to go back beyond the barrier between our worlds. It is strengthened with every passing moment. You, on the other hand, will be drawn back to your side unless I take steps to keep you here. When you are drawn to the other side, you could take some eggs with you."

Belial thought about it. Some small part of him felt compelled to help, wanted to, even though it went against his principles. If she had not caught him as he fell, he would be dead now. There were three options as best he could figure. Option one: take the eggs and be drawn back into his own world. Option two: not take the eggs and still get drawn back into his own world. Or option three: remain imprisoned here in this dragon tomb. "Fine, I'll take the books. How will you get them for me?"

"I cannot bring back the dead. But if it can be done, the information is in the Tomes, probably the one you already possess."

"Are you saying—"

"I'm saying that many things are possible and I'm still young and I do not know all of them yet. Things are almost never what they appear. For example, this mountain is not a mountain. This is not a volcano, or a cave, or any natural geological formation.

"What is it then?" His stomach lurched as he noticed the rhythmic pulsing of the surrounding walls. So slow as to be all but undetectable.

"You are swaddled in the coils of the oldest remaining dragon. When we were banished here and left to freeze, the last dragon mother curled up and raised her wings like tents above us." She ran her eyes over the walls, teardrops glistening on her cheeks like lava. "Her dying fires keep us alive, keep the eggs warm, but not warm enough to hatch. And though she still breathes, her fires are dying."

"Fine," he said begrudgingly, "but I will only take them on one condition."

"What's that?" She wiped her eyes.

"Come with me."

Azrael stretched her wings and flew as she had not flown in centuries. And for the first time she could remember, as the wind blew across her face and lifted her skyward, she felt alive. Deliciously and wholly alive. From this height, she could see the fabled four rivers winding like snakes from the ocean.

She knelt before the gates and the guardians with their flaming swords and then walked into the garden where no man or demon could ever go. The snakes slithered over her bare feet as she walked toward the center, toward the massive stump of an ancient fruit tree. She let her wings carry her up to it. It was taller than she was and wide enough to lie down on. Even now the surface bore a hard blackened sheen where it had been sheared with a flaming sword. She placed the ring carefully on a bed of fig leaves. From here, the full splendor of the garden stretched before her, as beautiful and fertile as it had always been, beneath a moving carpet of serpents. She launched herself upward. Getting in was the hard part; getting out was easy.

33

New Friends

Belial and the dragonling quickly gathered as many eggs as they could carry, seven in total. Belial carried four and she three. They left the shelter of the mountain together. As they ascended into the icy expanse and desolation, it struck Belial how like his birthplace this was. Free of the mother dragon's coils, he could feel the Pull drawing him back toward the realm of his imprisonment. In the open spaces, the girl shifted into her true form. She was larger than he might have ever imagined, the size of a tractor trailer. Legends claimed the dragons never stopped growing. Looking back over his shoulder at the not-mountain, he could believe it. The trek back took less time, for the dragon girl because she didn't have to carry and restrain him, and for Belial because he was being tugged in that general direction anyway.

Once they had traveled a suitable distance, they landed on a large glacier, careful to keep the eggs protected from the icy air. When the dragon girl shifted back to her human form, she was shivering, and her lips and fingertips were blue.

Belial, who until just recently had very little firsthand experience with the Pull, was finding himself quite adept at wrestling with the mysterious force. "Take my hands."

She eyed him suspiciously, but after a moment, she nodded and took his hands. They nested the warm, pulsing eggs in the makeshift basket formed by their interlocked arms. Belial cupped his wings protectively around her frail body. The partially enclosed space gave shelter not only from the razor-edged wind but from the noise as well. For Belial, this part was simple; he was being drawn to the place they wanted to go, but for the dragon girl it was a great exertion and one she had never made on her own before.

The world around them dissolved into white nothingness, dense and suffocating. At once, Belial felt a tremendous pressure that threatened to rip his arms loose at the shoulder. He redoubled his effort to maintain his grasp on the girl's slender wrists. With every passing second, she grew heavier. He wondered if the warring of these mysterious forces might rip him apart. The Pull closed around him like iron. The force that drew the dragon girl back to her wintry prison clung just as tenaciously. Her face, Belial noticed, was twisted into a mask of anguish. The eggs rocked to and fro, jostled by the turbulence. And with every passing second, he was aware of the pressure increasing. The dragon girl slipped, and he dug his claws in, piercing her scaled wrist and the tender flesh beneath. She did not cry out, only bore it in silence.

Many of the escaped demons had failed to find hosts. As a result, they were falling back into Hell. Belial imagined he could feel each individual demon slamming into the sand and ash and the corresponding increase in the pressure on his arms and fingers. "I won't let go," he grunted with great effort. She only nodded in acknowledgment, her eyes squeezed shut.

Long moments passed until they found themselves in a place of stasis between the forces that warred to possess them. He had not, could not, have imagined it would be like this. He thought fleetingly of how diamonds form from coal when caught by chance in the jaws of earth-moving forces. That seemed somehow more appealing than being dismembered.

So slowly that he thought he might be imagining it, they began to move. It took him a moment, in this place where there was no up or down, to discern that they were drifting back toward her Hell rather than his. Her eyes widened as they moved faster.

"Promise me," she said, "promise me you'll take them somewhere warm."

"Don't let go!"

"Take the eggs to warmth."

"I cannot carry them all," he said in dismay.

"Some are better than none." She smiled serenely and let go.

The girl vanished along with several of the eggs, lost in the void between worlds. Belial scrambled to maintain his grasp on the ones he still had, of which there were only three. He cradled them close to his body. They seemed drawn after her as if caught up in the wake of her departure. Without her resistance, the Pull threw him like a stone from a slingshot, and the eggs, for all their transdimensional reluctance, went with him.

Brooklyn sank heavily into the leather chair across from Kurt. Fatigue threatened to overwhelm her. Kurt poured two glasses of dark-colored liquid. He tossed his own back in one gulp and slid the other across the desk toward her. She took it and made a similar gesture, but with much less elegance. It burned her throat like fire and sent her into a fit of coughing.

An appreciative smile played across the old man's lips, and his eyes danced with amusement. No sooner had she put the glass down than he refilled it. "The second always goes down smoother." Brooklyn took it and found that the first had indeed burned most of the feeling from her throat. The liquor settled in the pit of her stomach like hot coal and spread like wildfire through her cold veins. Kurt cleared his throat uncomfortably. "Now we are even. Scales balanced. I saved you; you saved me."

"I believe you owe me an explanation, at least," she said.

Kurt shrugged noncommittally. "My throat hurts like hell. Now is not the time for talking."

"Let me look at your hand," she said in a voice that brooked no argument. He held it out to her, and she took it. "My God," she whispered, "you should see someone. I know you have doctors here."

"Probably right," he rasped, as he gently freed his hand from hers.

"So, what was the fantasy? How did the demon seduce you?"

He raised his eyebrows in surprise. "How did you—"

"Once it was done with you, it tried me."

Kurt poured a fresh drink and swilled it thoughtfully, not offering Brooklyn a third. "My family," he said gruffly. "The one thing I would do anything for."

"Do you think I'll ever see *my* family again?" The question tumbled from Brooklyn's lips in a rush, freed by the drinks. Kurt reached out his uninjured hand and took hers. Her hand fit inside his like a child's. Small and soft, where his were calloused and hard. It reminded her of her father and how close they had once been. Brooklyn pulled back. A look of hurt flashed across Kurt's face, but he quickly hid it.

"I'm sorry, I didn't mean—" he began.

"No, it's not that; it's just—"

"You don't have to explain." He leaned back in his chair, rubbing his eyes tiredly. "I like to think so," he said at last.

"Think so what?"

"That you will see your family again."

Brooklyn felt hot, stupid tears stinging the backs of her eyes. She quickly changed the subject. "What was that thing?"

"Some parasite from the depths of Hell, maybe."

Brooklyn snatched the feather from his desk, which had thus far gone unnoticed. She held it up. "And what does this mean?"

"That I am less lucky than you. It means I may never see my family again."

"But isn't your family . . . " She trailed off, not sure how to phrase it.

The corners of Kurt's mouth quirked up in amusement at her discomfort. "'Dead' the word you're looking for?"

Brooklyn nodded.

"In a manner of speaking, yes."

How could someone be dead in a manner of speaking? Brooklyn's mind was spinning, putting the pieces together. "You are trying to bring them back?" Kurt said nothing, but he did not deny. "And you believe demons can do that for you?"

"It's never simple as that. There're not angels and demons; there're worlds upon worlds filled with spirits, of all kinds. Good spirits and bad spirits and spirits that, like us, are somewhere in between. Some have no affiliation at all. They are not so different from us.

Brooklyn ran her fingers through her hair in a gesture of agitation. "I don't understand."

"Think of them like animals. Do you consider a great white shark evil, or dolphins as good?" His amber eyes flashed in the soft light cast by his desk lamp. "Their world is not so different from ours. Power means more than morality in either place. So, the question would be, do I believe that there are things powerful enough to give me what I want?"

"Do you?" Brooklyn whispered, feeling like a dimwitted pupil.

"I do. And there is one entity that I know of who has some power over life and death."

Brooklyn's mind turned toward the raven that had swooped seemingly from nowhere and ripped the invisible ring from Kurt's finger and vanished. "Are we talking about Greek gods here?"

"No, we're talking about lost gods. Gods for whom no stories remain. Whose worshipers are extinct, and whose power is diminished by obscurity."

Brooklyn's mind was spinning. Summoning demons could not be good. But she considered Kurt to be a generally good person. He was not doing this for money or for power, but for his family. That seemed noble, something she would do herself in his shoes.

Brooklyn thought of him defending her at trial and fighting for her above the cornfield. She owed him a lot, and she cared nothing for the laws of this world or the man who ruled it. In the end, it wasn't much of a choice.

"If I can help you see your family again, I'm in. Just tell me what to do."

34

Moving Forward

Brooklyn retired to Riley's room, which in some ways she had come to regard as her own. It was certainly more bearable than the room she had shared with David, still littered with his belongings. Constant reminders.

She entered the bathroom and ran a brush through tangled hair. The scratches on the back of her neck had dried into a patchwork of crusty blood. She wanted a shower but needed to sleep more. Instead, she bathed herself with a warm cloth, gently massaging the scratches and cuts, wiping away the smears of dirt and blood. Brooklyn opened her shirt on the now familiar barbed-wire scars from her previous battle. She couldn't help but run her finger along the raised flesh, tracing it like a familiar route on a map. It snaked from her heart up between her breasts like a tangle of thorny roots. All in all, she had fared much better this time. Brooklyn met her own eyes in the mirror and hardly recognized the tired, pinch-faced woman staring back at her.

Brooklyn made her way to the bedroom, shedding soiled clothing as she went. She did not bother turning a light on, and had settled heavily onto the edge of the bed to remove her socks when she noticed Riley snoring softly beside her. *So, he does sleep*, she thought with amusement. It suddenly occurred to her that in all the days they had been down here, she had never faced the dilemma of sharing a bed with Riley. He had seemed not to sleep, but then why would he have a bed otherwise? Her thoughts turned guiltily to David and how he might feel about her climbing into bed with another man, but she reminded herself gently that David was dead. It was a long way back to her old room, a room full of unpleasant reminders. Besides, she was already undressed. Brooklyn pushed her trepidations aside and slid beneath the blankets. It was a big bed; they could each have a side. In moments, Brooklyn was asleep and dreaming.

In her dream, Brooklyn stood on a cliff overlooking the sea. The waters were black in the dim light, an old, crumbling lighthouse perched nearby. Colored orbs the size of boulders orbited above her head, forming a giant halo-crown. Atop the lighthouse, a tall, slim man leaned against the iron railing staring down at her, his face shrouded in shadow. There was something intimately familiar in the set of his shoulders and the way he inclined his head, but she could not place it. The dream dissolved.

Next, she found herself draped in crude clothing made from animal hides and squatting inside an igloo with raw flesh in her hands. Her jaws pumped rhythmically as she chewed the tough, stringy meat, with a tickle of blood running down her chin. Despite having no shoes, the cold did not seem to bother her. Brooklyn's stomach lurched as her hands brought the meat to her lips and she savagely ripped off another piece with her teeth. From outside there came a terrible screeching sound, somewhere between the squeal of an engine belt and the call of a predatory bird. She crawled through the opening and stood up, shielding her face against the icy winds. The air knifed through her makeshift clothing, and the swirl of snow made it impossible to locate the source of the sound. Though blanketed in gray and white, the landscape was familiar. She recognized the mountain looming up before her and the empty place beneath it where her home should have been.

In her next dream, she found herself in a lab strapped to a stainless-steel table. On the table beside her, a young black man struggled frantically against his restraints. She tried to call out to him, but she could not move or make a sound. A great shadow filled her vision as a beautiful woman with silky black hair came into view. The woman drew a knife and drove it into the man's chest with one fluid motion. She withdrew the knife and turned to Brooklyn, raising it high over her head. Every fiber of her being screamed for action, but she may as well have been a mannequin. The woman brought the knife down with practiced precision between Brooklyn's breasts. She could not even open her mouth to scream as the agony rolled over her. With each beat, she could feel her heart squeezing itself around the blade. Each breath brought white-hot agony, but she could not stop breathing.

Brooklyn sat up, gasping. She clawed at her chest where the pain had been but found only the familiar scar twining like barbed wire beneath her fingers. Beside her, Riley slept like the dead.

The next morning, Brooklyn, Riley, and Kurt took breakfast together in the dining room. Kurt and Brooklyn took turns relaying to Riley what had transpired the evening before. As they spoke, his eyes widened in surprise and then pride as Kurt described how Brooklyn had fought off the creature and saved him. When they got to the part about the ring, the mood became more somber.

"My God, what have you done?" Riley said.

"It wasn't my fault, not really." Kurt's voice was low and soothing, but Brooklyn detected a pleading quality to it. "I'm sure if we just explain—"

Riley laughed derisively. "Whose fault was it, then?" he asked, temper flaring. "Who broke the law? Who stole the Ring of Solomon and lost it?"

Brooklyn waited for Kurt to explode. He was the one she thought of as passionate and hot headed. She had never heard anyone speak to him like this before, and she had certainly never heard someone admonish him. Instead, Kurt shrugged and said, "I know. What do you want me to say?"

"Help me understand the situation," Brooklyn said. "I mean, on a scale of one to ten, how bad is it?"

Riley turned to her. "It's sort of like stealing a nuclear weapon and losing it."

"Ah." She bit her lip thoughtfully. "So, how do we fix this?"

Kurt, still suffering from a sore throat, spoke around a mouthful of oatmeal. "I'm hoping nobody knows it was me. No one saw me take the ring. And I certainly don't have it now."

"Yes, but this will be investigated. You were the last person with Stewarth before he died. Who do you think they are going to come looking for first?"

"I never intended to linger long after my task was complete." Kurt steepled his fingers. "I have the payment." He gave Riley a meaningful look.

"What payment? What are you two talking about?" Brooklyn said.

Both Riley and Kurt ignored her question. After a moment Riley said, "You have all of—"

"All of *it*," Kurt cut in.

Brooklyn made a frustrated sound. "You may as well tell me. I'm in this with you now."

Kurt swept his caramel eyes over her appraisingly, and then his expression softened in surrender. "Do you recall what we spoke about last night?"

She nodded.

Kurt leaned back in his chair. "After my wife's murder, my son was in the hospital for a long time. He got better and worse and better again. I never left his side. I was hopeful, so sure he would recover. Until one night, I noticed a presence in the room with us. Beautiful woman with dark hair and raven wings standing beside my son's bed." Kurt's voice cracked; Brooklyn placed her hand gently on his. “I told her she couldn’t have him. At first, she seemed shocked that I spoke to her. I begged, and I threatened, but there was nothing I could do to stop her. I told her I would do anything to keep my son, and she proposed a deal.”

“What kind of deal?” Brooklyn asked.

“She wanted me to complete a task for her, and although she didn’t have the power to keep my son alive, she promised to prevent his soul from moving on, to reincarnate him. You know, let him be born again as someone else. In exchange, she wanted me to capture and deliver a thousand demons.”

“Capital offense,” Riley interjected.

“Yes,” Kurt went on, “a thousand death sentences, so I had to be cautious. Move slowly. We agreed upon a term of twenty years because she said I had already had twenty years with my son and I would not see him again until he’d grown to be that age again.”

Brooklyn withdrew her hand. She drew her brows together thoughtfully. “So, when Belial tried to kill the Heir, it was for something you did?”

“My deadline had passed, and I was far behind the quota I promised. So, I ensnared demons associated with the Wardens. It was foolish and reckless, but they are the easiest to get to because they are not so tightly constrained. Unfortunately, it drew unwanted attention, which led to”—Kurt shrugged helplessly—“all of this.”

“So, your son is alive out there somewhere?”

“Yes, but I will never meet him until I deliver my end of the bargain.”

“What do you think this death angel wants with all those demons?” Brooklyn asked.

“I believe she wants to use them somehow to preserve herself,” Kurt said. “She has visited me occasionally over the years, and shared that the ballooning population has become a threat to her continued existence. I don’t know the specifics, but she must attend to the death of every human being and as that has grown exponentially, it is becoming more and more taxing."

Brooklyn looked to Riley to see how he was taking all of this, but he seemed uninterested, as if he'd heard it all before. Perhaps he had. "So that's it then? You pay your dues, you collect your son, and you vanish? Leaving the rest of us holding the bag on everything you've done? Riley? Me? What do you think they will do with us when you are gone?"

It was Kurt's turn to place his hand on hers reassuringly. "Stewarth is dead, Brooklyn. I'll be leaving. That means you are free. You are of no value to Nathan Goodrum, or Father Logan. If I'm out of the picture, you can go home."

Kurt's words made her feel as if she had swallowed a stone. Brooklyn could not imagine what it would be like to go home. To face her family, find a job, sleep in her old room, hike up the mountain. She had wanted it. Wanted it more than anything only a few months ago. So much had changed. Brooklyn pulled her hand from beneath his, and said, "I'm not so sure I can." And without another word, she left the room.

Belial struck the ground on his back and slid several feet through ash and sand. He clutched the eggs tightly to his chest. When he righted himself, he could see chaos still ensued on the plains before him. Demons and spirits of all descriptions gathered around the places where the portals had opened, still jockeying for position, hoping one would reappear. Meanwhile, all around him, others were falling as he had fallen, being dragged by the forces of nature back to this pit. The eggs, which he had expected would continue to be drawn back to their place of origin, were not. Clearly, these things operated differently from place to place. And it made sense, for how else could the dragon girl have remained in the library? Perhaps they were bound by birth. Belial wondered, if the eggs hatched here, would they be Pulled here? Hopefully not. Right now, they needed a safe place.

The library was the safest place, but Belial suspected it was not warm enough for the eggs to hatch. He could bury them in the hot and arid sands, anywhere beneath the scorching soul sun, but if they were born here, the chances of their survival would be slim. The dragon girl would surely have perished if the Tomekeepers had not intervened, and they were not likely to soon forget her failings.

"Safe and warm." Belial repeated the phrase like a mantra, willing it to bring about some divine revelation. The solution did not come. There was only one place, both safe and warm, and Belial had no way to go back there.

35

Tipping Point

After a good night's sleep and breakfast, Kurt was feeling much better. He slipped into a heavy coat and pulled on his gloves before going out to the dog lot to check on the hound. It was disconcerting to open the gate without several dogs waiting impatiently on the other side. Kurt found his one remaining hound inside the doghouse, which had been built large enough for six or seven.

Kurt crawled inside, leaned against the wall near the dog, laid a reassuring hand on his head, and ruffled his floppy ears. "Hey boy, how's it going?"

The hound opened his droopy eyes in response and closed them again with a low grunt.

Kurt ran his fingers gently down the soft fur of the dog's side until his touch drew a concerned whimper as he reached the ribs. "Doc says you're going to be okay. Just going to take some time. Need you to hang in there." Kurt's back ached from hunching in the cramped quarters. He fumbled a can of Alpo from the folds of his jacket, dragged the metal food bowl close to the hound, and dumped its contents out. The dog nibbled with halfhearted interest and without rising. Kurt teared up. "You saved me. You and that damned girl. I'm going to make all this right. Everything's going to be made right again."

Back inside, Kurt let his heavy coat slip to the floor and busied his hands before the hearth until a fire crackled cheerfully. He took the bourbon and other liquors, and placed them in a dark wooden cabinet in the corner and locked it with a small brass key. Carefully, he coaxed the loose stone from the fireplace and returned what of the summoning book he had salvaged.

At last, he settled onto the sofa before the cozy fire and twirled the slender black feather between his fingers. Kurt craved rest, a deep, dreamless sleep before the fire, but, as always, that wasn't in the cards.

He sighed heavily and returned to his desk, drew a slender laptop from the bottom desk drawer, and powered it on. While he waited for it to load, he sorted through the backlog of mail in the tray on his desk. One letter with a familiar seal stamped in wax drew his attention; his stomach dropped as he lifted it from the pile and broke the seal. The missive was handwritten with a neatness that bordered on calligraphy.

Greetings Protector Levin,

Doubtless by now you are aware my father passed after you abandoned your post as his personal protector. He trusted you above all others, and it is clear his trust was misplaced. You were charged not only with protecting my father's life, but also the ring he wore on his finger. A ring that is now missing. If Solomon's ring is returned to my keeping promptly, I will strip you of your office, but allow you to live in exile as a token of my late father's esteem for you. If the ring is not returned, I will reclaim my birthright with overwhelming force. I pray you will see reason, find wisdom, and submit willingly to my rule.

Eric Stewarth

Rightful Heir of Solomon

Kurt let the letter fall. Icy fingers squeezed the air from his lungs. Time was against him. He thought fleetingly of calling Eric, of trying to explain, but no excuse even with the return of the ring could justify what he had done. Without the ring, he had no bargaining power at all. Kurt could only assume that the wake and funeral were the only things that had prevented the Stewarths from coming to confront him immediately in person.

He recognized the feather; Azrael had taken the ring. Some small part of him hoped she had taken it to return it before the Heir drew his last breath, but that was clearly misguided optimism.

Normally, he might consult Riley for advice. Political intrigue, posturing, those were areas where Riley excelled and Kurt fell short. But the time for scheming and maneuvering had passed. Things were openly hostile now, and Kurt found that strangely reassuring. He would rather know where he stood and what lay ahead than to languish in a quagmire of red tape and uncertainty. Kurt glanced down at the letter and noticed a line he hadn't seen before, scrawled down near the bottom of the page. Written in a hurried, cramped hand as if it were a hasty afterthought. It read: *Also, you will release the assassin into our custody.*

"The hell I will," Kurt mumbled to himself as he turned to his computer and reviewed his email—which was as poorly tended as the mail on his desk. He checked for the routine reports from the members of his guard placed on various assignments. When he got to the end of the list, one such report was missing. He scanned his inbox again quickly. One team—the team sent to North Carolina to make sure Brooklyn's family was safe—had not reported. In fact, they'd missed two reports now. Kurt snatched up the phone and dialed a familiar number.

No answer.

"Very good!" Riley shouted across the gymnasium.

Brooklyn smiled. "I think you're just going easy on me." The orbs spun around her in lazy circles as if she were the sun at the center of their universe. Riley pressed the button, and a volley of tennis balls came hurtling toward her. Brooklyn bent her knees, instinctively centering herself.

Tracking the collective trajectories of so many balls was impossible. Her spheres lanced out, guided by instinct and feeling rather than vision. They punched through the balls as fast as bullets and sent them careening wildly away from her. A trickle of sweat ran down her spine. She brushed the hair back from her face. “How many was that?”

“That was eleven.”

“What’s the most you have done without being hit?”

Riley shrugged. “About thirty.”

Brooklyn’s jaw dropped in shock. “Seriously? I thought I almost had this mastered.”

“It takes time. Be patient.”

Brooklyn shrugged aside her frustration.

“Let’s try something different for a while.” Riley gestured for her to put the orbs away. Then he tossed a new set. Instinctively, Brooklyn snatched them from the air with her mind. The effort was much greater; she had no connection to these. “It’s important for you to continue practicing with other things because there could very well be a time when you don’t have those with you. Besides, it will make you stronger.”

Brooklyn nodded. “I’m ready.”

Riley pressed the button, and a single tennis ball came hurtling toward her. Brooklyn flicked her eyes to one orb and willed it to intersect the tennis ball, but before she could make it respond, the ball whacked her hard in the stomach.

“See why this is important?”

Brooklyn nodded. “Again.”

“Bring them in front of you. That’s where the attack is. There is no reason to have them out of your line of sight. Narrow your focus. Do not maintain your hold on the whole orb, find the atom at its center, and will it to move. The rest will follow.

Brooklyn looked at him incredulously. "You want me to grab onto an atom? How is that even possible?"

"It's just something you get a feel for with practice. The key to moving large things is to first learn to move the smallest of things."

"Is that an old Chinese proverb or something?"

Riley did not reply; instead, he pressed the button again. This one struck Brooklyn in the forehead before she could react. Belatedly, the orbs spiraled between her and Riley, touching nothing but open air.

"I wasn't ready!" The next one struck her thigh with a solid thump, and then another one glanced off her hip. "Stop it."

The answer was a machine-gun fire of tennis balls raining down on her. One struck her mouth. Her eyes watered and she tasted blood. Brooklyn lost track of the orbs and they fell to the hardwood floor with a clatter. Frustration and anger rolled up her spine in a cold, murderous wave before she could stop it. Brooklyn stepped deftly to the left, avoiding three balls, and then a volley of dozens came hurtling after her as Riley adjusted the aim. Brooklyn saw white, and energy left her body in a whoosh, like someone had knocked the air out of her.

She slowly became aware she was lying on her back with her breath condensing into a white mist above her face. The floor was covered in a sheet of ice. There were tennis balls all around her, some pierced through with icicles. As Brooklyn sat up, she saw Riley coming toward her. Carefully picking his way across the slippery debris-littered floor. He knelt and placed his fingers against her throat, then checked her pupils.

"Fascinating," he breathed.

"What's fascinating?" she asked in confusion.

"I knew there was still some connection between you and Belial."

"Why did I pass out?"

"You just blitzed through thousands of calories in an instant. It was more than your body could keep up with." He placed a warm hand across her forehead and then coaxed her into a sitting position. "Completely inefficient. Pure waste of raw power. But if it could be controlled—"

"What are you muttering about?" Brooklyn snapped irritably. Her head ached, her mouth tasted of metal and blood, and black spots swarmed her vision.

"I'm just thinking. If you could learn to control this, direct it, and use it in a more efficient way, it would be an incredible weapon. Using it like this is more dangerous to you than it is to your opponent, though."

Brooklyn pushed him away from her. "You're a jerk." When she regained her feet, her legs were like jelly, but she would not let him see that. Brooklyn stormed out of the room and left Riley there on the ice, floundering in her wake for something to say.

36

Tough Choices

Kurt examined the feather thoughtfully. He could summon Azrael at any moment to make the trade, if he so chose, but what kind of life would he and Tyler have on the run from the Heir? Kurt counted himself among the most powerful of the Protectors. There were very few people he would hesitate to go head-to-head with on an even playing field. But this would not be a fair fight.

Again and again his mind was drawn to his meeting with Alexander Stewarth, and the demonic servants he held thrall without the aid of the ring. The Stewarths were an old family. They claimed the purest lineage back to King Solomon, the first holder and presumed creator of the ring. Their knowledge and resources were unparalleled.

His thoughts turned to Azrael and the demons he had hidden away from her beneath the mountain. He carefully guarded the knowledge that was the key to their imprisonment and control. It troubled him that she had stolen the ring. Only humankind could wield it, so it was of little use to her. Kurt wondered, not for the first time, what she wanted with so many demons. Might she draw sustenance from them somehow? Strengthen herself? He didn't know.

Kurt was doubly troubled by the radio silence from the men sent to watch over Brooklyn's family. He had dispatched their covert protectors the day of the judgment when it became clear that Kurt's precarious position as Protector was tied to Brooklyn's behavior. It would be all too easy for Nathan Goodrum to use her family to manipulate her into betrayal or defection. Now, with Alexander Stewarth dead, the situation had changed. Kurt had hoped to reason with the boy, buy into his good graces, and disentangle his fate from Brooklyn's. The hastily scrawled line at the bottom of the letter troubled him more because he could not pin down what they might want with her. To execute her, perhaps, or interrogate her regarding himself or Riley. Maybe both.

Kurt carefully wrapped his tongue around syllables that were never meant for human utterances, watched the silken black feather curl and char in his fingers, and tossed the remains into the fireplace. There was a rush of air and the fire guttered low. Then she was there.

"It is time to make the trade, then?" Azrael folded her wings carefully.

"Explain." Kurt raised his mangled hand and unwrapped the finger. His voice dripped venom, and he wondered if it was in his power to hurt her. But he knew the answer. If he could hurt her, he would never have needed to bargain.

"I do not explain myself to mortals. I am ready to give you your reincarnated child if you are ready to pay the price."

"What do you need with so many demons?" She did not answer him. She walked to the window and stared up at the cold, faraway moon. Kurt noticed how the moonlight spilled across her now unblemished face and turned her inky black feathers into shining points of light. "You cannot use the ring to control them, you know that?"

"Yes, I am aware," she answered without turning.

"I must return the ring to the rightful heir. It does me no good to gain my son and become a fugitive. I will not complete the trade until you return the ring." Kurt readied himself for her wrath, for threats and anger, maybe even an attack. None of that happened. She turned from the window and looked at him at last.

She crossed the room languidly like a jungle cat, cupped his cheek with one hand, and placed the other flat against his chest. For the first time since he'd known her, her hands were warm and pulsing with life. He was struck by how small she was. She'd always seemed bigger. Azrael rose on her toes and pressed her lips to his cheek.

"Oh yes, you will." And in the next instant, she was gone.

"I'm sorry," Riley said again, as he trailed Brooklyn down the vaulted hallways to his basement lab.

"Don't talk to me!" She hurried through the door and slammed it in his face. It only occurred to her after the fact that this was Riley's room and not hers. Be that as it may, the door remained tightly shut. He did not follow. Brooklyn gathered clean clothing and went to the bathroom for a bath. She carefully locked the door and set the water as hot as she could stand it. Brooklyn examined her busted lip in the mirror; it was swollen.

She sank into the tub, letting the warm water dissolve the remnants of her cold fury. Languidly tracing the barbed scar on her chest, her mind made its familiar rounds from David to Devin to her mom to her dad and around again.

Brooklyn held her hand above the water until a single fat droplet clung to her fingertip and fell. It paused in midair and returned to her fingertip. She did this again and again. It was almost as if she could turn back time. Brooklyn wondered if she turned it back for real, what she might change. The droplet fell one last time, crystallized into ice, struck the steaming water, and dissolved.

Belial headed for the library tunnel. It was the only refuge he could think of. He clutched the dragon eggs protectively to his body. It wasn't that he had a plan exactly, but he needed shelter and there were no answers to his problems out in the open. Presumably, no one currently guarded the dragon Tomes. He had promised the girl that he would take the eggs somewhere warm. Belial wanted to take them to the only place he had ever truly felt warm, with Tais, and bury them in the sand beside the sea. Belial fancied he felt life pulsing hotly within the eggs, but that was unlikely. The shells were as hard and thick as dragon scales and black as soot.

Belial made good time, having cleared the guardians from the path on his prior incursion. Soon, he stood before the majestic doors. Inside, the Tomes rested heavily on stone pedestals, much as they had on his first visit. Apparently unharmed by the fire and the flood that had followed. Belial half expected to hear his father's voice rumbling like a sea storm from some darkened corner of the room. Only silence greeted him.

Belial paced up and down the rows, eyes playing over the ancient and mostly unfamiliar words carved into the stone pedestals. There was, he suspected, enough knowledge here to make and unmake worlds, invaluable and unique information, and all of it worthless to him. He sat on the dais and watched the torchlight flicker eerily around the room. Shadows danced and played about him. These were his books now, he realized, assuming the dragon girl could actually give them away. Such treasure was like having a life raft in the middle of a desert, he mused.

Belial had long wished his father dead. Since the day Tais had been taken from him, Belial had suffered with a live, undying ember of hatred burning in the pit of his stomach. Learning of his father's death had not pleased him or angered him. He felt indifferent. His mind wandered, as it often did, back to Tais. He contemplated the curve of her nose and the quirky way it crinkled up when she smiled. Images and sounds as vivid as life he conjured effortlessly, and they stung more for their clarity.

Without warning, a jolt startled him from his reverie. Icy power flooded out of him. It was like an arrow in the heart pulsing electricity, and through the shock of it, he sensed the familiar presence of Brooklyn's mind. Her face swam before his eyes where Tais's had been an instant before. Then it was over. Belial reached for her with his mind, tried to reestablish the connection, but it was broken. Once again, he had only memories for company.

37

Line in the Sand

Azrael alighted in the shadows of an alleyway, and her feathered wings melted away into a stylish black trench coat she cinched at the waist. She hurried down the street, easily blending in with the throngs of humans busily going about their business. When Azrael found the place, she was shocked by how disgustingly appropriate it was. The lighting inside was poor, and there were tables and chairs in neat, militaristic rows, all of them empty. She wrinkled her nose against the stench of decaying meat and vomit, and took a seat near the door.

Azrael's thoughts wandered back to Kurt. To the look of incredulity on his face when she had kissed him. If a chaste kiss on the cheek elicited such a response, what other reactions might she engender? It was a shame, really, that he was so single minded and obsessed about his dead wife and son. These last twenty years could have passed much more pleasantly. Kurt's caramel eyes seemed to dance with life. Looking at them made her ache with the memory of all she had lost. Azrael had always been drawn to the vibrancy of life. When she had pressed her alabaster hand to the dark skin of his cheek, had he not leaned into her a little? Had she imagined it?

"So, you came?" a nasally voice inquired.

Azrael turned slowly, forcing her face into a mask to hide revulsion. As bad as her fate was, there were others who fared much worse.

"Don't act like you didn't smell me coming."

He laughed, and the sight of his teeth turned Azrael's stomach. "Lost in thought, I'm afraid." She smiled politely. "So you're really going to do this?" he said, settling lightly into the chair across from her. He withdrew a large plastic case from inside his jacket and placed it on the table. "Them's the blights." He made a great show of reaching into the other side of his jacket and rummaging around before withdrawing a large sealed envelope. "And them's the blueprints and locations."

Azrael dropped a velvet bag on the table. The drawstring loosened and a dozen perfectly cut blood-red rubies spilled onto the table and sparkled in the dim light. "Of course I'm going to do it. Why wouldn't I?"

"It's better I don't know then. When you fail, all the consequences is yours."

"And if I succeed, you profit with no risk? It is a win-win for you. I don't know why I even need to pay for this information."

"I help for free; I'm an ally. Now you pay. This is just business."

Azrael looked at him. Maybe she had misjudged. Perhaps this was the fate a coward and a worm deserved. She nodded politely. "I should go."

He didn't say anything, but the centuries of loneliness in his eyes followed her out the door and down the street until she turned the corner.

David opened his eyes and rubbed the sleep from them. Not to clear his vision, but more out of habit. He had discovered weeks ago that no amount of rubbing would restore his sight. Only darkness now. In a world of sound, smell, and touch. The narrow bed creaked as he sat up and rolled to his feet. His room, or cell, he wasn't sure which, was about four paces by six paces and contained a bed, a small table, and a lamp that seemed a mockery, as well as a sink with running water, a toilet, and a shower.

A single door opened into a hallway beyond, but the door was always locked from the other side. Meals arrived once per day at noon, and David had lost a lot of weight. He could tell by the way his ribs felt beneath his fingers. He stretched against the pain that still accompanied his healing wounds. Every day, David got out of bed for Brooklyn. He knew she was dead, they had told him that much, but he got up every morning because it might be the day he could avenge her. When his captors told him she was dead, they had apologized, saying they only ever intended to capture her. To get her away from Kurt because he was a bad man. David had nodded blindly, but he knew better. And inside, he nursed a murderous rage.

The voice came again into his head then, as it had the prior two mornings. The soft urging of a woman's voice. David wasn't sure if he was going mad, or if this was simply a cruel trick being played by his captors. "Let me open your eyes," the voice whispered. "Let's make a trade." It was maddening, because the voice seemed to be disembodied, coming from his own mind and from several places around the room at one.

David wondered, not for the first time, if this was some demon hoping to possess him as Belial had possessed Brooklyn. He would die before he let that happen. "I don't consort with demons," he informed the voice flatly.

There came a tinkling of breathy laughter. "And what about angels?"

Brooklyn stared mournfully into her closet. The selection was absolutely Spartan. She desperately needed to convince Riley or Kurt that a shopping trip was in order. With a sigh, she pulled down a pair of khaki pants and a knit sweater with the tags still on. The sweater was baggy and the pants too tight.

When she emerged from the bedroom into the lab, she found Riley hunched over his workstation. He looked up at her and then away sheepishly. "I'm really sorry about earlier," he said. He looked more like a child caught awake in the middle of the night eating cookies than like a man who had almost bludgeoned her to death with tennis balls. Quite unexpectedly, a bubble of laughter erupted from her lips.

"It's okay." She forced the smile from her face and nodded at him seriously. "But don't let it happen again."

"I won't. Promise." Riley smiled. He patted the bench next to him. "Come sit. I want to show you something."

Brooklyn settled next to him. He smelled of peppermint and lavender. Riley nudged the microscope's eyepiece toward her. Brooklyn leaned forward and peered into it, not sure what she was looking at. It sparkled with whites and blues and colors that seemed to move and writhe like living things. "What is this?"

"It's a sample of the ice you created. I decided to examine it because, based on my calculations, there wasn't enough moisture in the room to have facilitated so much ice and snow."

"You're doing it again." She laughed.

A hint of red colored Riley's cheeks. "Basically, I think you created water or somehow transported it to the room from somewhere else." Before she could speak, he went on hurriedly. "Water is fairly easy to create. I mean, hydrogen and oxygen are basically everywhcre."

"But why is that important?" Brooklyn asked in confusion.

"It is just interesting." He shrugged. "For one thing, it means that you can manipulate things at the atomic level."

"That's what I was trying to do when you bludgeoned me with all those tennis balls," she replied crossly.

Riley kicked a Styrofoam cooler at his feet. "There is more in there."

Brooklyn abruptly changed the subject. "Let's give the orbs a name."

"A name?" he repeated blankly.

"Instead of calling them 'the orbs' or 'the spheres,' let's name them."

"I suppose we could call them inanimate corporeal manifestations, or ICMs for short."

Brooklyn made a face at him. "Seriously?"

"Why? It is an apt description."

"Sometimes I wish I knew which parts of you were purely you, and which parts changed when you ascended with the Tomekeeper."

Riley looked hurt. "I was always smart, but now even though I have access to centuries of knowledge, I like to think my personality hasn't changed, but I don't suppose I would be the best judge of that." He shrugged. "How has sharing your skull with Belial changed you?"

Bloody images flashed behind Brooklyn's eyelids. She pushed them away.

"Soul stones," Brooklyn announced gleefully. "We will call them soul stones."

"But that doesn't make sense. They are not made of stone. It's a refined alloy that condense—"

"Yeah, but it's much catchier than intergalactic . . . whatever you said."

"Inanimate corporeal manifestations," he replied with mock exasperation. "Not that hard. You don't even have to remember what the words mean. Just call it ICM."

"Nah, I'm going to go with soul stones."

"Fine." Riley sighed dramatically.

Brooklyn became aware they were both smiling, and that they were only inches apart. He was gazing at her. She felt her heart flutter and speed up.

"I really am sorry about earlier," Riley said tenderly. And before Brooklyn could reply, he leaned in and pressed his lips to hers. He tasted of peppermint, smelled of lavender, and his lips were vibrant and warm and wet against hers. In that instant, the lab vanished as if the two of them had been sucked up in a black hole where the only sensations and the only light came from the touch of the other. Brooklyn had suddenly been filled with some vital part of herself that had been missing these last few months. She didn't have the time or the willpower to contemplate what that might be. The kiss went on and on, seeming to stretch into the distance like a road promising neither heaven nor hell, only adventure beyond the horizon. It was as if nothing had ever come before and nothing would come after. Dimly she was aware of his hand on her cheek and then in her hair, of her palm flat against his chest and then clutching into a fist with his T-shirt twisted inside. When the kiss broke, Brooklyn felt heat in her cheeks and her heart pulsing pleasantly in her ears.

She bit her bottom lip self-consciously. "So, I guess we're going with soul stones, then?"

His hands were still tangled in her hair when he spoke breathlessly. "Soul stones sounds amazing."

"What about angels?" David asked the emptiness in front of him. There was no answer. He sat on the edge of the bed and wished he could sleep all day, every day. In his dreams he could see, there were colors, Brooklyn was still alive, and they were both free.

David thought back to the day he left band practice and abandoned his friends to chase after Brooklyn. It had seemed dangerous, thrilling, and achingly romantic. He fancied himself a character from a book setting off on a quest, but now he wondered if all of them might not have been better off if he hadn't bothered. Brooklyn would still be alive, and he would still have his vision. When Father Logan had come by on the second day of his incarceration to ask if there was anything that he wanted, David had asked for a guitar. Father Logan had said he would see what he could do, but three weeks had gone by, and David had not heard another word about it.

Sometimes acolytes would stop by to pepper him with propaganda or read scripture from some sacred text he'd never heard of, or ask if he wanted to confess his sins. When David said he had nothing to confess, one of them replied that he had carnal knowledge of the demon's whore. Rage had filled David. He overturned the table and took the lamp in his hand and swung it wildly and blindly. He had driven them from the room, sent them scurrying like children before his unseeing wrath. Since then, no more casual visitors. His meals were delivered, his clothes laundered, and the dirty dishes collected in the morning. At first, he thought the lack of human contact would make him go mad, but he had grown accustomed to it.

It had been his choice to run, to flee the safety of Kurt's complex. Brooklyn was dead because of him. She had not wanted to go. David had pushed her. The thought wrung a sob of impotent rage from his throat.

David did not know if they watched him through cameras or one-way glass. The thought caused a shaky laugh to burst from his lips. Did one really need one-way glass to watch a blind man?

David dropped to his knees and scrounged around on the floor near the door until his fingers closed on the fork from the night before. Falling back to his haunches, he held it cupped in both hands. He tried to remember Kurt's words, his instructions, but no matter how much he tried, he could not will the fork to rise. Kurt had insisted that all people had the potential, some more than others, but all people were capable. David was not so sure.

Every day he found something to practice with, and every day he failed.

David sensed the vibration of two sets of footfalls coming down the hallway. He dropped the fork onto the tray with a clatter and scooted away, leaning back against the bed. When the key turned in the lock and the footsteps entered the room, David said, "Good morning."

Neither of them answered him. Nobody had spoken to him since the outburst. With mechanical efficiency, they collected the tray and withdrew, locking the door with a snick.

As soon as the lock clicked into place and the footsteps moved beyond hearing, the voice returned. "What do you want?" it asked insistently. "Let me light the way for you."

"I am beyond the reach of light now." David laughed bitterly.

"Are you content to live your life out as a caged bird?" Her voice was low and suggestive.

"Can you make me powerful? Powerful enough to escape this room and take revenge on my captors?"

"If you agree to be my prophet, I will make them your slaves. I'll give you the power to unmake the ones who wronged you, to crush their bones to dust and burn their lineages from the memory of the world. I just need you to agree. What do you say?"

38

Tumblers Turning

Kurt dialed the number again, and the call went to voicemail. He slammed the phone down. He was not sure what to do about Brooklyn's family. If Kurt told her, Brooklyn would bolt off to check on her parents, putting both herself and Kurt at risk. He could not afford the time it would take to chase after her now, not with Eric Stewarth issuing ultimatums. He might send someone else, he mused. Riley would be his first pick, if not that he needed Riley here. Not to mention Riley and Brooklyn had become very chummy lately. She would be apt to notice if he were missing, and ask questions.

Kurt itched to go himself. He suspected it was a trap. This was almost certainly the work of Nathan Goodrum. Sending his men alone against the Demonriders would be sending them to their deaths.

Kurt's mind was drawn again to the cornfield where they had fought over Brooklyn. Kurt had known they wanted to use her as a tool to bring him down, but it had been a shock to see Nathan Goodrum and Father Logan standing together.

Their two organizations had historically been the worst of enemies. The Demonriders, power hungry and wayward, had little patience for the maddening righteousness of the Prophets. Alexander had warned him that Father Logan was the dangerous one, but Kurt didn't see it. He was, as Riley would say, a pansy. *The enemy of my enemy is my ally.* Kurt was a little short on allies at the moment. He could claim only one, and he wasn't so sure of her anymore, either.

Kurt glanced at the black feather on his desk. He had found it there after Azrael kissed him, after she vanished. Left so he could call her when ready to make the trade. Kurt wondered if he might convince her to take him to Brooklyn's parents' home and back again.

Kurt touched his cheek, remembering the uncharacteristic warmth of Azrael's lips. It meant something that she was not cold. She was always cold. Not like ice, but in a way that spoke of the absence of life, the absence of heat, of long years and vast, empty spaces. Kurt looked away from the feather and pushed the idea from his mind. Kiss or no kiss, he was on shaky ground with her and must not trust her. That had become achingly clear. He flexed his stiff ring finger.

Kurt sighed and picked up the phone. "Send a tactical team to my office, at least six men." He paused thoughtfully. "Send one of the Adepts; ask for a volunteer."

"Okay. Yes," David said.

In the blackness of his unseeing, David sensed a deeper blackness, a shadow over a shadow. The shape of a woman, a dark silhouette. Her slender hand came toward his face and David felt a finger pressed to the center of his forehead.

The world exploded into light. The entire universe seemed to expand within the confines of David's skull. Brightness poured into his brain, and he could not squint or close his eyes against it. The light was inside him somehow.

David's eyes clamped shut and tears streamed from them. When the pain became so unbearable that David thought he may simply die, everything contracted to a single point, a sliver of glowing glass lodged in his brain.

David, dimly aware that he was lying on the floor now, saw the shadow woman was leaning over him. Warm lips brushed his forehead. A kiss a mother might have given a sick child, and then merciful darkness took him.

Brooklyn laced her fingers with Riley's. Nervous energy sang through her; she felt as giddy as a teenager on a first date. It had taken hours to convince Riley to abandon his experiments in the lab and take her to a movie.

Popcorn, in a container large enough to easily be mistaken for a five-gallon bucket, was wedged between them. Brooklyn did not know what movie they were seeing. It hadn't really mattered. She was thrilled to be away from the estate for a while. Popcorn had never tasted so full of buttery, salty perfection.

"This is better than the lab, right?" She watched his face, bathed in the glow of the coming attractions.

Riley smiled devilishly. "Definitely better."

Brooklyn squeezed his hand. They had traveled out of their way, gone two towns over as much to avoid bumping into Kurt as the Demonriders or the Prophets.

As the movie started, Brooklyn leaned her head against Riley's shoulder, and he wrapped his arm loosely around hers. It was the first time in a long time that she'd been completely safe.

Azrael lifted David gently and placed him on the bed. His chest rose and fell rapidly. She brushed his hair back. Despite everything he must have endured, his skin remained smooth and unblemished.

A thrill of elation ran through Azrael, an emotion so human that it caught her completely unawares. The pieces were coming together; the knot that had bound her, bound them all for so long, was unraveling. For the first time in thousands of years, she had a prophet. Azrael left David to rest. There was still much to do.

She found the place described in the papers easily. It was well protected, built into the heart of a mountain. Not a place to be flown into or out of. There were steel doors, cameras, electronic alarms that she did not fully understand. Going underground gave her pause as few things did. The worst deaths she had attended were underground. Her thoughts turned to cave-ins and collapsed coal mines, but she did not allow hesitation to stand in the way now. Azrael strode resolutely into the mountain.

Belial flipped through the pages of the Tomes randomly. Searching vainly for a word he recognized, a symbol, or an illustration, anything. A part of him thought he might fare better in the library at large, but his chances of being detected would increase astronomically out there. This room was rarely accessed, and then by the library's own researchers, the only ones who had any hope of deciphering these ancient glyphs.

Brooklyn? Belial called out in his mind. She had been here, and he had sensed her presence, the shape of her thoughts somehow familiar. Of course, she wouldn't hear him. The Pull probably restricted communication as well as travel. It only made sense.

Belial's eyes drifted along the rows of flaming torches. Not wall torches, but large stone pillars that rose from the floor to chest height and spouted steady streams of unearthly flame. Each torch was carved with an intricate dragon that wrapped and twisted around the column as if climbing a mountain. Their mouths opened near the top around the flames.

Belial wondered suddenly if his father had read any of these Tomes during the time he spent here, or the dragon girl, for that matter. They were—at least some of them—written in the tongue of her people. Belial wondered where the dragonling was now, if she had made it back to the shelter of the mother dragon's mountain, or had been lost in whatever lay between this world and the next.

Belial moved to the next Tome and found its pages filled with illustrations. These, at least, he had some chance of deciphering. He ran his clawed finger over a humanoid drawing with a great winged creature clinging to its back. The page was filled with inscrutable text. The next page held a complicated diagram with interlocking circles and dotted lines tracing paths of orbit.

Belial let the heavy skin pages slide through his fingers one at a time. Images and glyphs flashed by in shifting patterns like raindrops exploding on pavement. Vague impressions and half-formed feelings blossomed in Belial's mind. The flow of pages stopped on a crude sketch of five tribes, each bowed before a different god. Each god stood behind an altar with a human sacrifice. On the next page, he found an image of a hoard of people gazing up at a disintegrating deity. Silvery threads spiraled outward from its being into their opened mouths as it unraveled.

Belial turned to the next page where the people, now godless and in greater numbers, worked on a grove of massive stone buildings. Each tiny person with a silvery swirl on their forehead levitating stones into place.

Several pages of indecipherable script came before the next drawing. A man atop a great temple, arms raised, and below him all manner of spirits bound by silver chains, above him the merciless soul sun. For the first time, Belial desperately wished he could read the strange mixture of glyphs and scripts. He flipped the page to find the next one blank. Thousands of pages remained. All of them were blank.

The emptiness of the page throbbed like a toothache. Slowly, he pressed a claw to the tip of his finger. As the blood welled, he pressed his finger to the page and drew in broad, bold lines. The images seemed to swirl out from his finger of their own accord. The dragon girl with the eggs clutched to her bosom, eyes bright with uncertainty and hope. The slope of his own wings raised against the wind and the looping coils of the dragon mountain in the distance, lonely and desolate. As the images grew in detail, Belial relived the emotions, the struggle to hold on, and the loss that followed. The sorrow flowed from his finger until the pain turned to unfeeling.

When he finished, Belial sank to the floor, giddy with tiredness. He would draw more tomorrow. Images filled his mind. Images of Tais being swallowed by the sea, of the Pull breached in dozens of places by columns of eerie light, and of Brooklyn sleeping, unaware of his presence.

39

ON THE RUN

They walked through the historical district after the movie. Brooklyn tugged her hand free of Riley's and dashed across the grass.

"Take a picture." She laughed as she posed with her arm thrown lovingly around the neck of a statue, a soldier poised on a marble pedestal. She threw a leg over his outstretched arm so he appeared to hold her.

"Got it." Riley smiled as his camera phone flashed in the dim light.

Brooklyn disentangled herself and hurried over to see. They bent over the screen together. Brooklyn noticed Riley smelled different today: shampoo and cologne in place of the usual lab chemicals and peppermint.

"You smell nice."

Riley grinned self-consciously and slid his fingers through hers as they walked down the street.

His hand warmed hers.

"I'm getting hungry," he murmured. "There's a diner not far from here. It used to be a hangout for all the up-and-coming musicians traveling in and out of Nashville."

"That sounds great." It was the sort of place her dad would have liked to visit. Brooklyn pushed the thought away quickly. Tonight was a happy night. She deserved one carefree night, didn't she?

"They have this great omelet; it has mushrooms with—"

Strobing blue lights cut Riley short. They both turned to see a patrol car inching up to them along the curb. The window went down to reveal a shock of curly black hair framing a full face and a thickly muscled neck and shoulders.

"I'm going to have to ticket you for climbing on the monument, miss."

"Oh, okay," Brooklyn stammered. Her cheeks burned.

The officer's eyes narrowed, and he pushed the door open. He towered over them like a parent over unruly children.

"You're Brooklyn Evans." It was a statement, not a question.

"Evers," she corrected him. "How do you—"

The words died on her lips. Several things happened at once. The officer drew his gun and yelled at her to get on the ground. In the same instant, Riley—moving with inhuman speed—shoved Brooklyn to the left and dodged right. The officer's aim trailed Brooklyn for an instant and then wavered back toward Riley, but it was too late. The hesitation was all the time he'd had. The pistol fell to the pavement with a clatter. He swung wildly at Riley, powerful punches that would have crushed the slighter man with brute force. Riley batted the blows away almost contemptuously. Then, in a blur of motion, he struck the officer and sent him spinning back into his car. Riley hoisted his limp form upright in the seat and closed the door.

"You killed him. You killed a cop." Brooklyn heard the rising hysteria in her voice as if it were someone else's words. Then Riley was there with his hands on her shoulders.

"Look at me," he said firmly. His eyes were as large and earnest as twin moons. "He's going to be fine. We have to go. We can't stay here. Do you hear me?" Brooklyn nodded and let him take her by the hand and lead her away.

Belial slept. In the way his kind slept, which was more like a self-induced trance than true sleep. In his dream the sea rose up to tear her from his grip as it always did, but this time he shed the flimsy mortal skin he wore and plucked Tais back from his father's grasp with a furious beating of wings.

Belial imagined the way the air tousled her hair. In his dream, she looked up at his true visage and did not flinch. Looked with wonder, fearless and fragile.

Together they soared inland above the villages with their fires, sending lazy spirals of smoke into the sky. The others moved beneath them like ants. When Belial turned his face back to hers, she had gone pale with terror.

"What's wrong?"

Tais trembled now and gestured out to sea. Belial turned in the air, eyes straining in dismay. The sea was gone. It had withdrawn as completely as if it had never been there at all. As far as he could see, fish and other sea creatures were dying in the sudden absence of water.

On the horizon, mountains rose until they blotted out the sun. Even at this height, Belial could hear the shouts of horror rising from the people below. The mountains were made of water, and they were coming.

Belial flapped desperately to gain altitude. Tais clung to him with her eyes pressed shut. The water came from every side, and it rose higher than he could ever go and crashed down upon them, tearing her from his grasp forever.

Belial tried to take control of the dream. To remake it or end it, but he could not. His father's voice resonated in the water. "There were never choices. It was always going to happen just the way it happened. These fantasies are fruitless. Wait for me in safety until you are summoned."

The dream evaporated. The water was gone. Belial plunged into wakefulness. *It was just a dream*, he told himself, his heart slowing.

"Just a dream," he said aloud, as if that made it somehow more believable. His father was dead. The dragon girl had said as much. Belial would have believed it if, when he stood up, water had not trickled down his body and puddled around his feet.

To: Eric Stewarth

From: Protector Levin

Honorable Heir of Solomon,

I have received your letter and am hurt by your venomous tone. It was not so long ago that you spent your summers here in training with me as a boy. While you have a right to be angry, and the title of Protector is yours to give or take away, I urge you to give me the opportunity to explain my actions and the reasons for them.

Unfortunately, I can comply with neither of your requests. I beg you to see reason.

Sincerely,

Kurt Levin, North American Protector, District 1

Kurt licked the envelope and pressed the flaps shut. It was less than eloquent, he knew, but Riley had made his feelings on the matter well known at breakfast. And while Kurt would have welcomed help in penning the letter, he did not relish the idea of another exchange of harsh words.

Kurt busied himself with filling a tactical backpack and a duffel bag for an overnight trip. He was not sure how much longer he would be a Protector, but as long as he was, he had a duty to protect ordinary people from supernatural threats.

When the team stationed to monitor Brooklyn's parents had failed to report back, Kurt had sent a second team to assess the situation. They, too, had failed to report back. He could not in good faith send more members of his team into unknown danger.

Kurt slipped the spheres into a hidden jacket pocket and fastened a large, wicked knife to his ankle.

Before leaving, he scribbled a hasty note to Riley and left it in the center of his desk, where it was certain to be noticed. Kurt unwound the bloodied bandage from his finger and flexed it. The joint was stiff and swollen. Straightening it felt like stretching old boot leather. He doused it with antiseptic and rewound fresh bandages.

Kurt grunted as he shouldered his bags and moved silently toward the garage. If he hurried, he could be in North Carolina before sunrise.

When their car came into view, Riley stopped so abruptly that Brooklyn crashed into his back.

"What is it . . . ?" she began.

"SHHH." He pushed her back into the shadows, but it was too late. Blue lights flared around the parking lot, and a jumble of shouted commands assaulted her ears at the same instant. Boots pounded the pavement from several directions.

Brooklyn reached for her soul stones, but they weren't there. She cursed inwardly. She had worn a dress without pockets and thoughtlessly left them behind in the basement lab. Brooklyn stumbled as Riley shoved her back the way they came. They erupted through the shrubbery that marked the boundaries of the town monument park. She could hear the roaring of engines as some of the officers moved into position to surround the park.

"What do they want with me?" Brooklyn asked. Her heart flopped like a fish, hooked suddenly from the water, full of frantic impotence. Riley's eyes, she noticed, were twitching back and forth rapidly, as if dreaming.

"I don't know," he whispered harshly. "The important thing is we need to find our way out of this without hurting anyone, and we need another car." Together, they crouched behind a stone bench flanked by bushes. Officers dressed all in black tactical gear began emerging silently from the perimeter.

A sudden dread blossomed inside Brooklyn. This was a planned sting operation. Why would the first officer have known her name, and why were they waiting near their car? She was afraid she knew the answer, but there wasn't time to sort it out right now.

Twin spotlights shone up from the ground onto another statue and lit the immediate area in a yellow haze. How many statues did one little town need?

Brooklyn felt trapped. Anxiety and dread pressed like stones against her stomach and bladder.

Riley picked up three smooth sand-tumbled landscaping pebbles from beneath the bench. They whistled through the air, then glass shattered and the area was plunged into darkness. Tactical flashlights winked on all around the perimeter.

"At least we know where and how many," Riley said in a barely audible whisper. "They may have night vision." He sent more stones spinning into the leaves on the other side of the park; the sound continued as Riley manipulated the stones to create the sound of retreating footsteps. As silently as two ghosts, they ran down the edge of the park and melted back through the shrubbery with barely a rustle. They emerged on a side street lined with narrow loading docks and roll-up steel doors. Brooklyn followed Riley as he dashed from one door to the next, pausing before each to press his hand against it before hurrying on.

"What are you doing? We need to get out of here," she hissed at him.

Riley smiled at her victoriously. "No, we only need them to think we did." He closed his eyes in concentration and after a long moment, the door gave an audible click and rolled up enough to allow the two of them, lying flat, to slide underneath. "I just needed one without a padlock or alarm," he said, pulling the door down and latching it, "one that could be opened from the inside without a key."

The room they were in was pitch black, illuminated only by the faint red glow of an emergency exit sign. Slowly, Brooklyn's eyes adjusted and the vague shapes of mannequins and clothing racks materialized.

"It's a clothing store." She grabbed his hand in the darkness. "We need new clothes. The police know what we're wearing."

"New faces would be better," Riley joked. "We need light. But I don't think we can turn on the lights without drawing attention."

"I worked in a little store like this in high school," Brooklyn said. She searched the perimeter of the room, dragging Riley along by the arm. Her fingers found a door, opened it, and reached inside. "Here," she breathed triumphantly, "let there be light." And she flicked the switch to reveal a windowless employee break room. They both blinked against the sudden brightness.

Riley let the door close softly behind them. Brooklyn sank heavily into a chair. She felt as if tension and terror had stretched her nerves like elastic bands and now in safety left them loosened and sagging with exhaustion.

Riley moved efficiently around the room, taking inventory, checking the fridge for food, locating a television behind closed cabinet doors, and a radio. He flipped through the television channels until he found a news station out of Nashville.

"—thought to be terror attacks. Targets included several top secret Department of Agriculture facilities. Other targets rumored but unconfirmed. We will continue to bring you updates as they become available.

"Police investigators are asking for your help in locating this woman, Brooklyn Evers." Brooklyn gasped as her high school yearbook picture filled the television screen. "A person of interest in the suburban slayings of Northern Tennessee. Evers is believed to be traveling with a slight man, midthirties, with black hair and blue eyes. Both are considered armed and extremely dangerous. If you have any information, please contact your local law enforcement or call the number at the bottom of the screen."

Brooklyn stared at the TV blankly, even after Riley shut it off.

"Are you okay?" he asked, placing his hand gently on her shoulder.

"I have to turn myself in," Brooklyn said softly while winding a long strand of brown hair around her finger. "I can never go home, never be with my family again, unless I turn myself in and clear my name."

"You can't do that. If they're looking for you, they have evidence. Even if you convince a jury that you believe you were possessed by a demon, the best you can hope for is spending the rest of your life in a mental hospital."

"Maybe it's what I deserve." Her voice cracked. "I killed all those people and now I remember it. I dream about it every night. And when I close my eyes, I see dead faces as if they were burned into the backs of my eyelids. I killed them all."

"You did not," Riley said urgently. "You didn't. You were a prisoner inside your own mind and body. You cannot blame yourself for this."

"I should have resisted. Maybe I could've stopped him if I tried harder."

"You couldn't have. But you've done everything in your power to become strong enough to resist in the future. Don't you see you were a victim as much as any of the people he killed? In some ways, the things he did to you are worse because you have to remember them and relive them and accept that they happened."

"That's not how I feel; I just—" she began, but her throat seemed to close off the words and she felt tears like molten lava behind her eyes. *I will not cry*, Brooklyn vowed to herself.

"Everything will be okay." Riley patted her back soothingly. She reached for him then, and he opened his arms to her. Brooklyn buried her face against his chest and clenched her fingers savagely in the soft fabric of his shirt.

"It isn't fair," she murmured numbly. "I can never be with my family again. It isn't fair . . . "

"It's not," he agreed.

David sat up with a start. The sheets beneath him were soaked with sweat. The now familiar darkness greeted him as it always did. He rubbed the center of his forehead between his eyes, remembering the dream. It had been a dream, had it not?

Something foul touched his nose, drawing his mind away from troubled sleep. Lunch, he realized as he felt around on the floor near the door for the tray. It was a disgusting sandwich of some pungent cured meat. David ate it anyway.

There came an unexpected knock at the door. David dropped the half-eaten food and backed away until his fingers found the bed. He heard the door open and close, and the smell of after-shave filled the room.

"Hello, David. I'm Father Logan." The man's voice was smooth as silk.

"So, you're a priest?"

"A prophet, actually."

Prophet. Prophet. The word rang in David's mind like a gong struck over and over again.

"Prophet?" David repeated softly. "Prophet of what?"

"I don't think you are ready for the full explanation. There's still so much you have to learn."

"How about you just tell me why I'm here and why you've blinded me?" David was surprised by the frosty bitterness in his voice.

"You're here because I didn't allow my counterpart to execute you. Because you are untainted by demons."

"How generous of you."

"Yes, I thought so. You may yet prove useful in our efforts to remove the demonic stain from our leadership."

"You killed my girlfriend. Why would I help you do anything?"

"If Protector Levin had done his job, she would have never been mixed up in any of this. He's too soft; he tolerates Goodrum and his ilk. He believes they can be rehabilitated."

"And you don't?" David asked.

"No, I don't. I know better. Sooner or later, they all go back."

David shifted, leaning back against the wall. He thought of his training companions in the forest clearing. All were former Demonriders working to be free of their prior entanglements. He couldn't imagine the twins falling back into their old lives.

"You were with Goodrum. You attacked together. Do you think I'm stupid?"

"Of course not, just ignorant and naïve," Father Logan said.

David spluttered with laughter, "Well, thank you for your honesty."

Father Logan sighed theatrically. "'Together' probably isn't the right word. I prefer to think of our relationship like that of a hunter and his hounds. Unequal but mutually beneficial."

"Have you shared this analogy with Mr. Goodrum?"

Father Logan ignored the jab and went on. "The Heirs have forgotten their duty. Demon consorters, all. No better than the Demonriders. They have abandoned their legacy and forgotten the old stories. The parable of the three brothers and—"

"I don't care about any of this," David cut in. "I just want the hell out of here."

"Of course you do"—David felt a hand resting on his knee—"and after your initiation is complete and you acknowledge the divinity within, you will be free." The hand on his leg withdrew.

"What initiation?" His only answer was the latching of the door and the sound of Father Logan's footsteps receding down the corridor.

40

Escape and Capture

Brooklyn woke alone. The ghost of Riley's arm still prickling around her shoulder.

"Good, you're up."

She blinked the sleep from her eyes. "What's going on?" she asked blearily, trying to find his voice in the shadows.

"We are getting out of here; our ride is on the way."

"Kurt?"

Riley laughed. "Oh no. If Kurt never hears about this, that will be just fine with me, but of course with it on the news, that is unlikely. It's an old friend. Nobody you know."

"How cryptic." Brooklyn smiled as the familiar silhouette materialized above her. He pulled her to her feet.

"Listen, I'm sorry. I know this is not the date you had in mind."

She pressed herself against his chest. He smelled of sweat and peppermint. "This is exactly the way I imagined it," she deadpanned.

The next few minutes were spent raiding the store for clean clothing. Brooklyn splashed water from the bathroom sink on her face. She avoided looking in the mirror. The eyes there were haunted, she knew, a murderer's eyes.

She found Riley near the cargo door. "Hey," she breathed softly, "what're you doing?"

He smiled. "Waiting on our ride. How do you feel about riding in a hearse?"

Brooklyn grinned. "You're kidding, right?"

He didn't answer, but his eyes danced mischievously.

She didn't have long to wait. The familiar squeal of brakes and the low rumble of an idling engine announced their salvation. Riley lifted the door, and they slid under on their bellies.

Brooklyn stifled a gasp of surprise as the driver, a man no taller than her chest with a shamrock tattooed on his forehead, hopped down from the seat and opened the rear compartment with a familiar nod to Riley.

"In we go." Riley climbed into the back and held his hand out to her. Brooklyn saw the shape of a coffin filling the bulk of the space. She took his hand and felt the strength in his arm as he tugged her into the cramped space.

"The bottom panel is hinged. When we get close to the police roadblocks, you'll need to get inside and be still," the little man ordered gruffly.

"Thanks, Lucky," Riley said quickly as the door slammed.

"Lucky?" She arched her eyebrow.

"He's a leprechaun."

"Of course he is."

The car slid smoothly into the streets, weaving through the early morning traffic. Riley's eyes sparked like smoldering coals in the darkness as he looked at her. Brooklyn felt a blush rising under the intensity of his gaze. She spoke to ease the tension.

"Will Kurt know what has happened?"

"Undoubtedly. I think we must be on every news station by now, desperate criminals that we are."

"I don't understand how you are joking about this. How is this okay?"

His hand found hers in the darkness. "We are okay. Right now, here together, we are alive and we are okay. Right now is all there is, all that matters. We can't change what comes next by worrying." His other hand slid around her shoulders and drew her close. She let him, resting her head on his shoulder. Brooklyn felt the warmth of him through his shirt. He sighed. "And right now seems pretty good to me."

Something bubbled up in her chest, and her eyes stung with unshed tears. Everything he'd said was bullshit, but it was beautiful bullshit. Brooklyn pushed his arm from her shoulders, missing the weight of it almost at once, and turned on him.

"I'm sorry I didn't—" he began.

She pushed him hard against the coffin and pressed her lips over his. They stayed like that for long moments, Riley's eyes wide with surprise, and then she broke away. "I don't need you to be sorry. And I don't need your pity, either."

Riley was breathless and bewildered. "Okay, got it."

"I want you to look at me like I'm a whole person, not a charity case, or an interesting experiment, or an obligation."

"I don't think any of those things. I think you are amazing and strong. I just wanted to reassure you. That's all."

Brooklyn wanted to say something, but before she could find the words, blue strobe lights lit his face. Riley turned and lifted the hidden door in the coffin's side, and they slid into the velvety darkness together.

Kurt flitted like a phantom around the corner of the barn and let his eyes roam the field, muted gray by predawn light.

It was a pastoral scene he was familiar with only through the photographs sent by his team. Photographs that, he judged, had been taken from the east face of the mountain. He had crisscrossed that whole area in the last hour, straining his eyes and his awareness for any sign of life. It was as if his teams had never been here at all. The farm was strangely peaceful, everything as it should be, right down to the uneasy movements of large animals in the barn sensing his unfamiliar presence.

The western fields rustled restlessly, where cornstalks stood tall and dead and uncut. Kurt ghosted behind a large azalea bush as a light flicked on in an upstairs window. Through it, he glimpsed an older woman with sleepy eyes bustling about. There was something in the slope of her shoulders and the shape of her jaw that reminded him of Brooklyn. He felt a sudden irrational pang of guilt about not being forthcoming and bringing her along, but it seemed as if nothing was awry here.

Other lights bloomed like small fires in the darkness as the house came to life. In the sky, the first hint of orange sunrise rimmed the mountains and set the tasseled tops of the uncut cornstalks aglow. In the waxing light, Kurt noticed a lone figure on the front porch in a rocking chair, eyeing him keenly.

His first shocked urge was to take better cover, but instead, he stepped into the open and ambled casually up to the porch. The vague shape of a man resolved itself into an unfamiliar visage as he reached the bottom step.

The man's face was unfamiliar, but the mismatched eyes before him were seared into his memory. One filled with lightning and crashing waves, the other sunlight on blue water. Each spoke of the petulant and deadly moods of the sea.

"I don't believe I got your name last we met," Kurt said so quietly he wasn't sure the other man had heard.

"I don't make a habit of giving it out," he said casually.

"Fair enough. Think I've got a pretty good guess, anyway." Kurt climbed the steps and leaned back against the banister across from the man.

He was in the presence of a grade-two demon. Raw power radiated from it in dizzying waves. Kurt knew he should be afraid, filled with caution, but an unexpected wave of confidence and calm washed over him. The cards were on the table. No mystery or intrigue. This was a problem that could be faced head on, even if it were akin to facing a tank head on. "Prosidris, I guess the exorcism didn't stick?"

"They never do." Prosidris's voice was as soft as sea-foam.

Kurt wondered fleetingly if Erina knew what was happening. Surely, she would have warned him if she'd known this creature was back. "What are you doing here?" Kurt asked flatly.

"I could ask you the same. I could ask you a lot of things. I could ask why you've been summoning demons. I could ask why you've stolen the Ring of Solomon. I could ask you why you enslaved my son to steal the Death Tome." The demon reclined slightly in his rocking chair and twisted his host's lips into a sharkish smile. "Let your lies die on your tongue, Protector. I already know the answers. Let me answer some questions for you. Where are your men? Drowned by their own incompetence. Why am I here? I'm waiting for you or the girl because one of you will summon Belial, and that is all I really need."

Kurt felt cold all over. This creature knew too much. Kurt had known he was walking into a trap, but he never expected it to be something he couldn't outmaneuver. Kurt remembered joining his mind with the minds of the other Protectors, the way he had pressed this demon back, their wills expanding with all they could muster, only to have it thrust back by a force as vast and irresistible as an ocean tide. "I will not summon your son."

"I'll kill them. Kill them all if you don't." He jerked his head back toward the house at Brooklyn's family. "I'll even kill the little one. Now, let's be reasonable."

"Kill them then. I don't care." Kurt did care, he cared furiously, but he would not allow himself to be used as a tool for evil. "If you think you might force Brooklyn's compliance, you will need them alive." He kept his voice carefully neutral. "You won't have my help either way."

"Interesting sentiments for a Protector."

"Soon to be former Protector, I'm afraid." The knowledge of his men's deaths was like a knife in Kurt's heart. He had handpicked both teams for this assignment and sent them here to die.

"You don't look well, Protector," Prosidris said with mock concern. "Don't fret. Solomon's brats have always made fickle employers. I'm sure you'll land on your back somewhere." He paused as the full glory of the sun broke across the mountains. "Really, it isn't you I need. I trust that when you don't return, she will come looking for you or, finally free of you, she will come looking for her family. Either way, I'll be here waiting; patience has always been my greatest virtue. Until then, you'll keep me company."

"Don't move," Riley breathed into her ear as the back door of the hearse swung open. Brooklyn heard Lucky's voice, muffled but gruff.

"There. Nothing to see. You want me to pry the coffin open so you can do a cavity search of the corpse, or can I go now?"

"Yeah, yeah fine. Go on."

Brooklyn felt the door slam so hard it rocked the hearse like a boat. The car pulled away and sped up smoothly. After a few more moments, they spilled out of the coffin onto the floor.

"Claustrophobic in there," Riley gasped.

"I kind of liked it." Brooklyn winked at him conspiratorially.

"Good company, at least," he grunted.

Brooklyn smiled, and they lay together in the narrow space as the smooth pavement gave way to the crunch and bump of gravel.

"Thank you for being there with me," she said with a blush creeping up her cheeks, invisible in the dark.

"Well, they were going to capture us both." She felt him shrugging, though the light was too dim to see by.

"That's not what I mean. I'm talking about last night after the news."

"Oh," he exhaled, his breath breaking warm across her face. "You're welcome. It was nothing. I just wanted you to feel better."

"It was something to me." His eyes were large and luminous, the only part of him she could see clearly. Her palm found his chest easily enough and slid up along the curve of his throat to cup his cheek. They kissed then, by touch alone, in the darkness. The space allowed little movement, and without the possibility of more, the kisses grew long and languid, an end and a means to themselves.

Sometime later, when they both tumbled, flushed and breathless, into the cold air in front of Kurt's manor, they had to look at one another. Shyly, they watched the realization of what they'd done flicker in furtive smiles across the other's face. Seeking reassurances of their shared darkness in the first light of morning before they walked slowly, hand in hand, up the dawn-gray drive.

41

Costly Escapes

Belial watched the day dawn in the thick black lines of his blood as it swirled out onto the Tome's page. He lived again in the aching desire for Tais and her bitter loss. The image grew until colors and smells bloomed in his mind and he tumbled into the image of himself. His arms around her again looking into brown and green eyes. The water swelled over their naked hips. This was the part where he begged her to leave the water, warned her of the danger, but when he opened his mouth, the world froze and a strange voice hissed up from all around him.

"Do not etch your lies on my skin." Without warning, he was tossed back into his own mind and stumbled back from the Tome. The lines drawn in blood sizzled like grease in a frying pan, turned to ash, and fell away. The page again unblemished and beckoning.

Belial felt a coldness in his stomach as he opened a fresh wound and let the blood gather at the tip of his claw. When he touched the page, it seemed to draw the blood from him, tugging the memories from his veins.

They were in the sea as before, but Tais's brows were knitted with concern and his voice rolled from his lips in deep, soothing waves. "You are safe with me." His fingers deftly tucked a strand of blue-black hair behind her ear. "My father has promised to deal with this upstart king personally. He will never have your eyes." He kissed the lids then, delicately, first the green one and then the brown one.

"I do trust you," Tais shouted over the rising waves.

Belial circled her with his arms as the sea erupted and Prosidris rose up.

"Give her to me," Prosidris demanded without pleasantries.

Belial's thoughts were mired in molasses. Dread iced through his veins. "Why?"

"I've struck a deal with the king."

"Liar! You said you'd kill—"

"I said I'd deal with this king personally. I said the girl's father would never complete his bargaining. I've been true to my word on both accounts."

Tais clung to Belial, but her fierce eyes were turned on his father. Belial suspected she saw more, understood more, than he did. "You tricked me! I won't let you take her."

"You will." The certainty of his words crashed down on Belial like blows.

"And if I don't?"

"He'll kill you," Tais answered softly.

"Let him try." Belial bristled, looking past her to his father's tentacled form.

She kissed him and pulled free of his arms. Her eyes shone with unshed tears. "Be a good son today," she said in the rolling vowels of the Old Tongue. "I see the real you. One day, you will be a very bad son." She smiled sadly. "But not today."

Belial clenched his fists at his side and started forward. The sea crashed down over them. Belial was slammed against the driftwood where they'd hung their clothes to dry so many times. When the water receded, he was alone.

"Fool. Coward," he cursed himself as he looked down on the page at what he had struggled for so long not to remember.

The unfairness of being a fugitive gnawed away at Brooklyn's insides. Being with Riley helped her forget. She followed him, fingers laced with his, as he snaked his way through the maze of hallways in the manor house. They passed through a large room with a roaring fireplace, several dozen tables with white tablecloths, and the largest, most beautiful Christmas tree that Brooklyn had ever seen.

"How close to Christmas is it?" Brooklyn felt disoriented. "I just realized I don't know the date."

"Christmas is about two weeks away." Riley looked at her quizzically. "Are you okay?"

She realized, with a start, that this was the same room where she had stood trial. It looked so different, shrouded in decoration. Brooklyn could still see Stewarth on the dais pronouncing her death sentence where the nativity scene stood now. "I'm fine."

She followed Riley to the elevator and through another series of halls. They passed the room she'd shared with David. Brooklyn made a point of not dwelling on that thought. They came to a halt before a large oaken door she recognized as Kurt's office. Riley laid his hand against a stainless-steel plate just above the doorknob, and within a few seconds, the door swung open soundlessly. Riley crossed the room quickly to the ancient-looking desk and lifted a hand scrawled note and crossed to the window where the early morning light filtered through the treetops.

"Does it say where he is?" Brooklyn asked impatiently. She crossed the room and plopped down on the sofa in front of the fireplace. She watched Riley, whose eyes flitted with unsettling speed over the paper for at least the third time. Brooklyn noted the grim set of his jaw as he became more and more agitated. "What is it?" she asked again. When he didn't answer, she joined him at the window and plucked the letter from his fingers. Her curiosity turned to horror, and dread pooled in her stomach like mercury. "We have to go."

"He specifically says to keep you here. It's not safe for—"

"This is my family. We *are* going." Riley put his hand on her shoulder as if to stop her words.

"It isn't safe."

Brooklyn shrugged his hand off. "I don't give a damn if it is safe or not. That's my family. I'm going downstairs to get my soul stones and then we're going." She could see the conflict written all over his face. The desire to keep her safe warring with the desire to help her do what she wanted. "I'll be safer if you're with me," Brooklyn added softly. Then she turned and walked away.

Kurt watched in fascination as Brooklyn's father left the house and walked right by without seeing him. His troubled eyes seemed to slide over them both as if they could find no traction there. Kurt watched him until his puttering truck vanished from sight in the early morning mists.

"They may as well all be blind," Prosidris said, "for what little use they make of their senses."

Kurt said nothing. He had not expected such an old and powerful spirit to be uncomfortable with silence, but the less he answered, the more Prosidris spoke.

"I felt the world change the first time Solomon wielded the ring. The others were too stupid and too arrogant to realize how things were shifting. Belial included."

"Is there a point?" Kurt asked irritably.

"The ring is gone. Your world is regressing, so you must change with it if you hope to survive."

Kurt tasted bile in his throat. It was his fault.

"What's the harm in summoning my son? He has spent most of his life in your world as a Warden under the treaty."

"Do you know what the difference is between a spirit and a demon?" Kurt whispered so quietly that Prosidris stopped rocking to lean forward in his chair.

"Perspective?"

"Malice." Kurt reclined and peered at the entity across from him through half-lidded eyes. "Belial was a Warden, but now he's just a demon. He's broken Solomon's pact, and so have you."

Prosidris's mismatched eyes darkened until they conjured images of slimy predators so deep beneath the waves as to have never seen sunlight. "You, Protector, ring stealer, demon summoner, have no allies. Will you stand against me all alone?"

Kurt thought of his son, so near at hand. He could feel the power radiating from Prosidris in disorienting waves. This was not a winnable fight.

Demon summoner. Ring stealer. The words bounced around in his head.

Protector, whispered a smaller, less certain voice.

"Summon Belial, or give me Brooklyn Evers. I can be a powerful ally. I'm your best option right now. Your only option."

For the first time in a long time, Kurt knew what he had to do. The certainty, born from a lack of alternatives, settled in his stomach, warm and comforting. Tyler was out there somewhere, powerful and alive and safely anonymous.

"Yes."

Prosidris's eyes lit with triumph. A sharky smile split his face.

"Yes," Kurt repeated, "I'll stand alone."

The orbs slipped from Kurt's pocket and spun wildly toward Prosidris. Kurt dove from his seat and kicked a wicker table in Prosidris's direction. A thrill of satisfaction raced through him as he saw the demon's rocking chair go over backward and dump him in a jumble of furniture. Kurt leapt over the railing and it shattered behind him, splinters peppering his jacket before he touched the ground. Kurt twisted onto his back to face the house, raised both hands, and with a tremendous effort of will, ripped two wooden posts free of the house. The low porch roof, deprived of its supports, closed on Prosidris like a book with a satisfying clap.

Kurt rolled and came up on his feet, skittering backward away from the house, his eyes fixed on the place his enemy had been. The hair on the back of his neck prickled, and he sensed energy, lots of energy, flowing toward the house like a drawn breath. Kurt thought fleetingly of the three little pigs, and then the porch awning hurtled toward him like a truck. He dove to the side, but wasn't fast enough. The edge of the roof struck his thigh and sent him spinning into the barn wall.

Prosidris approached with predatory leisure. His eyes shone with a lust that gave Kurt the unsettling feeling the demon could scent the blood soaking his numb thigh like a shark.

"That was both foolish and futile." Prosidris gave Kurt a considerate look and drew his foot back and kicked him in the ribs.

Something inside him cracked. Kurt couldn't help it; he screamed. A hand that felt like a tentacle closed around his throat and lifted him, slamming him against the barn wall hard enough to rattle the structure and spook the animals inside. Kurt's mind reached for the orbs and couldn't find them. His fingers clawed at the thing around his throat. Darkness shrouded the edges of his vision. A savage slap jerked his face to one side, and the sting of suckers raking his cheek came a long moment later, accompanied by an insistent ringing in his ears.

Prosidris was speaking, but the words came from very far away and, try as he might, Kurt couldn't give the sounds meaning anymore. The face, at the end of the dark tunnel, smiled, then split open to reveal rows of jagged teeth. The stormy eye faced him, full of unrighteous wrath. Kurt's heart hammered in his ears. Far off, over the thundering of his heart, something roared. The sound ripped through his muffled hearing, and the face full of teeth exploded like a star.

Kurt hit the ground hard, gasped, and puked. When he looked up, he saw Brooklyn. Except that wasn't quite right. As his vision cleared he realized it wasn't Brooklyn. It was her mother aiming a shotgun at his face.

42

Hostages

Kurt's ears rang from the blast, but when Mrs. Evers gestured for him to stand with the barrel of her shotgun, the message was clear enough.

He stumbled ahead of her as best he could toward the house. Something in his left knee was damaged. A catch in the joint sent an unpleasant jolt through his leg with every step. She herded him around back to the kitchen door, the front door being somewhat inaccessible at the moment. Kurt could have taken the gun from her. At least, he was pretty sure he could have, but he didn't see the point. Inside, Kurt flopped down into a kitchen chair without being invited to do so.

"I want answers," the woman said matter-of-factly, as if the questions had already been asked and the answering was all that remained.

"Four, thirty-six, Brazil, photosynthesis." Kurt watched confusion, then annoyance, play across her delicate features. When she didn't take the bait, he said, "Oh, those aren't the answers you're looking for? Then you'll have to be more specific."

"Who are you? Where is my daughter?"

"I—" Kurt wasn't quite sure how to answer her about Brooklyn, and he didn't know how she had made that leap. But when Mrs. Evers jabbed the gun barrel against his chest, he decided maybe this was a situation that warranted the truth. "My name is Kurt

Levin. Your daughter is in Tennessee. I'm sure you've seen her on the news by now. And before you ask, no, she is not a serial killer."

"You are going to take me to her." It wasn't a question; it was a command. Tears stung the back of Kurt's eyes, but he refused to blink. He understood all too well what it was like to be separated from a child for reasons beyond your understanding or control.

"How about you put the gun down," Kurt said in his lowest, most soothing voice. "Put it down, and we can talk all you want. I'll answer any questions that I can, and I'll take you to see your daughter. That's fair, right?"

Mrs. Evers wavered. Obviously, she hadn't expected compliance. She eyed him dubiously. "How do I know I can trust you?"

"You saved my life out there. I don't take that sort of thing lightly. Besides, you're the one with a shotgun pointed at my heart. Seems to me I'm the one who has to be trusting right now."

She laughed shakily. "All right. All right." Mrs. Evers backed away from him until her hips bumped against the kitchen counter. She lowered the gun; the barrel pointed to the floor just in front of her feet. Kurt deduced from the easy, experienced way she held the gun that she could have it back on him in a blink. "All right, how about you start by telling me about that thing out there?"

Kurt took a breath. Either she would believe him or she would think he was insane and probably shoot his kneecaps off. He looked her directly in the eyes. "What you shot out there was a demon."

She nodded as if this were all very normal and expected. "My daughter, tell me her name."

"Brooklyn Evers, but I might have learned that from the news."

"And my other daughter? Did you take her too?" The gun barrel twitched up in his general direction and then settled back toward the floor.

"No, I'm sorry. I don't know anything about your other daughter. And just for the record, I didn't 'take' Brooklyn either." Kurt rolled up his pant leg to examine his knee. It was badly swollen and most of the skin had been scraped off on one side.

"Why is my daughter mixed up with you? Tell me what's been going on."

"Your daughter was possessed by a demon and—"

"I knew it!" Mrs. Evers leaned heavily against the counter. "I knew it. The erratic behavior. The memory loss. It all makes sense now."

Kurt blinked. He hadn't expected that. "She's fine now. I helped her, but she's made enemies, dangerous enemies. She's a wanted fugitive now. You understand why she didn't come home?"

"I saw her on the news," Mrs. Evers half sobbed. "I knew she couldn't have killed those people. My baby couldn't have done those things."

"You are right. She didn't. Well, she did, but it wasn't her choice. She wasn't in control."

Before either of them said more, footsteps pounded up the back stairs and the kitchen door burst open. Brooklyn's father's eyes darted from his wife with the gun held in her hands to Kurt and back again. Taking in the entire scene in the space of half a second. "Give me the gun, Jenny." He held out his hand for it, keeping a watchful eye on Kurt. His other hand had gone to his side to push a small blue-eyed boy behind him. "You stay right there, Devin. Don't move." He took the gun, letting his eyes flit away from Kurt only long enough to check the breach to verify that it was loaded.

This situation was quickly spinning out of control. Mr. Evers did not look like the sort of man who believed in the supernatural. He looked more like the kind of man who would assume the worst had happened to his daughter and shoot Kurt. "Mr. Evers, my name is Kurt Levin; I'm—"

Mr. Evers lifted the gun and pulled the trigger. There was a boom that rattled the windows. And blood, so much blood. Kurt felt the tears he'd been holding back for so many years spill down his cheeks in a gush.

All the air left Brooklyn's lungs as her house came into view. It looked as if a tornado had ripped the front porch off. Splintered wood littered the front yard all the way to the barn. Her dad's truck was parked beside the house with the driver's door standing open. "Oh my God, oh God. What has happened? Do you think they're okay?"

Riley squeezed her knee. "I don't know, Brooklyn. We're going to find out."

They parked at a distance and approached the house cautiously. The farm was alive with the sounds of morning. Sounds that Brooklyn had been accustomed to all her life and hadn't realized she missed until this very moment.

"Kurt is already here." Riley gestured to the tree line at the bottom of the fields, where Brooklyn could make out a truck disguised with tree branches. Just then, a muted gunshot rang out from the house. A flock of crows rose from the corn field beyond and filled the nearby trees with sounds of their disapproval.

Brooklyn dashed toward the house at a run. Riley's fingers clutched at her, but she slipped through them like cobwebs. She heard him behind her, calling her name in a frantic hiss, somewhere between a shout and a whisper.

Brooklyn rounded the house and went to her knees as her shoes slipped on the dewy grass. She scrambled up the stairs to the open kitchen door.

She saw Devin just inside the doorway, hiding behind her dad, who was holding a gun on Kurt. Kurt was slumped in a kitchen chair sobbing. Brooklyn pushed past her father to kneel beside Kurt.

She put an arm around his shaking shoulders and turned her eyes on her father. "What did you—"

The rest of her admonishment died in her throat when she saw her mom slumped on the floor, the front of her shirt torn ragged and stained crimson. Her lips moved soundlessly and dribbled blood.

"You shot Mom?" Brooklyn asked in disbelief.

"She shot me first." Her dad shrugged. "She kind of had it coming."

None of this made any sense. Brooklyn went to the floor with her mom and held her, cradling her head. As Brooklyn brushed the hair back from her mother's face, she could feel hot blood seeping through her jeans. Brooklyn looked up at her father again and saw a vast, unfamiliar intelligence behind his eyes.

"What are you?" she growled.

"Ah, I believe the correct question is: What do I want? I want you to summon Belial back to this world. Do that, and the rest of your family goes unharmed. Even your father if—" His eyes narrowed suddenly. "What have we here? A Tomekeeper playing house with humans? Found a way to study them up close, have you?"

Riley crashed through the open door on an invisible wave and slammed into the wall behind Kurt, arching his back and struggling against unseen force.

Kurt sat up straighter, eyes narrowing.

The demon waggled a finger at him. "Don't even think about it, Protector. You aren't fast enough, even with your little toys." Then it turned its attention back to Brooklyn. "So, what's it going to be, Princess?"

It inflected the last word just like her father would have, and it sent a shiver of revulsion up Brooklyn's spine.

"Don't," Kurt said, pulling himself upright in the chair and dragging his sleeve across his running nose. "Don't do it."

"She wouldn't be in this predicament if you had done what I asked you to do earlier. And we wouldn't have this mess," Prosidris said, gesturing to Brooklyn's mother.

"I don't know how to do what you want me to do," Brooklyn said.

There was a sudden flash of darkness, as if obsidian wings obscured the sun. In Brooklyn's arms, her mother made a choking noise and went still.

Azrael stood in the kitchen and watched the soul wisp away from the bloody body of Jenny Evers. "This is low, Prosidris."

He grinned. "We all do what we must do to survive. Even you, I hear?"

On the floor, a frozen Brooklyn cradled her mother's head, looking like a wax museum grotesquerie.

"They have enough pain in this world without you shitting on them."

"Sounds like Stockholm syndrome." Prosidris laughed. "Empathizing with your captors? Everyone I kill brings you a little closer to freedom." He smirked. "Unless you're ready to abandon your duties, fall, become a 'demon' like the rest of us? I know you feel the tug now."

"Fallen or not, I will never be like you." The weight of back-held time pressed against her. "Never." She spread her wings and vanished, taking Kurt with her.

Prosidris looked distracted for a moment, as if he'd lost his train of thought, but then said, "Oh, I can teach you how. It isn't hard, but we better hurry. People are dropping like flies in here."

Brooklyn shifted her mother gently back to the floor and stood up. She pointedly ignored the desperate look Riley gave her and noted the now empty chair where Kurt had been when she arrived. *Where did he go?* "Tell me what to do."

"Just remember him. Remember what it was like when he was inside your head. There is a ghost of him that lives in your memory. Latch on to that. When the shape of him seems so real you can almost touch it, smell it, and see it, give a mental yank, and let yourself go. Surrender to it."

43

Belial Returns

Belial turned the pages gently. He no longer needed to read the ancient text beneath the pictures because with a drop of blood he could live them. He suspected it was a secret that no one else knew. Otherwise, why would the Tomekeepers spend so much time researching these antiquated languages if they could just step into the memories?

After drawing the day beside the sea with Tais, he had been loath to touch the book again. But other memories burned in his mind like live embers, so again and again he poured himself into the book like a confession. To see his memories encapsulated here was strangely satisfying, but the Tome was selective. Some of the memories he'd drawn had bubbled and burned until the blood turned to ash and slid from the pristine vellum. He paused on the page where he clung to the dragon girl. Terraced coils of the dragon mountain loomed in the distance, and the eggs hung suspended between them.

There were so many other books in the room that he should have read, but he could not tear himself away from this Tome, this history of worlds. The uncertainty of his time here, which had once felt like a prison sentence, was now a gift he did not want to see ended.

He did not know if it was because the dragon girl had gifted him with the Tomes that allowed him the ability to see beyond the pictures and words. He thought often of his promise to deliver the eggs somewhere safe and warm and wondered if the secret to keeping that promise might be buried in one of the many volumes around him.

Belial was lost in just such thoughts when he noticed Brooklyn. The last time, she had drawn power from him and vanished in an instant. This time was different. She was summoning him. The library warped out of focus. *No*, he thought. He struggled to make himself heavier in order to remain here. When the impossibility of that became apparent, he cast his eyes desperately around for the eggs, but it was too late. He was drawn through the Pull. He spiraled between worlds until he saw her, a beacon in a sea of dim lights. She burned brighter than anything else, and he was drawn to her like a moth to a flame. The first time he had joined with her had been an act of desperation, but this was an act of compulsion.

He sank into her mind like a feather bed. The familiarity of her thoughts flurried around him. He drew a shuddering breath and relished in the familiar sensation of her lungs filling with air, ribs expanding. Belial smelled blood. The metallic ruin of it made his stomach lurch.

When he opened his eyes, he saw her father and—below the surface—his own father. Off to his left was a bloodied corpse he recognized as Brooklyn's mother. Belial felt a pang of sorrow at the sight and wasn't sure if it was his or Brooklyn's. She was strong enough now to keep him out, maybe even to push him out. Now he understood what had compelled her to call him back.

Brooklyn pushed her hair back from her eyes and sat up in bed. She could hear her mother and father bustling around downstairs. The smell of frying bacon drifted under her door. She checked her phone. There was a text from David asking if they could meet later. She sent a hasty reply with a smiley emoticon.

Brooklyn stood at the dresser and pulled her hair into a loose ponytail. She tugged on jeans from the day before and a shirt from the closet and padded downstairs, stifling a yawn.

Her dad was on the sofa watching cartoons with Devin, and for once he had on pajamas. He smiled as she walked through the living room, and Devin waved. In the kitchen, her mom was frying eggs. Scents of bacon, biscuits in the oven, and simmering gravy made Brooklyn's stomach rumble.

"Good morning, sleepyhead," her mom said. "I wasn't sure if you expected us to serve you breakfast in bed or what."

Brooklyn felt a smile tug at the corners of her mouth. "Oh, would you?" She slid arms around her mom's narrow shoulders and gave her a long hug. "I love you, Mom."

"I love you too, honey." She smiled.

Brooklyn squinted. For a moment she thought she had seen blood on her mother's lips, but it was just a trick of the light, or maybe some lipstick from the day before.

"What's wrong?" her mother asked, brows knitting together with concern. "Is everything all right?"

"Yeah, Mom. Everything is perfect."

Prosidris's mouth split into a feral grin. Belial was dumbfounded to discover that his father could make dentures look sharkish. "What have you done?" He gestured to Brooklyn's dead mother.

"She shot me first. Why do I have to keep explaining this to everyone?"

Belial could feel the power rolling from his father in sickening waves. "Why did you summon me?"

"The world is changing again. I need my son by my side. I don't know why you always seem so surprised when I save you. You would have died or become feral a long time ago if it wasn't for me. I make harsh choices. I do what must be done so that we can survive." His eyes narrowed shrewdly. "Do you have control?"

"I do."

"Show me." He stepped to the side, revealing the quailing figure of a young boy. Devin. He jerked his head in the boy's direction. "Kill him. Then I'll know you have your bitch on a leash."

"No!" The skinny man yelled, leaping onto the kitchen table.

Belial recognized him and plucked his name from Brooklyn's memories. "Riley! I thought you died?"

"You are a Warden! Do your job. Send him back to Hell!" Riley shouted.

Prosidris laughed. "Well, I'm glad we all know one another." With a flick of his wrist, he sent Riley spinning by the seat of his pants into the wall for a second time. "Let's get on with the demonstration, shall we?"

Belial pushed Brooklyn's hair off her forehead. Long hair was such a nuisance. "I won't do it."

"Oh yes you will." The words hammered him with their familiar weight, implied threats, and a supernatural compulsion to obey. His eyes flickered from his father to Devin and back again; he wasn't sure what to say. He did not want to kill the little boy, but if he refused, his father would probably do it with horrific flair just to make a point. "When they're all dead and she has nothing to live for, then she will submit. Be strong, son; do what must be done. I might not always be here to do it for you."

"Okay. Give me the gun." Belial held out his hands.

His father laughed. "Do you think me stupid?" He gestured to a large cooking knife on the countertop. "You can prove your loyalty and strength with that."

The boy watched him pick up the knife, terrified beyond tears or words, standing in a pool of his own urine. Belial could sense Brooklyn in the back of his mind, shrouding herself in fantasies. Willfully disconnected from reality. It was always like this.

Prosidris was quicker, smarter, and more powerful. His father always won.

44

AWAKENING

"Mom!" Devin cried out from the living room.

Brooklyn whirled so fast her ponytail swung across her face. She pushed through the kitchen door and skidded to a halt. "Erin! You're back!" Brooklyn wrapped her arms around her sister and lifted her off her feet.

"Put me down." Erin laughed. "I just went down the street to get juice for breakfast."

Brooklyn let her slide back to the floor. "You've been gone for almost three years. You vanished. The police searched; we searched . . . "

Erin pushed past her. "Mom, Brookie's being weird again."

Brookie. The nickname felt like broken glass in her stomach. Brooklyn reached up absently to touch the scar on her chest, but found only smooth, unblemished skin. Her head was spinning. It was all a dream. The whole crazy thing had been a nightmare. She followed her sister into the kitchen and stopped short. Her father stood near the door on the other side of the room, holding a gun. Devin crouched behind him, smiling. "W-what are you doing?" she stammered.

"Brought this in out of the truck to clean it," he said slowly. "What are you doing?"

Brooklyn looked down to see a large kitchen knife clutched tightly in her fingers. She didn't remember picking it up. "I was going to slice the biscuits."

"Well, slice them then," her mom said with a smile. Her teeth were red with blood. Brooklyn blinked, and the blood vanished.

"Are you okay?" Her sister's face twisted with concern. "I can do that if you want." She held her hand out for the knife.

"No! No. That's okay. I need to do this myself." Brooklyn hated what she had to do.

She concentrated until their concerned faces evaporated. Until she stood in her kitchen again, soaked in blood, facing her father. She moved unwillingly forward toward Devin. The morning sun sparked off the stainless-steel blade in her hand.

"Go on. Cut his throat so we can get out of here."

Brooklyn fought for control, expanding her will outward like a bubble filling her skull. Her fingers loosened around the knife. She squeezed them tight again. Belial pushed back, and it felt like supporting a tent against an avalanche. The tent collapsed, and the bubble popped. Icy numbness pressed in from all sides in a susurrus. Brooklyn gathered all of her willpower into a tight little ball in her chest. She fed it her sadness at being forced to leave her family and the uncertainty about her sister. The ball grew hot. She let the image of David tackling Nathan Goodrum sink into it, and the uncertainty and fear began to burn away. It hurt. A lot. The cold and numbness burning away.

"Trust me." Belial's voice echoed in her mind like a loudspeaker. There was desperation there. The ball in her chest seared like a flame. Brooklyn gave it the image of her mother bleeding on the kitchen floor. Then the bubble popped. Her will exploded outward in a hot fury, and Belial was silenced.

"No," she said aloud. An answer for Belial and his father.

Prosidris's eyes narrowed dangerously. "You will not ride my son like a pack mule, you insolent bitch." He lifted the gun and pulled the trigger.

Brooklyn raised the wedge of energy she'd been gathering and felt the massive blast pass its kinetic energy through the shield into her chest. The pellets screeched along her barrier, sending an agonizing series of jolts through her skull. "You're out of ammo."

"You cannot fight a force of nature." He flicked a finger, and the knife leapt from her fingers and hovered against Devin's throat.

"No, don't!" Brooklyn reached out for the knife with her mind. It twitched; the tip grazed the boy's throat and drew a line of red. He whimpered and shrank further into the corner, trapped. Sweat trickled into her eyes as she fought for control. The handle of the knife blossomed with frost.

"Your life is over," Prosidris growled. "Give up." He redoubled his efforts, and Brooklyn gasped as she felt her mental grasp slipping. The blade grazed Devin again, and he drew a terrified yelp.

"Maybe. But his isn't." The soul stones rose from her back pocket. A trickle of blood tickled her upper lip. The stones whistled through the air. One struck Prosidris in the thigh and another in the ribs. His grip on the knife wavered for only a second. Brooklyn's heart sank. She looked into her father's eyes, which no longer looked human. They danced with the fierce beauty of a sea storm. A trickle of blood oozed from one of his nostrils just as the third stone passed through the demon's eye and into her father's brain. Only after Prosidris's grip on the knife fell away did she realize Riley had been struggling alongside her the entire time.

Brooklyn sank to the sticky floor and wiped the blood from her face with the backs of her hands. She looked from her mother to her father and back again with a strange detachment. Riley knelt beside her, looked into her pupils, and touched the side of her throat with his fingers. "I'm fine," she slurred. "Check on Devin."

Brooklyn squinted through the darkness that shrouded her vision. Something with black feathered wings knelt over her father and then a light, bright as the sun, rose and faded away. Something dark blue and covered in tentacles lurched from his dead body and latched on to Devin. She reached for it with her mind, but there was nothing left inside her.

Belial pushed her back then. She couldn't shackle him anymore. He sailed free of her, collided with the tentacled thing, and wrenched it away from Devin, and the two of them drifted away to some other hell in a snarling ball of claws and teeth.

Brooklyn lay on the floor with her family and let the darkness settle over her like soft, warm feathers.

Kurt landed hard in his office. Azrael stood over him, brooding. "Go back for the others." Kurt coughed.

Her laughter was like tinkling glass. "No more errands. No more games. You bought one life, and it is time to pay. We finish our deal right now, or your child dies."

"Okay, okay." Kurt raised his hands in surrender. "I'll give you what you want, and you give me my son?"

"That was our original deal, more or less."

Kurt rolled to his feet and brushed off his pants. "We'll go through the cellar." Kurt wasn't sure but thought Azrael flinched, a momentary ripple in the otherwise smooth and placid surface of her face.

They arrived at a hidden entryway next to Riley's laboratory. Kurt reached through the stone with his mind to release the internal latch. "This whole place is built on top of an old missile silo. There's enough living space underground to survive the apocalypse."

Azrael said nothing.

Gradually, the path turned upward, and they emerged in an enormous cavern. The uneven topography of the ceiling spoke of natural formations, not the work of human hands. Kurt wove his way through the stalagmites to a crevice on the far side. He turned sideways to fit through the narrow passage. Within a few feet, it opened into a room lined with stone shelves carved into the rock walls. One shelf held a large wooden box covered in intricately carved symbols. The inlaid lid gleamed darkly with a large black Celtic knot, a triquetra.

Azrael beat him to it. Excitement made her seem almost human. Her long, pale fingers traced the shape of each rune and symbol. "How does it work?" she asked.

"Just connect the dots." He took her hand in his, noting again the uncharacteristic warmth, and traced her finger in a circle from the tip of the knot to the second and third points and finally back to where they started.

"Just a circle?"

"Yes. Now lift the lid."

Inside in individual slots, a thousand Celtic knots waited. Each pulsed with spiritual energy.

"It's beautiful." She closed the box gently and lifted it.

"Now it is time for you to uphold your end of the bargain," Kurt said.

Azrael flickered out of existence for a moment and back again. She smiled. "Your reincarnation has been delivered to your office. Our deal is done."

"I'm begging you. Please help Brooklyn and Riley. I can pay somehow."

There was no answer. She was already gone.

45

ULTIMATUM

The rattling doorknob woke David. He tossed the blankets aside and fumbled for the jogging pants they'd given him. Two sets of footsteps crossed the room quickly and pulled him from the bed by his arms. "What's going on?"

They didn't answer, instead hoisting his legs one after the other into the jogging pants, dressing him like a child. David thought of elbowing one of them in the face and making a run for it. He hadn't heard the door close. But run where? He was blind and didn't know the halls. Escape was a remote possibility.

He counted as they walked. Forty-seven steps on tile floors. Left. The soft change in air pressure of a door opening and another twenty-three steps—on carpet this time—left again. Seven stairs down to a landing, seven more stairs and through a squeaky door. They pushed through a heavy cloth and then their footsteps became hollow and loud. David became aware of murmurs and whispers and sensed many people gathered in hushed anticipation. He was on a stage.

"Welcome. All welcome." The voice belonged to Father Logan. "Today we begin the initiation of our newest brother." Muted applause rose all around David. "For thousands of years, our sacred order has guarded the spiritual purity of humanity. We have long fought against those unnatural forces that would twist and pervert our intrinsic divinity. We do not require dark spirits to be powerful. We do not welcome demons into our bodies. Do not consort with them or call them up from Hell. Ours is the power of unity. Our strength is togetherness. We are one mind, one body."

"One mind, one body," the assembly answered in unison.

"Together, we will rise up and eliminate the scourge that has festered in our leadership. Brother David has been misled. His eyes have seen vile things and judged them beautiful. Only through the trial of blindness can he learn to see things as they truly are. David. Will you drink from the cup of truth, open your eyes, and see?"

A smooth wooden goblet pressed into his hands. A slow chorus of whispers rose in unison from the crowd. "Drink and see. One mind, one body."

David lifted the goblet to sniff the contents and froze with the cup touching his lips. Suddenly, he couldn't move. It was as if he had drifted into a vacuum free of sound.

I wouldn't drink that if I were you. It was the angel's voice in his mind.

Why not?

Drink that, and your free will evaporates. At least as my prophet, I won't control your perceptions. Her hand cupped his cheek, and her breath was like an arctic breeze. She pressed her thumb between his eyes. *You don't need their poison. All you need is me.*

With a shudder, he opened his eyes. It was less painful this time as the information flooded in. She was a beautiful silhouetted shadow backlit by dozens of dancing flames, the burning lives behind her. The shape of the room came to him as well, an image in his mind, roughly sketched by brilliant blue lines of electricity running through the walls. David looked down at the cup. The liquid there shimmered silver and beautiful. *What is it?* he asked.

I don't know exactly, but I've seen what it does to the minds of the people who drink it. There is a reason the numbers of the Prophets have grown so fast.

Won't they force me if I refuse?

Faith! I'm here with you now. I'll tell you what to say.

David's ears popped as the sounds around the room resumed. Words bubbled up on his lips unbidden. “Father Logan, have you ever sipped from this cup?” David looked directly at him as if he could see and proffered the cup. The question, the look, and the gesture rattled Father Logan. David could not see the priest's face, but he perceived in other, deeper ways. In the subtle change of aura color around the false prophet and the kernel of violet anxiety that bloomed and grew in his chest. David pressed on boldly. “Well?”

Gray uncertainty drifted up from those in the crowd.

“Enough!” Father Logan bellowed. “Make him drink.”

“I serve the God of Death. Touch me and die.” David repeated the words without conviction or inflection.

The men beside him did not hesitate to force his head back and wedge his jaws apart. His heart pounded as he struggled. The wooden vessel smacked against his teeth. In a whoosh of wings, David stumbled free, his assailants lifeless at his feet. The cup dropped, and the contents spilled.

“Dark magician. Demon consorter!” Father Logan raised an accusing finger at him, and a murmur of assent rolled through the crowd.

David saw the indignation and wrath flow out of Father Logan and settle over the assembly in a sullen red web connecting each to the others and all of them to Father Logan. The room erupted in a chorus of homicidal outrage.

What happens next is up to you. Prove yourself a worthy prophet.

“I serve Azrael, God of Death; I welcome all who would join me, and death will welcome the rest.” David nudged one of the dead men with his toes, causing him to tumble from the stage with a thump of meaty finality.

Nausea-green uncertainty spread across the red tendrils of the web. The shouting faltered. David reached out with his mind. He could see the shape of his will coalescing in front of him.

The job of shaping it—that had once seemed impossible—was effortless now that he could see the task. He made contact with the web, and his awareness exploded into hundreds of minds. Panic and confusion at his presence ran rampant. He pushed the wild feelings away and moved through the web, spreading feelings of peace and calmness until, beneath the turmoil, he felt the manic undercurrents of Father Logan's mind.

David singled out a thread that ran to a blonde woman in the crowd. David pulled until the thread stretched and snapped away from the rest and attached itself to him. Father Logan let out a feral growl like a wounded animal, and more red light rippled across the web. David felt the woman's pain and horror in a crippling jolt as the mob dragged her to the ground and trampled her. The delicate filament connecting them winked out of existence.

"Mine!" Father Logan snarled.

David didn't know how he navigated the web; somehow he just sensed where to go, moving like lightning to the convergence, the place where all minds connected in a tangled mass to Father Logan. Red aggression pulsed through the filaments, and already the mob was clambering onto the stage to attack him. In seconds, they would do to him what they'd already done to one of their own. He shaped his will into a scythe and swung it cleanly through the convergence.

A sudden hush fell across the room as David became aware of the expectant attention of hundreds of minds. They were his now. All of them. A thrill of elation sizzled through him as they began to chant, "Azrael, Azrael, Azrael." He became so caught up in the moment that he failed to notice Father Logan had slipped quietly away.

Prosidris's power made him heavy. Belial twisted wildly in the tentacles that wrapped around him, tearing into his father's gelatinous underbelly with claws and teeth. The Pull dragged them down like falling stars. Every instinct screamed for Belial to spread his wings, to beat furiously against the inevitable impact, but his father's embrace made that impossible. Belial felt his unmaking approach. The final death. He envisioned his soul—as if he had such a thing—sluicing away into gossamer threads, twisting fractals, blue and bursting with brilliant futility. It might be worth it if it meant the world would be safe from his father, but it wouldn't be.

A sudden solidity spread across his skin, coating him like iron. His father's tentacles became transparent and insubstantial. He hovered between worlds, watching his father writhe and twist in his fall, fierce and terrible. The Pull fell away and Belial drifted upward, drawn back by an unseen force.

The world resolved slowly, the way sunrise robs the obscurity of darkness by degrees. Then at once it materialized, emerged whole before him, birthed from the shadows.

He stood opposite the skinny man, Riley, the Engineer, who hadn't died when they fought that night months ago. They were on the back lawn behind Brooklyn's house. The boy, Devin, was asleep on the man's shoulder and behind him, flames licked along the rafters and eaves.

"You set it on fire?"

"It seemed like the best way. We need to get the boy somewhere; I think he's in shock. I summoned you back because I was moved that you would sacrifice yourself to save him, and the rest of us, for that matter." The man stuck out his hand. "Truce?"

Belial pumped his hand firmly. "Just for today."

"Call me Riley."

"Belial."

"I know." He looked as if he wanted to say more, but the boy moaned, twisting his head, nuzzling against the man's neck.

Belial pulled his hand back and resisted the urge to wipe it on something. He had sensed something unnatural when they touched. This man was not possessed, but he was not wholly human, either. He was something else, something new. Curiosity gnawed at Belial, but there wasn't time. "Where are the others?" Belial cast an uneasy glance at the house, which was now fully engulfed in flames.

Riley answered by pulling a shiny black feather from his jacket pocket.

Belial recognized it instantly. "Are they—"

"No. At least, I don't think so."

"Are you going to take him back with you? Devin, I mean."

Riley gave him a strange look. "Too dangerous. Kurt thought he would be safe here. We set up guards but—" He shrugged helplessly.

"Kurt Levin is the cause of all of this. There's going to be a reckoning when I see him."

Riley turned to face him. "No, there isn't. What's done is done. We move forward from here together, or I'll send you 'back where you belong.' Your words, I believe."

"What are you going to do with the boy, then?"

"Put him safely beyond your father's reach."

"No one is safe from Prosidris, least of all me. There's nothing you can do. Hopefully, he won't be interested in the kid anymore."

The faraway trill of sirens rolled across the fields. Riley shifted the boy's weight and shaded his eyes, looking out at the ribbon of asphalt in the distance. Plumes of thick black smoke billowed from the house now.

"I thought about leaving him here for the firemen to find, far enough away from the house to be safe. Let them take him somewhere. Probably better we don't know where."

Without a word, they turned and jogged across the yard. Riley propped Devin against a tree, facing away from the flames where he was sure to be noticed.

The sirens were getting closer now. They sprinted for the tree line and watched until the firemen wrapped Devin in a blanket and the ambulance arrived and left with the boy. As they turned to go, the last remnants of Brooklyn's home collapsed with a roar and a hiss. Belial winced; it felt like a knife in the stomach.

Kurt hobbled up the stairs, ignoring his screaming knee and shouldering aside anyone in his way. He paused at his office door. Breathless, his heart hammered and his injured leg was on fire. He reached for the doorknob, then hesitated. His hands were trembling. What if Tyler didn't remember him? What if he resented being brought back?

Kurt steadied himself, took a deep breath, and pushed the door open slowly, quietly. Someone had stoked a fire and made the room stuffy and warm. Shadows danced and flickered on the walls in time with the soft crackling. He didn't see anyone in the room; his heart fell. Then he noticed a prone figure on the couch swaddled in blankets. Gingerly, he peeled the blanket back to reveal a face. Shock coursed through him.

"Brooklyn." The name escaped him in a sigh of disbelief and wonder. He sat down hard on the coffee table. "Brooklyn." There was dried blood on her face, and her hair was matted. How could this be?

Blood, he noticed, ran in fresh trickles from both her nostrils. The sight jolted him into action. Kurt scooped her into his arms. Her skin felt cold and clammy against his. As the blanket fell away, he saw her shirt still soaked with her mother's blood.

Brooklyn still breathed; for that he was thankful. Kurt limped to the medical wing, shouting instructions at the staff as he burst through the double doors. He placed her gently on a gurney. Nurses bustled around her, took vital signs, wiped her nose, and placed oxygen tubes in her nostrils. Somewhere along the way, Kurt was pushed back. He only caught glimpses of her as the doctor strode in from the back room with a clipboard and a stethoscope.

Kurt's thoughts moved slowly. He remembered the night he made the deal to save his son. At that moment, he would have sold his soul and burned the world down to save Tyler. Azrael had warned him that a soul was not personality, or identity, or memory, just a divine spark, a battery for life. If that were true, then why did his heart ache as they wheeled Brooklyn into the back room where Riley had been for so long?

"Into the miracle room," Kurt said to nobody in particular as he sat down to wait.

46

On the Head

Brooklyn drifted untethered in inky blackness, an endless sea of darkness and unfeeling. In the void, she had no dreams, no family, and no pain or pleasure. She did not exist. She floated outside the bounds of time. Centuries passed, civilizations rose and fell, and none of it mattered. Thoughts came sometimes, fragments of images, glimpses of a face she couldn't put a name to, and then they were gone just as quickly. Thoughts flashed sporadically like heat lightning and left her blinded by the afterimages. She preferred the numbness.

One vision bloomed blacker than the surrounding darkness. Perhaps she had been dragged into the deepest depths of the ocean by Prosidris. Drowned far beyond the reach of sunlight or warmth. *This is fear*, she thought, *this is hell*. But like all her thoughts, there was nothing to sustain it in the emptiness. It pulsed in the synapse of her mind, the last effort of a dying neuron extinguished. She did not have a body, a neuron, or a synapse, for that matter. She was the darkness and nothing more.

Somewhere in the recesses of her unconsciousness, the names of her family clattered against one another like bells, creating a terrifying cacophony. She was frantic to turn her mind elsewhere, and let these noisy thoughts evaporate like all the others, but they would not. This was harder. This was pain, and she wanted the numbness and the silence back.

Hushed voices assaulted her ears, as if they feared to wake her but intended to brave the task, anyway. Brooklyn felt a sharp pinch at the back of her hand and that's how she learned she had a hand. Slowly she grew a body out of the void, a sense of self built on a latticework of sensation. Scratchy blanket, cold toes, throbbing head. Bit by bit, she was born into pain, into life.

"Brooklyn, can you hear me? Can you open your eyes for me?" A man's voice coaxed her. Agonizingly, she did, only to have the bright lights force them closed again.

"I'm hungry," she croaked out. Her stomach felt like a shriveled prune. Strong hands helped her into a sitting position and guided a straw to her lips. Her own hands shook with feebleness.

She drank the broth greedily. The warmth of it spread through her like fresh blood. How had she become so weak? Had she become an old woman in this bed? Perhaps lying in a coma for a hundred years or more. "How long was I out?"

"About twelve hours." A cool hand smelling of antiseptic pressed against her forehead. "How do you feel?"

"Everything is bright and loud and my head hurts. Everything hurts."

"Good, very good. I think you're going to be just fine."

"I don't feel just fine," Brooklyn grumbled, and forced her eyes open. Even squinting, the dim lights were a violent assault. She slurped the rest of the broth, feeling wholly unsatisfied. "I'm still hungry."

"Let's give it a few minutes and see if you keep that down, then we can try something heavier."

She groaned in response and surrendered to the weight of her eyelids.

Sometime later, she was aware of a heavy hand on hers. She could think of no one it might be. Everyone who had ever loved her was dead. Riley! It must be. He must have escaped. She squinted against the light. It was Kurt. His familiar caramel eyes were soft with concern and something else.

"I'm glad you are okay." He smiled.

Brooklyn couldn't remember if she had ever seen him smile before. She smiled back tiredly. "Hey. How long have you been here?"

He pushed her messy hair back from her forehead. His hand was cool and heavy. "I never left."

She took his hand in both of hers. Brooklyn wanted to say: *I don't have anyone*. But that was pathetic. Instead, she said, "Thank you." Maybe he understood, anyway.

Kurt opened his mouth like he wanted to say something and then thought better of it.

"What is it?" she asked.

"I wanted to say I'm proud of you. You were very brave back there. And don't think you don't have family; you do."

Azrael watched the slow, strange expressions that played across David's face. The Prophets milled around uncertainly below the platform, dazed in the wake of the sudden leadership change. She could almost make out the inky gossamer threads of shared and misguided beliefs that bound them together into an impressionable hive mind. She wrapped her arms around David and whispered behind his ear, "Dismiss them. I'll be waiting in Logan's office. You'll find the way."

The office was sparsely decorated and unremarkable in every way, save for a bookshelf with an eclectic collection of religious and supernatural texts. She had not expected so much of the occult to pique the good Father's interests. She ran a pale finger along the spine of *Divine Demons of the Fall* and pulled a copy of *Blood Gods: A History* from the shelf. The cave drawings and description-based sketches pictured in the book were outlandish and exaggerated, but she recognized the garish visage of many old acquaintances and noted the absence of just as many, lost to the obscurity of time and human memory. A fate worse than death.

It was several minutes later when David stumbled awkwardly through the doorway. She stretched her wings lazily, as much to impress her visage upon his new sight as to relieve tension. "Now that we've addressed your sight, let's move on to your oversight." He nodded unflinchingly, so she continued. "Father Logan seems to have escaped your notice."

David shifted from foot to foot like a little boy in the principal's office before he spoke. "He is no longer a threat. Without his followers, he is—"

"Blind," she finished for him. "Blind but not dead. Not a threat, you think? I'm sure he thought the same of you just a few hours ago."

"Blind?" David asked, as if the word itself were offensive.

"You started this day with no eyes. Now you have hundreds scattered throughout this compound. You only need to look through them."

His expression shifted from confusion to concentration, then to disbelief and awe. "Unbelievable."

"The Prophets have many conclaves around the world, still bound to Father Logan. Thousands of shining eyes. Will they be his, or will they be yours?"

"Ours," he said firmly. The notion brought a smile to her lips.

"Ours indeed. Come then." She spread her arms to embrace him and her wings to carry them. "Let them choose you or death."

47

Sins of the Father

Kurt had just slipped—half against his will—into a fitful sleep when the alarm trilled overhead. The exhaustion of the past few weeks evaporated. Brooklyn bolted upright in bed, looking as grumpy as a bear roused from hibernation.

"Stay here," Kurt commanded softly as he slipped from the room and closed the door gently behind him. Beyond the doors of the medical wing, the halls bustled with activity. He found himself swept along in a torrent of clomping boots and frenzied energy.

At the eastern staircase, he broke free of the throng and climbed to the third floor. The stairs emerged into a quaint common room that overlooked the southeastern fields. The house's evening shadow speared across the fields like an accusing finger at the loose clusters of soldiers assembling themselves to surround the manor.

Kurt took it all in at a glance. The sun glints of prone snipers on the ridge crests to both the right and left, the larger numbers of mixed-rank soldiers at the main gate, and though he couldn't see from here, he suspected a look out his office window would find the back of the manor equally besieged.

There were faces he recognized. Nathan Goodrum leaned heavily against one of the few shade trees in the expanse of grass, his coterie spread in a loose circle. They looked pale and sickly down to the last man. Demonriders deprived of their demons. It made sense—if they thought Kurt held the Ring of Solomon—that they would face him demonless to deprive him of a weapon that might be turned against them.

In the far back, Eric paced between his mother and the other Protectors, Brianne and Michael. The set of Eric's slender shoulders spoke of ruthless determination, but already sloped with an age-inappropriate weariness that grieved Kurt even now. A boy forced too soon to take on too much. He yearned to put a comforting arm around those shoulders, but it appeared the days of discussion were dearly departed.

Directly below Kurt, a line of his own men poured from the main entrance and formed a semicircle. The snipers on either side shifted restlessly. Bloodhounds on taut leads. Kurt pulled a piece of paper and a pen from a nearby table and scribbled a hasty entreaty for a peaceful discussion. He deftly folded it into a paper airplane, raised the window, and sent it spiraling toward Eric. It bobbed and wove, born on the invisible tendrils of his will. Every eye traced its graceful arcs until the weight of so many expectant gazes came to rest on the pasty boy they called leader. Kurt watched long enough to see the message read and Eric's face harden. He crumpled the paper in his fist and dropped it at his feet.

Eric strode forward and raised a bullhorn to his lips. "Protector Levin stands accused of murder, conspiracy, and treason. In one minute, we will enter. Surrender now and be forgiven. Stand with the traitor and die."

One minute came and went twenty times over before the blended forces were properly organized to make the assault. Kurt felt helpless fury as the seconds ticked away without clever options presenting themselves. Maybe there were no clever ideas to be had. Sometimes there was only the obvious way, no matter how messy and dangerous. Again and again, he agonized over what words might sway Eric from this path. In time, the boy could be made to understand. In time, working together, Kurt was sure they could reclaim the ring from Azrael. With Brooklyn safe and the deal concluded, he owed no allegiance to the God of Death.

One at a time, the seconds slipped away until there could be no more time for thought. Somehow, he'd imagined them advancing in the neat orderly lines of a well-drilled army. Instead, they came at a run like a pack of wolves. Kurt snatched two cue balls from the pool table and flung them from the window. They sped up, striking the snipers almost simultaneously. He immediately missed his orbs as someone wrenched the balls from his mental grasp, leaving a dull ache between his eyes. Brianne. It could have only been Brianne. Gun fire erupted from both sides as Kurt ran for the stairs. The cue balls trailed him, crashing blindly through the walls.

The Adepts would wait for him or Riley to direct them. He found them, as expected, just within the entryway, shifting uncomfortably in borrowed body armor. Tessa gave him an uncertain smile, as always, seemingly oblivious to the effect her blackened teeth had on others. When this was over, he'd pay to get them fixed if she wanted. Beside her, Raul stood stoically, eyes averted. The muscles in his jaw flexed rhythmically. Saul. Saul had volunteered to accompany the second team to Brooklyn's house. Saul was gone. Kurt felt a pang of guilt. Raul didn't know yet about his twin. Or maybe somehow he did. The other four Adepts were new and still had that pale, strung-out look of recently failed Demonriders.

"Follow me. Stay close." Together, they pushed through the rear ranks.

The field was alive with gunfire, though none of it had been directed at them yet. The Adepts crowded close behind Kurt as they entered the fray. He shaped his shield into a concave wedge. A loose pack of demonless Demonriders advanced along the left flank under cover of gunfire. Kurt searched their faces, but Nathan Goodrum was not among them. Many of the faces he had identified from the third floor were lost in the rolling terrain and chaos of battle. "Tessa, deal with those." He gestured to the Demonriders with contempt.

She smiled with fierce enthusiasm and slipped through the shield like a wraith. From somewhere within the folds of her faded Army jacket, she produced three circular blades that gleamed dully in the overcast morning light. Kurt didn't see the results. His attention was drawn away by a flurry of automatic gunfire pelting the right-hand side of his shield, but he heard the wet screams of the Demonriders cut short. The bullets against the shield felt like a jackhammer between his eyes. Thankfully, his men returned fire before his shield could buckle.

A gurgled shriek jerked Kurt's eyes back to the left. Tessa was on her back dragging herself on her elbows, two of her own blades stuck bone deep in her upper thighs. Blood soaked the front of her pants and trailed wetly as she dragged her useless legs. Nathan Goodrum stepped over the corpses of his fallen men. His cruel smile, paired with his sickly pallor, gave him a feral look as he advanced on Tessa. Kurt took a deep breath and flared the shield out, reworking the wedge into a cylinder large enough to encircle Tessa. The effort was excruciating. Unlike a wedge, a cylinder had no single point of focus. The same properties that made a circle excellent for containing demons also made it very inefficient as a shield. Raul and one of the new Adepts, a petite blonde girl, ran to Tessa and dragged her back.

Another spray of bullets pounded against the shield, forcing his focus away from Tessa. When Kurt turned back, Nathan Goodrum was gone. Two of the new Adepts carried Tessa back to the manor, safely behind a line of armed men. Kurt, Raul, and the remaining three pressed forward until they arrived at the crest of the first hill. It was the first defensible position, far enough away from the manor to prevent a sudden rushed entry, but close enough to prevent them from being cut off from retreat.

With a cursory look around for more gunmen, he let the shield fall with a pop. Those who remained with him spread out in a loose semicircle. From this vantage, he could see the field again. The motley army consisted of a left flank of disorganized Demon-riders looking withered and pale even at a distance. The Heir's household guards were in the center, each cradling a machine gun, near the other Protectors with a small group of Adepts. Beyond the Protectors, Eric and his mother, ringed by personal guards, appeared to be having some sort of argument. Kurt held the hill as his armed guards brought the line forward and descended halfway.

Kurt directed the Adepts to support the advancing line and intercept any interference from power users on the other side. He watched as they trailed the soldiers, casting uncertain glances at one another. *Christ! They reek of inexperience.* Gunfire erupted on both sides. "Shields!" he bellowed, raising his own again, small and efficient this time. A shrieking roar raced from the ridge to his right. A moment later, the front door and the men who guarded it were blown apart. Fire clung to the wreckage, licking hungrily. He scanned the hills, looking for the source of the rocket. It was the whine of a second launch that gave him the location of the shooter. The rocket struck ground behind the left flank. The concussion from the blast battered Kurt's shields down, and a spray of scalding sod peppered him. Bodies were tossed in a dozen directions and dead before they hit the ground. Kurt wrenched a knife from the boot of a fallen man and flung it at the reloading rocketeer. Guided by his power, it sank to the hilt between the second and third ribs. Too little too late. The damage was done.

48

Punishment of the Child

Brooklyn woke to screaming. A mixture of voices rose like a cacophony of dying birds. One shriek rose above the others and was shushed by a rush of low, soothing words. The scrambling footsteps of running medics made tiny ripples in the IV bag's fluid. Brooklyn struggled to sit. Once upright, she carefully pulled the needle from her arm and tugged the oxygen nubs from her nose. She found her clothing laundered and neatly folded on a nearby table.

The inhuman screaming faded into drugged moans and then stopped, leaving a vacuum of silence. Brooklyn eased out of bed and had to steady herself as a wave of dizziness blackened her vision. After it passed, she dressed, ignoring the protest of aching muscles, and slipped quietly from her room.

There were gurneys in every bay. Groans interspersed with quick bursts of medical directives met her ears. Through a partially opened curtain, she spotted Tessa on her back with shiny circular blades sticking out of both legs. Bile rose in her throat. Brooklyn swallowed and moved on. Just as she reached the exit, a nurse burst through and almost bowled her over. She tried to bypass Brooklyn, but Brooklyn grabbed her arms firmly. "What's going on?"

"War," she blurted, impatiently shoving Brooklyn aside.

The hallways beyond the medical center were deserted. She tried to jog, but quickly became winded. Black spots swam before her eyes, forcing her to sit against the wall with her head between her knees for several moments. Down the hall, Brooklyn found a window that looked out over the fields and the battle that raged there. From this distance, details were obscured by dust and smoke. An explosion rocked the house; cracks spider webbed across the window inches from her nose. She stumbled back the way she'd come and found the stairwell that would lead down to Riley's lab. On the way down, Brooklyn detoured by the kitchen to grab food. She was probably going to need the energy.

In the dining hall, dozens of women and children huddled, talking. Boys, obviously too young to be fighting, stood solemn watch at the entrances. Brooklyn felt ashamed that she had lived here for so many months and knew no one. She did not know so many people lived and worked here. The guilt was compounded because recognition lit their eyes, and they admitted her to the kitchen without question. She quickly rummaged through the pantries, grabbing snacks, a bag of semisweet chocolate chunks, nuts, and a handful of cookies off a cooling rack. Brooklyn dashed back to the stairs, eating as she went, ignoring the inquiring stares that followed.

Once she reached the lab, she rummaged through drawers, dumped out boxes, and flipped the mattress off the box springs, looking for weapons. She needed her soul stones desperately, but they were lost in the ruins of her old life. In the end, Brooklyn came up with a small razor-edged disk and a combat knife that got strapped to her thigh. She finished the last of the cookies, tore open the bag of chocolate, and took the stairs back up two at a time. She grew breathless almost immediately, but blackness did not threaten her vision anymore.

On the first floor, she heard a woman sobbing and a commotion from the dining hall. Brooklyn followed the sound. Strange men, pale as wax paper, herded everyone into one corner of the room. Knives danced in her stomach.

"Hey, you, get over here against the wall," one man screamed at her.

She came forward stiff legged. Her mind whirled through plan after plan. She was vaguely aware of the sobbing she had heard earlier becoming more distant, moving away from her down the hall. One of the sickly-looking men grabbed her shoulder and shoved her roughly toward the huddled women and children without bothering to take her weapons. None of the men had guns, which made her suspect they didn't need them.

As she stumbled into the crowd, a thin woman grabbed her arm. "My daughter. My daughter. They took her. You got to do something. Can't you do something? Get us out of here!"

"Who took her?" Brooklyn asked, trying to extricate herself from the vise of bony fingers.

"The leader. Nathan Goodrum." A new dread blossomed inside Brooklyn and threatened to wring all the air from her lungs. David's face swam before her eyes, unbidden. She pushed it away. "You got to do something. You're the only one who can do something. Please!"

"If Goodrum has your daughter, she's probably already dead. There's nothing I can do." Brooklyn winced at the unintentional cruelty in her voice, and continued less harshly. "There's five of them and one of me. What can I do?"

"Anything! Something?" Brooklyn pulled her arm free of the woman's grasp and stumbled away. She had to get away; she couldn't listen to this anymore. Her head throbbed and her eyes ached. Her mom's bloody corpse haunted the backs of her eyelids. The woman with her hopes dashed, sank to the floor and wailed. Brooklyn squatted and covered her ears, trying to block out the sound. The screams became Devin's.

Brooklyn felt ashamed. Five unarmed men. Pale and sickly looking at that. What would David do? She already knew because he'd done it for her. She slid a finger inside her shirt where the scar above her heart ran like a thorny vine, Nathan Goodrum's gift to her. He'd murdered David. Now he had this woman's daughter. He was here. He'd dared to come here, the arrogant bastard.

"Come on." Brooklyn took the woman's hand and pulled up. "Here's what we're going to do."

The woman nodded her understanding, and they separated, threading through the crowd, whispers spreading around them like wildfire.

Brooklyn glanced around the crowd. All eyes were on her. Several of the women gave nods of affirmation. She nodded herself and reached beyond the five men and slammed the dining hall doors and locked them with a thought. The men flinched and turned toward the sound.

That was all it took. The prisoners moved in unison, a human wave that crashed and broke over the startled Demonriders. They were dragged down and trampled before they even fought back. Brooklyn looked away. She'd seen enough blood.

Kurt used his mind to scoop handfuls of dirt into the eyes of the opposing gunmen. Blinded, they were easily picked off. His line advanced, stepping over the fallen men. The other Adepts hurled stones and blades. Some of the newer ones froze. A boy no more than nineteen, a mop of brown hair, died with a blade in his chest because he couldn't raise a shield. Kurt flung the knife back at its owner with such force that it passed all the way through her throat hilt-first, but that didn't bring the boy back.

He glimpsed Eric pacing in the distance and turned toward him. If only they could talk, they could end this madness. He dashed forward but met heavy resistance. Kurt plowed through soldiers and Demonriders alike until he came up against Brianne. Steel blades floated outside the wedge of her shield, daring him to take another step. She arched an inquiring eyebrow above her wizened eyes. “Going somewhere?”

“I just need to talk to Eric. We can sort this misunderstanding out.” The words sounded absurd, even to himself.

“Return the ring, and flee into exile. Please.” Compassion and duty warred in her voice and expression.

Kurt shrugged helplessly. “Don’t have it.”

“My God, what did you think was going to happen? Why would you take the ring?”

To summon a horde of demons to fulfill a twenty-year-old contract with the God of Death in payment for the reincarnation of my son. “It’s complicated, Brianne. But you know me. Know the kind of person I am . . . I had every intention of returning that ring before Stewarth died.”

She looked troubled. “I thought I did, but we both know where good intentions lead.”

Kurt couldn’t dispute that. He’d set quite a literal precedent recently. But aloud he said, “Talk to him for me. Tell him to give me time. I’ll find a way to get the ring back. If he kills me, where’s the benefit? He still won’t have the ring.”

“It’s more than that, Kurt. Eric has named a new Protector.”

He couldn’t hide his shock. “Who?”

She nodded to the rows of pale soldiers. “Take a guess.”

“No. Hell no!”

“As articulate as always.” She smiled sadly. “He’s committed. He couldn’t back down now, even if he wanted to. Goodrum has always wanted to be a Protector. Giving it to him is the safest thing Eric can do right now. He can’t afford to have them as enemies without the ring. You put him in this situation.”

Kurt felt a stab of guilt. He knew it was true. Everything was happening now because he had set the clockwork in motion long ago. But then, that wasn’t right. None of it would have happened if they hadn’t attacked his family. Trying to trace the causes and effects back into the murk of memory made his head ache. "I don't want to fight you. Any of you. There must be another way."

"Surrender. Nobody else has to get hurt. I'll ask him to go easy on you. He likes you. He looked up to you once. He's angry and hurt right now, but I'm sure he'll see reason with some sound guidance."

Kurt considered being sealed away in some dungeon away from Brooklyn. Rotting while everything he'd clawed for over the last twenty years evaporated. He couldn't let that happen, couldn't throw it all away, not after all these years finally reunited with his son, no, daughter, he corrected himself. He'd come too far already. "No, Brianne, I can't do that."

Power bristled between them like heat lightning. Kurt recoiled, realizing this might be a fight he couldn't win. "It's nothing personal," Brianne said.

A second later Kurt clutched at his throat. Where his shirt collar had tightened—seemingly of its own accord—and cut off his breath.

Brooklyn dashed down the hallway, ignoring the pounding in her ears. She swallowed the last of the chocolate from the bag. The path was easy to follow, marked by askew pictures and intermittent bloodstains.

She arrived unexpectedly outside Kurt's office. A pitiable whimpering pierced the heavy wooden door, sounding all the more forlorn for it. Brooklyn pushed it aside, her stomach coiling and uncoiling by turns like a yo-yo.

"Brooklyn!" Nathan greeted her without turning. He squatted over a series of symbols painted on the floor. A girl faced Brooklyn, bound to a chair beside Nathan. She sobbed as blood ran down her arm in rivulets and pooled in a wooden bowl in her lap.

Goodrum casually dipped two fingers in the bowl and continued drawing the symbols with absolute focus.

Why does there always have to be so much blood? "What are you doing?" She tried for an air of casual curiosity but didn't quite filter all the trembling from her voice.

"It's obvious Kurt doesn't have the ring. He could command an army of demons if he did. So, there's no reason we should be weakened any longer. Want me to summon yours, too?" He smiled knowingly.

"I'm not like you," Brooklyn blurted out, disgust dripping from every word.

"Not yet," he agreed, "but I could teach you to take the reins, to shed your emotions."

"Shed my humanity, more like. I've seen how you live. Like robots. I'd rather die." She knew she should be choosing words more carefully, but they bubbled up, unstoppable, from the tight knot in her chest.

"And you might at that." He dipped his fingers into the bowl again.

Brooklyn inched closer. He seemed oblivious as she lifted a pair of scissors from Kurt's desk. Even as she began to cut the tape that held the girl in the chair, he didn't move to stop her. He scrutinized the symbols, making small adjustments.

"I'm surprised you're alive at all. You wouldn't be if that poison had gotten to your heart," he said absently. "I guess you can thank your big blind fool for that, if you ever see him again."

Brooklyn's heart seized, declining for several long seconds to beat. Did she dare to hope? Could he mean David? David had saved her, but he wasn't blind. Hadn't been, anyway.

The girl, freed from the last of the tape, bolted from the room with a guttural sob. The bowl tumbled and splattered blood across the wall. Brooklyn watched it drip down in parallel lines before she spoke. "I don't know any blind fools."

"The idiot that tackled me off of you."

"You killed him. You or one of them." As she said it, hatred dredged up images of stabbing the scissors into Goodrum's throat.

Nathan looked up, smiling in disbelief. "Is that what Kurt told you to keep you from searching? To keep you safely under his thumb and out of the way?" A look of pity tugged the corners of his mouth down. "What a mind fuck. I'm sorry."

Brooklyn wasn't sure if he was mocking her or not. She touched the barbed scar above her heart. The scar he gave her. It tingled and ached. Or was that her heart beneath? She couldn't tell. False hope is real poison. Aloud she said, "You're lying."

"I have no reason to lie to you. Kurt is corrupt. A traitor, a hundred times worse than any of the rest of us. I would have gladly killed you that night to ruin him, but that's no longer necessary. In fact, I'm glad you are alive."

"He's really alive?" Hope blossomed, painful and raw inside her. Thoughts tumbled through her head, vying for attention. Kurt had saved her from Belial, from execution. He'd had no motive but goodness that she could think of, but he'd tried to keep her confined here every moment since. Whether for her own safety or for selfish reasons, she didn't know.

"He was alive the last time I saw him. About a week after I gave you that." He gestured to the twining scar.

She pulled her shirt up self-consciously. "Where is he?"

"Father Logan had him, last I knew. I've since parted ways with that pious prick." He stood and moved uncomfortably close to her. He took her wrist in his stained hand and pulled the scissors from her grasp. A trickle of fresh blood smeared her palm where she'd clenched her fist around the blades. Goodrum flicked her wrist, casting droplets into the center of the painted symbols that began to pulse with a reddish light. He stepped away to stand in the circle once more. "Let me teach you how to control rather than be controlled. Then you'll have the power you need to get him back."

The hair on the back of Brooklyn's neck stood up. His words mixed with that garish red light tugged at something primitive inside her. Primal desires for safety, power, and something darker she couldn't name.

The light intensified around him. "I need an answer, Brooklyn."

49

Minions of Death

Azrael danced across the battlefield. Whirling among the whizzing bullets like a harem girl, wings trailing like scarves. They followed in her wake, a grotesque coterie of misshapen demons. The first ten she would train to sever souls from the dying. Freedom was coming. She could taste it, smell it, feel it like a spray of hot arterial blood against her alabaster skin. The demons dashed from body to body, not as fast as she could have done it, but because of them, she would soon not have to do it. "No more the slave of death," she hummed contentedly to herself. Azrael passed beyond the fighting to perch beside the king without a ring. He would be a delicious boy if he didn't scowl so much.

"For Christ's sake, he must have the ring. There are demons everywhere out there. You see them?"

"They are not fighting," Del Stewarth commented as she passed the binoculars back to her son. "Can't tell what they are doing."

"All it means is he lied about having my ring. My ring!" he repeated petulantly.

"You will lead without it if you must. If it is not recovered today, then we will let all of our allies believe it was, anyway. If they believe you have it, they will submit."

"Bluff my way through the next fifty years? That's your plan? Just hope the Demonriders never call me on it?"

Azrael flickered away. Their bickering bored her. Across the field, Kurt struggled with Brianne, clawing at his shirt collar as it suffocated him. She waited patiently. His would be the last soul she would personally sever from this realm. Poetic justice. Beyond him in the house, Brooklyn, freed from a lifetime in Death's shadow, shone like a meteor burning up in the atmosphere. It was fitting that these two should perish here. The living reminders of her transgression erased on the eve her shackles fell away. Freedom even from memory, freedom to be reborn, reinvented.

It was a clever gambit, Kurt thought with admiration as his face purpled. So intent they always were on holding shields against projectiles that they seldom considered the weapons already behind the shield, let alone around their own throats. Brianne hadn't gotten old in this world by being stupid.

His shield fell first and then he fell, too. The panicked need for air clawed at his sanity. Thoughts rattled uselessly against the inside of his skull and clattered to a halt. Brianne's shoes were coming toward him. Slow, deliberate steps. He tried to look up and couldn't. The shirt collar tightened mercilessly whenever he moved. He wondered with sudden terror if his eyes might pop out and roll across the grass to be crushed under the heel of her shoe. *Shoe. Shoe.* The word lodged in his blood-deprived brain, a mantra without a meaning, the answer to a forgotten question. It was the half-suffocated madness that gave the answer, a dim flash like the last light of a dying ember.

Shoe. He mouthed the word soundlessly. The shoe was coming down, down out of the growing darkness like a plane landing. Before it landed, he moved it with everything he could muster. She tumbled with a cry of shock, and air rushed into Kurt's lungs, setting off a series of gasping coughs. Under other circumstances, he might have felt guilty yanking the feet out from under an old woman, but not right now.

Around the battlefield, the gunfire intensified amid frantic shouts. Kurt felt what his spotted vision couldn't see. Demons. A lot of demons. *Brooklyn!* Kurt rolled to his feet, but Brianne was faster, striking him across the jaw with a metal baton. He spun and fell again. Beyond Brianne, the pale, expectant faces of the Demonriders turned skyward as if in prayer. Energy pulsed soundlessly across the open fields, and then the screams started.

Isn't she worried? Of course not, he thought groggily, spitting blood onto the grass; they were her allies. Brianne had risen to one knee, the club in her hand drawn back threateningly. "Don't move," she hissed through clenched teeth.

He moved. Rolling out of her reach. She lunged for him and struck the ground where he'd been. Her leg buckled and dumped her in the grass. Scrambling backward, free of the bubble they'd occupied, he cast his eyes around the larger battlefield. They were losing. Men he'd known for years lay lifeless and riddled with holes.

Raul, ringed by Demonriders, slashed wildly with the blades in his hands and those that floated around him like bloody satellites. It made a frenzied blur of blood and steel unlike anything Kurt had ever seen. *The boy has talent*, he thought, but there were too many of them and with their demons, they were much stronger now. Kurt watched helplessly as the Demonriders ripped Raul's weapons from his grasp and plunged them into his torso over and over again. Kurt lanced out with his will and tried to wrest one of the daggers away, but the attempt was shrugged off almost effortlessly. One of them, a young man with close-cropped red hair, glanced over at Kurt. He smiled and winked before he vanished back into the midst of the battle.

He had seen enough to know this fight was lost. "Retreat!" Kurt bellowed over and over. It was too late. The Demonriders formed ranks and pressed forward. His men's guns were yanked from their grasps, some with such force that fingers caught in the trigger guards were broken. The bulk of those who heeded his cry turned to run and were cut down from behind. Those who stood their ground were crushed underfoot as the line advanced and everywhere, on both sides, the shadow of death danced with her demons.

50

Homecoming

Brooklyn watched Nathan change before her eyes. As he spoke, the fanatical urgency drained from his voice. The animated expression on his face hardened into a mask of careful control, and his gestures stilled. His eyes darkened as the internal struggle resumed. When next he spoke, it was in the familiar, chilling voice of the Demonriders.

"I will summon him here now, and you will take control." It wasn't a question; it was a directive.

She took a small step backward and shook her head.

"Yes, you will. No one has ever successfully taken long-term control of a grade-three demon; under my direction, you will be the first."

Brooklyn unsheathed the knife at her thigh and raised it between them to ward him off as she inched still further away.

Goodrum laughed an otherworldly laugh. She felt the knife go taut in her hand. Brooklyn struggled to keep her grip on the handle as he steadily increased the force until the tendons in her wrist screamed and her fingers sprang apart. It was a power so vast and executed with such restrained finesse that she knew she could never hope to match it.

"Don't do it for me. Do it for yourself and for your blind lover. I'm offering you the strength to save him, the strength to be free of Kurt and all the rest of them. The Ring of Solomon is lost; the line of heirs is broken. Our power is unchecked now. The days of taking orders from a Protector or even an Heir are almost done."

"You don't offer freedom; you offer slavery."

"I offer power. The only 'slaves' are those too weak to deserve it, like those failures Kurt 'rehabilitates.'" He took a step toward her.

She took another step back, reaching back, fingers brushing the doorknob. Brooklyn turned the knob and yanked. Nothing happened. It was as if the door were nailed shut.

Nathan continued, as if he had not noticed her futile attempt to escape. "This is the one." He pointed to a symbol on the floor, the only one not glowing. "This will bring him here."

Brooklyn's hand dropped numbly from the doorknob. Her eyes followed the intricate interplay of lines. It was oddly familiar with edges sharp as icicles and inner swirls that conjured the essence of snow and great empty plains of permafrost. Beneath the guise of desolate ice, she sensed the fervent heat of life in the Arctic, flames of hope standing in defiance of the cold expanse somehow. It was as complicated and beautiful and unfathomable as Belial himself. As she gazed at it, the depths of meaning resolved themselves. There was a true heat there too, an unexpected, volcanic passion threatening to rupture the icy exterior.

"Do you know why blood is such an important part of summoning?" Goodrum went on without pausing for her to answer. "All spiritual life came from the First Mother, a single source of creation, and the source of all sustenance. In those days, much as now, there was a separation between the spiritual and the physical aspects of the world. The mortal world and all that lived within it died, but they also multiplied. That was something the spirits could not do. They lived forever, but depended on the First Mother for any new creation and for sustenance. Then, the legends say, she became enamored of the way creatures of the physical world grew independent and multiplied without taxing their creator. She grew exasperated with her children and their eternal dependence on her, so she abandoned them, giving her blessing to humanity instead."

"What blessing?" she asked.

"Will, dominance, strength. Souls, if you will."

"She changed us?"

"Yes," he answered with restrained jubilation, "some legends say that as humankind has grown exponentially, so too has the blessing." Nathan smiled slyly. "Here's the kicker. All the spiritual world was suddenly cut off from its source of sustenance. They don't need this food to continue existing like you and me. They can go for thousands of years, but over time, they grow weaker and less substantial."

Brooklyn released the doorknob, leaning back against the cool wood as Nathan continued. "Somewhere along the way, they discovered what they craved wasn't really gone. It was trapped within people, particularly within their blood. I'm sure you can guess what came next."

Brooklyn swallowed, her throat suddenly dry. "Slaughter? War?"

"Blood sacrifice. They took the sustenance however they could. Some established themselves as gods and demanded blood offerings. Lesser ones found other ways to harvest what they needed. Incubi and succubi were born. They became dark and terrible. They became demons, and by taking sustenance from humanity, they bound themselves to us inextricably."

"What does this have to do with Belial or me?" She wasn't sure she wanted to know the answer.

"You are symbionts. You make each other stronger. The only question is who holds dominance."

Brooklyn bit her lip thoughtfully. "What does it feel like to—you know—ride a demon?"

"Terrifying at first, like hang gliding in a hurricane. And then you just feel powerful. You are powerful. You are—"

"No longer human," she finished softly.

He looked to her uncomprehendingly and then down at his own bloodstained hands. When he raised his eyes again, they were cold and dull and hard like granite.

"The battle is over, and Kurt Levin will not be returning to protect you this time." He crossed the space between them in a heartbeat, pinning her against the door. He smelled of sweat and blood and something vaguely floral. Nathan touched her cheek, and she shuddered inwardly, but didn't flinch, unwilling to give him the satisfaction. His finger left a smear of blood as he traced down the side of her throat to the beginnings of the black scar that peeked out from the top of her shirt. "Maybe I'll keep you as a pet."

Why do I never have my soul stones when I need them? she thought as she grabbed his finger and twisted it away from her chest. "Don't touch me."

His eyes widened in disbelief as heat leached from his finger and frost burned its way over his skin. He lurched away from her.

"I think you better find a warmer pet." Brooklyn flung the door open and darted out before he could recover.

His words chased her down the hallway. "Belial is the only thing special about you. Without him, you are nothing! NOTHING!"

Belial spotted the smoke first, black billows over the trees. "There's nothing else for miles around. That's Kurt's house." Riley's knuckles tightened on the steering wheel as he sped into a deep curve, tires chirping indignantly on the narrow two-lane.

They were brought to a sudden and screeching halt by a barricade of military vehicles and a number of armed men in fatigues. One of them approached with an automatic rifle hanging loosely from his shoulder. "Road's closed. You'll need to go back and detour around the—" his eyes widened with recognition when he saw Riley, and widened further in shock when he saw Belial, who had neglected to hide his true form.

He made an unintelligible grunting noise and jerked his rifle up. Riley reached through the open window and grabbed the barrel. He yanked hard, causing the soldier to stumble face first into the door. Riley kicked the door open, sending the man rolling away from the car. The other men were slow to react. Riley slammed the shifter into reverse and floored it. Automatic gunfire followed them as the men scrambled into jeeps and trucks.

Belial ghosted out of the car and stood in the road, drawing himself up to his full height, spreading his four wings. He let the bullets pass harmlessly through him as their focus shifted from Riley's backward escape to him. He lumbered forward, baring his teeth threateningly and growling. Several men in the front row almost fell down in their haste to retreat. These were contracted men with little idea what they'd gotten themselves into.

When Riley had been given a sufficient head start, Belial flew up, hugging the treetops as he approached Kurt's manor. The scene before him reminded him of Hell save for the presence of vegetation. The odor of voided bowels, piss, and blood permeated the air. The sheer human wreckage, twisted and mangled bodies, made him shudder, and beneath the revulsion he hungered. Belial could sense Riley's location in the trees below as he circled the west side of the compound. Dispassionately, he watched Brianne struggle with Kurt, and resisted the urge to swoop down and help her finish the job. The part of him that yearned to fulfill his duty, to exact justice, was overridden by his more pragmatic thoughts and the promise he'd made Riley. Kurt had faced Prosidris and lived, even triumphed briefly. That wouldn't be allowed to stand. Perhaps punishment for his crimes was still in the making.

Belial's attention was drawn suddenly to the summoning. He felt a breach in the Pull as the demons came through to rejoin their Demonrider hosts. He turned his course eastward, gliding low over the eaves of the manor to rejoin Riley.

They stood together in the tree line, surveying the field below. The Demonriders and the Protectors cut through Kurt's men with ease. "We need to help," Riley said. Belial wasn't listening. He felt Brooklyn as she drew power from him. She was inside the house and she was in trouble. "Are you listening?"

"Brooklyn's inside." Without further explanation, he took off and sailed through an upstairs window. The sound of shattering glass reminded him he should have ghosted. It didn't matter; the sound would be lost in the battle below. Inside, Belial reached out again and again, but could not sense her. She was on this floor. That was the only thing he was sure of from their brief contact. He bounded down the halls, shifting forms as he went to maximize speed. He flung open every door he encountered. In one room, a young mother and two small children huddled in the middle of a bed and screamed upon seeing him. Most of the rooms were empty. As he moved systematically toward the northeast corner of the house, the hallways began to look familiar, modern sterility giving way to plush, old-world extravagance. Hardwood paneling, period lighting, and thick carpeting smeared with blood. At the corner where this hallway met the next, he entered Kurt's office. The heavy wooden door hung ajar, wrenched partially off the hinges. There was a lot of blood here, a summoning circle with a patchwork of demonic sigils, including one that was strangely familiar. It sent a shiver of anticipation and dread through him.

His eyes traced the swirl and swoop of lines on the floor; his essence written in blood. It conjured memories of snow and vast, empty spaces. The stubbornness of glaciers and the muted terror of deep, icy waters. The tension of temperature, hot and cold, at war within a single being, but there was so much that it didn't capture. So much had changed. Even in the last year. *I have changed.* The thought was a strange one for one as old as he. It took him by surprise. He turned a bowl of congealing blood upside down, filling in the gaps, erasing himself from the floor. Afterward, he turned and jogged down the northern hallway. It didn't do to dwell, and for once—he vowed—he wouldn't let the girl down.

51

Fleeing Friends

Riley sighed in exasperation as he watched Belial disappear through the window. Below, Kurt stood almost completely alone against an army. He was retreating one step at a time into the burning wreckage of the manor's entryway.

Eric's amplified voice echoed between the two ridges that flanked the valley below and reverberated up into the trees. The Demonriders pelted Kurt's shield with such savagery, Riley wasn't sure how he summoned the strength to maintain it.

In the valley to Riley's right, a line of soldiers emerged from the tree line and stepped deftly over the corpses of the house guards to enter the rear of the estate. Kurt was being surrounded.

Riley let his focus shift, surrendering control to the other part of himself. His eyes flicked across the scene below with stunning speed and clarity. He perceived small details he would never have noticed otherwise, and time seemed to slow down. Riley lanced out, focusing on several dozen targets at a time. The gunfire petered out as the soldiers fumbled with their weapons and discovered the safeties were engaged. One of the men swung his rifle to the side as he worked to release the safety. Riley helped him and then depressed the trigger, sending a spray of bullets into the other soldiers. Several of them went down.

Sweat sheeted down his ribs and back. He'd done all he could do. Even small tasks were taxing at this distance. Desperately, he dug through his pockets until he found the soul stones he had recovered from the wreckage of Brooklyn's house. He dashed through the edge of the trees, staying hidden as much as possible, although he suspected no one was looking in his direction. When he got as close as safety allowed, he drew back and threw the stones in a long high arc toward Kurt. They fell short, but unable to wrap his mind around them, it was the best he could do.

Riley turned and dashed back the way he'd come, angling down for the back door. He leapt over the bodies of the guards without slowing down, mentally drawing his own soul stones from his pocket as he went.

The soldiers had a significant lead on him, but he assumed they would be moving straight ahead to attack Kurt from behind. Riley ran full ahead with no thought of stealth or his surroundings.

Just as he reached the foyer, the floorboards rippled under his feet and a wave of hot air flung him back. His eyes clenched; he reached instinctively for the soul stones that had been wrenched from his grasp. He sat up and looked stupidly around, intensely aware of his own heart thudding over the ringing in his ears and of the burning wetness that covered the right side of his face. Smoke and heat seared his lungs with every breath, and he heard the pitiful moans of other people around him, the soldiers he'd come to stop.

A low groan shuddered through floors above as the house settled on weakened supports. The wreckage of brick and marble before him had once been the foyer, and flames danced triumphantly around a hole in the floor where Kurt should have been.

Nathan Goodrum caught her before she reached the stairs. Brooklyn knew instinctively that she could not defeat him. His words rang in her mind, and she knew they were true. There was nothing special about her; the only thing she had was Belial's power, and she couldn't control that reliably. It was more of a reflex than anything.

He cornered her in the bathroom. The finger she had frozen looked angry and purple. His expression was one of controlled hatred. It promised cold, passionless violence. "Soon you will beg for the poisoned knife again."

Brooklyn shuddered inwardly at the implications. He took a step toward her, but the floor lurched beneath him. A mirror fell from above the sinks and shattered. Brooklyn braced herself against the windowsill as the house settled noisily back onto its foundation. Before Nathan recovered, Brooklyn launched broken shards of mirror at his throat.

He batted them away easily. With an impatient wave of his hand, the partitions separating the toilets screeched free of their brackets and crashed down on top of her. The impact caught her just above the right temple and drove her hard into the tile floor.

The floor was cool against her cheek. Brooklyn felt numb and tired. Oh so tired. She might have slept, right then, right there, on the floor beneath the rubble, if not for the incessant whooshing in her ears. Brooklyn twitched her head irritably, trying to block it out. The whooshing, no, whispering, she realized foggily, was growing more insistent. She tried to understand, to focus on the words, but she was too tired. It felt like trying to identify the sound of individual raindrops during a thunderstorm.

Breathing was agony. The act of inhaling required her lungs to bear up all that was on top of her, and then the weight pressed down, wringing the air from her lungs like water from a dishrag. Brooklyn wondered vaguely what it would feel like to stop, to quit trying, to let go.

There were footsteps nearby, and she remembered she was not alone. Careful, calculated footsteps, the sound of glass grinding on tile. The whispering intensified. Brooklyn wanted to plunge her fingers into her ears, but her arms were pinned at her sides. She could not move at all. And the voice, she realized, was inside her head.

Belial? she thought.

The noise resolved itself into words. *Let me in. Let me help you. I'll leave as soon as you are safe. I promise.*

It was tempting. It was also exactly what Goodrum wanted. *I'd rather die.*

She could sense his frustration as he tried to say more. *No*, she thought more firmly, and then just like that, he was gone, leaving her at last to die in peace.

Belial growled in frustration. He'd finally found Brooklyn when she'd gone up like a flare. A sudden scorching light that was there for a heartbeat and gone. He wouldn't be the only demon that had sensed that power when she lost control. He had glimpsed enough of her thoughts to know who she faced. Belial knew he could not stand against Nathan Goodrum in his true form. He was too insubstantial, too easily banished by someone who knew how. Riley was in the building, but far below him, and Brooklyn didn't have much time. Belial hated everything about what he was about to do.

He found the mother and her two children where he'd left them. Under other circumstances, he might have changed his form and lured her from the room, or made himself invisible, but there wasn't time. He dove into her. The children screamed as the monster vanished inside their mother. Another time, she might have thrown him off. But these were not other times. He was free of the Pull, and terror and shock worked against her. She raged and struggled, but it was too late. He viciously shoved her into an obscure corner of her own mind and locked her there.

"It's okay. Mommy will be right back," he said in her silky voice. He disentangled himself from the children. "Stay here, be quiet, and don't let anyone else in." Their eyes were solemn and round and full of tears as he turned away and latched the door against the begging and shrieking pleas.

When Belial arrived, Goodrum was lifting the bathroom partition with one hand and dragging Brooklyn out by her hair with the other. Belial slipped up behind him, planning to snap his neck quickly, one smooth motion like a golf swing. The crunch of glass gave him away, and Nathan whirled around, letting the divider drop back on Brooklyn's legs. Nathan's eyes flicked over him, cold and calculating. He saw a waif of a girl, nothing else. He came forward and tried to shove Belial back through the bathroom door, but Belial grabbed Nathan's arm, pivoted, and stuck out his foot. Nathan stumbled and pitched forward. Belial slammed his fist into the back of Goodrum's neck hard enough to crack the bones in his host's hand.

Nathan had touched him, so now he knew that he was more than he appeared. His smile was feral when he righted himself. Belial heard Brooklyn gulping air greedily behind him.

"Belial. I presume?" he said by way of greeting. "You seem to have a penchant for wearing women's clothing. Gender issues?"

Belial chafed against his limitations. He longed to summon a blade of ice and plunge it into Goodrum's heart, but he was hobbled, unable to manifest fully in this body. Why did Brooklyn have to be so damn stubborn? He lashed out with his uninjured fist. Goodrum slapped it aside and delivered a backhanded strike that sent Belial spinning into the door.

"Care to try again?" Goodrum mocked.

Belial did try again. Half a dozen particularly nasty shards of mirror shot off the floor. Goodrum's shield was flawless. The glass was not turned aside. Instead, it appeared to be moving in slow motion through a viscous liquid. The glass ground to a halt, hanging suspended in a haze of energy. With a wink, he launched them back. Belial was slow to shield, and one of the shards buried itself in his left side and drew a yelp of agony. Blood seeped fast and hot. Belial doubled over, slicing both hands as he tried to pull it out. Fear and shock coursed through him in wild fits he couldn't quell.

Goodrum took a triumphant step forward and crumpled unexpectedly to the floor like a marionette with cut strings. Belial was confused for several seconds. He and Goodrum shared a look of mutual agony and disbelief. Then the bloodied glass clinked to the floor, and he understood. Brooklyn. She'd hamstrung him. Both legs.

Goodrum rolled onto his back and sat up, staring at Brooklyn with undisguised hatred. "You little bitch." A hysterical laugh bubbled up from his throat and echoed eerily around the bathroom. He was losing control. This was not the disciplined reaction of a master Demonrider.

Belial released his host, relieved to leave the panic and pain behind, and latched on to Goodrum. It was the fatal distraction. It freed the demon within. It looked out at him from Goodrum's eyes with a burning, alien lust that Belial could not give a name to, struggled for a moment to make its legs work, and failing that, released its hold, and vanished into the Pull.

With an effort, Brooklyn freed her legs and stood gingerly. She stepped over Goodrum, who was staring in catatonic disbelief at the wall. She knelt beside the woman Belial had vacated, and checked her pulse. "Dead," she announced clinically. "Who was she?"

"Just some girl." He turned away from Brooklyn, stepping over the girl into the hallway. *Just some girl. It was always just some girl. Her name might have been Tais.*

52

David Rises

David saw everything through his Prophets. Thousands of eyes with the singular purpose of feeding him information. A hive mind that hummed with images and sounds. Eyes in the political epicenters of all the world powers. Even eyes on the burning remnants of Kurt's house and the wicked smile playing across his winged mistress's lips. He wondered if she saw him through the other man's eyes. She was so beautiful, he thought, as the eyes he gazed through darkened in death.

It was more than that, this newfound gift. He saw lines of energy. He understood telekinesis at last, and though he was still pretty terrible at it, he was making more progress seeing than he'd ever made by feeling. Over the last few days, he'd learned to navigate the compound by following the cool blue lines of electricity oscillating in the wiring.

Information came to him as he needed it. If he didn't know it, but one of the Prophets did, then he did too. And, he suspected, it could work in reverse. When he felt hunger pangs, food was seldom long to arrive. Carried by hands eager to please. All of his needs seemed to be anticipated, even his baser desires were indulged without comment or complaint.

At first, he had relished the idea of exploring the thoughts and feelings of others, but if they had complex thoughts, he couldn't hear them.

David sighed and reached for his guitar, a gift from Azrael. He wasn't sure what it looked like, but the cool curves of slick wood and the warm tones were intimate friends. His fingers found the familiar shapes of the chords as he strummed and sang softly. He was still learning to close his supernatural eyes. Music helped. At times, he felt like the music was almost visible, a faint cloud of color shrouding him from all the visual noise. A wall to protect his sanity.

At night he tossed and turned, jumbled dreams, the restless work of a thousand humming minds. On the nights Azrael came to him, he slept like the dead, cradled against her breasts, wings enfolding them both into a cocoon of warmth and silence.

Other times they made love until he fell back amid the pillows, shadow blind, sated, and suddenly mournful for Brooklyn. She never asked him what the matter was. She just drew him close against her as if to hide him from grief.

Azrael alighted in the hours before dawn, a few miles north of Elberton, Georgia. It was one of her favorite places to think on this continent. The mysterious Guidestones towered over her, their inscriptions hidden in the darkness. She pulled the plastic case from her cloak pocket and examined it. She sensed the potential locked away in the inner chambers. Disease eager to live, grow, and spread, but in some ways an antibiotic for her. A medicine to cull the infection that was slowly tearing her apart. The demons were a reprieve, but they were slow, inefficient, and taxing to control. Often enough, Azrael still found herself flickering to bombings and earthquakes because she couldn't yet use her fledglings all at once.

Azrael spread her wings and fluttered up to crouch lightly on the capstone. Despite spring, the air chilled her, a sensation she was still getting used to. Occasionally headlights moved like persistent fireflies across the winding two lanes. Stonemasons headed to work, no doubt.

How often had she made the distinction? The God of Death, not Murder. The case buzzed in her hand as if the larvae inside knew her hesitation. She shook it irritably until the noise subsided. From fertility and life, to death, and finally to murder. Had she been the last to fall? The last to seek the divine light in the blackness of blood? She didn't know, but there was no going back. There had never been a way back. She knew that now.

Azrael began in India, raining the larvae across the crop fields. Then she moved to the Ukraine. Argentina. Brazil. All the top producers of corn. Finally back to the United States, streaking across the Midwest, trailing a blight of certain famine behind her. Afterward, she rested back atop the Guidestones as first light made the ten inscriptions visible. She touched the top one with her toe.

Maintain humanity under 500,000,000 in perpetual balance with nature.

Guide reproduction wisely—improving fitness and diversity.

Unite humanity with a living new language.

Rule passion—faith—tradition—and all things with tempered reason.

Protect people and nations with fair laws and just courts.

Let all nations rule internally resolving external disputes in a world court.

Avoid petty laws and useless officials.

Balance personal rights with social duties.

Prize truth—beauty—love—seeking harmony with the infinite.

Be not a cancer on the earth—Leave room for nature—Leave room for nature.

Lofty goals. But whether instructions for an end or for a new beginning, Azrael couldn't say. She planned to find out.

53

Would You Go With Me

Belial and Brooklyn jogged down carpeted hallways and dashed down a back stairwell. Twice they hid as soldiers or Demonriders passed by. Smoke and sulfur clung to the air around them. At the second floor, Brooklyn leaned heavily against the wall, panting and rubbing her eyes.

"Let me help you," Belial implored.

"No," she wheezed.

He couldn't blame her, really. Not after the situation he'd put her in. The life and family he'd taken away. When she looked at him, he could see hatred at war with necessity. Hatred would always win, it seemed. Brooklyn slid down the wall to sit on the floor, her expression slack and disoriented. She mumbled something about food, slurring the words. Belial looked around furtively. They could not stay here; she wouldn't let him in, so he had to find another way.

Bodies littered the second-floor hallway. Fighting had spilled over into the house as the Heir's men moved floor by floor and room by room to bring the survivors under control. Those who resisted died bloody. Belial found a Demonrider with a partially crushed skull, one eye emulsified, but he was still warm, recently dead. Belial shivered with dread. There were few things worse than this. He braced himself and melded with the corpse.

The first shock of pain stabbed like a thousand needles. So much agony. Oxygen-starved tissues, the dying heart, not to mention the eye, a white-hot hell all its own. The brain, bruised and jellied, didn't hurt so much as scream of an alien wrongness. Organic thought was an impossibility. There was only pain and a desperate grief for the loss of oxygen.

It took a willpower he hadn't known he possessed to remain wrapped in that damaged carcass. It took more to restart the heart. An excruciating determination to complete each beat. Breathing was its own chore as well. Slowly, things began to hum again, soulless but alive. The brain staunchly refused to do its part, but that was okay. Belial could do the thinking for a little while.

He returned to find Brooklyn fully unconscious. Belial lugged her to her feet, draped her arm across his shoulders, and wrapped his host's arm around her waist, pulling her tight against him to stay upright as they shuffled down the stairs.

At the first floor, they stumbled, feet dragging, down a smoke-filled hallway. Belial saw recognition and shock in the eyes of a couple of Demonriders, but no one stopped them as they shuffled past. He'd chosen his host well, it seemed.

At the next stairwell, Brooklyn was more lucid and hobbled down the first flight on her own. He helped her down the second. As they passed under the upstairs entryway, they had to climb over rubble where the floor had collapsed. A man above yelled down through the hole for them to halt, but they kept going. Hurried boots clattered away from the hole, yelling instructions.

"They're coming," Brooklyn murmured.

Belial just nodded. The effort of keeping this body alive was wearing him down. He wasn't sure speech was a possibility, anyway. His vision fuzzed, and strange bursts of color and light ghosted across his good eye. There was no resistance to his presence, no other life, nobody home. Coagulated blood dripped sluggishly from the damaged eye in time with every forced heartbeat.

They found the tunnel that led to the underground garage. There were rows of cars, the personal vehicles of those who worked and lived here, and cars for work use. None of them had keys in them. The footsteps were in the basement now.

Belial steered them across the garage. Maybe they could find a place to hide until an opportunity to escape presented itself. The next area was a service area. There was a car on a hydraulic lift dripping oil, apparently abandoned during service work.

Belial spotted handlebars jutting from a dusty tarp. As they neared, he snatched the tarp free to reveal a dirt bike with the key in it. His vision darkened, prompting him to renew his efforts to maintain the heartbeat. He struggled to help Brooklyn hoist her leg across the saddle.

He flicked the switch to the on position and lifted the dead meat of his leg onto the kick starter. His first effort was weak, barely spinning the engine. He tried again and was rewarded with a satisfying grumble that quickly died. Boots clattered across the garage floor, and men shouted for him to stop. He kicked again, and the engine pinged to life noisily. He revved the engine and released the clutch all at once, numbed fingers refusing to obey. The bike jerked, almost dislodging them both, and died. The smell of gasoline and exhaust filled his nostrils. Rifle lasers danced across his arms as he kicked the bike to life and opened the throttle fully and dropped the clutch again. The bike reared onto the back wheel, lurching forward. Gunfire erupted. He leaned left and right, zigzagging toward an open bay door.

They exploded into the field beyond the manor house, but were ringed by chain link. The only way in or out was through the heavily guarded gate up the driveway. Belial swung the bike in a wide looping arc and hauled ass toward the house with Brooklyn shouting directions in his ear. Screams and gunfire were wiped away by the wind and the growl of the engine. He zipped by the house, angling up the adjacent bank. Behind the house, he swerved, narrowly avoiding the carcass of a large hound riddled with bullet holes. He heard Brooklyn's gasp of outrage, but then she was shouting and pointing. Belial followed her finger to a break in the trees. They vanished into the underbrush a moment later, limbs whipping them as they tore up the narrow footpath.

Brooklyn clung to Belial, ignoring the corpse coldness that seeped into her fingers. They emerged at the picnic area that had served as a training ground months earlier, and where she'd freed Kurt from that awful demon he'd summoned. It seemed more like years than months had passed.

"The road is that way." She pointed through the trees to their left. Belial gunned the engine, and they lurched forward again, weaving through the trees without a trail, skirting sideways along the steeper ridges, descending. Several times, they almost tumbled or veered off an embankment, but somehow Belial always righted their course. She fought to stay awake, to not be the burden that dragged them down.

They fell into some sort of game trail that moved with a strange grace through the thickets that jerked the handlebars and welted their faces and hands. They followed it down to where it slid steeply into a ditch. Belial stopped at the top and asked her to get off. She did, though her legs trembled and dropped her onto her butt. He rode the bike down and toppled into the ditch. After he righted it and managed to get it onto the road, mostly by spinning and grunting, she slid down the bank and remounted behind him.

They saw the smoke before they reached the town, black clouds billowing from multiple sources. Sirens blared and firemen directed their hoses at one inferno and then another. All Main Street burned. A diversion, Brooklyn realized with loathing. A way to keep the local officials occupied during the assault on Kurt. They barreled straight through it. The heat, pounding from both sides, made her want to bury her face in Belial's shirt, but the fleeting reflections they cast in the fire-warped store windows were terrible and beautiful.

Brooklyn didn't recognize herself anymore. This woman, tired and regal, pale with dancing flames reflected in the hollows of her eyes, and Belial, his true form lay bare beneath the translucent dead flesh. They flickered from store to store as if giving chase in a strange game of hide-and-seek, haunted woman and her monster. The last reflection twisted their features, blending them into one being. Chiseled ice, sharp edges softened by femininity, the four wings spread with staring eyes—eyes she recognized as her own—and in each pupil the world burned. Then they were through the inferno and the wind was cool against her fevered cheeks.

They had not gone far beyond the town when the motorcycle lurched to one side and then the other before being righted again. Brooklyn clung to the bloodstained jacket that Belial wore. Her heart hammered. Though after the last few days, she didn't think a wreck should be so terrifying.

Belial coasted onto the shoulder of the road. He put his foot down, but the leg buckled and they both tumbled into the dewy grass.

Brooklyn wiggled free and heaved the dirt bike off of him. He wasn't moving. She went to her knees, cradled his head in her lap, and looked for life in the undamaged eye. It was dull and dead, but the corpse's lips moved anyway. She put her ear close until she understood. "I promised," he said, but he was already gone.

Brooklyn pushed the lifeless body aside with disgust. It was just some Demonrider again, nobody she knew or cared about. She lifted the dirt bike and opened the throttle, kicking the starter over and over again until it sputtered to life, smelling strongly of gasoline.

She pulled away, wobbling at first, trying to recognize the road. It was vaguely familiar, a road she'd seen and not cared about so many months ago when Belial had been in the driver's seat. This road had led her into this strange new life. Brooklyn didn't have much hope it would lead her out again.

A few miles later, a familiar drive appeared. It might have been a mistake, but Brooklyn had encountered kindness here once, if all too briefly. After a moment's hesitation, she wheeled in.

The driveway meandered lazily around trees too large and troublesome to be cut. Until at last she rolled between waves of freshly tilled earth, stretching almost to the horizon with fertile promises.

A whitewashed farmhouse loomed ahead. She'd never seen it by the full light of day. Brooklyn rolled right up to the porch steps and propped the bike on the kickstand.

She knocked on the door, behind which she hoped to hide, rest, and heal. She knocked and knocked. No answer.

Brooklyn slumped into a nearby rocking chair to wait. Her head pounded dully. She wiped her nose, relieved to find her fingers came away dry. As adrenaline faded, the pain returned in nauseating waves. She focused on it, intent on experiencing each excruciating moment fully, for it forced her mind away from her mom and dad, Devin and David, Kurt and Riley, and Belial too, truth be told. The physical pain had an anesthetic effect on her grief. The losses were stacked like giant Jenga pieces, threatening to tumble and crush her. Brooklyn closed her eyes just for a moment.

It was sometime later, when strong but gentle hands woke her from the emptiness of sleep. The sun was slipping behind the mountains, and the cicadas chorused loudly. The largest woman she'd ever seen stood over her with tears shining in her eyes. "I never thought to see you alive again," Mrs. Mays said. "Wasn't sure you was when I first saw you. Come on, let's get you fixed up."

54

Circles of Hell

Riley, like all the surviving Adepts, had been locked up until there was enough time for further evaluation, but it didn't seem like that time would ever come.

His meals came three times a day. The food tasted the same as always. The house and kitchen staff had been retained, apparently. They even brought his tea with lemon, just the way he liked it.

He'd hoped to be kept in one of the basement cells, a part of the complex he was intimately familiar with, in the hope that an opportunity for escape would present itself and allow him to slip into the tunnels that crisscrossed beneath the mountain.

Instead, he gazed out from a window overlooking the fields surrounding the manor. He could break the glass, but the drop was sheer. Even if he survived the jump, they would find him broken and immobile the next morning.

Riley fully expected to be executed within three days, but days spiraled slowly into weeks. He counted them into the double digits.

Always waiting to be taken away, he slept lightly—attuned to every sound. As the days dragged by, boredom drove him to reconsider the four-story jump from the window. Minutes blossomed into hours under the tension of uncertainty.

Riley might have gone mad if not for the companion he carried inside.

In solitude and silence, they spoke the language of thought and image, an intimacy that superseded words.

The memory of Kurt swept away by smoke and fire—a fabricated image taking the place of the blank shock left by the violence of the explosion and concussion—haunted Riley.

During the days he imagined the conversation he would have with Goodrum, securing his release and an apology with his wit and righteous anger moments before stepping over the Demonrider's corpse and going to free the others, if they still lived. Delusions of grandeur.

At night, he dreamed of something closer to reality. A trial for treason and a prompt death. A nightmare that gave a strangely soothing counterpoint to the monotony and uncertainty of waiting.

He wondered if the other Adepts were imprisoned and left to rot, or if this hell was reserved for him as a relative of "the traitor." What loyalty did they owe Kurt? Precious little. They were free to serve another master, but Riley knew he could never do that. Kurt was family, and family was worth dying for. Such thoughts agitated the companion he carried inside. Images stirred in his mind, urging him to reconsider his cavalier attitude about death. Images of himself kneeling before Goodrum, feigning fealty followed by images of a knife in Goodrum's back. The message was clear, if unrealistic.

"You are just worried about your final death," Riley said aloud. "It is the price we pay to experience life. You knew that when you signed up."

There was no answer.

He inspected the inner workings of the door lock with his mind, as he'd done every day. It was unlike anything he'd ever encountered before. Endlessly complicated, moving parts with obscure and perhaps irrelevant purposes. It was like trying to solve a Rubik's Cube blind.

Blasting the door from the hinges also occurred to him, but he soon discovered it had a steel core and anchors that ran deep into the wall. Riley wondered if it had always been so, or if these were special accommodations just for him.

He looked to the mountains beyond the fields where the setting sun gleamed dully on the two-lane that wound like a scar across the face of the nearest mountain.

That's where Brooklyn and Belial had been when he was captured. They had abandoned him. He supposed it was to be expected from a demon, but Brooklyn?

They were there and moving fast away when he'd cut Belial free of the Celtic knot, knowing it would be taken, and not wanting Goodrum to have another demon on a leash.

She didn't even know you were here. How could she have known? his companion demanded.

Belial had to get Brooklyn out of here. It was what Kurt would have wanted, her safe. Kurt would have wanted him safe too, though, wouldn't he? Riley wasn't sure. They were family, but Kurt had never approved of his "arrangement." Kurt the demon summoning Protector. Kurt the hypocrite. This was all his fault anyway, so Riley wasn't sure why he cared about Kurt's approval.

The next day, he screamed and pounded on the door until his hand throbbed in time with his racing heartbeat and his throat burned. Anything was better than this. He would jump. He snatched the thick comforter from the bed. He would drop it down along with the mattress to soften his fall, even if only by some minuscule amount.

Riley punched the window. It didn't break. He punched it again and again until blood smeared the glass. There was a useless phone on the nightstand, like a movie prop to taunt him. He threw it hard against the glass. Nothing.

He snatched it with his mind and launched it at the glass with everything he had. The phone shattered into a dozen pieces.

He seized the whole of the door with all the power he could muster and strained to rip it free of its moorings. The wall creaked and groaned, but the door didn't budge. He held his breath as the pressure between his eyes spiked into pain so sharp he thought his eyes might pop out. He closed them just to be safe. There was nothing but the door. He had to get through that door. Riley pushed with everything he had. When the blood trickled over his lips, he redoubled his efforts.

Kurt would have been strong enough. Brooklyn would have puzzled out an escape. His thoughts ran sluggish as the blood. In the back of his mind, his companion screamed. Real words! But they sounded like gibberish. Real words. How long had it been?

Images of himself dead in a pool of blood flashed like a broken strobe. *I'll heal. I always heal.* His finger found the puckered scar below his sternum for confirmation. *If we are truly dying, then tell me your true name, then we will know everything about one another. It's time to trust fully. You promised you'd tell me before we die.*

He waited. The sound of his breathing rattly and wet. No answer came.

Hours later, he stared up at the beaded board ceiling. Beautiful natural wood with hundreds of dark-brown knots spread like stars in the sky. "I'm not dying." He counted the stars, sometimes losing his place and starting again. He repeated his mantra each time he reached a new hundred. "I'm not dying."

Each time he said it, a part of him wished it weren't true.

No more secret tunnels. Belial strode through the double archway into the library. The guards moved to block him, and he sidestepped the first, raking razor claws across the leathery scales of his throat with a satisfying ripping sound. He summoned spikes of ice from the floor to impale the other and snapped her neck with a savage twist. Energy coiled eagerly inside him like a wound spring.

The doors to the Tome room stood slightly ajar and unguarded. Light from the dragon torches inside flickered into the dark hallway sporadically, giving the shadows life. The doors opened soundlessly at his touch. Inside, displayed on the empty dais, where the Tome of Death had resided, were the dragon eggs he'd so carefully concealed.

As he stepped inside, the doors slammed behind him with a boom. His father—Prosidris, Belial wouldn't call him father anymore—stepped out of the shadows behind the eggs. Belial started forward, teeth bared.

"Uh uh uh," Prosidris chided, placing the tip of a shark-tooth dagger against an egg. "What is it that always brings you back here?"

Belial stopped short, his rage swelling impotently inside him. "It isn't you."

"You are not one of them, you know. Not human. You can never be one of them, never be so weak because you are my son."

"I'm not your son anymore."

"You *are* my son, and that's why it pains me to kill you, but your betrayal was absolute. First though . . . "

Prosidris drove the dagger into the dragon egg; steam and blood hissed out around the blade. A keening sound filled the room. The dragon torches flared indignantly, and a strong wind fluttered the pages of every Tome until they all shone blank. Identical renditions of the scene before him appeared in bold black strokes. The last lines were finer and depicted Belial shocked and afraid. Shame flushed through him and he steeled himself against cowardice. He could rush Prosidris and save the last two eggs, at least one of them, maybe. There wouldn't be enough time to stab both. Prosidris raised the dagger over a second egg, and Belial lunged.

The attack caught Prosidris off guard. He stumbled back. Belial pressed the advantage, putting himself between his father and the two remaining eggs. He slashed out with his claws aiming for the throat, but the shark-tooth dagger sheared his claws neatly at the knuckles.

Belial replaced them with icy razors and slashed again, but the ice shards turned to harmless water on contact with his father. A wave of energy rolled back, slamming him into the dais and overturning it. The eggs tumbled to the floor and rolled into the shadows. The wave of energy that struck him receded back to its source, an ocean tide dragging Belial like detritus along the stone floor toward Prosidris. He scraped his remaining claws against the floor for purchase. He could see the pages of the Tomes turning in unison, images being recorded.

The last of the receding energy washed over Belial, and he stumbled to his feet. He launched spikes of ice at his father, but they vanished inside a wall of water that cascaded from nowhere. The wall rushed to meet him, engulfing him in a sphere of greenish brine. For a moment he was defeated again, on the beach with Tais, but then he remembered the dragon girl, the eggs, and Brooklyn.

Belial closed his eyes and concentrated. Slowly at first, and then more rapidly, the water hardened around him into a giant misshapen ball of ice. His father's grip on the water weakened, and he willed his icy creation to accelerate, slamming Prosidris against the wall with a thunderous shattering of ice, stone, and, he hoped, bone.

Belial scrambled away without checking, eager to reclaim the eggs and escape. The shadows obscured the eggs. He ran his hands along the floor in the dark corner. Nothing. His stomach clenched into knots; he glanced over his shoulder at the icy rubble. No movement. He moved along the wall systematically until his finger brushed something hard and smooth. One of the eggs.

Belial quickly ran his fingers over the shell, checking for cracks. He didn't feel any.

The tinkling of falling ice chilled his blood. He looked back to see the large chunks shifting as Prosidris struggled to free himself. Belial spread his wings, opening all the eyes. The shadows retreated from his scrutiny, and the other egg shone like a black jewel under bright lights.

He snatched it just as Prosidris rose from his icy sepulcher. Belial dashed for the door. A wave of energy helped him along, slamming into his back and smashing his face against the door. The pressure was immense, but he managed to curve his body protectively around the eggs.

Prosidris's footsteps approached leisurely, crunching ice, but Belial couldn't even turn his head to see. As he drew closer, the pressure increased. "You'd be . . . a fool . . . to kill me," Belial choked out.

"Why's that?" Prosidris asked as he pressed the shark-tooth dagger's tip against Belial's back behind the heart.

"The Tomes—"

"What about them?"

The pressure lessened enough to speak. "I can read them."

"So can—"

"Fluently."

Prosidris paused. Belial bit his tongue against saying more. He waited through long, excruciating moments as his father weighed the possibilities.

"Perhaps you still have some use to me, then."

"I'll only do it if the eggs remain safely with me; otherwise go ahead and kill me now."

The blade dug deeper, and a long, uncomfortable silence stretched out. "You'll remain within these walls, as will the eggs. You'll translate at my leisure. You will submit loyally to my wishes, or you'll go to your final death." The dagger tip twisted slowly. "Well?"

"Yes. I'll do it." The pressure fell away, and the dagger withdrew, but the pain in Belial's heart didn't lessen.

"Welcome home, son."

55

Between Sea and Sky

It surprised Brooklyn to find the cut on her palm the most nagging and persistent of her injuries. It healed slowly and hindered her usefulness around the farm long after her cracked ribs were mended and the headaches stopped. Every night, Mrs. Mays took Brooklyn's hand in her larger ones and dabbed a poultice of unknown origin on the cut. Day by day, the infection and redness faded until the pain gave way to a strange tightness when she spread her fingers.

The months Brooklyn spent healing at Mrs. Mays's farm were the most peaceful days she could remember since early childhood. Sometimes they talked, but most often they spent the days in quiet companionship. In the mornings, they gathered eggs and milked the cow. After breakfast, Mrs. Mays worked the corn rows while Brooklyn prepared lunch. In the evening, after milking the cow again, they sat on the porch in the rocking chairs until well after sunset bled the world of color.

One such evening, Brooklyn stared sullenly over the cornfields, fading in the dusk. She flexed her hand against the tightness and traced the raised barbs above her heart. The place where the field sloped up to the tree line drew her gaze over the corn tassels. It had been dark and chaotic, but she thought that was about where she'd been standing when Goodrum tried to kill her.

She thought of him often, especially the things he had said. Was David alive, or was that a lie aimed at cruelty? Was Kurt trustworthy? How had he known for certain David was dead? Her thoughts circled in on themselves endlessly when her hands were not busy. Brooklyn brushed the hair back from her forehead and—in the darkness where Mrs. Mays couldn't see—let frost blossom from her fingertips until she felt the connection. Belial in her brain and she in his.

Her thoughts continued to spiral around those she'd loved and lost until he'd seen enough and asked, *Wouldn't it be better to decide what to do next instead of worrying about what is already done?*

It isn't so easy, she grumbled. *I have nowhere to go but home, and you said it burned. I couldn't drive a dirt bike across Tennessee and North Carolina, anyway.*

You have to figure out the next move for both of us. You promised that you—

I know what I promised, she cut in. *I have lost Devin, David, Riley, and Kurt. Who do I search for? Where do I go?*

I don't know, but not choosing is a decision too. Pick somebody before you lose everybody.

I've been healing. It takes time. I need to be one hundred percent before—

Draw from me. Use my strength. You can control it better now. It doesn't take much energy to read bedtime stories to my father, he said bitterly.

"I need a car," Brooklyn muttered aloud.

"What for?" asked Mrs. Mays.

Ask her if she has a car, Belial urged.

Shut up, Brooklyn said, letting the frost go before he could reply.

Losing his followers was the most bitter pill Father Logan had ever swallowed. It was improbable, he would have even ventured impossible, and he wasn't sure how the blasphemous little infidel had managed it. It irked him because he prided himself on his cunning. And because it had brought him to this most humbling moment in which he waited impatiently for an audience with the newly appointed Protector Goodrum. A title that embodied the very essence of oxymoron in Dravin's opinion.

"He'll see you now," the receptionist, Lauren, said with a pretty, practiced smile. He smiled back. Lauren was someone he very much thought he might enjoy getting to know better under less dire circumstances. He gave a nod of thanks and followed her down the hallways to Kurt Levin's former office, noting the sway of her hips and the effect it had on him. This, he thought, was simply the result of being in a building where so few people were actually human. Lauren was very human.

The office was different from when he'd visited it last. Goodrum had stripped it of any reminder of Kurt. The couch was new, modern, though the refinished mahogany desk remained along with a fresh bottle of bourbon and drinking glasses. "It's good to see you again, old friend," Dravin offered by way of greeting.

"And you as well." Goodrum stood and offered his hand.

Father Logan perceived it as soon as they touched. Goodrum was wholly human. He was demonless, and had been long enough to kick the withdrawal, judging from his healthy pallor and bright eyes. "Did you recognize the error of your ways?"

Goodrum laughed. "It seems people don't trust a Demonrider to be a Protector."

"When did you start caring what other people think?"

"It's the price of politics and old age, I guess." He smiled, but Father Logan thought he saw malice in the other man's eyes.

"I apologize. I didn't come here to pry. It seems your good fortune heralded my misfortune. Since we've worked cooperatively in the past, I thought you might see fit to assist me with a little problem?"

"I might. How little?"

"I've lost a number of followers to someone else. I need him removed so I can reclaim them."

"How many is 'a number'?"

Father Logan sighed, fiddling with the vial in his pocket. "All of them."

Goodrum's eyes widened in disbelief. "Who?"

"It doesn't matter. I just need—"

"If you want my help, answer my question."

"David Sterling." Dravin waited patiently for Goodrum's fit of laughter to end, before continuing, unabashedly. "I should have let you kill him when you wanted to. Now I'm asking you to do it for me."

"You come to me, a Protector, to contract a murder? I'm hurt!"

Father Logan felt his patience wearing thin, but bit back the retort that rose like bile in his throat. "Obviously, it wouldn't be you personally. The Demonriders still answer to you, or have you lost that privilege in your 'condition'?"

"They answer to me!" Nathan roared, slamming his hand on the desk. "I can summon my demon in an instant if need be. His will is broken to mine."

"Of course. I didn't mean to suggest otherwise. No offense intended." Dravin paused until Goodrum gave a nod of acquiescence, then said, "May we have a drink while we talk?"

Goodrum reached for the bottle and glasses. "I didn't think you imbibed. Isn't it against your code or something?"

Dravin shrugged. "Politics and old age?"

Goodrum laughed and slid a glass across the desk. "The only thing worth a damn that Kurt Levin owned."

Father Logan sipped the bourbon. The taste and burn foreign to him. "So, will you help me?"

Goodrum tossed back half a glass in one go. "No. Help yourself."

"How would you propose I do that?"

"Find the bitch. David and his followers will do what you say if you hold her."

"So go after the head to control the body. Seems I've heard that somewhere before. Read it, I think."

Goodrum shrugged with disinterest. "Call it what you will. You overthink everything."

Dravin ignored the jab. "*Meditations on Combat.* Isn't that it, right there?" He gestured to the bookshelf behind Goodrum.

Goodrum put his glass down hard and swiveled to look. "For Christ's sake," he mumbled.

Father Logan spun the lid off the vial in his hand and poured the contents into the last of Goodrum's bourbon.

"No, this is a genealogy of families that trace their lineage back to Solomon." He dropped the massive leather-bound tome on the desk.

"To the Solomonians!" Dravin held his glass up to Goodrum, and they both drank.

Brooklyn watched Mrs. Mays putter out of sight in her old truck. It had taken Brooklyn more than an hour to convince the old woman to leave her here alone. The jagged remnants of her childhood home cut a stark profile against the overcast sky.

As she approached the house, Brooklyn felt her soul stones in the rubble, pieces of herself reconnected, resurrected. She pulled them free by touch, easing them over boards, under blackened rocks, through the maze of debris until they rose—gleaming, like a family of phoenixes—from the ashes of her life. They spun, weaving a new pattern, almost of their own accord. When the hum began, she felt as if she guided them not on paths through space but by sound, instinct adjusting speed and course until the agony of loss was made corporeal.

Her feet carried her forward until she stood in the center of the maelstrom of deadly projectiles, weaving a pattern around herself with lethal grace. Here was a melody unlike anything ever heard by mortal ears. The music converged and harmonized with something deep inside her. She lost track of where the song came from. It felt as if the sounds were living emotions seeping from every pore of her being. Brooklyn let her soul expand until the melody became her, defined her, seemed to kill her and resurrect her anew. She wasn't sure what was happening, if she created it or was created by it. Images conjured by her mind danced and flickered in the blur of the stones' passing. Ocean-deep grief flooded from her. Feelings too dark and vast to be conveyed by words were given voice by the three stones. The song rose and crescendoed, echoing and dying against the mountains of her childhood.

In the exhausted silence that followed, she dried her eyes with the heels of her hands and bunched her hair on top of her head to let the sweat on her neck evaporate.

Afterward, Brooklyn rummaged in her father's workshop until she found the things she needed. She poured gasoline on the half-burned remnants of her family home and tossed a match. The flames leapt to life with a sudden whooshing sound. She watched the crackling fire finish unmaking the only life and home she'd ever known. She wasn't sure she could have gone back, anyway.

With that done, she opened the double doors of the barn to reveal an old Ford tractor and a Chevy Cavalier. The car shone in the dim light, flawlessly maintained by her father for the day her sister would return and claim the keys. The engine started almost instantly.

Brooklyn stopped at the end of the driveway; everyone was lost. She couldn't go forward and she couldn't go back. Her heart wouldn't let her hide any longer, either. She couldn't go to the police to inquire about Devin. She was still a murder suspect. Kurt and Riley were long lost. David was allegedly alive and a prisoner to Father Logan, but she had no idea where. In the end, the only person she could help was the one who deserved it least. The one who had cost her everything.

The drive to Driftwood Beach took almost ten hours. Brooklyn couldn't find a radio station that wasn't buzzing about the world's failing corn crops.

Entomologists from around the world opined about the origin and rapid growth of the never-before-seen corn beetle and its bizarre immunity to pesticides.

Economists rambled about the effects on world markets and predicted changes in the costs of meats and plastics, the impact on gas prices, and even the growing scarcity of popcorn and whether it was because of an actual shortage or mass hoarding.

Conspiracists theorized about culprits of an agro-terror attack and the evasive nonanswers from the Department of Agriculture and other officials about the older species of corn missing from secure government storage facilities and seed banks around the world.

Zealots shouted for repentance and predicted the apocalypse.

Brooklyn remembered the little red-and-yellow beetle Mrs. Mays had captured in a mason jar. It had just looked like any other bug to her, but within days, the fields had gone from green to yellow to brown. She shut the radio off. The silence was comforting. Brooklyn found a cheap hotel in Brunswick, paid cash, and promptly passed out.

Sunrise found her on Jekyll Island, picking her way through the tree graveyard, a mile-long tangle of ancient trees, their eroded roots rising like gnarled fingers against the dawning sky. Brooklyn found a place deep enough within the tangles to be shielded from sight or disturbance. Tiny crabs and spiders skittered away from her footfalls in the cool white sand.

Brooklyn brushed her arm across the ground until she had a smooth surface to work with. Belial's symbol spiraled into the sand from her frosty fingertip. She could feel his anxiety as he watched through her eyes. She was aware of his father's presence, imperial and all consuming, as Belial's gaze drifted to the eggs basking near the heat of the braziers, then back to the page as he explained to Prosidris what he saw. He willed the tension to leave his body as the last lines were drawn and the symbol neared completion.

Brooklyn cut the pads of her fingers, allowing the blood to trickle into her palm and pool there. The timing was critical. She closed her eyes, seeing as he saw. It happened as if in slow motion. He dashed toward the eggs, and Prosidris reacted as if having anticipated the movement. A column of water erupted around the eggs. Belial dove through it. Quicker than lightning, Prosidris placed himself between Belial and the massive doors. Belial groped for the eggs in the column of water, his fingers brushing them several times before he found them and clutched them tight to his chest. *Now!* he thought as loudly as he could.

Brooklyn poured the blood from her hand, taking care that it didn't unmake the symbol scrawled in the powdery sand. Her connection with Belial was suddenly severed and gave way to blackness. The surrounding sand exploded, filling her eyes and nose, forcing her to turn away.

When the dust settled and she cleared the grit from her vision, Belial stood before her, regal and tall in his true form, wings cupped tightly against his body, eggs clutched to his chest, and a look of wordless agony on his face. He fell to his knees, tried to extend the eggs to her, and failed. They rolled to a stop in the soft sand. Belial fell. Face first. A small spartan-looking dagger in his back between his wings.

Brooklyn pulled it out. There he lay, stretched out like an offering, the demon that took her freedom and ruined her life. She knew the weapon in her hand could end him. She felt the elemental power of it thrumming through her arm. Brooklyn could smell blood on the blade . . . almost taste it. She felt a frantic need clawing in the back of her throat.

"I want you to," Belial choked out, coughing up something wet and black. "If it's between dying here or falling again, I choose the dagger. Make it quick and clean." He subsided into a fit of coughing, more tar-colored blood stark against the white beach.

"You ruined my life." The words burst from her lips involuntarily. "They're all dead because of you. Everyone is dead." Brooklyn took a half step back. Her voice sounded thready and high. "It's all your fault."

"Yes. It is," he broke in. The wounds on his back closing up as he spoke. "It's all my fault. I took your freedom; I made you a fugitive from the police and the scions of Solomon. Because of events I set in motion, your boyfriend became involved and is now a prisoner or dead. Because of my father and, by extension, me"—his voice grew sharp with bitterness—"you are an orphan."

The last word hung in the air between them like a curse. Brooklyn blinked. "So, give me one reason why I shouldn't kill you right now."

"You must have one, else why am I still talking?"

"Devin," Brooklyn said softly, "and me. You saved me when you didn't have to."

"I didn't save others who have counted on me."

Brooklyn remembered snatches of a dream, a dark-skinned girl on a beach, Belial beaten back by the ocean. She considered him, vulnerable and prone. The dagger thrummed eagerly. He was a demon, an opponent of humankind and free will, a parasite unable to remain for long without a host. She didn't want to kill him. She knew once the Pull took him he would be as good as dead anyway. No choice was a choice, too. Every road led to his destruction, save one. "Tell me about these eggs. Tell me why you risked everything for them."

He told her.

"Dragon girl? Does she have a name?"

"I'm . . . not sure." He sat up, cross-legged, and even so, she noticed he was almost at eye level with her.

"What do you know about these eggs?"

"Not much. Bury them deep in warm sand. Maybe one day they hatch. I don't know when or how long. Or—"

"Or what will hatch?" she finished grimly.

"I trust in her goodness"—he looked away—"just like I trust in yours."

"And are we both fools for trusting in yours?"

"Probably."

Brooklyn nodded absently. She was thinking of the parable about the Cherokee boy who rescued a freezing rattlesnake. The snake begged for help and promised not to bite. The boy had nursed it back to health, shown the snake every kindness, until one warm spring day it bit him. Before he died, he asked the snake why it bit him. The snake replied, *You knew what I was when you picked me up*.

Brooklyn felt a tug as Belial turned translucent. She pulled, and he solidified again with an expression of pained concentration on his face.

"What could I do to help you?" Her voice seemed lost in the surf, but he tilted his head in thought, his wings stretching and settling back into place.

"I won't ask it of you."

"You don't have to, but if you so much as think about biting me, I'll take your head off."

His face twisted in confusion. "Why would I bite you?"

"Metaphor. I'm in the driver's seat. I'm calling the shots. You can't deal with that, then go to Hell, literally, and work through your daddy issues."

"I can deal with it," he murmured.

"Good," Brooklyn said, and stuck the dagger through her belt.

After they buried the eggs beneath several feet of sand in the driftwood-sheltered alcove, Brooklyn walked down to the open beach, kicked her shoes off, and left them behind. As Brooklyn walked in the warm surf, she thought about her sister, the first great loss in her life. Erin's face had become shadowy and vague in her memory. When did that happen? Would her parents fade as well? The thought put a weight in the pit of her stomach. In her mind, Belial stirred in restless sleep.

Brooklyn nodded as she passed other early morning beach goers. The ocean seemed alive to her today, in a way she couldn't explain. Somewhere behind her were David, Riley, and Kurt, and further beyond them the smoking remains of her decimated family. And here she was with an inhuman ally and nothing to go back to.

She stopped walking and waded into the ocean. The water slapped her thighs, soaking her shorts. For most of her life, Brooklyn had opened her eyes in the shadows of mountains. They had stood around her as comforting sentinels, immovable and permanent. When she looked up at them, her eyes were drawn to the ridges and hollows. The paths of passage shaped over thousands of years were clear to her. Always she knew where to go. They gave the horizon height and shrouded her small, manageable world in an illusion of safety.

Gulls crisscrossed above her on silent wings. The world had suddenly grown larger, and the way unclear. The mountains of her childhood were no more. The world was changing. She was changing, too. She'd have to if she wanted to survive. They would come for her, and there were no easy paths left. Let them come.

She would be ready. Waves lapped harmlessly at her ankles as Brooklyn gazed out where the horizon vanished between the sea and sky.

Signup for my Newsletter to get notification of upcoming novels, author recommendations, and exclusive content

About Author

Tony Galloway is the author of Solomon's Ring, the first book in a trilogy he began writing shortly after college. Mr. Galloway balances his part-time writing habit with a day job and a family of six. Besides fiction, he has written and published articles on various DIY automotive topics. Mr. Galloway lives and writes in the rural North Georgia mountains.

For more information, visit the author's website at: http://www.tonygallowaywrites.com or subscribe to his newsletter for updates on future books.

Printed in Great Britain
by Amazon

53672969R00227